THE
MARTHA'S VINEYARD
BEACH AND BOOK CLUB

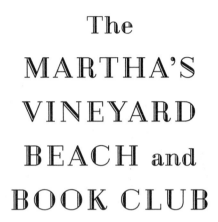

The
MARTHA'S
VINEYARD
BEACH and
BOOK CLUB

A Novel

Martha
Hall Kelly

BALLANTINE BOOKS

NEW YORK

Copyright © 2025 by Martha Hall Kelly

All rights reserved.

Published in the United States by Ballantine Books, an imprint of Random House, a division of Penguin Random House LLC, New York.

BALLANTINE BOOKS & colophon are registered trademarks of Penguin Random House LLC.

Hardback ISBN 978-0-593-35491-9
Ebook ISBN 978-0-385-69705-7

Printed in the United States of America on acid-free paper

randomhousebooks.com

2 4 6 8 9 7 5 3 1

FIRST EDITION

Book design by Barbara M. Bachman

To my mother, Joanne Finnegan Hall,
who inspired this book with her stories of growing up
on lovely Martha's Vineyard during World War II

THE
MARTHA'S VINEYARD
BEACH AND BOOK CLUB

1

MARI

2016

I HOISTED MY BACKPACK OVER MY SHOULDER AND JOINED THE crush of people streaming down the ferry's gangplank.

I'd made it to Martha's Vineyard at last, that storied island. I'd heard it was almost too charming. That Princess Diana had stayed there. Lots of presidents. Carly Simon and James Taylor once upon a time. There had to be something cool about it.

I stood under the canopy and scanned the people coming to meet their friends and families. Mrs. Devereaux had been so vague in her letter. *Take the 9:30 ferry. I'll fetch you in Vineyard Haven.* Had I gotten the day wrong?

I wiped the sweat off my upper lip. I'd forgotten my sunglasses and was beyond jet-lagged from taking the red-eye from L.A. to Boston.

An amped-up bridal party pressed by me in a haze of Miss Dior, gold Mylar balloons bobbing above them; matching straw hats identified them as *Bride* and *Bride Squad,* as if the world didn't know. I stepped back to let a couple not that much older than me walk by, a toddler in the father's arms and a sweet-looking mutt leashed behind. The perfect family.

I walked across to the gray-shingled terminal building, the asphalt radiating heat, and sat cross-legged on a bench, watching the crowd of rich-looking tourists, flannel-shirted farmer types, and lunch-tote-carrying workers from the mainland. Were some headed to those stately white houses that lined the harbor, the ones probably built by men with names like Ichabod, the kitchens done over with double Sub-Zeros and too much white marble? Life was good for people here in almost-too-charming land.

I held my suede fringe bag close, one of my mother's favorites. My high-waisted jeans and halter top had seemed right at the time when I left L.A., but from the few stares and glances cast in my direction, I now knew I looked out of place. Not that I cared much about dressing for others. I dressed for joy. And my dwindling bank account.

I'd eaten nothing since the peanuts on the plane, because the ferry snack bar offered only industrial-looking clam chowder and some shriveled hot dogs. And a ten-dollar deck of playing cards featuring a vintage Martha's Vineyard map, which I'd bought in a moment of impulse and regretted as soon as cash changed hands.

I called Nate's number. "This is Nate. Sorry I'm not here right now, but we'll talk soon." Why did he never pick up? He was always so busy with his tech start-up, which was taking forever to start up.

I sipped my bottle of club soda, an economical drink since the bubbles made me feel fuller, and watched my fellow passengers match up with their rides. A white Range Rover arrived, and the bridal party wrangled their balloons into the car and piled in. Soon a white-haired woman wearing a pink button-down shirt waved to the perfect family, and off they went, the mother fussing over the daughter or daughter-in-law.

It made me miss my own mom. Not that my mother would've worn anything remotely buttoned down. If a shirt didn't have a seventies vibe, Nancy Starwood wasn't wearing it. We'd spent hours browsing the L.A. thrift shops as a team, hunting through the racks on Melrose, on the lookout for band T's and vintage Levi's. All the shop owners loved her charming way and always saved her the good stuff.

Soon the crowds thinned. *Where is Mrs. Devereaux?* I checked my phone and found it nonresponsive. *Maybe a new phone with some battery life would be a good thing to save for.*

I turned the golden bracelet on my wrist, a habit I'd just acquired.

Before I left L.A., I found the circle of gold hearts in the electric-pink sock my mom used to store her jewelry in. The hearts were kind of corny and the bracelet wasn't really my mother's style—or mine, either—but it gave me an odd sort of comfort now.

I approached a woman wearing an orange vest, who stood waving cars onto the ferry to return to the mainland. "Where's the closest public phone? My ride hasn't shown up."

"Across the street," the woman said. "Vineyard Bikes will let you use theirs."

I dodged cars and hurried into the shop. Bikes filled every inch of the place, even hanging from the rafters, and I ran one finger along the seat of a tandem bike resting against the wall. That much togetherness would be a mistake no matter how good the relationship.

A guy I guessed was in his mid-thirties, maybe two years older than me, stood bent over an overturned bicycle, his hair pulled back in a messy bun. He spun the wheel with a satisfying ticking sound. I basked in the cool darkness of the place and admired his strong-looking back, a body part underappreciated in men.

I waved. "Hey."

"Hey." He looked up and tucked a stray lock behind one ear. "Great bag."

I ran one hand down the suede, taken aback that a male human had admired a piece of my clothing, a first for me. "My mother's. I'm sorry, but the person I was supposed to meet is a no-show. Mind if I use your phone?"

He nodded toward the counter. "Have at it."

I dialed the number from the letter, and while it rang, I considered the bike man's profile and decided if he'd been born in the seventeenth century he could have passed for a Flemish painter or composer.

"Is it always this crowded here?" I asked, phone to my ear.

"It's an August Friday, so yes. March, not so much."

I liked the way he said *Mahch* in that famous Massachusetts accent.

I hung up the phone. "No one there."

I stepped to the window and checked the ferry terminal again.

After paying my mother's funeral expenses, I couldn't afford a long cab ride.

"I'm here from L.A. Just flew into Logan this morning. How much to rent a bike to ride to Chilmark?"

"Twenty bucks a day." He glanced at me. "But it's a tough ride." He straightened, brushed off his jeans, and gave me his full attention. "Used to biking?"

"I went on a Berkeley trip once back in college—toured Hershey, Pennsylvania."

"Oh, that garden spot."

"But it was really fun, actually." I shooed away the image of my ex-boyfriend, Justin, riding off with Jennifer Sibley down Chocolate World Way.

"Well, you'd be fine biking the flat roads along the coast, but the roads Up-Island are hillier. Trust me, just take Stagecoach Taxi."

"How much would that be?" I asked.

"Around sixty bucks."

I pictured the inside of my wallet and the two twenty-dollar bills and change there. At thirty-four I should have been well past the back-packing phase of life and able to afford a taxi. Just a late bloomer, my mother had said. "That's kind of a lot for me right now . . ."

He reached up into the rafters and pulled down a pale-green bike, a surprising feat of strength, and I stepped back to watch. I'd always found men who did physical labor more attractive than their office-working counterparts.

"I get it. It's possible to live out here without a lot of money, but you have to be creative. I can do it for ten if that helps."

"It does, thanks."

He went to the counter and hovered his pen above a form.

"Name?"

"Mari Starwood."

He smiled. "You could be a movie star with that name."

I'd actually been christened Marigold Violet Starwood, named after a British soap my mother had a passing fancy for, but I rarely shared my full name. Not because I didn't like it; more to avoid people's same old jokes about it.

"Are you an actress? Being so . . ."

"So what?" I asked.

"I don't know." He searched my face for a few long seconds. "Beautiful."

I glanced away, hiding my smile. He was just flirting, but that wasn't a word I'd use to describe myself. *Interesting,* perhaps. But black hair and Elvira-white skin wasn't the most sought-after vibe in L.A., where blonds ruled. Just the thought that there might be a more relaxed beauty standard here in the land of farmers and fishermen made me feel newly buoyant.

I told him I had to leave tonight on the seven-thirty ferry. I'd scored a quick turnaround flight out of Boston for less than three hundred dollars round trip.

"You'll want to stay longer. It's a unique place. The air alone here helps people reconsider things."

"I need to get home. I'm moving. Going back to school for physical wellness. Hoping to make a bit more money so I can afford a bigger place." I forced myself to stop oversharing with this random stranger and pulled the deck of cards from my bag. "Can you show me where I'm going, on this map here?"

I liked the easy way he leaned his forearms on the counter, rested the deck of cards on his palm, and pointed to various spots as he spoke. "The island's bigger than some people think—twenty-three miles long. There are six towns. We're here in Vineyard Haven, one of the two main ports. You're going to what they call Up-Island, to Chilmark. Lots of farms up there. At the other end is fancy Edgartown. It's like New England Land at Disney World. You need big bucks to hang around there. The bar at Atria has amazing two-for-one gin gimlets on Tuesdays, though."

"I have to go to Copper Pond Farm, wherever that is."

He stood a little taller. "That's a very cool place—huge piece of property. Used to be an Army base just above it. Highest spot here. Now kids go there to make out."

I felt an absurd rise of heat in my cheeks. What would Nate think about me chatting up the bike man? "I'm meeting a woman from there. For a private painting class. Supposed to be starting at eleven."

"Elizabeth Devereaux? She's famous."

"I know. We studied her work in an art class." I'd taken Intro to American Painting during my wanting-to-be-an-artist phase at Berkeley. Not that I was any great painter or anything. Elizabeth Devereaux would probably think my work was a total joke.

"Wow. For one of her one-on-one workshops? I thought she didn't take students anymore."

"I wrote and told her how much I love her work and she accepted me," I said, aiming for vagueness. He didn't need to know the real reason I was here.

"Well, Mrs. Devereaux's a private person. I paint a little, too, and met her once, at a gallery opening last year, but I've only seen her farm from the water. It's gated, and they say the dirt road is in terrible shape. Out here, seems the more exclusive the property, the worse the potholes."

"There were no photos of her online. What's she like?"

"A bit brusque, but very kind to the artist community here. She loved talking shop but not much about her personal life. I asked her about her farm, and she just changed the subject."

"She's ninety-something?"

"Still an amazing talent, though. Said she paints every day. Were you an art major?"

"I wish. I love to paint. I had to major in something that would pay the bills, though. Communications. But I ended up in the health-food industry." I'd never actually graduated, after my scholarship ran out. I tried not to think about the blender station at the Jamba on Wilshire, where I whipped up Mango-A-Go-Go's and microwaved sandwiches, the elder statesman of the baby-faced staff.

The bike man leaned in over the counter. "Devereaux paintings go for more than this whole shop's worth. You're lucky to get in with her."

"Who's lucky to get in with her?"

We turned and found a woman standing in the doorway, dressed in a comfortable-looking pair of paint-spattered cargo pants, which I instantly wanted, and a gauzy linen shirt. Tall and thin, she wore a wide-brimmed straw hat, her white hair plaited to one side, down across her chest.

"Mrs. Devereaux—"

"Ronan, isn't it?" she asked with just a trace of a French accent. "So this is where you spend your days? You should be painting." She stepped toward me. "Are you Miss Starwood, by chance? I figured you might be here chatting. All the girls seem to find their way to Ronan White." Mrs. Devereaux just stared at me, lost for a moment.

"Yes, I'm Mari." I shifted in my shoes. How did she recognize me? She continued to gaze at me. "Are you okay?" I asked.

Mrs. Devereaux seemed to emerge from her trance. She turned and started out the door. "Let's get going, shall we, if we're to get some painting done? Mustn't dawdle."

I looked back and found Ronan watching me go. And part of me wished I was on my way to drink gin gimlets with him instead.

I FOLLOWED MRS. DEVEREAUX through the parking lot to a yellow convertible jeep with its top down. Despite some rust along the door bottoms, it was in great shape for a vehicle that was clearly much older than I was, and I slid into the passenger side, the leather seat hot through my jeans.

Mrs. Devereaux turned the key in the ignition, and the sun glinted off a thin gold band on her left hand. *Is there a Mr. Devereaux?*

I'd never seen anyone drive a stick shift before, and Mrs. Devereaux was a master at it, surprisingly strong. "So what's life like for you out in California?" she asked. "Do you paint a lot?"

"Whenever I can. Mostly portraits. I build stuff, too. Just made a little dollhouse for my boss's niece."

Mrs. Devereaux's gaze lingered on me again, this time for a longer moment.

"Is everything okay?" I asked. "I could drive if you're feeling light-headed." It was the kind of offer I often made without thinking, but I hadn't driven a car in five years, since my mother sold the Mustang, never mind a stick shift.

"Oh, no. Never felt better."

I sat back and tried to relax as we drove along the main street of the harbor town, past an organic-food shop and a drugstore, along with some T-shirt shops. "Welcome to Vineyard Haven," she said.

"Cute town." I loved the boutiques, a nice break from the Glendale Galleria.

"Had a terrible fire here in 1883. Everything burned, clear down to the water, if you can believe it."

We passed a sweet storefront with books displayed in the plate-glass windows. Bunch of Grapes Books. I turned in my seat. "Was that Allen Whiting's book in the window? Amazing landscapes."

"Yes. Great art books. A person could spend all day in there. You know, why not stay the night in my guest room? Come back and browse. And it'll give us more time to paint."

For a private person, she was pretty free with the invitation. And I hadn't really intended to do any actual painting. More just fact-finding. "Thank you, but I need to get back. Nonrefundable flight."

"Do you read?"

"Mostly nonfiction. But now I'm reading all my mom's old novels. Makes me feel closer to her." I pulled a worn paperback from my bag, my mother's copy of *Valley of the Dolls*, which I'd found when I was cleaning out our closet. "Read this on the flight. It's a wild one. Drug overdoses and stuff. Good, but pretty unrealistic."

We passed a cute coffee bar with café tables out front, advertising matcha lattes.

"Whatever happened to plain black coffee?" Mrs. Devereaux asked.

"Matcha's good for you. At least that's what Gwyneth Paltrow says. And tastes amazing."

"Blech," Mrs. Devereaux said, waving the idea away.

We passed a vintage-clothing store with a few dresses hung outside, swinging in the breeze. My mother would have liked the vibe of the town—a little corny, not trying too hard to be cool. I ran one finger along my heart bracelet.

Mrs. Devereaux glanced over. "Pretty."

"My mother's," I said. "I think she got it from a thrift shop." It pinched me to look at it, but it felt good to have inherited something, no matter how small, from my mom. The Medi Clinic doctor in Los Feliz had floated Lexapro as a way to treat the sadness. But I didn't want to forget my mother. I just wanted her back.

"You like vintage clothes?" Mrs. Devereaux asked.

"Yeah. They have great energy. Love guessing the past in them. And they're always well made. Plus, thrifting's good for the planet."

Mrs. Devereaux nodded, as if that had some deeper meaning.

"This farm we're going to. How long have you lived there?" I had limited time to get my real questions answered.

She checked her side mirror. "Off and on for a few years."

"Ever get out to Los Angeles?" I asked.

She looked over at me. "No, never."

We drove by a restaurant advertising warm lobster rolls and past a bank with a Spanish-tile roof that looked like it belonged in Carmel-by-the-Sea. It was a cute town with great exploration potential if I came back one day. But once she opened up to me and I got what I came for from Mrs. Devereaux, I'd never need to return.

We continued Up-Island along an untraveled road arched with ancient trees, and I breathed in the honeysuckle air, feeling renewed. It was such a different vibe from the West Coast. The light made everything seem crisper, and there was a wetter, briny sweetness to the air, none of that woodsmoke and cedar scent of L.A.

We passed what Mrs. Devereaux said was the old Alley's General Store and then lots of sheep meadows, and later she veered onto a dirt road and drove through an open gate. Off to the side was a blue farm stand, metal buckets of white lilies there for sale.

We drove along, as she expertly skirted most of the washtub-sized potholes, and I held on to the door handle. "Is there someone who can fix this road?"

"It keeps the curious away," she said with a smile.

Soon the wild cry of gulls and terns met our ears, and we emerged from the woods to a hazy blue sky and a sweeping lawn that ran to a bluff overlooking the water. A small, two-story stone-faced cottage stood off to our left, a white-painted picket fence along the front of it, which had surrendered to a glorious tangle of creamy-pink climbing roses, white lilies, and foxglove. A magnificent old barn stood to our right, a rust-colored cow grazing near it, and rows of emerald-green plants grew up the hill. I'd never set foot on a farm before. Unless you counted Knott's Berry Farm.

"Wow." I stepped from the car. I liked the smell of the farm, the roses, the freshly mowed hay and the salt air, and even the manure. "You live here by yourself?"

"I do."

"Is this your family home?"

"Oh, no. Just taking care of it for a friend."

"Lucky you." I shielded my eyes with one hand and took in the old barn, newly renovated. They'd done it right—updated but not too modern, with black-framed architectural windows and a cedar-shake roof. "Cool barn."

"It's a dairy farm, but we also grow potatoes and hay."

We walked toward the edge of the bluff, where two easels stood next to canvas camp stools. Just seeing those easels made me regret my decision to leave without taking the painting class. Mrs. Devereaux was probably an amazing teacher.

I waved toward a clearing on the hill where an enormous boulder sat, surrounded by a grove of tall curly-branched trees, which swayed in the gentle wind. The scene was a familiar one. "That big rock," I said. "And those trees. You've painted them."

"Oh, the *beetle*bungs. Aren't they just marvelous? They grow all over here, Up-Island. The bees love the blossoms, and you should taste the honey."

I watched the branches bob and the leaves flutter. "They're almost alive, like women dancing."

"I like their scientific name, *Nyssa sylvatica,* nymph of the woods. Sometimes I think there's something magical about them. They helped the family that lived here get through a lot."

I turned and took in the vista, the waves lapping the shore and the low islands in the distance. "Amazing view."

Mrs. Devereaux waved across the landscape. "The property runs from cove to cove. Salt Cove to the right, with the sandy beach, and Pepper Cove to the left around the bend—not much beach to speak of over there. Just an old boathouse." She shielded her eyes with one hand. "In the distance are the Elizabeth Islands. Named by explorer Bartholomew Gosnold in 1602."

"After you?" I asked.

Mrs. Devereaux laughed. "Oh, no, after Queen Elizabeth. And he named the Vineyard after his daughter Martha."

"Thank God this property hasn't been developed," I said.

She nodded. "We're very lucky."

Just the thought of some big mansion being built here, or cluster homes with asphalt driveways, made me a little sick.

Mrs. Devereaux gestured to the cottage's stonework. "You can see the seam in the front where it was flaked. Cut into sections to be moved."

I craved a quick look at the inside of the house. "Do you have a place I can plug in my phone, Mrs. Devereaux?"

"In the kitchen. Help yourself. I don't stand on formality here. Kitchen's at the back of the house."

I slipped into the cottage, the entryway cool and shaded, and let the screen door bang behind me. I passed a narrow staircase to the low-ceilinged living room; a threadbare velvet sofa was set between its two windows. I stopped short at the frameless paintings of varying sizes hung above the sofa, all of which featured the same subject: the boulder in the far field. Each caught the massive stone at a different time of day or different season, one under a covering of snow, each with different light and color, much like Monet's thirty haystack paintings.

From my jeans pocket I slid a page I'd torn from my art textbook, which showed a photograph of my favorite painting, *Untitled. A landscape. E. Devereaux, 1992*, printed below it. The big rock. Those beetlebung trees.

I continued on to the kitchen, with its wide white porcelain sink, knotty-pine cabinets, and round oak table, the finishes so worn and lived-in that the room must have been the heart of the house. Somewhere along the way that part had been an addition, tacked on to the older stone front of the house. It smelled good in there, like sugar and wood ash and vanilla extract. I admired the old stone fireplace and the little model tugboat on the mantel. I was a big fan of fireplaces in kitchens, and I stepped closer to read the inscription carved into the wood: *Deal justly, love mercy, and pay all debts.* I ran a finger along the words carved there. That was such an easier, simpler time.

An HGTV star might rip out the old paneling and replace it with shiplap, but to me it was perfect as it was. I wanted to bake banana bread or can something in there.

I found a cord and left my phone charging on the counter, and on my way out I stopped at the entryway closet; its door was open a crack. I found it packed with clothes and ran one hand along the variety of smallish-sized men's shirts and jackets hung there, loving the feel of the rough wools and cashmere I never got to wear at home.

I found my way back out to Mrs. Devereaux, who stood on the bluff at the easels, picking through a faded cigar box full of paint tubes.

My gaze wandered to the beach below, past a weathered gray shack to a wide plum-colored pond, iridescent as a dragonfly's wing, the sand a coppery brown around the edges.

"The colors look so different on this coast," I said. "More intense somehow. That pond . . ."

Mrs. Devereaux swished her paintbrush around in a baby-food jar of turpentine. "That's Copper Pond. Gets that aubergine color from minerals in the soil. Has magical properties, they say." She waved the brush in the direction of the woods behind the house. "On that hilltop above us, there was an Army camp—loaded with tents, filled with soldiers."

"Who built this house?" I asked.

"That would be old Ginny Smith's grandparents. Started farming here in the 1800s, off the boat from England via the mills in New Bedford."

"Who lived here last?"

"Ginny and her three grandchildren. All gone now. Few remember them."

I shut the paint box, my heart beating a bit faster. "Mrs. Devereaux, do you know anyone by the name of Nancy Starwood?"

Mrs. Devereaux set down her brush and turned. "Is that why you're really here?"

"I'm afraid I haven't been completely honest with you. Though I'd love to paint with you, I'm not here to take your class."

"Oh, really?" she asked, not at all shocked by my revelation.

"I found your name among my mother's things. She passed away this spring."

Mrs. Devereaux held the easel to steady herself. "I'm terribly sorry for your loss. What happened?"

"She had a brain aneurysm at the library where she worked."

"Sudden." Mrs. Devereaux looked down at her hands. "I see."

"At least it happened in the place where she was happiest," I said.

We listened to the waves lap the distant shore.

"So why are you here?" Mrs. Devereaux asked.

"Before she died, she'd been planning a trip, I think. And I found your name—first in the search history on her computer and then written on the back of an envelope. The words *cadence* and *briar* were written there, too. Names, maybe? Strange ones."

"No stranger than Marigold Violet. I like that your mother named you after a soap."

Something buzzed, warm and deep in me. "I don't—"

"I guess I haven't been totally honest, either. I was actually expecting your mother here, but then I received your painting-class inquiry and noticed the similar last name. I had no idea she'd passed."

"Why did you contact her to begin with?" I asked.

"She reached out to me."

I wrapped my arms around my waist. "Why? Did she know you? My family has no connection to this place."

"I'm afraid you're wrong."

"But my mother never set foot out of California in her whole life."

Mrs. Devereaux picked up her paintbrush. "I think you'll find you're mistaken about that, too, Miss Starwood."

"I don't understand."

"It's an extraordinary story, really. And it all started with the Smith girls."

2

BRIAR

—

Copper Pond Farm,
August 1942

IT WAS MY BROTHER TOM'S TWENTIETH BIRTHDAY, AND OUR DOG, Scout, and I watched the party from up in the barn hayloft. Half of the island stood packed in there wishing Tom well; the other half stood down on the distant beach, cooking the lobsters, silhouetted by the raging bonfire. It was easy to count our blessings from up there. A bounty of lobsters and corn and Gram's Portuguese bread. The most generous and loyal friends, many of them once Mum and Pop's. And a farm that somehow provided for us no matter the season.

But it wasn't all rosy, of course. Some days felt like we were all sailing the river Styx on our way to Hades; every day was something new to dread. Hitler's Nazi storm terrorizing Europe. Gram's illness. German U-boats downing American ships just off our shores. But none of us saw the big one coming. That we would kill one of our own. That surprised us all.

Scout sniffed the air as the lobster scent drifted up from the beach. Our guests gathered at the table—Gram's church ladies, Tom's work friends, farm neighbors; even Sharkey Athearn from the post office, who liked no one, came—and not just for the free supper. We were all there for the charm. Tom had it in buckets, and everyone wanted their little piece of it, me most of all. Since our parents died in a car crash in Boston when I was six, Tom had been the kindest stand-in father. And I wanted to give him his birthday gift.

To pass the time, I picked burrs from Scout's coat and dropped them below onto my sister, Cadence, who stood flirting with the Mayhew twins. I'd managed to land a nice collection of them on the shoulders of her sweater without her realizing. Little did the twins know she'd never grant either of them a date, saving herself for some future perfect man to take her off the island to New York City. Cadence had gotten the largest proportion of beauty in the family genetic lottery, the famous MacNeil look from Gram's family's side—anthracite-black hair with natural curl and thick-lashed eyes so startlingly blue that folks often stopped and stared. I didn't resent her for it. I was always more comfortable disappearing.

Cadence felt a burr land in her hair, pulled it out, then glared up at me in the loft and stomped off, probably to find her friend Bess and dance with her, causing the unattached men there to stare at them longingly. Just another fun night for Cadence.

I'd rigged an old record player to a speaker Gram brought from church, and a few people danced. Others gathered around the world's longest wooden table, just plywood on sawhorses, which Gram covered with newspaper, the traditional lobster-night tablecloth. The chairs were my favorite part. Everyone knew to bring their own, and I loved seeing them drawn around the table, a striped canvas beach chair pulled up between a velvet-seated dining chair and a paint-splattered step stool, as varied as we islanders ourselves.

Our grandmother bent to light the candles in the jelly jars scattered along the table, her white hair blue in the candlelight. Gram was the backbone of that community. Happy to help those who needed it and ever vigilant for those too proud to ask. As long as she was doing for others, Ginny Smith didn't feel so poor.

It was the perfect vantage point up there to count bald spots— a surprising number on women as well as men. And I'd spotted five silver flasks drawn from pockets to refresh Coca-Colas and ginger ales, a new record. Wartime was stressful.

I felt the loft shake as Tom climbed the ladder, bottle of beer in hand, and he settled next to me in the hay. "What are you doing up here? Counting stuff again?"

I leaned in to him, so close our shoulders touched. "Scout likes it up here."

Tom sipped his beer. "You carry her up and it takes six people to get her down."

I smiled, barely able to keep the secret—my surprise birthday gift for him. A night sail like we used to take. We'd shove off at midnight and camp on the beach over at Pasque. I'd already made the sandwiches.

He rubbed Scout's ear. "You two coming down? I'm gonna say a few words."

We were lucky the Fates had smiled on us and let Tom stay out of the war. He'd enlisted in the Army after Pearl Harbor, gone all through basic training, even Ranger School, and had been assigned a desk job in Washington. But he was granted an emergency leave to come home when Gram developed a heart condition no island doctor could treat. She'd already lost one son to the first war, and the Army granted her grandson an indefinite stay and all of us a sigh of relief.

"Since when have you said only a few words?" I asked.

Tom bit back a smile and tipped his head to one side. "Fair enough."

I considered Tom as he watched the crowd below. He wasn't what you'd call classically handsome. Individually, his features were nondescript, bland in an average American sort of way. But most every island girl agreed that when his supreme good nature filled in the blanks, it made him one of the best-looking boys there.

"Tyson says hi, but he has to leave," Tom said, trying to sound nonchalant.

I watched as Tom's friend Tyson Schmidt, the grandson of our next-door neighbor Conrad Schmidt, stepped out of the barn doors.

"Please stop trying to get me together with him," I said. "It's not going to happen, trust me."

"Well, I asked him to have your back. Keep you out of trouble."

"I don't need his help." We were quiet for a moment, watching the crowd. "I saw it again."

Tom turned to me. "You have to stop, Bri."

That morning, from up in my tree, I'd seen a German U-boat just off the coast of our farm and called it in to the island tip line.

"They didn't believe me. But I know what I saw."

"You've phoned in six times. I hate that they call you . . . you know." He took a sip of his beer.

"Just say it, Tom. Briar the Liar. It's not like I don't know."

He set his warm hand on mine. "I'm worried about you. Come down and join the living, Port."

I loved that nickname. We'd sailed Pop's old catboat together so often we called each other "Port" and "Starboard," since I sat on the left side of the boat and Tom to the right. He'd taught me to sail when I was six, as soon as I could swim. It was the one thing I had that my sister Cadence didn't.

"Please?" he asked. "Talk to some kids your own age. And I need you down there when I give my big speech."

I tried to hold back my smile. There was only one thing it could be. "You're announcing your engagement."

I found Bess in the crowd below, helping Gram set a steaming platter of corn on the table. Tom had met his match with Bess Stanhope, who'd lived with us since becoming estranged from her wealthy Edgartown family. She was beautiful in that slightly masculine, patrician sort of way and could talk to anyone. And, best of all, she didn't let him get away with much, which he actually liked, something no other woman had ever been able to do. She even taught him some French. "*Je t'aime plus que la vie elle-même,*" Bess would say, in her excellent boarding school French.

"*Je t'aime plus,*" Tom would reply, one of the many phrases Bess had taught him. Because he really did love her more.

Tom ran his fingers through his short hair. "I can't ask her yet. I have to get over to Falmouth to buy the ring." He sipped his beer. "Okay. Two more guesses."

I was afraid to ask but dove in. "You're going to take the desk job in Washington?" I held my breath, hoping that wasn't the answer.

He hesitated. "Um, nope. Guess again."

Relieved, I thought for a moment. "The Burbanks are ready to harvest."

Tom had made a big bet on planting this new variety of potato and he was sure they would be much sought after, with the obsession with frozen French fries in America.

"Not for another two weeks at least. Did you and Cadence step up the watering?"

I nodded.

Tom sat back on his knees. "Well, that's your three guesses. Now you have to come down and hear for yourself."

"Maybe."

"I hope so. Life's short, Bri. We have to enjoy every minute."

I stayed put and let Tom climb down the ladder. Scout and I watched him descend and go to the head of the table, as someone tinged a glass.

Tom shoved his hands into his trousers pockets and perused the crowd. "Thank you for coming tonight to celebrate my twenty years in this wonderful place. We may be on the front lines out here at sea, but there's no one better to handle it than islanders. Yankee ingenuity'll win this war. And speaking of the war, I have something I want to share with you all." He paused. "I ship out tomorrow morning."

The crowd buzzed with concern, and I sat up as if stung.

"I was lucky I got to spend some time with Gram, but now my outfit is being mobilized." He pulled a tan beret from his pocket and put it on. "I just found out I've been assigned to the Seventy-fifth Ranger Regiment."

I covered my mouth with both hands. A Ranger. Of course Tom would choose one of the most dangerous parts of the Army. The premier light-infantry unit and special-operations command. The lightning bolt on the patch said it all. They went in first and struck without warning.

Tom pressed his palms together. "Sorry I didn't tell you all, but there was no guarantee they'd take me. I'll be deployed soon from Fort Moore, Georgia. But I have a favor to ask." He paused and the crowd leaned in, the table candles lighting their faces. "Please take care of one another and my sisters, and my girlfriend, Bess, and our Gram. Keep supporting her farm stand, as if you need any more reason to eat Ginny Smith's donuts."

Laughter trickled through the crowd. "More glazed crullers!" someone called out.

Tom smiled. "And read any book my sister Cadence forces on you. She means well, I assure you, and you may as well just surrender once she locks in. I know we all have to ration our driving, but please give my sister Briar a ride to work if you see her walking on the street, since I won't be here to drive her. Right, Briar?"

He looked up to the hayloft, and thirty pair of eyes turned toward me. I shrank back. Why did he always *do* that? There was something in their gazes that I couldn't place as they lifted their faces to look. Like when the organist hit a wrong note in church and everyone turned. They didn't have to say, *Oh, the weird sister who wears the strange clothes.* It was all over their faces.

"We all have limited days on this beautiful earth," Tom continued, and the guests returned their gazes to him. "We need to work together. And no one's better at that than islanders."

Gram raised her glass. "Hear, hear!"

"While I'm gone, continue to live in the sunshine, swim the sea, drink the wild air. Thank you for one last night of lobster and your love, as I go off to fight for us to continue to do that as free people. And to the adventure of a lifetime. I couldn't have asked for a better gift for my twentieth."

He held up his glass and someone at the table softly sang, "*First to fight for the right, and to build the nation's might,*" the Army fight song, and most stood and joined in. "*Proud of all we have done, fighting till the battle's won, and the Army goes rolling along.*"

I tried to stave off the dizzying feeling that the world was shifting on its axis. How could my brother be leaving the next morning? Tom and I would not be going night sailing anytime soon. I held Scout close, as the bottom of my world dropped out and I felt myself falling. On my way to Hades.

3

CADENCE

August 1942

BESS AND I STOOD BOTTOM-TO-BOTTOM IN THE SNACK-SHACK kitchen of the Bayside Beach Club, each cooking with one hand and reading a novel with the other, an art we'd perfected during our summer of hard labor there.

By August 1942, the war had changed so much at the Bay, as it was known by locals, a private beach-and-sailing club situated along the harbor in Vineyard Haven. Our colleague Delia Murray was fired after her naval-aviator brother flew so low over the club that the manager, Mr. Wespi, called the Coast Guard. And then the cook, Roscoe Olivera, went off to enlist, leaving us to both cook the food in the barely ventilated kitchen and serve it, for no additional pay. The war had even taken Tom, and we would miss him stopping by every day at lunch.

I crossed the bluestone terrace, where a group of clubwomen sat lunching at one of the glass-topped tables, and took in the chaise longues lined up along the perfectly smooth beach that a hired man combed each morning. Here the toddlers, their blond hair bleached white by the sun, shoveled shells into pails and staggered across the beach, sand clinging to their terry-cloth diaper covers. The lucky ones. Insulated from much of the hardship of the war. And, come fall, they got to go home to Boston or New York.

Beyond the beach in busy Vineyard Haven Harbor, sailboats of all sizes bobbed as the steamship *Martha's Vineyard* arrived at the dock to discharge her passengers from the mainland. The boat Tom had left on that morning.

I tried not to think about Tom heading to war soon and approached the table of clubwomen, whom Bess called "the Richies," since they were all from elite families around the area, most from nearby West Chop. They were holding one of their last book-club meetings of the season, and Lindy Carmichael, their leader, sat at the head of the table. It was hard to stand before them dressed in my baggy uniform dress and dirty apron and—the worst part—hairnet. Each of them wore the same sleeveless shift dress from the Tog Shop in Edgartown, just in slightly different colors.

I asked them if they needed anything else, and one said, "Ketchup, I suppose," as if doing me a favor, finding something for me to go fetch.

With so many of the male club members enlisted or engaged in war-related business off-island, that place felt more like a girls' summer camp for wealthy women, who shared bottles of chardonnay after tennis while their children played under the lifeguard's care. I marveled at their rigid pecking order, in which wealth, it seemed, mattered most, then physical appearance.

Not that I counted in all of it. Once, the nephew of a West Chop matron well known at the club had asked me to a bonfire on Black Point Beach. I told him, "Maybe," reluctant to inform him that staff were forbidden from socializing with club members. When his aunt got wind of it, she immediately shipped him back off to school, where he'd be safe from the draft, and from me, of course.

Lindy held up the book. "Next week, we'll be reading this—*The Song of Bernadette*. Everyone have their copies?"

I had already read the book, given to me by a club member, and wrote that *it had the directness and verbal clarity of a drama, while at the same time the naïveté of folklore.* I maintained a healthy side business writing book summaries and reviews for the members who enjoyed the social aspect of these meetings more than the actual books. Mr. Wespi had no idea that I had provided those to six Bayside members the previous month, earning more than my weekly snack-bar check. And it was good practice if I was to ever get to New York City and find a publishing job, something that would solve so many problems for our little family.

But the publishing world was in flux and not hiring for many entry-level spots. The war had created shortages of paper along with the other things required to produce books, like cloth for covers, the copper used to make the printing plates, and chlorine that bleached the paper white.

Bess and I collected books that members left behind, or we found them at the dump, where we went for a variety of items.

Do these women even know how lucky they are to have new books?

Winifred Winthrop lay out on the beach on a chaise longue, in all her bronzed glory. From New York City, she'd been on the island all summer at her house on West Chop, after she and her husband separated when he moved to a banana plantation in Honduras. She was Bess's and my favorite customer, since she said little and tipped generously, out of the sight line of Mr. Wespi, and left us her *Vogue* magazines once she'd read them. She raised one thin-wristed hand and shook her gold charm bracelet, as she did whenever she needed ice water or a whiskey sour, and I hurried over.

"Thank you, darling," Winnie said, as I poured water into her glass.

Winnie represented physical perfection to me: tall, perfectly tanned, and impossibly chic in the sandals she had custom-made in Mykonos. I marveled at the idea that somewhere in Greece there was a shoe pattern hanging in a cobbler's shop with Mrs. Winthrop's name written on it in Greek.

Winnie picked up the newspaper and read aloud. " 'Up-Island Happenings,' by Cadence Smith. Your column is very funny, you know. I look forward to it every week."

I barely breathed. "Thank you, Mrs. Winthrop."

"Humor is much harder than straight drama. It's very well done."

She moved on to the obituaries, and I hurried into the kitchen to find Bess. "You won't believe what Winnie said."

"Did she sleep here last night? That woman doesn't leave the beach. She's getting wienie-roast skin."

They say you should have one friend who always makes you laugh and one who lets you cry, and Bess Stanhope was both. I shared every-thing with Bess. My books. My father's old razor, which we used to shave our legs. Even a bed once Tom shipped out.

"She said my column is well written."

"Well, of course it is. Everyone reads it. Even Mr. Wespi."

Just the thought of the club manager running about the place with his springy step, tilted forward on the balls of his feet, made my stom-ach hurt. The Wesp had almost fired me the week before for eating a quarter of a peanut butter and jelly sandwich a child had left on a plate.

"He's vile," I said.

Bess ate the last of her French fries. "Let's just make it to the end-of-season closing. Every penny counts."

Our paychecks were laughably small, but combined they were vital to keeping the farm afloat.

"Hey—there's a new officer up at Peaked Hill. Supposed to be good-looking."

Somehow Bess always knew the minute a new male under fifty stepped onto the island.

"Oh, really?" Not that we had much contact with officers, since they kept to themselves more than the enlisted men did.

I looked out the one window toward the club's front path, to the little white wooden RESTRICTED sign. Mr. Wespi stood there pointing it out to a young couple who'd tried to enter club grounds. He always made such an embarrassing scene, thrilled to flex his manager muscle with anyone even vaguely non-white or with a name like Cohen, unless they were some sort of royalty, however obscure.

"Members only," I heard him say, as if they'd failed his unspoken test. He firmly steered them back toward the street, while the members pretended not to see.

Bess turned a page. "Did I tell you Mr. Wespi said I should put socks in my bra to fill out the uniform better?"

I slid a stack of plates into the dishpan. "Don't tell Tom that. He'll run back here and defend your honor."

I wished I could stuff those words back in my mouth. Bess was keeping a brave face, but I knew from our talk late last night that she was having a terrible time with Tom's departure, having expected a ring from him before he left. We'd all cried as Tom left that morning, but she had sobbed in such a heartbreakingly pitiful way, long after the ferry had sailed out of sight, and her face was still swollen. At least work was a distraction for us both.

The screen door banged open, and Mr. Wespi bounded in. "Miss Stanhope, I've warned you about reading on the job."

A compact, mole-like man, who wore his orange hair swooped across his forehead and had freckles that comingled to give his skin a blotchy look, Mr. Wespi seemed to be everywhere and nowhere at once.

Bess shut the book and looked at him with the benign expression she'd developed during years of humoring boarding school teachers at Brillantmont in Switzerland. "Yes, Mr. Wespi."

"And shake that fryer basket. Mrs. Rayburn said the fries were too greasy." He leaned closer to Bess. "And I know you two have been helping yourselves to them."

Bess frowned. "How can you say that, Mr. Wespi?"

"Well, we're going through an extra quarter bag a day, so someone's eating them." He turned to me. "Now, I know your family has come on hard times, Miss Smith, but food has gotten expensive because of this war."

I sent him a little salute. "Understood, Mr. Wespi."

"Good. Now get out there and take the burgee down."

Since the war began, the job of tending to the club flag had fallen to Bess and me. Each morning and night we trudged to the flagpole near the beach at the back of the club. There we raised and lowered the little burgee, which was embroidered with the Bayside Beach Club insignia, crossed white oars on a navy-blue field. We found the ritual embarrassingly pretentious, since all present were required to stand and salute, and we thought there was enough of that sort of thing happening in Germany already.

Mr. Wespi left, the metal service bell tinged, and I turned to find club member Holly Jantzen's head and shoulders framed at the service window. A Jantzen of the sportswear Jantzens, she wore a beach cover-up and a straw hat with ball fringe along the brim. I liked the hat very much and hoped I'd see it at the West Tisbury dump soon, since the Richies had their maids bring their castoffs there at the close of each season. According to dump etiquette, we followed the "give-a-little-take-a-little rule," always leaving something in exchange. It was a pretty nice dump and had become our department store of sorts. First floor, women's clothing. Books on mezzanine.

Holly put her arm around her thirteen-year-old son, who stood next to her. "I just wanted to tell you it tastes like there's sand in little Reggie's ice cream again." The pom-poms on her hat shook as she handed me a white cup—chocolate, I could see through the fluted paper.

I took it. "So sorry, Mrs. Jantzen."

Holly pressed her chest against the window shelf. "Go ahead, taste it. I'll tell Mr. Wespi I gave you permission."

I wondered how I'd gotten to a place in my life where, at nineteen years old and more widely read than Oscar Wespi would ever be, I had to seek his permission to taste ice cream. I dipped a fresh spoon into it and held back a groan at the creamy chocolate goodness.

"It's just a few ice crystals, Mrs. Jantzen." I took a second bite and resisted knocking back the whole cup. I had to admit it was excellent soft-serve ice cream, though I despised Mr. Wespi's unnatural love for the hulking machine that produced it.

"Oh, yes—this happened by the end of last summer, too. I guess you need to clean out the machine again."

"Actually, I just did it this morning." I had come in at the crack of dawn to clean out the machine, to make sure I didn't spend a second more than I had to at that place.

"Well, looks like it needs to be done again. I'll tell Mr. Wespi."

"Oh, please don't bother him with it, Mrs. Jantzen. I'll get right on it."

"And one other thing." Holly checked her surroundings and slid a paper bag across the shelf of the service window toward me. "I need to give you this."

I peeked into the bag. "A book?"

"I'd like to hire you if I can. Left a dollar on the title page." She leaned in farther and lowered her voice. "Isn't that how this works?"

"What?"

"You read it for me. And I get, you know, a summary. I'm not accustomed to doing this sort of thing, but Dot Higginson said—" She reached to take the bag back. "But if it's too much trouble . . ."

"No." I grabbed the bag. "I'll do it."

"And there's another fifty cents in it for you if you can get it to me by Friday."

"I'll see what I can do, Mrs. Jantzen."

Once she left, I showed the book to Bess, who'd resumed her reading at the fryer basket.

Bess glanced at the cover. "*Song of Bernadette?* They get all the good ones. Can I have it when you're done?"

"Sorry. It has to go back to the customer so she can bring it to her meeting." I opened the book and inhaled the new-book scent—my favorite. "I wish we could just sit around and talk books all day."

Bess sat on the counter. "We should start our own book club."

"And we'll actually talk about the books." I tasted a fry and then shook more salt onto the batch.

"We can have a burgee of our own," Bess said. "I'll embroider our new symbol on it—a book and a wineglass full of Ginny's beetlebung-honey wine. We'll sit on the beach at the farm and eat the leftover potato chips from here."

I took another fry, picturing the two of us sitting on Gram's faded canvas beach chairs, gorging on books all day, the waves lapping our toes. "We can call it the Island Book and Wine Club."

Bess dumped frozen French fries into the fryer basket. "How about the Martha's Vineyard something?"

"The Martha's Vineyard Book and Wine Club?"

"The Martha's Vineyard *Beach* and Book Club," Bess said. "No Richies allowed."

I adjusted my hairnet. "*You're* a Richie, Bess."

"Not anymore. And promise me we'll vet our members carefully."

"Done," I said, as we each toasted our new club with a French fry.

I hurried back out to the terrace to clear the tables and Winnie strolled by, now dressed in a black piqué shift over her swimsuit, her raffia tote in one hand. She stepped closer to me, bringing a lovely wave of patchouli and clove. "You know, I read *The Sound and the Fury* review you wrote for Lindy. It's quite good. I have a proposition for you. Have you ever thought about working in publishing?"

I blinked, a bit lightheaded. "You mean for money?"

"I'm having some friends over for drinks at the yacht club."

The Edgartown Yacht Club was the Vineyard's most exclusive enclave, and it made the quaint Bayside Club look like a sandwich shop. Despite the yacht club's fondness for thrifty soup swaps, its membership was reserved for those of *Mayflower* lineage—"the Pilgrim People," as Bess called them—and for longtime yachtsmen whose ancestors had once sailed home to Edgartown Harbor, hulls laden with sperm oil and baleen, after whaling the Pacific. I had only seen the yacht club from the water, when we'd sailed our catboat into the harbor, all the beautiful people sipping their cocktails on the porch, the pennants flying.

"They're Putnam girls," Winnie said. "Coming up on the company yacht to entertain some clients."

By Putnam did she mean G. P. Putnam's Sons? Putnam published all the greats. James Fenimore Cooper. Edgar Allan Poe.

"Do you work there, too?"

"Not yet, though they never stop trying to hire me. We're friends from school. They'll want to talk shop, but it might be fun for you. Cocktails at four."

"I'll be there," I said, completely and pleasantly numb. "Thank you, Mrs. Winthrop!" I called out, but Winnie had already gone off to the parking lot.

I hurried back into the snack shack. "Can you cover for me? Winnie just invited me to cocktails with her publishing friends."

Bess grabbed my hands. "You're kidding."

"I have to be there at four."

"You'd better go soon so you can change. I'm assuming you're not planning to wear that uniform."

"I'll leave now. Gram can drive me."

"I heard that, Miss Smith." Mr. Wespi came to the service window. "If you want your paycheck, you won't be going anywhere."

4

BRIAR

—

1942

I STEPPED INTO MY FRIEND CONRAD SCHMIDT'S HOUSE, NEXT door to ours at the farm, to investigate the strange box I had found in one of the cupboards there. The house was a ramshackle old place, completely uninsulated, what he had called "the camp," built into the side of a wooded hill along the shore. Since Mr. Schmidt had died, his grandson, Tyson, who lived in Mr. Schmidt's elegant primary residence in Vineyard Haven during his summers home from boarding school, used the house for an occasional visit to the beach.

My footsteps shook the floor as I slipped in through the screened porch. I loved the smell of that old place, of mildew and salt water, but I was still sad every time I walked in. Mr. Schmidt and I had spent so many happy days here, talking war strategy after combing the beach for what we called our treasures and making models together.

I was still reeling from Mr. Schmidt's sudden death a month earlier, and I'd taken to wearing his green wool jacket most days, despite the heat, to keep him with me still. But I was finally ready to deal with the locked box I'd found. There was probably nothing interesting inside, old papers, maybe, sentimental keepsakes. But I'd never encountered a puzzle I couldn't solve, and it gnawed at me that I couldn't figure out how to open it.

I turned on the shortwave radio in the kitchen and a voice startled me. "*Come in, Sailfish Five.*"

Shortwave radios were prohibited for civilians during the war, but the Navy had provided them to fishermen. This included one for Gram, since she had been known to do her share of floundering, and they told her to monitor the airwaves and report any questionable activity. "Get rid of that thing," Gram had said to me when it interrupted her quiet baking time with staticky bursts of chatter. She much preferred the hulking radio Pastor Harshfield had given her when the congregation gifted him a newer model, which she'd placed in our front parlor.

So Mr. Schmidt had put Gram's shortwave in his kitchen and set it to receive calls from his friends that he called "the Squad," who shared information they'd gathered from a variety of sources, mostly from Coast Guard radio monitoring. After Conrad died, I still chatted with them now and then, and carrying that on made me miss him less. I got to know their code names for things. They called subs "red hots" and torpedoes "eels." And they believed me when I told them things.

Another call came in. *"Anyone hear about the U-boat sighted off the Cape?"*

I stepped closer to the radio.

"It surfaced and made contact with a Portuguese fisherman out of Falmouth in his two-stroke boat, which had live pots in it—one for fish, one for lobster, to keep them alive until he made it back to shore. He's out last night making seafood stew, sitting on his boat, when up comes the U-boat."

"Jesus."

"So these Kriegsmarine guys board his boat, see he has no radio, take all his lobster and all his fish and his stew that was on his little stove. Give him a case of schnapps and leave."

"Did he report it?"

"Not with Portugal being neutral. He was afraid to go to the authorities and he just threw the schnapps overboard. Then he phoned it in once he got home."

"Did he say what model U-boat?"

"Nope. Hey, have you seen something happening on the North Shore beaches? Major deliveries on Lambert's Cove. Points west."

I picked up the mic. I'd been all over those beaches, checking out the deliveries. "I got a good look," I said. "Crates marked U.S. Army. Bales of barbed wire. Last week they were trying to land some sort of amphibious vehicle."

"Probably practicing for beach invasion down the line."

The impending event on the island's North Shore beaches had them all hypothesizing madly. It was widely known to island residents that Martha's Vineyard would be the site of intense military maneuvers, but when they would happen and the adjacent details were an actual national secret.

I turned the radio down. That was all I needed, Gram knowing I was talking to grown men about war stuff. She would take the radio away in a heartbeat. I wouldn't tell Gram about the metal box I'd found, either. She'd have me give it to the police or something.

I'd discovered the box in what Mr. Schmidt called his "medicine closet," a hidden cupboard next to the fireplace that was probably used to hide booze during Prohibition. After he died, I found that the medications had been cleaned out and replaced with that metal box, which was impossible to open.

I went to the closet to get it and stopped to examine the framed photos on the wall. One of his beloved wife, Maria, who'd died years ago. Another of Mr. Schmidt's grandson, Tyson, as a toothless grinning baby. I smiled to think of the now almost-six-foot-tall Tyson as a newborn and wondered if he cried much as a child. He had become a remarkably even-tempered eighteen-year-old.

"Wasn't I a cute little bugger?"

I turned, startled to find Tyson there behind me, blond and tanned, like something out of a military-uniform catalog, an Army private's stripe on his arm. A familiar-looking girl trailed him, dressed in a two-piece swimsuit, cherry-red nail polish on her toes. It was the barely literate Shelby Parker of the Boston Parkers, summer West Tisbury residents; like Tyson, she was a Connecticut boarding school student. Miss Porter's. I had seen her all over the island, hanging around with fellow summer kids, usually looking at herself in the reflection of a shop window or the closest puddle. Not that she was so fantastic-looking, with her flat hair and squinty eyes.

"Oh, wow, is that Briar the Liar?" Shelby asked. "Does she just hang around here in your grandfather's house all day?"

"I'm right here," I said.

Tyson barely looked at Shelby. "Hi, Briar."

Shelby checked her face in the old mirror in the entryway.

"How was Hotchkiss?" I asked.

He smiled. "Good. Enlisted man now, though."

"Where've you been all summer?" I made an awkward wave toward his uniform. "Besides basic training."

"Traveled all over the country. Arizona. Louisiana. South Dakota, if you can believe it."

Most of the boys around my age annoyed me, but there was something about Tyson that I liked well enough. He was interested in more than just football and getting drunk at bonfires. He actually knew almost as much about Joan of Arc as I did. It wasn't anything remotely romantic, but I could talk to Tyson about my brother, and it helped lessen the terrible ache of missing Tom.

"Didn't know you'd be here today," I said.

"Shelby wants to swim."

Shelby stepped out onto the screened porch and looked left along the beach. "I want to ride in that boat."

"The *Tyche*?" Tyson asked. "That belongs to Briar's family."

"So?"

"It's a catboat and kinda hard to sail," I said, happy to have a little something over her. "My mother named it. Tyche is the Greek goddess of chance. She capriciously dispenses good and ill fortune."

"Got any chips?" Shelby asked.

We both just looked at her, and then Tyson turned to me. "So Tom shipped out okay?"

Shelby perked up. "Tom Smith? He's cute."

"Seventy-fifth Ranger Regiment," Tyson said. Just hearing that made me want to cry.

"Like a forest ranger?" Shelby asked.

"No," Tyson said. "Like the bravest guys in the military—they go in first."

Perhaps reaching the limit of words she understood, Shelby moseyed away to the kitchen and came out holding the shortwave.

"What's this?" she asked.

"Don't *touch* that, Shelby," Tyson said.

"Jeez. O*kay*." Shelby frowned and shuffled back into the kitchen.

The last thing we needed was Shelby Parker ratting out our shortwave.

Tyson returned his attention to me. "You must miss Tom already."

I liked his expression—concerned but not pitying. He and Tom had been summer friends for years, but with Tyson going off to boarding school each fall, they were only as friendly as a summer person and an islander could be.

"Yeah. Hopefully he'll be home on leave in a couple of months. We should have you over to the house if you're around."

"I'd walk over hot coals to get to your Gram's cooking." Tyson's gaze wandered to Shelby, who stood again at the entryway mirror, now on her toes and craning her neck to see her swimsuit bottom from behind. Tyson watched, mesmerized, as she bent to roll her breasts up higher in her swimsuit top.

Tyson forced his gaze back to me. "Well, if there's anything I can do, you have my number. I know you're shorthanded without him."

"I'm hungry," Shelby said as she wandered by us back to the kitchen, the pale half-moons of her fanny cheeks escaping her bathing-suit bottom. She turned up loud dance music on the regular radio.

"Just so you know, we're selling the place," Tyson said to me over the music. "So if you have any stuff around the house, you might want to take it home."

Something close to panic flashed in me. If they sold the camp, I would lose my last connection to Mr. Schmidt. And I needed to get the box out of the medicine closet. "Sure," I said. "Where are your parents?"

"They just left. Traveling until Thanksgiving, so I'm stuck with it all." Tyson looked about the room. "They've got realtors coming by soon."

"I can help you box up your grandfather's things. I have six twelve-by-twelve boxes, and that should fit a little over seventeen hundred cubic inches, so altogether just over ten thousand. That should handle it."

No wonder I had no friends. I'd somehow become old "Popcorn Harry" Collins, who would recite multiplication tables and Bible verses while he strolled the Oak Bluffs beach selling Darling's popcorn bars from his baskets.

"Thanks." Tyson leaned in. "And I haven't told Shelby yet, but I'm shipping out soon, too."

I felt a warm gush of pleasure through my arms that he'd told me before Shelby. And then the shifting sands of despair. Everyone was leaving.

"When?"

"Waiting to hear, but I'll keep you posted."

Shelby turned off the music, wandered back to the porch door, and tapped her painted toe. "Can we just *go,* Tyson? I have to be at Seven Gates for a parental clambake at five."

Her father worked in Detroit for Ford Motors, and the Parkers spent their summers at Shelby's mother's ancestral home in West Tisbury, boarded up for the season when I'd checked it out during my winter wanderings.

Tyson nodded my way. "Briar should come, too, right?"

Shelby seemed puzzled by that and, for the first time, addressed me directly, training her squinty eyes on me. "I guess. If you want. My parents don't let us drink anything but wine, but my brother has some scotch in his golf bag."

It felt kind of good to be invited somewhere by a summer kid, if you could call that an actual invitation, but I itched to get back to opening my metal box.

"No, thanks." I nodded toward the beach. "Tide's coming in. You'd better get down there."

High tide was the best time to swim on the North Shore, before low tide turned the beach into a vast plain of rocks and seaweed.

Tyson sent me a little wave, the couple made their way to the stairs, and I breathed freely again. That was a perfect example of why I didn't have friends my own age. It was all too complicated. I envied Tyson's relationship with Shelby, though I didn't get what he saw in her, beyond the extra helping of estrogen and the bathing-suit stuff. I accepted the fact that I'd never have a soulmate. Joan of Arc never married, and she led a productive life.

I watched Shelby and Tyson descend all fifty-two concrete stairs to the rocky beach, and a shiver went through me. The same stairs Mr. Schmidt fell down to his death. If only I'd been there to lend an arm like I always had, it might have been different.

I hurried back into the house, pressed the panel next to the fireplace, and the door swung open with a satisfying little spring action. I slid out the box, the smooth metal cool in my hands, and set it on the table for a good look. It was dark brown, the size of a small shoebox, and pretty heavy. I'd tried every numeric permutation I could imagine, sliding the combination-lock numbers with my thumb, but the lock wouldn't release.

It was German-made, of that I was certain. I ran my fingers over the embossed words on the lid. *Buro des Zahlmeisters.* Purser's Office. It looked relatively modern and, if from a ship's purser's office, had probably been used to hold military paychecks aboard a German ship. I shook the box and felt something move around inside.

I itched with curiosity. Surely Mr. Schmidt put it there? Maybe one of his friends gave it to him? I never saw it when he was alive. If he were here, he'd tell me to use my resourcefulness and intuition to puzzle it out.

I took a knife from the drawer, slid it into the seam between the base and lid, and pressed, but the metal was too strong. I could take it to an auto-repair or boatbuilding shop and have them pry it open, but then they'd see the contents. What if there was something of a sensitive nature inside? I needed to protect Mr. Schmidt's legacy.

I slid the box back into the cabinet and pressed the door closed. I wanted that combination so badly. And there was only one place to get it.

5

CADENCE

THE MORNING THE SOLDIERS CAME TO THE FARM, BESS AND I STOOD out in front of the cottage, snipping flowers for Gram's farm stand, lilies and foxglove that grew along the low white picket fence, the bees still buzzing in some. I tried to brush off the sting of the reality that I wouldn't be meeting Winnie's publishing friends anytime soon. After Mr. Wespi kept Bess and me under house arrest the day before and watched us reclean his ice cream machine, we rode our bikes home and staggered into the cottage, our aprons streaked with chocolate. The Wesp had withheld my one phone call, claiming Edgartown was a toll call, and by the time I used the drugstore's phone to reach the yacht club, Winnie and the Putnam ladies were long gone. I'd missed the possibility of a high-paying New York job in exchange for a paycheck of three dollars and sixty-three cents.

I breathed a lungful of sea air and took in the hazy view, the morning fog still burning off the slope, baring one shoulder of the beach beyond. How lucky we were to live in that heavenly spot, Copper Pond shimmering down below, our young turnips planted along the lower field. Not a terrible place to be while I awaited my life in New York. But what would my parents have said about the rusting tractor and the blue paint peeling off the cottage's front door? Though it was August, we'd even gotten used to the coal buckets of rock salt left on either side of the front door, complete with metal scoops, which we used to melt ice and snow on the front walk. Chances were, they'd probably stay there until next winter. All I needed were more hours in the day and a steady income to get that place back in shape.

Gram was inside, cleaning up after breakfast, during which she'd performed one of her bizarre soothsaying rituals, predicting our futures "in the cup." It was too hot to drink warm tea, but Gram brewed loose oolong, poured some into one of her mismatched flowered teacups, and drained the water back into the pot.

Gram was either a gifted clairvoyant or just committed to the role. She held the cup high and circled it around her head three times, then peered into the bottom of it and announced her prophecies. As embarrassing as the ritual was, Gram had foretold some important events. My parents' fatal auto accident. And Briar's broken rib from falling out of her tree. Briar claimed Gram was 85 percent correct in her predictions. But, like all of Briar's assertions, they were only loosely factual.

"Will the *Gazette* like my latest column?" I'd asked Gram. My weekly column was due later that morning.

"They love every column," Bess said. "Ask a better question."

I crossed my fingers. "Will I ever move to New York City?"

Gram avoided my gaze. "Ask another time."

Why does she always deflect that question? "You can be very annoying, Gram."

"You'll miss me when I'm gone," she replied with a smile, her pat answer to anything.

Gram stepped out into the sunshine on the grassy bluff at the side of the house and hung her wash on the line, her stockings sagging over ankles thick as soup cans. She wore her black oxford church shoes everywhere, whether she was weeding potato plants or taking in wash for islanders who couldn't fend for themselves. As good friends often do, Gram had come to look like her church friends and was often indistinguishable in that hardy flock of New England women her age, with their topknotted gray hair and ample bosoms, which had long ago succumbed to the effects of gravity.

A breeze puffed the skirt of Gram's good dress, a faded flowered cotton she washed every day, her work apron tied at the waist. I'd saved almost three dollars toward the blue shirtwaist she'd admired in the window of Lillian's dress shop on Main Street. *One more thing I can help with once I get a publishing job in Manhattan. I'll buy Gram a whole closet of dresses.*

Gram took down some dry sheets and then pinned Briar's brown corduroy pants to the line—my sister's favorites, even in ninety-degree weather. Tom had tried to get Briar to wear one of my skirts once, but she wouldn't budge. I worried about her ghoulish strategy of watching the newspaper for the obituaries of older people, usually men on the smaller side, whose wardrobes she admired, full of good moth-free cashmere and wools, and then shopping Vineyard Thrift Shop exactly ten days after they passed, when their clothes typically wound up there. It didn't help her social life to dress like Little Lord Fauntleroy.

Gram had just gotten to the chorus in the church hymn she was singing—my favorite one, where the willful young boy drowns in a water-lily pond—when we heard the sound of pounding footsteps along our little dirt road. Bess and I lobbed our flower nippers into the tin bucket.

"My God," Bess said, pulling off her work gloves. "Men."

The soldiers came, running in unison, two abreast. We watched them approach, an endless stream, tanned and fit, dressed in Army green shirts and shorts, each with a fully loaded pack on his back. For an island with a winter population of five thousand, it felt like a glorious avalanche of males ready to defend our little island, so vulnerable out there in the sea, nothing but ocean between us and Europe.

Bess linked her arm in mine, releasing her rich-girl scent of Arpege and cold cream. "I think those are the Cape Cod Commandos. Over from Camp Edwards. Tom told me they've been training up at Peaked Hill."

"They must be lost," I said. "Probably don't realize this is private land."

"There goes our nude sunbathing," Bess said. "Though maybe it's our duty to the troops to continue."

I brushed the dust from my overalls and stood taller, hoping for at least a smile from one of the soldiers, but they only snuck a few glances at us.

"I know what you're thinking," Bess said. "Any one of them could get you off this island."

"I suppose." I searched the boys' faces and felt more sorrow than anything. Some looked barely out of high school and were training to battle the Germans. Or the Japanese. Half of my graduating class had already gone. One day they were out floundering and checking lobster pots; the next they shipped out. I could barely think of our Tom arriving in Europe soon. At least that was what Gram had seen in the cup.

"They're the ones with the good-looking commanding officer—Major Gilbert," Bess said. "Sue Mayhew said she saw him at Larsen's, and a woman there thought he was so handsome that she got dizzy and had to sit down and apply a cold pack of fish ice."

Gram came around to the front of the house, blinding-white sheets billowing in her arms, and joined us to watch the men. "Poor boys. Most of them won't see Christmas."

The soldiers turned, nimble as a flock of birds, and headed down the hill to the beach.

With growing alarm, I watched the troops head toward the newly planted turnip field.

I called to them, "No, stay up here on the road—you'll kill the plants!"

A jeep brought up the rear of the procession, the driver wrangling a large map, which flapped around on his lap like a trapped seagull.

I stepped into the road and waved my arms. "You there!"

He braked suddenly, the scent of burning rubber in the air. "Do you always stand in front of oncoming cars?"

"Do you always read maps while you drive?" I asked.

"Get the fish ice," Bess murmured.

"Kindly move aside, miss," the driver said. "While it's still daylight?"

From Bess's reaction, I assumed this was Major Gilbert, of Larsen's fame. He wore the light-brown uniform all the Peaked Hill officers did, and he seemed older than me, perhaps twenty-five to my nineteen years. My first impression was that he certainly seemed good-looking enough, perhaps the handsomest man I'd seen in my life, with his wide-set light eyes and nice chin, somewhat lanky and well-built from what I could see with him sitting down. But his smug air ruined the whole thing.

Bess had left out the part about him being British. I approached the driver's side of the jeep. "You must be lost. This property is private."

He turned to Gram. "Are you the owner, ma'am?"

Gram nodded. "I am. Virginia Smith. Most call me Ginny. This is my granddaughter Cadence and her friend Bess Stanhope. I have another granddaughter and a grandson, Tom, off in the Army."

He returned the nod. "Major Gilbert. Peaked Hill. Under different circumstances I'd be fascinated with the intricacies of your family tree. But right now I need beach access."

The way he drove matched his cocky attitude. While we civilians drove so carefully, under the thirty-five-mile-per-hour "Victory Speed" to preserve rationed gas and precious, old rubber tires, he drove at a breakneck pace.

I shook my head. "So you just run across our land willy-nilly?"

He looked down at me. "Worse luck, I'm afraid. My orders are to seize any property I see as vital for military training. We'll be here awhile."

I took a step back. "The whole farm? This is how we earn our living. You can't do that."

"As your new neighbors to the north, I regret to inform you that it's a *fait accompli*. A done deal, you might say."

"I know what a *fait accompli* is, Major. Who can we call to appeal this? Your men can't simply kill our new crop."

He folded his map. "If you write to Washington double-quick, you might hear by the new year."

Gram draped her sheets over the fence and walked up to the jeep. "We're happy to do our part for the war, Major, but perhaps your men could use the road to get to the beach? That way they wouldn't run right across our fields."

"Sorry to push in, Mrs. Smith, but we need the most direct route."

I leaned closer to him. "I don't think you understand. We depend on those crops to survive. And we can barely run this place as it is, with my brother gone. He just shipped out. He's an Army Ranger. So we rely on that income more than ever."

"A Ranger? He must be quite a soldier." He paused for a moment. "I'm sorry he had to ship out, but during wartime, things like this cannot be helped, can they?"

I wiped the sweat from my temple. I loathed that crisp British way of speaking that so often ended with a question, as if anyone else had a say.

Bess stepped to the gate. "Cadence writes a column in the *Gazette*. Delivering one today, in fact. It would be a shame for your general to read how you drove a local Vineyard family into poverty."

The major barely looked at Bess. "She can write whatever she likes." He turned to Gram. "What's the quickest way down to the beach? The roads here are confounding, I must say. South Road. Middle Road. No rhyme or reason to this place."

Gram set one hand on my shoulder. "Cadence gives an excellent tour of the island—though most men have a hard time keeping their eyes on the road when she's the guide."

"Gram, please." I willed myself to melt into the dirt.

The major glanced at me. "I'm sure there's rather a queue for your charming granddaughter's tours, but right now I need to get to the beach, before my men decide to swim for the mainland and escape me."

"Who would blame them?" I asked. Though I thoroughly disliked Major Gilbert, something about his dismissal still wounded me.

I hurried to the front hall and brought back a carton of books I'd been collecting. "You can at least bring these up to the base and distribute them to your men."

He glanced at the box. "My men don't have time for literature and aren't exactly clamoring for books, except comic books. They're Americans, after all."

"Yesterday one of your men borrowed a book from our farm-stand lending library. He left a very nice note. You could at least take the books up there and offer them."

He turned to Gram. "The quickest drive to the beach?"

"Just follow this road down," Gram said. "Mind the potholes, but you'll see the beach soon enough."

"Don't drive on the sand, though," I said. "Birds are nesting."

"All right, then." He prepared to drive off.

"Do come back for tea sometime, Major," Gram said. "I can make you a Cornish pasty if I have enough flour."

"No offense, Mrs. Smith, but I shudder to think of the poor pasty coming out of an American kitchen." He glanced at the cottage, the broken gate, the rusty tin bucket, the sheets draped over the fence. He probably thought we ate squirrel and pulled our own teeth.

"My mother was a Killigrew from Cornwall," Gram said.

"Is that right?" the major asked, clearly skeptical.

"Buried beneath the floor of the altar at St. Budock Church."

"I know St. Budock's well," he said. "If you have to die, there's no better place to do it than in Cornwall."

"She made Cornish pasties for the miners to take in their lunch pails, and she baked their initials into them. In case they didn't finish half, they could save it for later. The men fought over those little pies. You should come for tea, and I'll make one for you."

He smiled at Gram. "Good day, Mrs. Smith." He glanced at Bess and me and drove on. "Ladies."

The jeep rumbled off down the hill, as hot dust sifted onto us. I set down my carton of books and kicked the rusty bucket into the road with a clatter. "I can't believe this," I said to Bess. "How could he be so rude to Gram? And how could Gram be so nice to him? If he ever did come, he'd be a most annoying guest. Certainly turn up his nose at her tea-leaf reading."

"I'm glad you spoke up," Gram said.

"What the heck, Gram? He basically just took over our farm and you stood there and let him."

"Well, I was trying to appeal to his sensible side."

"He doesn't have one." I tracked his jeep as he made his way toward the beach. "How are we supposed to get by without the turnips? Tom would have a fit."

Gram gathered her sheets from the fence. "Well, if you can't move heaven, then just raise hell."

"I certainly will." I watched the men on the distant beach, running with full packs. "He works them to the bone. And they'll be here every day. Ruining the place." I still had time to add the major's little visit to my column.

"We've still got the potatoes," Bess said. "And he seems like the perfect man for you, Cadence. Except for the horrible, pompous part. He's pretty funny, actually, and the best-looking man on this island right now by far."

The major's jeep had made it to the beach, and he sped along the shore on his fat new tires, leaving deep ruts in the sand. Would he kill all our birds? "I'd never date such a foul human."

Gram smoothed back my hair. "Well, that's terribly inconvenient, since you're going to marry Major Gilbert." She turned and stepped toward the house.

"Please, Gram," I called after her. "That's ridiculous."

"Oh, no, it's not," she added with a shrug. "I saw it in the cup."

6

BRIAR

I CAME TO WORK AS USUAL AT THE VAN RYPER MODEL COMPANY in Vineyard Haven, eager to get my hands on the combination to Mr. Schmidt's box. It felt like home there at my workbench, the ocean lapping the beach outside my window. I loved the hush of that place, all of us quietly sanding and sawing, the scent of poplar wood and shellac in the air. It was my last day of temp work, and I hoped my boss, Mr. Reed, would need me again soon.

I was lucky to work now and then at Van Ryper Models, one of a network of souvenir-model shops the Navy used to supplement its production of military war models. Recognition models, to help soldiers identify enemy ships and planes. And, even luckier for me, every ship model we built came with a thick file of research meant to ensure accuracy. American intelligence provided ship blueprints and aerial-reconnaissance photographs of the various vessels, even a copy of the ship's operations handbook so we could get the most minute shipboard details right.

For the last model I'd built, the handbook included chapters for toilet maintenance, kitchen-knife sharpening, and proper condom storage. All precisely detailed, in true German style. If Mr. Schmidt's box had been in the purser's office of a German ship, the combination to the lock might be listed in the ship's manual.

Not that borrowing anything classified from the government was casual for me. I'd done it before, here and there, but it always made me feel like my stomach was about to fall out onto the floor. Just going into the classified room during the course of my work was a big deal. Mr. Reed treated it like entering the Hohensalzburg Fortress or something, with a whole system of key checks and protocols.

I gathered my green boiled-wool coat close and glued the railing of my last Japanese destroyer model. In my miniature world, the tiny parapets and smokestacks formed a safer and more orderly place. Soon there was no beloved brother going off to war across the Atlantic Ocean, zigzagging past German U-boats. No sick grandmother. No friends that stopped coming around once I talked too much about model-making.

Mr. Reed came and admired the wooden tray of all those scale models before me. "Your paints made this so much more realistic-looking, Briar," he said.

I liked that Mr. Reed allowed me the special privilege of bringing my own paints from home.

"I'll miss you, Briar," he said. "Hopefully I'll have more work soon."

"Mr. Reed, do you mind if I get my own folder from the classified room? I just need to check the Japanese schematics one last time." A pinch of guilt nipped at me for lying to him.

He handed me the key. "No need to sign in. Just get it back in there stat."

"Of course, Mr. Reed."

I steeled myself against the jitters. Borrowing a classified document could get me in real trouble. I'd read in the paper that a model maker at a similar shop in New York was just caught discussing the Japanese submarine he was working on. And two weeks before, a model shop in Wisconsin reported that an employee smuggled out a copy of a top-secret schematic inked on his hand, allegedly to show his son. Both men were serving sentences at the United States Disciplinary Barracks at Fort Leavenworth. I'd borrowed classified docs before. I just had to be extra careful.

I stepped into the classified room and closed the door behind me, huffing quiet little breaths to stay calm. The one eyebrow window above me gave scant light, and I yanked on the chain for the overhead bulb, illuminating the metal file cabinets against three walls.

The scent of cedar was strong in there and reminded me of Gram's bedroom closet. What would she think of what I was doing?

I pulled out the gray metal drawer marked *M* and found *Master File Drawings of German Naval Vessels*. I slid out the file, opened it, and paged through the blueprints and top-secret photos of the ships. Where was the handbook? I heard cars pulling into the driveway out front and upped my pace, flipping through the papers. At last I came to the tiny handbook, wedged between two photos. I opened it with shaking fingers and flipped to the purser's office chapter, where I found three pages of combinations. I pulled the pages out, folded them, and slipped them down the front of my shirt.

"Looking for something?"

A flash of fear went through me as I turned to find my colleague standing in the doorway. It was harmless Jerry Whitcomb, who worked at a bench near mine.

"Maybe I should be in the Secret Service," he said. "You didn't even hear me come in."

I sighed. "Just double-checking a schematic."

"For your Japanese subs? In the *M* drawer?"

"Oh, right." I dropped the handbook back into the file and closed the drawer.

Jerry leaned against the doorjamb, settling in to deliver one of his unsolicited little discourses. "Like the Jap subs, U-boats have to stay on top of the water most of the time, you know. Need to recharge their batteries every few hours. Like a shark that has to come up from the depths to breathe."

I stared at that thirty-year-old man, astounded by his ability to underestimate me, though for me it was a daily occurrence with men in general.

Something about my silence must have registered with him. "Of course you know that, don't you? You're the granddaughter of Zeb Smith. He made models for Teddy Roosevelt, didn't he?"

"I'm busy, Jerry."

"You're wearing men's clothes again. You like Joan of Arc, right? She wore men's clothes, too. That why you do?"

"Joan of Arc wore men's clothes because she'd been assaulted by the English when she wore women's clothes. And maybe she just liked them better."

"Anybody ever mistake you for a guy?"

"No, how about you, Jerry?"

He paused and then chuckled at that. "See that U-boat again? I believe you, ya know. Anytime I hear someone call you Briar the Liar, I say, 'Whoa. Briar Smith knows her stuff. If she says she saw a U-boat, she two hundred percent did.' "

"Thanks."

"Hey, you hear that a U-boat surfaced last night at sunset, just outside the harbor at Menemsha, and the soldiers demanded Richie Mayhew give up his swordfish? Then the Krauts just took it and went on their way. Gettin' to be like an A&W drive-in around here, Germans ordering their dinner."

"Anybody catch the U-boat's call letters?"

"Not that I know of. Waitress at the Beach Plum Inn said she had two bearded guys with accents come in, and she swore they came off a U-boat. Saw them cuttin' their meat in the European way. Cops took 'em away, but I haven't seen a thing about it in the *Gazette*."

They were probably keeping it hush-hush so the tourists wouldn't get scared away. No one wanted to laze on a beach with Nazi Kriegsmarine soldiers tripping over them. Of course, Cadence did her part with her column, keeping a positive tone at all costs.

I closed the file, returned the key, and went back to my desk. I made sure Jerry wasn't looking, took the pages from my shirtfront, and slid them into the false bottom of the old cigar box I kept my paint tubes in. I sighed with relief as I shoved the cigar box into my knapsack.

All of a sudden I heard men's voices in front of the shop, and Jerry peered out the window. "Wow, it's Captain McManus."

"Are you kidding?" I asked.

"It's no big deal. Just another security check. Like last week."

The month before, McManus had been promoted to island FBI chief, and he'd instituted weekly checks at the shop. I was out sick when they visited last.

McManus came in and stepped toward Mr. Reed's glass-walled office, staring at me as he went.

Mr. Reed pushed himself back from his desk. "Frank."

I pictured the pages in the cigar box in my knapsack. There was no way he'd find them.

"Good to see ya," Mr. Reed said, and closed the office door.

Captain McManus sat and angled himself for a view of the workers in the room. He was somewhat new to the island—moved here with his wife five or so years before, and she'd died from cancer—and I'd seen him around. He didn't fit my impression of what an FBI captain would look like off-island, crew-cut and fit, ready to chase down criminals. McManus was well into his sixties and not exactly a men's fashion model, in his thick black-framed eyeglasses, stained khaki trousers, and too-tight navy-blue windbreaker. And with that paunch, he wasn't running anywhere. But it was Martha's Vineyard. Not exactly crime-ridden. If criminals were running, it wouldn't be far.

For the amount of glass around it, Mr. Reed's little office was remarkably soundproof, but sitting so close to it, I could make out words if I listened hard enough.

"Who's the kid?" McManus asked. "She wasn't here last week."

"Briar Smith," Mr. Reed replied. "One of my best temp modelers."

I bristled at the word *kid*. At sixteen, I probably knew more about the U.S. military than McManus did.

"Jesus, Everett. You let a teenager handle classified documents?"

McManus glanced at me through the glass, and I quickly averted my eyes.

"Smith—she's the one that's been bugging the tip line with false alarms," McManus said. "And I hear she was cozy with a sympathizer."

"Conrad Schmidt? Nah. Born in Germany, but he was no sympathizer. Decorated by Pershing himself. He was a fine man."

"You're a German lover now, too?"

Mr. Reed leaned back in his chair. "Heard you just took Bert the Barber from his shop and put him under house arrest. Just for being Italian."

"In case you didn't notice, Mussolini declared war on us when Hitler did. We can't be too careful."

"Jesus, Frank—Bert was right in the middle of a shave."

"Maybe you don't understand the Fifth Column and how it works. There are scores of German, Japanese, and Italian sympathizers living in this country, actively working to take us down from within."

A drop of sweat trickled down my back. It was too late to remove the pages. What if they caught me with them? Would they punish Mr. Reed, too?

McManus lit a cigarette. "Where'd you find her?"

"Got her name from the hobby shop in town."

"The hobby shop."

"I'm under the gun here, Frank. We have to use temps to keep up with the workload. And she's faster than three guys."

"What's to stop her from yakking to school pals about top-secret stuff? Maybe swipe a few things?"

"She's a good kid. Graduated early and keeps to herself, some sorta genius. Taught herself German."

"Interesting. They don't offer that at Tisbury High."

"She's no thief, Frank. Certainly no spy. Brother's an Army Ranger."

"Impressive." McManus crushed out his cigarette and strode to the door. "Mind if I lead the employee search today?"

"Be my guest." Mr. Reed followed him out and addressed the employees. "We're closing early today, everyone."

We all knew what that meant. We were to leave a clean workbench and endure a quick security check. I shakily slid the strap of my knapsack over my shoulder and joined the line.

As we shuffled forward, I watched Mr. Reed and McManus do a cursory check of my colleagues' belongings at the table near the door, making a little chitchat here and there. When I approached the table, McManus reached for my knapsack and removed the cigar box. Up close I got a bird's-eye view of that windbreaker, the cuffs stained with some sort of greasy stuff, and I wasn't thrilled about him touching my belongings.

"Coat and boots off, Briar," Mr. Reed said with a smile. "Trouser pockets inside out."

As the captain pawed through the jumble of paint tubes in my cigar box, I slipped off my coat and pulled out my pockets so they hung like donkey ears, my heart thumping against my shirtfront.

McManus attempted a smile, and I tried not to look too hard at his teeth, which may have been dentures.

"I've heard a lot about you, Miss Smith, though you probably overheard the whole conversation."

I nodded. "I did, actually."

"Visit the classified room today?" he asked.

I tried to sound nonchalant. "Checking a schematic for my Japanese sub."

"Your sub?" he asked with a smile.

"The recognition model I'm building for the Navy."

McManus dumped the paints out of the cigar box. "Mr. Reed tells me you knew Conrad Schmidt."

I nodded, unable to breathe as I watched him wedge his thumbnail under the cigar-box bottom and try to peel it up.

"Family friend?"

"He lived next door to us, and we just became friends. He liked to walk the beach."

"I see." McManus held the box up to the light. "You've phoned in a few U-boat sightings to the tip line."

I ran through my options. If I was honest, he'd come snooping around Mr. Schmidt's for sure.

"Guess I've been reading too many magazine stories."

McManus set down the cigar box and lifted the jacket from the table. "Yours?"

"Mr. Schmidt's," I said. "I started wearing it after he died."

He nodded, perhaps a glimmer of sympathy in his eyes. "When I was in Germany years ago, everyone there wore one of these. Tyrolean, they call it?" He showed me the label. "Says *Made in Düsseldorf.* Did Schmidt go back to the fatherland often?"

"Not that I know of."

"My sources tell me his house is for sale."

I swallowed hard. "Yes."

"I may come over and have a look-see."

I met his gaze. "Swell."

"And how about you come to the office and we take a fresh set of fingerprints?"

I looked to Mr. Reed. "We already did that here."

"Oh, I like to do my own. We can get to know each other better."

"Sure, I guess."

McManus swept the paint tubes back into the cigar box. "Good, then. You're free to go." He handed me an ecru card. "Come see me for those fingerprints. And I suggest if you get the urge to phone in another false alarm, you channel your imagination into writing a fiction story for one of those war magazines."

"Good idea." I slipped the card into my pocket. "See you later."

"Hope so," he said.

I walked out into the parking lot, relieved to have made it out undetected.

I headed for home, vaguely unsettled. I was happy I'd made it past McManus and was eager to open the box but puzzled by an annoying gnat of unfinished business. Why had he been so nice? He suspected me of something, but what was his plan?

When I got back to Mr. Schmidt's house, I pulled the box from the fireplace cupboard, set it on the kitchen table, and slid the pages of combinations from the cigar-box bottom. One of them had to open it, but with my luck it would be the very last one, so I started at the end of the list, wheeling the dials with the tip of my thumb. I tried the lock after each one, with no success, and my thumb blistered. It was going to be a long afternoon.

Finally I keyed the right combination and the lid opened with a satisfying click. I stared at the contents, almost unable to believe I'd done it.

I was in.

UP-ISLAND HAPPENINGS

———

By CADENCE SMITH

THIS AUTHOR, WHO HASN'T EVEN BEGUN TO GRAY AT THE temples, remembers a time when there wasn't a single restaurant Up-Island, and now they're popping up like morels after a spring rain. Our newest eatery, Hortense's, on State Road, conceived on the notion that a malted milk and a sandwich counts as a fine supper, is a sheer delight. Now that, due to wartime shortages, chicken à la king is the new steak, you may want to be first in the door. If you don't mind dining next to the man in the suspenders who may have delivered the lettuce that morning, give it a whirl.

The chamber of commerce, tasked with ensuring that cheer and gaiety run rife at all times here on the Vineyard, assures the vacationing public that this beautiful island and its equally hand-some sister, Nantucket, are virtually unchanged since the war's inception. Except for the deluge of handsome servicemen, all continues exactly as in prewar days. We hear that the residents of Chappaquiddick still cross the channel at Edgartown without sighting periscopes and sleep well in their undefended outpost, among the wild roses and beach grass.

Speaking of handsome servicemen, the dauntless Tom Smith has gone off to add his considerable might to the U.S. Army's 75th Ranger Regiment and will no doubt be sending back up-dates soon.

If you think of all Englishmen as well-mannered to a fault and with a fondness for queuing, Major Gilbert of the British Allied forces, new to Peaked Hill base, may alter those precon-ceptions. Here from Camp Edwards, he is whipping his Cape Cod Commandos into fighting shape at Copper Pond Farm

Beach. His first task was to bravely take on a detachment of young plants; he wiped them out and emerged victorious, perhaps with his eye on other crops to take on. What the good major is reading is apparently a national secret, but his men are enjoying *War and Peace* from the farm-stand lending library and hoping for less of the former and more of the latter.

Books continue to be scarce due to wartime shortages. In West Tisbury, Joanne Finnegan is reading her aunt's copy of Mary Shelley's *Frankenstein*, limited to daylight reading due to blackout regulations. "It's for the best," Joanne said. "It's much too nightmare-inducing to read before bed."

And who is this week's book winner of *For Whom the Bell Tolls*? It tolls for thee, Sue Seligman. Please pick it up at Ginny Smith's farm stand and pass it to your neighbor once you read and review.

7

CADENCE

—

1942

BESS AND I WOKE AND RAN WHOOPING DOWN THE HILL TO THE beach, carrying the burgee Bess had made for the Martha's Vineyard Beach and Book Club. She'd sewn that little flag beautifully, the letters *MVBB* cut from Gram's old floral calico apron and sewn with Bess's Swiss boarding school–taught Breton stitches onto a triangle cut from a pink terry-cloth dish towel. We hoisted it up the rusty flagpole near the beach shack and then sat on Gram's wooden folding chairs, close enough to the surf to wet our feet. It was our inaugural meeting, and our first book was *The Song of Bernadette,* since I'd found three copies in the Bayside Club lost and found.

I'd tried bribing Briar to come by promising some old *Scientific American* magazines I'd found at the dump, but she practically ran from me and claimed she had work. I was not surprised, since she called fiction "the scourge of all mankind," but I knew she'd join us one day.

Bess and I agreed that we'd all vote by secret ballot for the books we would read in the following months and carefully vet any new inductees for compatibility and like-minded reading taste. But then Gram just invited a friend of hers from church, Margaret Coutinho, two years ahead of me in high school.

"She makes the best linguica sandwiches," Gram said, as if that mattered for a book club. "And she has little family here to speak of, so it's the Christian thing to do."

Margaret's Portuguese ancestors had come to the island during the whaling days, when the ships would stop in the Azores to add crew, and many of the sailors settled on the Vineyard. Her parents had gone back to Portugal to take care of her grandfather, and she lived with her aunt in Chilmark. She seemed pretty easygoing and worked at a drugstore, where she got free products sometimes, *and* she had a car with four good tires, which she was allowed to drive anytime, since she made deliveries. All of that qualified her in Bess's eyes. Driving with Margaret rather than in Gram's truck, we wouldn't have to worry about Fred Leo—our policeman, ever alert for wasteful wartime joyriding—stopping us to ask, "Is this trip really necessary?" And I liked that Margaret could quote whole passages of *Sense and Sensibility* and referred to our house as Barton Cottage and to Briar and me as the Dashwood sisters, so she was in and joined us that day on the beach. If we counted Gram and Briar, we already had five members, a number Bess and I considered respectable.

A wave washed over my feet, and I sank them deeper into the sand. Nature's pedicure.

"I've typed up some initial book-discussion guidelines," Margaret said.

"We haven't even read the book yet," Bess said. "Let's just play cards."

Margaret leaned forward in her chair. "My cousin Sheila in Tewksbury is in a book club and says their credo is: *We will make the world a better place by first being better ourselves by reading, then sharing what we know with others, simply and humbly.*"

Bess put on her sunglasses and leaned back in her chair. "Our credo is: *We don't ask what the credo is.*"

"At their meetings, they pass around a wooden spoon," Margaret said. "Whoever has it is the one that may speak."

"Sounds unhygienic," Bess said.

"We should do something for the war effort," I said, water lapping my ankles. "A New Bedford club is doing a book drive for the troops. It was in the *Gazette.*"

"Hardly anyone can get new books right now," Bess said. "I've been on the list for six months at the library for *The Day of the Locust,* and they say it may be another three. There are only old fishing magazines left on the shelves."

Margaret nodded. "And if people have books, they're keeping them." She rubbed suntan lotion on her arms, from a bottle of Gaby Greaseless Suntan Lotion she'd nicked from work.

Not that Margaret needed it for her gorgeous skin that Bess and I were so jealous of, which she'd inherited from her beautiful Portuguese mother. Even in December, Margaret looked sun-kissed, and in August she barely burned, while we went lobster red.

We filled Margaret in on Major Gilbert's visit to the farm the day before and what an ass he'd been.

"I've been collecting books here and there," I said. "I'd love to give those to the troops." I had my sacred Never-Lend collection of books, mostly ones that had belonged to my mother, but was always on the lookout for good titles for my "Up-Island Happenings" column giveaways.

"Major Gil would have a nervous breakdown if you just started handing out books to his men," Bess said.

"Who cares?" I asked. "Let's just drive up there and do it."

"We can call it Books for the Boys," Margaret said. "I'll make bookmarks to distribute, featuring the book-club logo."

Bess sent me a distressed look, clearly regretting not requiring a trial period for new members.

Just the thought of bringing books to the troops made me more optimistic about the world. It would make a serviceman's day so much better, having a good book to come back to. Hopefully some kind souls were doing something similar for Tom, wherever he was. As a librarian, my mother would have loved the idea, since she lived to spread the joy of a good book. No one read as much as Emma Smith, and I was grateful every day that I'd inherited her love of reading.

I stood. "Why should we be cowed by Major Gil? If we can't move heaven, we'll just raise hell."

Bess smiled. "Now, there's a credo."

—

AFTER A QUICK DIP in Copper Pond, the three of us drove up to Peaked Hill, the trunk of Margaret's car weighed down with three cartons of books to hand out to the troops. I'd included a few pristine novels I'd found at the dump, probably discarded by summer people after they'd either read them or just said they did. In the mix was the latest title everyone was reading, *The Moon Is Down*, and lots of science fiction, and some good Faulkner I'd found at a thrift shop.

We showed our IDs and made it through the sentries easily once I told them we'd come at Major Gilbert's request. Margaret pulled into the gravel parking area, and we stepped out of the car and took in the view. It was the highest point on the island, where we came as kids, long before the Army had claimed that spot. We called it Top of the World, since there were fewer trees back then and we played on the massive rocks, still there by the bluff. Wee Devil's Bed. Stonecutter's Rock. How quickly that base had become the nerve center of coastal defenses for the island.

We looked out over uninhabited Noman's Land, an island the Navy used for practice bombing, and in the far distance Buzzards Bay on the mainland. We could see the entire North Shore of the island from up here, almost to Vineyard Haven, though I could not see our own house, directly below. I hadn't expected the base to be so sprawling and efficient, uniformed men hurrying about. At the heart of the camp, sun bounced off a silver Quonset hut, and white canvas tents stretched out in neat rows beyond it.

I kept an eye out for Major Gilbert, braced to be thrown out of there the minute he discovered us. Had he seen my column? All over the island, readers were waking up to it that morning.

Two soldiers dressed in mechanic's coveralls hoisted a massive truck tire by a chain onto a tripod of birch trunks, while others headed toward the largest tent of all, what must have been the mess tent, peaked like a circus big top. Tom was probably eating at a similar one that very moment, wherever he was.

"Mortar pits," Margaret said, pointing out along the edge of the bluff. "Machine-gun nests."

Are they expecting Germans on our shores any day? We went back to the car, and Margaret popped the trunk to reveal the three cartons of books. A few soldiers noticed us and headed toward the car from the direction of the mess tent.

"Let's go, ladies," Bess said, handing one soldier a T. S. Eliot book to consider. "I know. Cat poems. But they're actually quite fun."

Soon, soldiers crowded around the trunk, flipping through pages and skimming book jackets, as if browsing the aisles of first editions and leather-bound treasures at Argosy Book Store in Manhattan, which I'd seen in a magazine once.

I handed one private *The Heart Is a Lonely Hunter.* "This is one of my favorites. Starts slow, but stay with it."

Others picked up their pace and ran toward the car, dog tags flapping against their chests. I recognized some of them as Major Gilbert's Cape Cod Commandos.

Bess smiled at the men milling around us. "What an extraordinary sight. Every woman's dream right now."

"Choose your book," Margaret called out. "Courtesy of the Martha's Vineyard Beach and Book Club."

"Have *The Great Gatsby?*" one soldier asked.

"I'd like that one, too," said another.

"Sorry, no," I said. "But we have Fitzgerald's *The Beautiful and Damned.* A much bigger seller."

All at once, Major Gilbert came striding from the direction of the Quonset hut and waved off the gathered men. He wore what must have been his training clothes, Army-issued shorts and a T-shirt, which fit him so well it was hard not to stare. Apparently, he trained alongside his men, and it showed.

The major stepped toward the trunk, about to slam the door down, but all three of us rushed to sit on the edge.

"I figured it was you when they called and asked if I'd allowed this," he said.

"The men love them," I said. "Not one asked for a comic book."

"It disrupted their lunch. And may I remind you all that this is a military installation?"

I heaved the final box from the trunk and set it on the grass. "Well, they'll have books to bring with them when they leave. Souvenirs of their time here."

"Maybe you don't understand what these men do, Miss Smith. They train to fight in combat. There's no room in their packs for these."

I clapped the dust from my hands. "Perhaps keep them as a lending library for the next group?"

"Maybe we also keep the local paper on display, so my men can find your column, which includes a derogatory mention of their ill-mannered commanding officer? Thank you most profusely for that. I received a call from Camp Edwards this morning, inquiring if I've been disturbing the locals."

"Well, I hope you said yes to that one," I said. "Have you read it?"

"I've had the unfortunate pleasure."

"Then perhaps make amends with the locals and allow them to distribute the rest of their books. And stop running over their crops."

Major Gilbert looked out to sea and then back at me. "If you don't remove yourselves from the premises this minute, I will gladly have it done for you. And if you write another thing about me in that column or set foot up here again, I'll requisition that whole bloody farm and send you all packing." He walked off. "Is that clear?"

8

BRIAR

1942

I LIFTED THE LID OF MR. SCHMIDT'S BOX, JUMPING OUT OF MY skin with anticipation. Why had he left this in his medicine cabinet? Was that what he wanted to tell me about before he died from his fall down the beach steps? I shivered at the thought of poor Conrad's body, twisted and lifeless at the bottom of the concrete stairs. I'd been the first to come upon him, his body still warm.

Scout scratched at the screen door with a pitiful whimper.

"What is it, girl?" She had just been out to do her business and would have to wait. It was only a squirrel, no doubt.

From the cold metal box I pulled a manila envelope and a black leather jeweler's box. I opened the envelope first and found two photographs. One was taken in the woods somewhere and showed a large gathering or rally, with people dressed in Nazi uniforms, arms raised, saluting the swastika-adorned flag. The other was of a typical German house, with a decorative swastika arranged in bricks under the front eave. I looked closer at the street signs. ADOLF HITLER STRASSE. GOERING STRASSE. All named after Hitler and his close friends. How did Mr. Schmidt get these? Had he kept his Nazi past a secret?

I opened the jeweler's box next and found a ring, which I'd once seen described in a magazine as a Nazi honor ring. A shiver went through me as I turned the silver band in my fingers and examined the grinning skull with hollowed-out eyes set between two oak leaves.

Frederick the Great had started that lovely tradition of using the skull in military insignia, but I didn't know much else about it.

I held the ring to the light and searched the inside for an inscription. *To Kuno.* I set it back in the box. Kuno? Why would Mr. Schmidt have it? Was it a fake? Those had been springing up at hobby shops everywhere. Nazi-flag replicas and toy Lugers. No, it was the real thing— I could tell by the heft of it alone. Why did Mr. Schmidt not tell me about it? It didn't make sense. Conrad had been a decorated captain in the Marines during the Great War. But what had he not told me?

Sandra Granger could fill me in. She owned and operated Martha's Vineyard's best—only, really—military- and marine-antiquities shop, Island Treasures. That second word was possibly an attempt at New England sarcasm, since the shop, found down near the harbor, had never seen anything close to treasure. Mostly she carried old whaling antiques, heavy on the scrimshaw, and a bunch of World War I artifacts, most of them American but with some German and Russian items here and there.

The eighty-year-old proprietress had been friends with Mr. Schmidt for a few years, knew even more than I did about military paraphernalia, and seemed to be pretty discreet, which was essential. But would Sandra call the cops on me for having such a piece? I had a feeling a lot of her goods had come to her by way of a no-questions-asked policy, the kind of wink people in her trade gave to customers. She probably wouldn't rat me out. Not if she could profit from it.

I kept the ring and the pictures and stowed the metal box back in the cupboard, feeling a fuzzy, wrapped-in-cotton disconnection from the earth. Sandra would help me make sense of it all. There was no way my best friend had been a Nazi. Had he had some connection to the U-boat I'd been seeing?

I took Mr. Schmidt's binoculars, stepped to the porch, and scanned the sea, checking the horizon for any glint of sunlight off metal. My arms ached after a while, and just as I was about to quit, my eye caught a flash and I refocused. My whole body went cold as a fence-like run of metal partially emerged from the water.

My heart thumped. They were waiting for something. It was the deepest part along the North Shore, thirty fathoms at least, but why would they park themselves there? U-boats had only six hours of battery life before they had to resurface to recharge, but why do it right there in the shadow of an Army base? Not that the Army lookouts could see directly below the base, into Pepper Cove. The Coast Guard shore patrols had trouble accessing that rocky cove, as well, and had sworn in Gram to keep an eye on it, a job they often assigned to coastal fishermen. But even Gram doubted that what I'd seen was a U-boat.

I set the binoculars down. Though I'd glimpsed only the very tip of the conning tower, I knew it was a U-boat. But I had to be certain. I didn't care how much they'd laugh at me—if I was 100 percent sure, I'd call it in again. It was too important to let my stupid pride get in the way.

I refocused and saw it even better than before, the whole top of the U-boat just barely submerged.

I scrambled down the cement stairs and ran along the beach to the call box, grabbed the receiver, cranked the handle, and a familiar voice came on the line.

It was Joe Presley, my least favorite of the shore-patrol dispatchers.

I bent and caught my breath. "I saw it again. German sub, just off Pepper Cove. I need Coastie backup to scare them off."

"Aw, jeez. Is this Briar Smith?"

I heard laughter on the other end. "Is it Briar the Liar again, Joe?" someone asked.

I pictured them at that big oak desk they sat around all day, their sweaty armpits showing pink through their cheap white short-sleeved shirts, smoking and telling dumb stories, transcribing low-priority calls in their fat logbook.

"You've come in here to the office, as well, haven't you? Skinny kid wearing a parka hottest day of the year? Joan of Arc hairdo. I remember you."

I paced the beach. "I saw the conning tower."

"The *what*, now?" Mr. Presley quieted for a second and then attempted a gentle tone. "Folks've been seein' whales quite a lot."

"Off the North Shore? No. It's a U-123. I just know it."

"We've had the pleasure of your call before, Miss Smith." I heard the cover of the logbook slap against the table. "Lemme see . . . says here you called on August second and reported a cork life vest found washed up on Salt Cove Beach. August third reported seeing a Nazi U-boat off the North Shore. You insisted, and I quote, 'Nazis are watching us and are gauging the best time to come ashore.'" He turned a page. "Then August fourth. The incident with the flare gun. We don't need to rehash that one."

"It's the same U-boat I saw that day." I paused. "May be the *Leopard.*"

"The *Leopard?*"

Someone chuckled on Joe's end.

"The sub they say took down the *Port Nicholson* off P-town?"

"Yes."

"So, you think a German submarine is sailing offshore in shallow water, right below a U.S. Army base."

"It's completely secluded over there and sixty-five feet deep in places. They can't see it from up at the base."

"You memorize the maritime charts for fun?"

I didn't share that on Saturday nights eighty-two-year-old Conrad Schmidt and I had often sipped iced schnapps and quizzed each other on the marine navigational charts. Just the thought of Mr. Schmidt pinched my heart. He would have believed me.

"Take any pictures of this U-boat?" Joe asked.

"No, but I know what I saw."

"Look, Miss Smith, there's a reason the Coast Guard has strung call boxes around the perimeter of this island. And it's not for you and me to have chatsies every day. You're fifteen, right?"

"Sixteen."

"Go on over to the Jive Hive. Meet some normal kids. Play checkers."

"I want to take it out before it torpedoes any more ships. I know what a German U-boat looks like."

"Of course you do. I'll log this call in, but you've now officially been warned to cease and desist, and your name's been added to the list monitored by the police and the FBI. So, unless you have solid proof, stay off this line. If you want to help, knit socks for the boys."

"Can you just—"

The line went dead. I hung up and surveyed the water, darkness now falling. The sub had probably descended when they saw me at the call box. By now they might have already gone off somewhere.

Or maybe they were still sitting out there, radios silenced. Watching.

I walked on toward home. I wouldn't even tell Gram and the others. I was used to being called Briar the Liar, and I didn't want to embarrass them any more than I already had. But I knew what I saw.

9

CADENCE

WE HELD ANOTHER BOOK CLUB MEETING THE NEXT MORNING, since Margaret had completed a lengthy series of discussion questions we hadn't gotten to, which caused Bess to scribble me a series of notes saying she wanted to change our address and not tell Margaret. At least Gram had baked some of her Surprise Cookies for us. Those were always a big hit, since each cookie contained a whole chocolate wafer baked inside, resulting in a rapturous comingling of brown sugar and crunch. Thank goodness Gram was a genius at bartering, doing any number of small jobs in exchange for sugar and flour coupons.

We gathered at the kitchen table, for easy access to milk for the cookies. Briar again did not attend, but Gram was there with us and, being a fast reader like my mother, had finished *The Song of Bernadette* in a flash. How good it was to be in that kitchen, so cozy. Long ago, Grandpa Smith had built that room with his own two hands, an addition onto the back of the house, out of pine from our woods. He wasn't the best carpenter in the world, and it was uninsulated, so it was cold in the winter, but it almost doubled the size of the house, and we spent most of our waking hours there.

After a short but rousing book discussion, we circled back to our philanthropic agenda.

I took a second cookie and bit into it, realizing the actual surprise was how many you could eat in one sitting.

"I was thinking," I said. "We know the troops want books but can't carry them in their packs. What if we made a size that they could bring with them everywhere?"

"Like a paperback?" Bess asked. "They already make those."

"Even thinner," I said. "Like a pamphlet, but a full-length book. It would fit in even the fullest pack."

"I suppose," Bess said. "You'd need something like tissue paper, though."

Gram shuffled through a kitchen drawer and then lobbed a pad of her airmail stationery onto the table. "Can you type onto this?"

It wouldn't be perfect, but at least it would get the idea across.

"I could draw the cover," Bess said.

"I can type, too," Margaret said. "I broke all the records in my correspondence class."

For such a mild-mannered person, Margaret had a braggy side, and I was starting to share Bess's irritation with her.

"Too bad we didn't have an Emerson one to give Tom before he left," Gram said.

We wrote six prospective titles on slips of paper and tossed them into Gram's empty red cookie jar, and Gram did the honors.

"*The Sun Also Rises,*" Gram read from the slip of paper.

"Hemingway it is," Bess said.

We spent the next seven hours making our little prototype. Margaret read the text aloud from my personal copy, a well-loved first edition I'd found at a thrift shop, while Bess sketched a matador and bull as a possible cover. Gram fueled it all by making us cheese sandwiches and iced teas.

"If we get this done, can we bring it to the USO dance tomorrow night?" Bess asked. "Maybe Major Gilbert will be there and will take it straight to the top. Bet he's a good dancer."

I kept my gaze on my typing, all the anger coming back. He was the last person in the world I wanted to see.

IT TOOK US ALL the next day to finally finish our prototype, and it was dark by the time Bess and I flagged down one of the Fisher boys for a ride to the USO dance. The three of us sat up front, me in the middle, the music turned up, and heard the commentator break in with news of Japanese advances in the Pacific.

Ever since Pearl Harbor the previous December, the whole nation had been on edge, and we all huddled in the parlor each day, listening to Roosevelt's chats; it seemed that Germany alone was an overwhelming force, never mind Japan. And Italy, too. I pushed away thoughts of Tom sailing across the Atlantic to who-knew-where in Europe. Tom would want us to have some fun tonight. I felt in my pocket for the little book we'd made. Bess's cover had turned out so well—she'd drawn the matador and bull from memory, having been to the largest bullfighting arena in Spain, Las Ventas, with her governess.

By the time we made it to Main Street, the USO hall was lit up and packed with couples dancing, as the strains of "Serenade in Blue" eased out into the sweet night air. Those dances were getting a reputation. Gram didn't even let Briar walk by the USO and look in while a dance was going on; she made me drop her off at the underage get-togethers, held on Wednesdays and Fridays in the Jive Hive, above Association Hall. I'd stopped taking her there, though, since Briar went reluctantly and sat, wearing sunglasses and a trench coat, reading war magazines, while her peers danced and played checkers.

The USO hall was thick with cigarette smoke, and the scent of shortbread and coffee made my stomach growl as Bess led the way toward the punch table. I looked forward to relaxing a little. Maybe Bess and I would dance with a couple of GIs or, better yet, dance together, since we knew we'd be safe from our toes being trod upon, liquor breath, and wandering hands.

We edged past girls talking with men dressed in every sort of uniform. The island was chock-full of servicemen, from the shooting range at Katama, to the Army station at Peaked Hill, to the new Navy airfield being built in the middle of the island to train aviators to land on aircraft carriers in the Pacific.

We danced a little together and got some punch.

"It's more crowded in here than Brooks Brothers at Christmas." Bess searched the room. "I don't see your future husband."

"It's just as well. He's such a killjoy. Maybe it was the boarding school they all went to so young, where they probably were bullied and worse. Though you are a product of it, and you're not a horrible boor."

I felt a presence behind me and turned to find Major Gilbert there. Had he heard me? What difference would it make? I was fine with him knowing how I felt.

Bess offered her confident, wealthy-person handshake. "Good to see you again, Major."

It was a shame he was such a lout, because he really was a fine-looking human, and that wasn't just the punch talking. The uniforms made all the soldiers more handsome by half, but in the case of Major Gilbert it was quadrupled, and the girls in the room openly stared at him.

He shook Bess's hand and then nodded to me. "Miss Smith. You're looking well. Staying off the roads?" Was he hoping to sweep our acrimonious past under the rug for the sake of public civility?

I returned the nod. "We drive on the right side of the road, Major. Just a reminder."

"No arguments here."

"So have you decided if you're going to allow my family to protect our livelihood or let us descend into poverty?"

He looked around the room. "Usually, I greet acquaintances before launching into . . . whatever this is."

I sipped my punch. "Well, you're in America now, Major."

"Indeed."

He stepped closer and leaned down to speak in my ear over the music, and I breathed in his essence, of starch and bay rum. "You might like to know, I'm thinking about directing my men to go around your lower field."

"Oh." I looked up at him. "Since when?"

"Captain Feldman over at Camp Edwards suggested I consider it."

I smiled. "Oh, your boss made you."

"Not exactly my boss, but he has an idea that he thinks will help community relations."

I studied my empty punch cup. "I see."

"Wanted me to ask if you could . . ." He searched the crowd. Clearly, it was hard for him to beg a favor. "He'd like to know if you'd write something good in your column for us."

It was fun seeing him squirm. "Depends on the event, I suppose."

"He has a particular one he'd like to highlight, actually. He wishes to speak to you directly about it. You may have read that some war exercises will be taking place here. Overrunning the island, perhaps."

"Uh-huh."

"He'd like to solicit the help of the good folks here."

"So he wants me to write about the maneuvers to make sure people are okay with their land being flattened?"

He nodded. "That's right."

"I'm sure you see the irony here, Major. How can I request that of my readership when my own land is being trampled? You'll have to do more than think about redirecting your men."

He studied the dancers and then returned his gaze to me. "Fine. I'll make sure they don't cross your fields. But you need to make a genuine appeal. Feldman is worried that the citizens here will raise bloody hell about their gardens getting trod upon by the maneuvers."

"These islanders are more patriotic than that, Major. But I suppose I can do as he wishes."

He seemed relieved. "May I give him your number to ring?"

Bess handed me a slip of paper and a pencil.

"And maybe I'll think of something good to say about you, too, Major," I said.

He finished his punch. "That may take some doing." He looked at me and I met his eyes, barely able to look away. Despite evidence to the contrary, I knew we both felt a similar pull of attraction. I'd felt it before from men, like the urgent energy of excited bees.

He scanned the room. "You could say I'm a convert to the idea of my men reading."

"Why the sudden change?"

"I still stand by my belief that they can't bring books into battle, but I have to say there have been many fewer fights among the men since you brought those books."

"How big of you to admit you were wrong, Major."

He sipped his punch, his gaze on mine. "Even if a horrible boor?"

A warm flush crept up my neck, and I busied myself jotting down my phone number on the paper. "I can also admit when I'm wrong, Major." I handed him my number.

He took it and started to reply, when a blond woman inserted herself into our threesome.

"There you are," she said. "I'm famished, and they only offer sweets and punch. Do let's go."

And was it my imagination or was the major disappointed at her arrival? Surely she'd seen me hand him my number.

The major nodded toward her. "Miss Smith and Miss Stanhope, may I present my friend Amelia Wilmont?"

Bess and I just stood there and took her in, overwhelmed by her presence. I'd never met an Englishwoman before, unless you counted Virginia Woolf and Emily Brontë between the pages of their books. She was nothing like what I'd envisioned an English rose might be, more Teutonic than Tudor, built with good hips for childbirth, as Gram might say. She wore her platinum-blond hair smoothed back into a low chignon, and seeing her dressed in her ballet-pink skirt and crisp white blouse, her low Capezio heels barely broken in, sapped my strength.

I shook her hand, regretting my choice of saddle shoes and gray pleated skirt. "From the UK?"

"Here writing for the BBC."

I tried not to stare but could barely take my eyes off her pearl stud earrings, so simple and chic.

"Nice earrings," Bess said.

"I'm mad about South Sea pearls." Amelia stroked one earlobe.

"From a South Sea factory, maybe," Bess murmured to me.

"Well, isn't she just extraordinary?" Bess asked Gil. "Cadence is a writer, too, Amelia. Has a very successful column in the *Gazette*."

I wanted to run from the building, being compared to the almighty Amelia.

"You don't say?" Amelia asked, trying hard to look interested.

"They asked me to do a story on this little island out here on the front lines. Thought it was a good excuse to see Gilbert."

A black snake of envy slithered in me.

"That's Cadence's dream," Bess said. "To write and live in a major metropolis." She sent Major Gilbert a pointed look. "She'd love London, I'm sure."

"New York City, hopefully, one day," I said.

Amelia brushed a phantom speck off her sleeve. "It's not as glamorous as it sounds."

"Amelia makes it all seem easy," the major said. "Even the queen is a fan."

Amelia smiled at him. "She does have good taste."

"How do you know Major Gilbert?" Bess asked her.

"Interviewed him after he escaped from a German POW camp."

I turned to Major Gil. "You were captured?"

Amelia answered for him. "Battle of Narvik."

"Norway," I said.

"Was captured by the Germans, but he outwitted them by being their friend, didn't you, darling?"

The major handed his empty cup to a USO hostess. "Hardly." He checked his watch. "If you're hungry, we should be going."

"You wouldn't believe the intrigue," Amelia said.

"Do *tell*," Bess said, with a glance at me.

"Once he was back on English soil, we compared notes and found that our families were actually close in days past. Lord Gilbert and my mother used to *date*, before he met Gilbert's mum, the duchess."

"You don't say?" Bess asked.

"He had to endure a terribly deprived childhood, I'm afraid. He was born in a drafty old castle, poor thing." Amelia turned her weary gaze to me. "And where do you live—Cadence, is it?"

"On a farm. Just downhill from the Army base."

Amelia linked arms with Gil. "Peaked Hill is mad fun. I had to dress like a nun when I was up there, with all those rowdy boys. You should hear the whistles when Gilbert's not there to tame them. So don't venture up there if you value your reputation."

Bess leaned in and muttered in my ear, "I think she's dating your future husband."

Amelia smiled. "Or just wear those farm clothes and they won't be tempted to look." She sipped her punch. "Saddle shoes are marvelous for dancing, but they're absolute man repellents, I think, don't you? Not that you don't wear them splendidly, Candice. And one can't wear one's best things on a farm."

"Yes," I said. "Secondhand clothes don't get ruined during farm-work."

"Good on you, putting castoffs to use during wartime. I'd never be able to live on a farm. Couldn't do without my silk and pearls."

"I'm sure you couldn't."

Had Amelia ever worn denim? She'd certainly never seen a stalk of asparagus outside of a can. She may have been accomplished, but she wasn't exactly interesting.

I slid the book from my pocket and handed it to Major Gilbert. "Thought you might like to see what we made with our book club."

The major took it. "Hemingway? Quite a nice cover."

Bess smiled. "Thank you."

He flipped through the tissue-paper pages. "You got a whole book in here?"

"Almost. And the foreword, too. So the troops can take books with them everywhere."

"Impressive," the major said. "You don't waste any time, do you?"

Amelia plucked the book from his hands. "I've been with the men near the front lines, and the last thing they're thinking about is reading. They want women and food, in that order."

"You're wrong there," I said. "They want books. Need them, I think. As much as food and water."

"Well, that's a good one." She handed it back to me and pulled the major closer. "The boys all do want socks, though. That's a helpful thing for you to focus on."

I turned to the major. "If you could mention our book to Captain Feldman, it would help. Give me someone in Army public relations I can talk to?"

Amelia tugged on the major's arm. "Are you quite finished here? I'm positively boiling. I need champagne and something divine for dinner."

If she was expecting to find a restaurant in that little town with gold faucets in the ladies' room and diners who sipped their soup softly, she'd be disappointed.

As they started off, Gil turned back and reached out. "Good to see you."

I shook his hand. "Same here, Major." What a lovely handshake he had, warm and just firm enough.

"Thank you for the books for the men and for—"

"Don't worry, Major. I'll make sure you get a good mention in the column."

He was about to reply, but Amelia yanked him through the crowd.

Bess watched them go. "Should we tell them this is a dry town or let it be a fun little surprise?"

"They'll go to Edgartown," I said.

"Old Major Gilbert is not so bad after all, am I right? And Amelia is so threatened by you. Like a wildebeest protecting her mate. She could tell he likes you."

"Those two are made for each other."

"I'm surprised he didn't offer more help with the book," Bess said.

"We can't give up on it. If he won't help us, we can write to Washington. I know it's a good idea."

The record inside the hall changed, and Bess led me outside onto Main Street.

We walked off arm in arm, up the sidewalk, into the darkness, past the sweet honeysuckle hedges perfuming the night, the sound of "Stairway to the Stars" drifting out after us.

Bess nudged me with her elbow. "That's a sticky wicket, old Amelia with her mitts all over your future husband."

"Stop calling him that, Bess. I really don't care."

There would be others, just as attractive, when I got to New York City someday.

"Born in a drafty old *cah*-stle." Bess mocked Amelia's accent, which she knew would get me laughing. "You should see some of those places, *Candice*. My roommate, second year at Brillantmont, invited me home in the height of summer to her Scottish castle, and I had to wear a vicuña coat to bed at night, it was so cold."

"I wouldn't mind."

"Oh, yes, you would. And they had one decent shower in the whole place. For twenty-two bedrooms, can you believe it? Same bar of soap for us all. So don't date old Gil for the castle. Do it for that chest. I've seen the Parthenon Marbles, and the river god Kephisos has nothing on our Gil."

I'd only just stopped laughing when a car pulled up alongside us and stopped.

Bess clutched me closer. "Who is it?"

The driver's side window rolled down. "There you are." It was Winnie Winthrop. "Don't just stand there, for goodness' sake. Get in, both of you."

10

BRIAR

—

1942

I BURNED THE CLASSIFIED DOCUMENTS IN GRAM'S FIREPLACE AND headed out, eager to get to Island Treasures to see Sandra. I'd even dressed up a little, in my best dungarees, a plaid shirt, and one of Tom's ties. I caught a ride with a fisherman who was on his way to Vineyard Haven. We'd had to cut back our driving, since gas and tires were rationed. Seventy-five tons of rubber went into making a battleship, not to mention the life rafts, gas masks, and tank tracks being manufactured for battle. I was happy to ride with a neighbor if it meant Tom might benefit.

The fisherman dropped me at Sandra's house, and I walked around back and into her shop, the scent of mildew the dominant fragrance of that place, with underlying notes of stinky feet and clam chowder. There was only room for maybe two customers at a time—not that I'd ever seen another soul in Island Treasures—and two dirty old curtains led to some sort of back room. Most of the space was taken up by three glass display cabinets crammed with Sandra's collections. It was so dark and cluttered, it gave me the creeps, the type of place where they'd find human remains in the basement someday and everyone would pretend to be surprised.

The proprietress, octogenarian Sandra Granger, lay on her bologna-colored faux-leather BarcaLounger, legs up, munching on oyster crackers from a little cellophane bag. She napped and ate her fried-clam meals while lying in that chair, and I tried not to think about the amount of tartar sauce spilled on it.

She glanced up at me. "Close the door—the flies are driving me bonkers." Sandra had a great voice. You could hear every cigarette she'd ever smoked in each gravelly word. And, as Gram would say, she had a Massachusetts accent "as thick as a truckman's wrist."

"Haven't seen you since Mr. Schmidt's funeral," I said.

Sandra dropped the BarcaLounger footrest, struggled to her feet, and stood at her main display case, silhouetted against the closed venetian blinds behind her. "I still expect to see him walk through that door."

A former hardware-store employee turned antiquities dealer, Sandra wore her salt-and-pepper hair in a short style she said she cut herself, over the kitchen sink, and men's bifocals. Her face was remarkably unlined, probably from setting foot outside only when forced for her entire life.

"Nice outfit," Sandra said, through an inhale of cigarette smoke.

She was a big fan of my wardrobe.

I perused the glass cases. "Where did you get all this new stuff?"

"For God's sake, you know I don't share my sources. But let's just say I have some pickers with important friends, who like a little sexy time. I still got it, ya know."

I wasn't sure what "it" was and didn't want to think too much about it.

"You just here to talk, Briar, or you going to buy something?"

A dedicated grouch, Sandra had a demeanor that'd been imprinted on her after many years at Abby's Hardware, which Cadence called Crabby's on account of the gruff staff. In the long New England tradition of cantankerous hardware salespeople, they gave every lucky customer a generous helping of contempt along with their deck screws. Sandra had also picked up another habit at that store: a pretty loose way with the profanity. This caused Gram to avoid her on Main Street, but she took it easy around me, maybe because of my age.

Sandra suffered from severe epilepsy, and fainting was a real concern. She probably shouldn't have been smoking or on her feet so much. At eighty years old, she got most of her exercise by knocking back her anti-seizure drugs with her regular coffee.

Sandra rubbed smoke out of her eye. "Or maybe you brought me something good that I can actually sell?"

I'd found lots of old stuff, which she'd sold for me—no big money, but it kept me in modeling supplies. An authentic Nazi fork I'd found on South Beach, probably off a downed U-boat, was my biggest score. A helmet liner I first thought was a horseshoe crab was another find. Sandra had also sold a gold tooth I'd found in the pocket of a sport coat from the dump; that seventy-five dollars went straight to Gram.

I stepped to the main case. She had some pretty cool things, especially the war paraphernalia. I bent to examine a couple of nice German World War I knives and a helmet, then continued on to the scrimshaw in the next case: an enormous whale tooth etched with a whale hunting scene, and part of a jawbone with lines of ye olde poetry in curlicue script carved into it. The whole scrimshaw thing, which everyone on the island seemed to love, saddened me. Whalers chased down some poor sperm whale minding his own business, boiled his blubber, and then etched pictures of his violent death into his own bones. All for lamp oil when a candle would do.

"Ever wonder if sailors went on those two-year whale hunts just to get away from their families?" I asked.

"I'd sail to Madagascar to get rid of *my* husband," Sandra said. "If he hadn't died already."

I smiled. She was one of the funniest people on the island.

I slid Mr. Schmidt's photos out of my pocket. "I wanted to ask you about these. Promise me you won't tell anyone?"

"I'll be as quiet as the grave." Sandra adjusted her glasses and examined the pictures. "You should be paying me for this, you know."

I waved toward one of the people with arms raised in a Nazi salute. "Recognize where this is in Germany? I found them at Mr. Schmidt's house."

She shook her head. "No clue. Just another bunch of Krauts partying in the fatherland. So what else is new?"

"Look closely at the street sign in the other. It says *Adolf Hitler Strasse.*"

"They love that friggin' lunatic back there. Do you know how many babies have been named after that sick bastard?" She handed the photos back to me. "Probably Conrad's family snapshots." She pulled an *NS Frauen-Warte* magazine from under the counter. "These magazines are more valuable than caster sugar right now. Have a supplier out of Boston. Brings 'em back from abroad. They're full of pics like those." She opened to one black-and-white photo of Germans on a street saluting as Hitler's motorcade went by. "Hailing their führer. It's all over the newsreels, too. Makes me wanna puke."

"But Mr. Schmidt was no Nazi."

"So far as we *know*. Just because you two made models and drank schnapps together doesn't mean he didn't have some skeletons in that closet. He'd read *Mein Kampf*."

Why had he never told me?

Sandra took another drag of her cigarette. "That book was a slog, I tell you."

She'd read it, too? Where did a person even get a copy?

"What about Mr. Schmidt's grandson, Tyson?" I asked.

"Never met him," Sandra said, pinching a piece of stray tobacco off her tongue.

Something about the way she said it seemed less than truthful.

I picked up the photos and started saying my goodbyes. Naturally she tried to buy the pictures, but I told her they weren't for sale.

"It's like I'm the public library or something," she said. "Folks bringing things in here for info but never selling."

I patted my pocket. "I might have something else you'd like."

"Oh, yeah?" From under the counter she pulled her little black receipts book, which was held closed with an enormous rubber band, trapping in what must've been fifty old receipts. Always her opening salvo to a sale.

I slid the ring from my pocket and offered it to her. "Found this in his house, too."

She looked at the ring for a moment, as if frozen. "Holy shit," she finally said.

I tried again to hand it to her.

"God no," she said, waving it away. "Take it and go."

"What's wrong?" I asked.

She stepped back from the counter, barely able to take her eyes off the ring. "That didn't wash up on any beach."

"You have to tell me why you're acting this way," I said.

"Just get it out of here. And don't tell anyone else you have it. Or neither of us will be around much longer."

11

CADENCE

—

WINNIE OFFERED TO DRIVE US HOME AND WE CLIMBED INTO her Italian sports car, Bess in the minuscule back seat and me in the front, so low to the ground. Though it was dark, Winnie wore her signature sunglasses. Halfway to the farm she stopped, put the convertible top down, and we flew through the night, stars flung across the sky.

Winnie drove as I knew she would, fast and decisively, even with only the car's parking lights to guide us, due to blackout regulations. Her gold bangles jingled as she downshifted. I breathed in her exotic perfume as we rode shoulder to shoulder, the scent of spicy jasmine and sea spray in her tousled hair. At that pace she'd get us there in record time, and I willed her to slow down so I could keep feeling the cool wind on my skin after the heat of the USO hall. Winnie was on her way to a party at the Gay Head cliffs home of a friend who was hosting a Dutch cheese heir and his family.

"They'll probably all want to get naked and cover themselves with clay," Winnie said, over the sound of the engine. "I'd invite you, but they're doing a silent retreat."

I tried to keep my hair back. "No problem, Mrs. Winthrop."

"Winnie, please. We're not at the beach club anymore." She sent me a sidelong glance. "You were a no-show at the yacht club. Something better came up?"

"I'm so sorry, Winnie, but Mr. Wespi had me stay at work. I called and they said you'd left."

"The girls were disappointed not to meet you, after I'd talked you up so much."

"She was heartbroken, believe me," Bess said from the back seat.

I felt our little book in my pocket and considered showing it to Winnie. Would she think it sophomoric, a grade school art project cobbled together?

"I'd like to show you a book our book club made for the troops," I said.

"Well?" Winnie shifted. "Don't hold me in suspense."

I slid it out of my pocket and pinched the pages closed to keep it from blowing away. "It's a full-length book, just easier to carry."

She snuck a glance at it. "I love it. Show it to the girls. They've been here a week now, and we're reconvening at the yacht club for a last hurrah before we go back to New York. Cocktails, day after tomorrow. Hopefully you can make it this time."

"Yes. I will definitely be there." I turned to Bess, and we soaked in the joy of it. A second chance.

Winnie stopped at the head of our road, and Bess and I unfolded ourselves from the car. "Let's say five o'clock?" Winnie asked.

"I'll be there with bells on," I added, one of Gram's favorite expressions, and cringed at my own words. Why did I always sound so corny around Winnie?

Winnie asked me to grab four stems of lilies from the farm-stand flower buckets, presumably as a silent gift for the Dutch cheese heir, handed me a five-dollar bill for the cashbox, and zoomed off.

Bess and I stood and watched her taillights fade into the darkness. "How does she drive at night with sunglasses on?" Bess asked. "And I don't think she's heard about Victory Speed."

"I don't know, but I'll make it this time. I'll sleep on the club doorstep if I have to."

THE NEXT MORNING BESS woke me, clutching her belly in pain.

"I don't think it's appendicitis," Gram said. "Wrong side for that."

Gram liked to think she was a doctor. But she'd probably learned the little she knew about appendicitis from the children's book *Madeline,* so I drove Bess to the Stanhope family's doctor's office in Edgartown, posthaste.

We were wary, entering town, and on the lookout for Bess's mother. Bess had been living with us at the farm for almost a year, estranged from her wealthy parents after she fell in love with my brother Tom. I had been delivering some bluefish pâté to the Stanhope house when I worked at the A&P, and Bess answered the door. We became fast friends, and once I brought her to the cottage and introduced them, Tom fell hard for her and she for him. It wasn't long before those two were inseparable, and one day Bess just never went home.

Mrs. Stanhope did everything she could to get her only child to come back, but Bess wouldn't budge. She said she'd rather live with us, scraping to get by, than return to her difficult mother, and Gram welcomed her as one of her own.

Dr. Von Prague's office was located behind his home, a neat Cape Cod–style house on Peases Point Way. By the time we got there, the pain had dissipated somewhat, and I helped Bess out of the truck. Gram's old Ford with the rusty running boards and bald tires seemed so out of place at Von Prague's house, with its white picket fence and powder-pink shutters, the sun shining off the crushed-oyster-shell driveway.

"Is he expensive?" I asked. We didn't have a family doctor, just hoped for the best about most ailments or took Gram to the hospital to her heart doctor.

Bess shook her head. "The nurse will put the charge on my mother's account. Their accountant pays the bills. She'll never see it."

Bess was short of breath by the time we walked up the stairs to his office over the garage, and I stayed with her in the exam room as the doctor entered. He glanced at us both with cold pale-blue eyes and said, "We don't allow guests in our exam rooms." He had hair as white as bleached whalebone and a bedside manner to match.

Bess took my hand. "I don't go anywhere without Cadence."

He washed his hands in the sink, took Bess's recent medical history, and then gently probed her belly with his fingers. "When did you complete your last menses?"

"Maybe April some time," she said.

He looked at her over the top of his glasses. "Bess Stanhope. You don't keep a calendar?"

"No, actually. I live on a farm now."

"With the Smith boy?"

Bess looked at me. "*Tom.* Cadence's brother. I suppose everyone here knows."

"Your mother mentions it now and then."

"Of course she does," Bess said.

The doctor stepped to the sink and washed his hands again. "Looks like we're having a New Year's baby."

Bess and I exchanged a look, mouths agape. Tom's baby.

"How wonderful," Bess said, with a wide smile. "It's what I've always wanted. We talked about a baby. Tom will be so happy."

I embraced Bess. "No wonder you've been so tired."

Bess was right. Tom would be the happiest man in the world, and Briar, Gram, and I would be right there with him. A child to raise in a home full of love.

"I need to write to Tommy today. Will you help me, Cadence?"

I nodded, eyes blurred with tears. Tom would be a marvelous father. And Bess a doting, loving mother. "He'll want every detail."

I didn't want to ruin the happy moment, but it was hard not to think about Bess's mother and the specter of whatever unpleasant business she would bring down on us all when she heard the news.

"How long have your ankles been swollen like this?" the doctor asked.

Bess looked at me. "I don't know, a few days."

He took Bess's blood pressure and then removed his glasses. "Is the father willing to make an honest woman of you?"

"*Honest?*" I asked.

The doctor barely glanced at me.

"Tom left for active duty last week," Bess said, her voice shaky.

I held her hand tighter. Just hearing those words made it more real.

Dr. Von Prague scribbled something on his clipboard. "Your blood pressure is much higher than I'd like, and the edema in the legs is troubling. The abdominal pain may be early contractions, so I would consider going back home for a while, on bed rest, until the birth."

Bess shook her head. "That won't be happening."

He took the stethoscope from around his neck. "Sounds like a wedding won't be happening, either, at least not anytime soon. This is a high-risk pregnancy, Bess, and you can't be stuck on a remote farm, an unwed mother. You'll need funds for specialists. Live-in nursing care when you come home. Not to mention decent maternity clothes."

"The Smiths take good care of me."

"I'm willing to bet you're anemic," he said. "How are you eating?"

Bess glanced at me. "Fine."

I had to admit he had a point. While Gram tried her hardest to provide good meals, we hadn't had red meat in recent memory and, though we lived on a farm, ate mostly potatoes and corn. And with Bess out of commission now, unable to help farm the crops as usual, we'd have even less.

He washed his hands again. "Frankly, I find it disgraceful that a serviceman would leave you this way. It speaks to his character."

I could barely see straight, hearing him criticize my good brother.

"Tommy didn't know," Bess said. "It's my fault as much as his."

I tried to keep my voice steady. "How can you criticize a young man who's risking his life for this country?"

"I protect my patients, Miss Smith."

"Well, he's off protecting our country."

The doctor dried his hands and turned to Bess. "I'll see you back here in two weeks for more tests. In the meantime, my nurse will give you some vitamin tablets, and I want you toes up and no lifting. Call the office immediately if you have any spotting."

"Please keep this confidential, Doctor. I need some time before I tell my parents."

"You won't be able to keep it from them much longer, obviously."

Bess got dressed, and we waited at the nurse's station for her tablets.

When the nurse asked about payment, Bess suggested that she charge the Stanhopes' account.

"I called when you got here," the nurse said. "Your mother refused."

Bess waved that thought away. "Just tell her I'll pay her back."

"Tell her yourself," a familiar voice behind us said, and we turned to find Lydia Stanhope standing there, dressed in a white boucle suit and pearls.

"*Mother.*" Bess stiffened, and my whole body went cold.

I took Bess's arm and we hurried out of the office, down the stairs, but Mrs. Stanhope followed.

"What a way to find out your only daughter is about to ruin the family name—a phone call from a *receptionist.* I was in the middle of a club meeting and had to run out and leave them all there in the living room."

"Then go back to them," Bess said over her shoulder.

Mrs. Stanhope rushed after us. "I've never been so embarrassed in my life. I don't know how I'll tell your father." She called after me. "So you're Tom's sister who introduced them?"

I kept walking. "I am."

"Word at the club is that Bess Ann and your brother had their first date at the town dump, shooting rats. I suppose you arranged that, too?"

Bess and I passed Mrs. Stanhope's black Cadillac idling in the courtyard, her beefy gardener at the wheel. We tried to make a break for Gram's truck, but Mrs. Stanhope grabbed Bess by the wrist. "You're coming home."

Bess wrested herself away. "Let me *go,* Mother."

"It was one thing playing farm girl, even starting to sound like them, dropping your *r*'s. But now *this?*"

"*This* is a baby, Mother. I'm as surprised as you are but never happier."

"How can you do this to us? We've given you everything. Brillantmont. The clothes. And now to hear this is a high-risk pregnancy. You'll need specialists."

Bess walked off toward Gram's truck, oyster shells crunching beneath her feet. "I don't need your money."

"It will kill your father and me both. But I suppose that's why you're doing all this."

"Is he back from Newport, there with his niece? Seems like every man has a niece in Newport these days."

Bess and I got in the truck.

"I won't let you ruin the Stanhope name, Bess Ann," Mrs. Stanhope called to us as we pulled out of the driveway. Only then did we finally breathe.

Bess checked behind us as we drove off toward home. "She means it, you know."

"A *baby*, Bess. Don't let her steal the joy. We need to write Tom straightaway and tell the others soon, too. Briar will be over the moon. Gram, too."

Bess just folded her arms across her belly. "You don't know my mother, Cade. She'll never let this happen."

UP-ISLAND HAPPENINGS

———

By CADENCE SMITH

IF YOU'VE GROWN BORED OF TOO MUCH SUNSHINE, TIRED of lolling on the beach with nothing but a warm sarsaparilla and a tedious novel on your towel, and have started longing at the noon hour to hear the friendly tinkle of cracked ice being bounced around a cocktail shaker just for a change of pace, take heart. Our peaceful haven here Up-Island is about to see some sensational, large-scale maneuvers taking place, according to Capt. H. G. Feldman, speaking to me all the way from Camp Edwards, across the sound in Falmouth.

The war games are likely to start sometime in the coming weeks, and the Army is announcing the plan, hoping to gain the cooperation of the public. In case damage is done during the maneuvers, to fences or stone walls, or to that all-important tennis-court net, the captain asks property owners to be good sports. The only detail available is that "enemy" troops from Camp Edwards will arrive by boat along the North Shore.

Don't let it stop you from soaking up the sun on Lambert's Cove Beach in the coming days, since no live ammunition will be used. An astute observer might assume that the purpose of the training is a landing on some shore a long distance from Martha's Vineyard, but no explanation can be made officially. Just move the beach towel aside if a slew of young men in combat boots comes hastening past, and enjoy the show. You might even get a glimpse of good Major Gilbert, fearless leader of the island's Cape Cod Commandos, as he takes them through their paces.

And in case you need even more energizing good news, there

is now an official book club associated with this column: the Martha's Vineyard Beach and Book Club. Our next book is ready to make the rounds on the island: the incomparable Virginia Woolf's *Mrs. Dalloway*. Come and pick it up at the farm stand, lucky winner Carol Zimel Cohen, and remember to pass it to your neighbor when finished. She may be shoreside, watching the boys practice winning the war, but she'll be back in a jiff.

12

BRIAR

1942

I STOOD THERE HOLDING OUT THE RING. "I'M NOT LEAVING UNTIL you tell me why you're acting so weird."

Sandra hurried to the front door and pulled down the shade. When she came back to the counter, her hands shook as she switched on the desk lamp. Her reaction sent chills down my spine but made me feel important for having something so supposedly dangerous in my possession. Had Mr. Schmidt been in some sort of trouble? Maybe his fall down the stairs was no accident after all.

Sandra slipped thin gloves onto her hands. "I'm risking my life telling you this."

I found that hard to believe, since her histrionic co-workers at Crabby's had infected her with a taste for melodrama.

"My God," she said as she took the ring from me and placed it on her velvet display tray.

"Obviously Third Reich," I said.

She examined it with her jeweler's loupe. "It's a Totenkopf ring, aka the *SS-Ehrenring*—the SS honor ring." She met my gaze. "It means dead person's head. It's an award ring, given only by Himmler himself. To his most trusted and beloved men. Of pure German blood. His master race."

"Ever seen one before?" I asked.

"No." She held the loupe to her eye and read the inscription inside the band. "Whoever this Kuno is will be looking for it, and let's just say they won't play nice."

I bent and looked closely at the skull's gaping eyes and loose mandible. "The Nazis have really embraced the skull."

"Nothing like scaring the crap out of someone when you arrest them," Sandra said. "And they see old death staring 'em in the face."

"No one knows I have it."

"Are you one hundred percent sure about that? You might be surprised about who's out here on this island. Trust me, you don't want some Nazi knocking at your door. But you'd probably never hear them coming."

I was startled by the sound of a shortwave radio crackling to life in the back room, and Sandra evaded my gaze. What did an antiquities dealer need with one of those?

"I'm not worried," I said. "We've got the Army base just above us."

She blew a spitty little sound through her lips. "Please. Like that'll help you. Assassins are stealthy. And that's where you'll find your spies. Your double agents. Your traitors. They get off on being so close to the secrets." Sandra gave me a penetrating look. "Especially that Brit major, Gilbert."

I stepped back, surprised to hear that name. I'd overheard Cadence and Bess talking about him—that Cadence was actually infatuated with the so-called bane of her existence, who led his troops across our property each morning. "You know him?"

"Came in here with one of his men, all pissed off, since I'd sold the kid a German helmet. Said his men aren't allowed to purchase 'spoils of war,' in that uppity accent of his. How was I supposed to know? Half of my inventory comes from soldiers helping themselves to battlefield spoils. Told him a deal's a deal, and the two of them swung outta here in a jeep."

I rolled my eyes, mostly to get Sandra to like me. "Brits."

"He's one to keep an eye on. He knew a lot more about German stuff than most. Referred to the helmet liner as a *helmfutter*. There's something shifty about him."

"Noted."

She weighed the heft of the ring in her palm, suddenly less afraid, perhaps bolstered by the thought of a substantial commission. "I suppose I can take it off your hands. Get you at least two grand."

"*What?*"

"I'll sell it on the q.t., with no connection to you. In Boston or New York City."

It was tempting to just get rid of it. And we could use the money. But how would I tell Gram I'd suddenly found two thousand dollars?

I plucked the ring from her palm. "I don't think so."

Why the quick reversal? Could I even trust Sandra? I had a feeling that it wouldn't take much for her to turn on me. All McManus would have to do is dangle one free shoreman's fried dinner and she'd spill her guts.

"Jeez. I'd already wrapped my mind around the deal."

I exhaled. "What about all that assassin stuff?"

"Just an initial reaction. We'll be fine. It'll sell quick. I want this outta here as much as you do."

"And you really won't squeal to anyone?"

She held up one hand. "God as my witness."

"Fine." I handed her the ring, relieved to have it out of my possession.

She opened her black book, wrote a receipt for the ring, and handed it to me. *One National Socialist jewelry piece on consignment.*

I pocketed the receipt. "I'm counting on you, Sandra."

"Only my best customers will hear it from me. I want to live to see another day."

THERE WAS NO ONE home when I got back to the cottage. I found a note on the kitchen counter from Gram that said Cade and Bess were out and that she was with her church ladies. It was starting to get dark, and it was hard to shake the creeps after all the scary stuff Sandra had been throwing around. Like some bad guy was going to come find me here—clearly an overreaction.

But the ring came from somewhere. Maybe Kuno was Himmler's pet name for Mr. Schmidt. Maybe they knew each other from the old days? I felt a little sick imagining it. But there was no way Mr. Schmidt had been a Nazi. And it wasn't like Himmler just sent it here in the mail. Someone had brought it from Germany. I had to go with my gut, not with paranoid Sandra, whose brain was probably scrambled from all that nicotine and fried food. Part of Sandra's business was drumming up anxiety.

Scout stood by the front door and whined. Was someone here? Maybe walking down on the beach? I listened for the sound of a car engine. Had McManus come by to search the place? No. He would come during the day.

I opened the front door and Scout took off down the path to the beach. With just enough daylight left to find my way, I followed the sound of waves hitting the shore and passed the darkened boathouse. I emerged from the woods onto the beach, and Scout was already running down the shore. She only ran after squirrels, but there were none of those along the beach.

I hurried after Scout as she rounded the bend and found her tearing toward something that had washed up on the beach in the distance. A seal? Dead seals and small whales sometimes washed up along the south coast of the island, which was open to the pounding surf, but rarely here on the quieter North Shore.

I slowed as we came nearer the form, and my stomach dropped.

"Scout," I called ahead. "Careful."

13

CADENCE

I WORE MY HEART BRACELET TO SEE WINNIE AND COMPANY AT THE Edgartown Yacht Club. The humble little piece that Tom gave me for my sixteenth birthday wasn't exactly Daisy Buchanan's pearl necklace, but it had always brought me luck.

I made it past the club manager's inquisition at the entrance, stepped into the dining room, and took a moment to soak it all in. Bess and her family had been members at the yacht club forever and she'd described it, but it was much more impressive than she'd made it out to be, with its high ceiling and wraparound view of the harbor, all the island's finest yachts and sailboats moored there. I loved the nautical richness of it all: The dining tables with their starched white cloths. The red, white, and blue ship pennants hanging from the rafters that made it feel like a birthday party. That's what it was like to be rich. A celebration every day.

To my right, a long mahogany bar ran the length of the room, and men already sat there, so early in the day, smoking their cigarettes and cigars, drinking scotch or something. "Sunday sailors," my father had called them. I checked my lipstick in the reflection in the glass as I passed through the dining room to the porch beyond, where Mrs. Winthrop stood, her back to the railing. No doubt Winnie would be relieved I'd actually made it.

I headed out to the porch and found Winnie there, looking so relaxed and elegant. She wore a white sleeveless figure-hugging dress with a square collar, and, best of all, she was barefooted and stocking-less, her toenails painted the perfect shell pink. Near her sat two women at a grouping of wicker chairs around a low cocktail table.

"Come here this instant," Winnie called to me, and waved her empty martini glass. "Ladies, this is Cadence Smith. The friend of mine from the beach club I told you about."

The porch overlooked a lovely panorama of ocean and harbor, the green of the water somehow prettier, the French-blue sky more vivid, than it was on our side of the island. The little *On Time* ferry shuttled cars to and from Chappaquiddick Island in the distance, using their horns and bells to narrowly avoid sailboats large and small, crisscross-ing the harbor. The harbormaster drove his skiff by, a suntanned couple sitting arm in arm in the bow, a sweet little flag at the stern flapping in the breeze. Out to their yacht? It was like a storybook.

"Do sit down, my dear." A redheaded woman patted the cushioned seat next to her. "Here by me. I'm the most interesting one."

I smoothed back my hair, feeling like a calf at the ag fair, the subject of their piercing gazes, and wished I'd had something more appropri-ate to wear than my brown plaid skirt and dingy yellow blouse.

Both of Winnie's friends were dressed almost as beautifully as she was. The blonde wore tortoiseshell sunglasses and an organdy print dress with the perfect white mushroom cap of a hat. The redhead wore a navy-blue dress and a chic little nautical hat I'd seen while flipping through a copy of *Vogue* at Leslie's Drugs. They'd all removed their gloves to show off their rings and manicures, but it was the shoes that caused me to stare. They both wore tan-and-white spectator pumps, the "it" shoe of the moment and impossible for normal humans to find in shops.

The blonde called for a waiter to get me a drink and I sat, suddenly afraid to say a word for fear they'd think me a hick with no business coming to New York City. What did people even talk about in publish-ing circles?

Winnie waved toward her friends. "Cadence Smith, meet Celia St. Germain, the blonde, and Dolores Reinhart, the redhead."

"Winnie tells me you are school friends?" I asked.

"Radcliffe," Celia said, in a most casual way, as if it were the A&P.

Dolores beckoned Winnie. "Then Celia and I went to Putnam. Still trying to get Winnie here to join us."

Winnie sat next to Dolores. "Cadence lives on a farm. You should see the flowers at their farm stand. Lilies to die for."

"My Gram sells donuts at the stand, too." I felt the color rise in my face. "And I sell my beetlebung honey."

Celia watched a mahogany speedboat cruise by. "Beetlebung? That's a new one."

"Beetlebung trees grow all over here. They have very hard wood, and the early British colonists crafted casks known as beetles out of the wood, pounding them together with mallets made of the same wood, called bungs."

Dolores put out her cigarette. "This island is endlessly fascinating."

"See what you learn when you leave Manhattan?" Winnie asked.

I felt my scalp sweat. Could I do nothing but recite the encyclopedia?

Winnie rescued me. "We're all big fans of your column, Cadence."

"You've read it?" I asked Celia.

"Win read a few to us that she'd saved," she said. "New York has been beset with a plague of allegedly funny columns, but yours is actually good. The one about chicken à la king being the new steak. Dolores almost collapsed a lung laughing."

I had to take a deep breath, a little lightheaded after hearing that.

Winnie leaned in toward me. "The girls have been lunching with Willis Todhunter Ballard most of the day."

"*Say Yes to Murder* Ballard?" I asked.

"He's keen to go on safari," Dolores said. "And we've had our fill of discussing the poor water buffalo he's so eager to hang on his wall."

"I reviewed *Say Yes to Murder* in my column," I said, and instantly regretted it. I'd have to be honest.

"And?" Celia asked.

"I wrote, *It's a Hollywood homicide that detective fans will follow with mounting interest.* But to be honest I found it a bit convoluted."

"*Convoluted* is being kind." Dolores looked me up and down. "Aren't you a rare bird, a literary thing out here on Más a Tierra?"

How good it was to talk books with people who had actually read all the classics, like *Robinson Crusoe,* and even knew the real island Defoe had based it on.

"At least there are no cannibals," I said.

"Beautiful *and* funny," Celia said. "They'll have their knives out for you in the city."

Winnie lit a cigarette with her gold lighter and snapped it closed with a satisfying little click. "Cadence also writes book reviews. Damned good ones. Charges beach-club members a dollar a pop to do a synopsis of their monthly book-club pick."

Celia threw back her head and laughed. "That's a hoot."

Dolores kept her gaze on her drink. "Look out, Mary McCarthy."

"I love her book reviews. And her debut, *The Company She Keeps.*" I pressed one palm to my chest. "I admire all of Mrs. McCarthy's work."

Celia waved at a passing boat. "So does Mrs. McCarthy."

"Do you type?" Dolores asked.

"Sixty words a minute," I said.

"Well, don't tell anyone or you'll end up being a secretary," Dolores said. "You want someone else typing your words. All the autumn hopefuls bunk together at the Cosmopolitan Club, like a litter of kittens. You need to get there early this fall to get the good spots at the publishing houses."

"There's a whole Vassar wing," Celia added, lighting a cigarette.

Just the mention of a Seven Sisters school plucked at something deep inside me.

Julia Howe from my class at Tisbury High was the only Vassar student I'd ever known. Julia had been my rival for yearbook editor and got the position because her father owned a camera shop in Edgartown. How could I compete with those girls?

"Where did you go to school?" Dolores asked.

I withered at the question. I hadn't even applied to college, much less Radcliffe or Barnard, though my English teacher Mrs. Moss had practically begged me to. How was she to know I couldn't leave Gram and the farm, never mind pay for even part of it? And I'd been too ashamed to tell her. Of course, there was the worst part, too: that I'd never actually gotten my high school diploma. I fell into a terrible depression at the end of my senior year, on the anniversary of my parents' death, and just couldn't get out of bed. Tom helped me through it, but the weight of my farm chores and helping Gram with Briar was too much, and I never went back.

"The Tisbury School," I said, hoping it sounded upscale.

"She means college," Winnie said.

"I never went—too much going on at home. But I've read six hundred and thirty-two novels. I have them listed by a five-point ranking system, from *Anna Karenina* to *Zaynab*."

"Imagine that." Dolores exchanged a glance with Celia. "I'd like to see *your* list."

"Well, that's quite a curriculum in itself, Cadence," Celia said. "Better than anything you'd have gotten at Bryn Mawr. You should come work in New York."

"You mean as an editorial assistant?" I asked. I'd seen that job title in the classified ads in copies of *The New York Times* that members left around the Bayside Club.

"It's exhausting work," Dolores said. "But you'd do a bang-up job."

I searched their faces. Was this just talk or were they serious about me coming? My whole body buzzed with happiness. "How do I register?"

"All the girls show up and it simply sorts itself out," Dolores said.

"And you'll need to have a working knowledge of martinis," Celia said. "It's a prerequisite in publishing."

Winnie tossed a pack of Pall Malls into my lap. "And know your way around a cigarette."

Dolores stood and offered her martini to me. "Here, take mine."

"I don't think—"

At their urging, I tipped my head back, braced for the taste, and let the gin run down my throat, smooth and cold.

Celia tapped her cigarette ash into an empty cup. "And so it begins."

It didn't take long to feel like I was floating down Lethe, the river of forgetfulness in *The Scarlet Letter*, and I suddenly understood why Dorothy Parker was so mad about martinis.

Winnie set her empty glass on the porch railing behind her. "Word around the Bay is, Cadence has a book club."

I marveled at how quickly I felt the calming effect of the alcohol, warmth spreading outward from my belly. "Yes. It's only five people so far. We sit on the beach and drink wine and talk about books."

"Sounds like breakfast at Mother's house," Dolores said. "Does this club have a name?"

"The Martha's Vineyard Beach and Book Club," I said.

Celia stubbed out her cigarette. "I like it."

Winnie tapped her watch. "Cadence, don't you have something you wanted to show the girls? We need to get going."

Celia opened a compact and checked her lipstick. "Picking up Somerset Maugham at the Colonial Inn to take him over to Chappaquiddick for dinner. He won't drive, wants to save wear on his tires."

Somerset *Maugham*? What would these women think of our hastily typed little book?

I ran my finger along the hearts of my bracelet for luck and then slid the book from my pocket. "We made a prototype for a special book for the troops. My brother, Tom, couldn't fit his favorite book in his pack when he was shipping out, and I thought it would be good to make one that the soldiers could take with them anywhere."

"What's your brother's favorite book?" Dolores asked.

"*Emerson's Essays.*"

Celia crossed her legs. "Is Tom single?"

"Celia, please," Winnie said.

I slid the prototype from my pocket and held it out in front of me like a butcher showing a choice chop. "It is a whole book and fits in a loaded knapsack. We tested it."

"*The Sun Also Rises.*" Dolores took it from me and held it by one end and shook it. "Not sure you can call this a book. It's light as a feather duster."

She handed it to Celia, who flipped through the pages. "That's the whole point, dear." She turned to me. "You got a whole book in here?"

I nodded. "Just about."

Celia handed it to Winnie. "Are you kidding, Dolores? This will be bigger than pinups."

Dolores shrugged. "If you say so. You can see right through the pages."

"It's a prototype, for goodness' sake. We'd have to use different paper, of course."

"Think that's doable?" Winnie asked, handing the book back.

"Anything's doable." Celia held it out and considered the cover. "But is Hemingway too expected?"

"How about *Last of the Mohicans*?" Dolores asked.

"Good one," Celia said.

"How about *The Great Gatsby*?" I asked. "Some of the soldiers were asking for it."

"Oh, I don't know," Celia said. "It didn't sell as well as his others. Bit of a flop, I'm afraid."

"Well, why not include it?" Winnie asked. "And add some Zane Grey and Steinbeck."

Dolores toasted with her glass. "They'll feel very patriotic to be included. The authors will be happy, for once."

Lightheaded, I held on to the rattan arm of the chair. They were actually discussing publishing our books. "We chose this one from Gram's cookie jar. Folded up six titles on paper scraps and drew one."

Celia shook her head. "Gram's cookie jar. She's just too much, Win. Can we keep her?"

Dolores clapped her hands together, suddenly all in. "I haven't been this excited about a book since I read *Ben-Hur*."

"Mildred Young Johnson is a good friend of ours," Celia said. "Former Navy librarian, and much nicer than any of us. We'll call her up and make her do this."

I couldn't take the country grin from my face. "Wonderful."

"But you should give serious thought to coming back to Manhattan with us tomorrow," Winnie said. "Pitch it yourself."

"We'll put you up at the Cosmopolitan," Dolores said. "And come back with us on the Putnam yacht, *Never Moor*. It's docked in Menemsha."

Celia waved for the waiter. "King Carol of Romania once owned it, so the upholstery's a bit flashy, but it gets us where we need to go."

"I'd love to come," I said, numb with joy.

"There's a Cordon Bleu chef on board," Winnie said. "He makes the best salmon mousse you've ever had."

As if I'd ever had salmon mousse. But I wanted to try it. I wanted to try everything. I couldn't wait to tell the book club.

Celia raised her glass. "And in the meantime, let's have another round to celebrate our Cadence's move to Manhattan. Mark my words: You're going to run more than book clubs, my girl."

14

BRIAR

1942

As I drew closer, I recognized the form on the beach as a man. He was clothed in a thin T-shirt and a pair of underwear and lay face down, one ear to the sand. He was extremely pale, his skin a milky blue-white, probably suffering hypothermia and shock from exposure.

I checked my surroundings and saw no one on the beach, then knelt and felt the man's neck. I found a pulse, thready but there, and glanced at the call box along the shore. *Not yet.* Why get the authorities involved if I didn't have to? Would they even believe me enough to come? I could attend to his medical care.

He'd nearly drowned. How long had he been in the water? Living on an island, I'd seen my share of water-related accidents and knew that a victim had only four to six minutes to survive a brain deprived of oxygen, after which recovery was generally considered impossible. I pressed on his back, with no luck, then pushed more vigorously, causing him to dislodge a quart or more of seawater. But I knew I had to pile on blankets to get him warm to fight the hypothermia.

Was he a fisherman? Perhaps. I considered the wilder possibility that he came from the U-boat. I looked out to sea, darkness closing in. Was it still off our shore? I pictured seventy men lying in their shallow bunks out there in the darkness, radios silenced, saving their battery power. Were they watching?

The tide was coming in and threatened to swamp him, so I ran around the bend and up the beach to the boathouse, grabbed a waxed tarp and blanket, and ran back. I dragged him onto the tarp, covered him with the blanket, and pulled him toward our old boathouse, a gray-shingled box set on concrete pylons.

It was dark by the time we made it up there, and I hauled him over the threshold, my clothes drenched in sweat. I switched on a table lamp, which lit the knotty-pine walls of the high-ceilinged room. It had been Grandfather's place to play cards with his friends back in the day; he'd furnished it with a small round table and chairs, a sagging velvet sofa, and equipped it with a small water closet.

I sat next to the man on the green-painted floor, caught my breath, and examined him for the first time with the benefit of lamplight. Would he wake and thrash about violently? Attack me? For the moment he looked peaceful, sleeping there. I didn't recognize him from the Menemsha docks or from church. If he was local, I would have seen him at Alley's General Store at some point.

Since he had a beard, it was hard to tell his age, but I judged him to be no more than twenty-five. He was slender and of average height, and the skin on his arms and legs appeared smooth and nearly hairless, with no sign of exposure to the sun. He fit the profile for a Kriegsmarine cadet. On the more compact side. Being at sea for a few months would explain the beard. But why had he just washed up like that?

How could this be happening on our little island? I'd never felt more alive, unraveling the puzzle of who he was.

He wore no life preserver. Did his fellow soldiers throw him out? Did he ditch his ship? Desertion was serious—the Nazis killed deserters. And he was probably not a spy. Spies were better organized and prepared, sent ashore with U.S. dollars and always in German uniform in case they were caught, since spies in civilian dress were more likely to be executed. According to the Hague Conventions, a combatant attempting to gather information while in uniform had to be treated as a prisoner of war.

But perhaps it was a spy mission gone wrong. Eight German men had just been tried in Washington, D.C., for coming ashore from

U-boats during what they'd called Operation Pastorius. Was this somehow connected to them?

Suddenly the man's whole body began to shake. I took a second blanket from the sofa and smoothed it over him, then headed for the door. Gram would know what to do.

15

CADENCE

1942

I WAVED GOODBYE TO WINNIE AND HER FRIENDS AS THEY WALKED off, just as Margaret and Bess pulled into the yacht-club parking lot to pick me up.

Margaret laid on the car horn and waved from the driver's side window. "Cadence! Over here!" she shouted.

I hurried over to them and ducked into the back seat, hoping Winnie wouldn't rescind her offer after seeing my friends in Margaret's car with the falling-off bumper.

"You won't even believe how it went," I said. "They told me I should work in New York City and it's like a litter of kittens and I told them about our book for the armed services and they know a former librarian—"

"Wait." Bess turned to me. "Slow down. Breathe."

I exhaled and gathered myself. "I met Winnie's friends, and they want me to come to New York City."

Bess leaned in. *"What?"*

"Celia St. Germain was there."

Margaret looked at me in the rearview mirror. "From Putnam? You met her?"

"Dolores Reinhart, too."

"Teddy Roosevelt published with Putnam," Margaret said.

"They promised to try to get the books for the troops made. Said they'd be bigger than pinups. And it turns out that social drinking is important to a girl's career. Cigarettes, too. You'll never get anywhere professionally unless you smoke."

"So, are you going to New York?" Bess asked.

"They want me to pitch to a former Navy librarian friend of theirs. Can you believe it? On the Putnam yacht."

"Putnam has a yacht?" Bess asked. "Business must be good."

Bess was not at all impressed by the yacht, since she'd been on so many, courtesy of her boarding school friends. But her parents had never owned one, since they were that rare breed of Boston Brahmin and notoriously avoided the crass shows of wealth flaunted in places like Newport and Palm Beach.

"It's for entertaining authors and clients," I said. "It's called the *Never Moor.*"

"From 'The Raven,'" Margaret said. "They published Edgar Allan Poe."

"They're leaving tomorrow."

"*Tomorrow?*" Bess asked. "How long will you stay?"

"No idea. But they have a chef on board and will put me up in a hotel."

On the way home Margaret stopped to deliver a prescription, and when we arrived at the cottage we found Gram sitting in the living room, listening to the radio.

"You won't believe it, Gram," I said. "I'm going to New York on the Putnam yacht."

"That's wonderful, dear," Gram said, and returned her attention to the radio.

"What do you wear to a literary meeting?" Bess asked. "A dress, I would imagine, though perhaps they all wear suits."

We hurried to my bedroom, and Bess watched me heave three suitcases from the closet. "For a person who barely leaves Chilmark, you have a lot of luggage."

I clicked open the suitcase lid. "I've been waiting for this day." *Will I have time to see Rockefeller Center? The Statue of Liberty?*

The front screen door banged, and I heard Briar talking to Gram.

"Cadence?" Briar called out.

"In here!" I replied.

Briar came to the bedroom door, and I turned from the closet. "What, Briar? Is it Gram?"

"You need to come down to the boathouse," she said, her face ashen. "I found something."

16

BRIAR

———

1942

I LED THEM ALL DOWN TO THE BOATHOUSE, WITH BESS HELPING Gram to take it slow at the rear.

Cadence took me aside as we walked. "Gram shouldn't be out like this at night, Briar. She can barely breathe."

"It's important, trust me."

Cadence walked next to me in silence, but I knew what she was thinking. *Yet another Briar drama about nothing.*

I stepped into the boathouse first.

"My God," Cadence said when she saw the man on the floor. "Who is it?"

I approached him. "I don't know. I found him on the beach."

Bess crouched over him. "Is he even alive?"

"Just unconscious," I said. "He almost drowned. Shock from exposure. Hypothermia."

Bess ran up to the house to get supplies.

"We have to call the police," Cadence said.

"Get him to the sofa," Gram said.

Cadence set her hand on Gram's arm. "He needs a doctor. I'll call an ambulance." She started to turn away.

I pulled her back. "Wait. Let's get him stable first."

Cadence kept her gaze on the man. "But we have no idea who he is."

We woke him enough to get him settled on the sofa, but he lost consciousness again.

"Has he spoken at all?" Margaret asked.

"No."

Gram put a hand on the man's forehead. "He needs to change out of that wet shirt."

"It's no one local, right?" Cadence asked.

I shook my head. "No."

"We'll get him fixed up," Gram said, in her element, no doubt eager to stir up some of her tinctures and potions. "I'll make a poultice up at the house."

Margaret stroked his hair. "Poor thing. Almost drowned."

Bess returned with a basin and towels, more blankets, and some of Tom's clean shirts and trousers.

As we pulled back the blanket, through the man's wet shirt I saw the outline of something taped to his torso. I lifted his shirt to find a rectangular length of waxed paper taped to his chest.

Cadence leaned closer. "What's in there?"

I gently pulled off the tape and paper to find a pamphlet calendar, written in French, and a thin leather case the size of a deck of cards.

"He's French?" Gram asked.

"Maybe," I said, though I suspected he was not. Hitler based his submarine operations out of Lorient, France, on the western coast. If this man had come off a U-boat, it was possible that France was the last place he'd been.

Bess took the leather case from me and opened it to reveal a photo. She held it up. "Look."

It was a picture of a child, not more than a year old, looking at the camera with a grave expression.

Bess returned her gaze to the man. "His son or daughter maybe."

Cadence paced. "We need to call someone. He could die here."

Gram ran some cool water in the basin and drew a towel down the side of the man's face. "He's already coming around."

"*Mutti?*" the man muttered, with his eyes still closed.

Gram turned to me, her eyes wide.

"He's German," Cadence said, breathless.

Bess set the blanket over him again. "Does it really matter right now? He's hurt and needs us."

I could only nod, amazed my suspicions were true. A warm thrill coursed through me. In some ways this was the opportunity I'd dreamed of—a German soldier ready to answer anything I asked. I could finally use my German skills. It was a dangerous situation, of course, and it had to be handled smartly.

Margaret hurried to the bathroom, came back with a cup of water, and helped him sip from it.

"Please help me," the man said weakly, in good English. "I am just a medic, not a criminal."

"This is just like what happened on Long Island." Cadence headed for the door. "I'm calling the police."

"Not yet, Cade, please," Bess said. "Just hear him out."

"What's your name?" I asked.

"Peter Muller. I cannot go back to them. I'll do anything."

"Why are you here?" I asked. "I know you came off the U-boat that's been sitting out there."

He stared at me for a long moment. "I had to get away. I didn't sign up for what Hitler's doing. I am just the ship's medic."

"Why is your English so good?" Cadence asked.

"I was raised here in America." He patted his chest. "Where is my photo?"

Bess handed him the little leather case. "A beautiful child."

"My daughter, Anna." He opened the case and looked at the photo. "She's with my grandmother in Minnesota."

"How old is she?" Bess asked.

He looked at the picture. "Already three now."

"How long since you've seen her?"

"Too long. Since she was an infant."

"Why did you jump ship?" I asked.

He struggled to sit and then gave up and settled back down. "My grandmother is a Mennonite. Our family moved to Minnesota from Germany when I was a child, and I was raised in a household of non-violence."

Gram stepped closer to him. "God-fearing people."

He nodded. "I hate what Hitler is doing. I finally left last night. I knew I'd rather die than remain a part of that."

"But they'll come looking for you," I said.

"No. I staged my own death. With pig's blood from the galley, on the clothes I left behind."

"But they have binoculars," I said. "They'll see you here."

"They have only limited focal range from out there." He paused and looked at Gram. "I would like to defect."

"How did you end up in Germany?" I asked. Had he just made up this elaborate story? It was hard to tell. But the details seemed unique enough to be true.

"My parents took me back, to Hesse, when I was in middle school, to wrap up the family's estate. We ended up staying and I married. My mother and wife took our infant to Minneapolis when the war started and I was conscripted."

"So they're waiting for you there?" Bess asked.

He shook his head. "My wife got sick on the voyage over, and my mother, too."

Gram tapped herself with the sign of the cross. "God help them."

Bess crouched near him. "But the baby survived?"

"She did. Thriving with my grandmother, last I heard."

Gram sat next to him on the sofa. "Thank the Lord, raised in a Christian household. Nazis have disavowed God."

"I'm so sorry," Bess said. "All while you were on that U-boat, separated from them."

"I was a farmer like my father—we grew all our own food—but the Kriegsmarine trained me as a medic since I'd birthed calves. And I was assigned to a U-boat. Once we downed a ship, I knew I couldn't stay."

Cadence clearly wasn't buying his story. "So you had no idea what the U-boat was out there to do?"

He turned to Cadence. "Of course I was aware that we would confront the enemy—I was trained to bandage wounds and suture—but I didn't know our exact mission. It was terrible knowing I'd been a part of causing so much pain and bloodshed."

"How awful for you," Bess said.

"You don't know the horror of it, hunting ships with human beings aboard like that, the men cheering at the kills, and adding another pennant to hoist upon our arrival home."

Cadence went to the door. "I'm sorry, but this sounds implausible. We have to call the police now."

Peter reached out one arm toward Cadence. "Please. I love this country. I'm not a threat to anyone. I just need to reach my daughter. My grandmother is not well."

I weighed his claim of fealty to the United States. Was he making it up to save his skin? I had no idea about the process, but helping him defect wouldn't be easy. And all of us would be liable, too, if we didn't turn him in soon. We were probably already harboring a criminal in the law's eyes.

"Sleep now," I said. "We'll talk more later."

After he fell asleep, I stepped to Cadence at the door.

"You're not actually thinking of keeping him here?" Cadence asked.

Bess, Gram, and Margaret joined us. "What if this were Tom far from home?" Bess asked. "Wouldn't we want someone to care for him?"

"These are the men Tom's fighting," Cadence said. "Gram, you swore a Coast Guard pledge to watch the shore for invaders. We have to turn him in."

"We need to know more," I said. "What would the defection protocol entail?"

"You just want to study him," Cadence said. "You must be having a field day, seeing a Nazi up close like this. But this isn't some spy game, Briar. We have to turn him in and be done with it. His story sounds so fake."

"Let me go and talk to Captain McManus about defection."

The thought of finding and turning over a German who wanted to defect was appealing. Someone would finally believe me about something. But it had to be handled delicately. Peter was innocent and practically American. He didn't deserve to die in the electric chair, no matter what Cadence thought.

"Head-of-the-FBI McManus?" Bess asked.

"I know him a little from work. Maybe we can hand Peter over quietly. When J. Edgar Hoover announced they had found those German saboteurs, it created a riot. Roosevelt had no choice but to execute them. Maybe we can do this secretly somehow."

"Fine," Cadence said. "Go talk to McManus tomorrow." She sent Bess a pointed look. "But don't get too attached to him. As soon as we figure out the best way, we're turning him in."

17

CADENCE

—

1942

WE ALL WORE WHAT BESS CALLED OUR FUNERAL FACES AS MARGA-
ret drove us to Menemsha to give Winnie and pals the bad news. I sat
in the back seat, imagining the looks on their faces. Win and the Putnam ladies would be crushed by my inability to join them, and would
exclaim that no one could sell the project as I could, and would insist on
giving me a rain check for another time.

Why did some German have to wash up on our beach at that moment? His story seemed bogus. He'd suddenly embraced his deep
Mennonite values and staged his own death in order to reunite with his
supposedly sick grandmother and daughter? It wasn't a stretch for him
to assume Gram was a church lady. He'd made it all up to prey on her
sympathies. And they all bought it so easily. I tried to picture the German, with his slender build and scraggly beard, in the simple clothes of
the Mennonite faith, but it was hard to imagine. He was there for some
other nefarious reason and would be the ruin of us all.

I watched Margaret as she drove. Would she blab about Peter to
someone at the drugstore? We barely knew her. Though, as we drove,
she didn't seem all that concerned about the Peter situation and had
seized the opportunity, with us trapped in the car, to review in detail the
pros and cons of choosing *Madame Bovary* as our next month's book-
club pick. Bess, eager to stop her, tried turning the radio up, but Margaret just spoke over it.

"I know it's a racy book and Ginny may not vote for it, but it's a true classic, and I'd love to reread it and discuss."

"We've all read it already," Bess said.

"But that's the beauty of it. We don't need multiple copies. We can just discuss it. I do enjoy Flaubert." She looked at me in the rearview mirror. "Did you know he used to yell the sentences he wrote, at the top of his lungs, to make sure they sounded right?"

"His neighbors must have enjoyed that," Bess said.

"I've put together something for us to play called 'book bingo,' with so many good questions. Like: What annual event does *Madame Bovary* have in common with Martha's Vineyard?" She paused. "The Agricultural Fair, right? Though not this year, of course, on account of the war, but isn't that fun?"

"Eyes on the road, Margaret, dear," Bess said.

I tuned them out, raking through my own difficulties. I wouldn't be going to New York City on the yacht anytime soon, or at all. It had been a stupid pipe dream to begin with, since Gram needed a heart operation and, naturally, any extra funds had to go toward her procedure at Massachusetts General Hospital in Boston, not to me for running around Manhattan. Even if we didn't have a German in our boathouse.

At least Briar was finding out more from Captain McManus and we would be done with Peter soon. I was desperate to have it behind us. With our property crawling with Army commandos, we played a dangerous game by harboring him, even for one day.

For moral support, I brought Bess and Margaret with me to the dock. I waved to Winnie as she walked toward us, sandals clacking, from the direction of what must have been the Putnam yacht, the seventy-foot cruiser parked alongside the distant dock.

"Wow, look at that," Margaret said, gazing out at the yacht.

"Nice," Bess said, unimpressed.

But I could barely breathe, confronted with all that seafaring magnificence. With her sleek white hull and teak deck, and *Never Moor* painted in gold leaf at her stern, that boat was a beauty and stood in almost comic contrast to the run-down swordfishing and lobstering boats around her.

Winnie was dressed for travel, in a yellow sundress, chic tortoiseshell sunglasses, and a navy-blue, polka-dotted silk scarf keeping her hair back, knotted at the nape.

She made it to us, and I introduced Bess and Margaret.

"Where's your valise, for heaven's sake?" Winnie asked me.

I handed her the booklet prototype and told her I wouldn't be coming due to Gram's ill health.

"Well, family comes first," she said, taking the booklet. "I'm just along for the ride, but I'll make sure Celia and Dolores know. They'll be disappointed. No one can sell it the way one of you can."

I smiled at that. "Thank you, Winnie, but—"

Margaret raised her hand. "I'll go."

We all turned to consider her. While I appreciated the gung-ho attitude for the cause, Margaret hadn't conferred with Bess and me. And the thought of her taking my place on my dream trip didn't sit well at all.

Bess perked up at that. "Great solution," she said, clearly happy to be rid of her.

Winnie looked Margaret over and shrugged. "All right, then."

"But you don't have your overnight bag," I said, part of me hoping that might derail the plan.

"Oh, we'll pick up a few things for her," Winnie said. "And don't worry, we'll have her back next week."

"No rush," Bess said, probably happy she didn't have to play book bingo.

I took Margaret aside. "With the Peter situation . . ."

She held up her hand in a Boy Scout salute. "Mum's the word."

Winnie started off toward the yacht. "If you're done saying your goodbyes, we need to get going. Chef's making Welsh rarebit and says terrible things in French if it's allowed to get cold."

I watched Winnie and Margaret amble to the Manhattan-bound boat that I longed to be aboard. Even with the flashy upholstery.

The two of them turned and waved to us.

So much for the ladies being sorry not to have me. Now Margaret would be the hero, selling the book.

I waved back to them. "Sell it hard, Margaret," I called out, ruing the day Margaret Coutinho joined our club.

THE MERCURY HAD HIT ninety degrees by the time Bess and I returned to the farm. We craved a swim but found Major Gil's commandos training on the beach in the distance, doing some sort of relay races. There would be no swimming for us, with them down there all day. Perhaps it was better, after all, since the doctor had told Bess to relax. Not that she had been following his orders. She needed to do more reading and less weeding.

Determined to continue the appearance of normalcy while we waited for Briar's information from Captain McManus, Bess and I convened a book-club meeting in the cool, dark living room. As soon as Briar returned, we could turn the German in and get back to normal. Finding out about Peter would send Peaked Hill into a tailspin. Major Gilbert would certainly be surprised—the hick farm girls found a German spy. We'd be heroes, until they realized we'd been harboring him.

Gram hurried in the front door, holding the white basin. "He's coming along."

"Oh, good," Bess said. From the way she fawned over Peter, you'd think he was her long-lost lover. Perhaps she was replacing Tom with him in her mind.

"Once Briar gets back, we're making the call," I said. "We just need to work out the details."

"You could do the Christian thing," Gram said. "Go down to the boathouse and check on him now and then."

"We have book club, Gram," I said. "And he's probably happy for the time alone to rest. Are you joining us?"

Gram went to the kitchen without a reply, and I opened my copy of *The Song of Bernadette*.

Bess stood and went to the window. "Hold on. We have company."

A knock came at the front door and Major Gilbert stood there, his form dark against the screen. "I'm terribly sorry to intrude."

It was good to see him. He'd clearly had a good workout that morning, and I forced myself not to look at how the perspiration made his T-shirt cling to his chest.

But I needed to make it quick, having a German in our boathouse and all.

"We're having book club," I said.

"Just wanted to tell you that your boat is at risk of floating away down at the beach. Tide's coming in, I'm afraid."

"Oh, no. My sister left it there." Briar had failed to use the sand anchor again.

"My men are holding it, but they can't do it forever."

"I'll take care of it," I said. I stepped out into the front yard. "I'll go get the sand anchor from the boathouse and bring it to you."

He followed me. "No need, Miss Smith."

"I don't want your men holding our boat from the tide all day."

He started back down to the beach. "Oh, I sent Private Jeffers round to get it."

"You *what?*" I called after him, a dull buzz in my head.

"I sent Jeffers to the boathouse for the anchor. He's getting it now."

18

BRIAR

1942

MY STOMACH WAS DOING BACKFLIPS AS I FOLLOWED THE ADDRESS on the impressive card that Captain McManus had given me, which was stamped with a gold embossed seal. The black coffee I drank was probably burning an ulcer the size of Buzzards Bay in my belly. I was careful not to wear Mr. Schmidt's Tyrolean jacket again, just an argyle vest over an oxford cloth shirt Tom had worn as a boy and corduroy pants.

I found the office, in Vineyard Haven above the A&P, *Federal Bureau of Investigation* lettered discreetly along the bottom of the wavy glass on the door's window. I entered a reception room that didn't exactly match the fancy calling card, and McManus opened his office door and stepped out. He seemed even more disheveled since I'd seen him last, dressed in almost the same outfit. Did he wear that dirty windbreaker to bed? But despite his sloppy appearance, something about him scared me no end. "Sneaky good," Mr. Schmidt would have called him.

"Miss Smith. What can I do for you?"

"Sorry I didn't call first. But I'm not so great with details."

"Oh, really? You seem pretty buttoned up to me."

I took a deep breath. I'd have to watch every word with him. "I've been thinking about what you said."

He sat on the corner of the desk, his thick glasses magnifying his eyes, the lenses dirty as a bug-flecked car windshield. "I'm tingling with anticipation."

I sat in the chair across from him, jittery. "That was great advice you gave me about writing a story. There's a contest in *Total War* magazine, for a piece about a true crime. I could win a trip to Atlantic City."

"Fun." He lit a cigarette and stared at me for a long second. "I'm not a literary editor, Miss Smith." He thought for a moment. "Heard you called in another U-boat sighting."

He was certainly well connected on the island.

I shrugged. "They tell me I was mistaken."

He brushed cigarette ash from his tie. "I make my living off mistakes, Miss Smith. Keep 'em coming."

Contrary to outward appearances, McManus was an ambitious guy. Sandra told me that, since his wife died, he'd been itching to get back to Boston, and she hypothesized that he might need some sort of big arrest to get him noticed. Looked like he thought I might be his ticket to a score.

"About that article," I said. "I'm thinking I'll write about the Germans they caught in June that came ashore."

"Operation Pastorius?" he asked.

"Any thoughts on how it was handled?"

He shook his head. "I can't comment on that."

I slid a pad and pencil from my pocket. Men lose their minds when they think someone's actually writing down their thoughts. "Just off the record?"

He shrugged and looked out the window. "Gotta say, Hoover did a great job grabbing those guys."

"Your dauntless FBI leader."

"They're calling for him to get a medal," he said.

"Who's doing the calling?" I asked. "His office?"

McManus smiled. "Not bad for a sixteen-year-old."

"So what happened exactly?" I asked, pencil ready. "The newspapers only say so much."

"Pretty simple. A couple of months ago, eight German naturalized citizens came ashore from U-boats, some on Long Island and some in Florida, sent here by Hitler himself. The ones in New York approached a Coast Guard patroller and tried to bribe him to look the other way. Few days later their leader turned them all in."

"It seemed like a fast trial."

"Less than two months. They move quickly with these things in time of war. Closed-door military tribunal to preserve wartime secrecy. Six were sentenced to death. The two that turned them in got prison time."

"The six were executed by electric chair?" I asked.

"Alphabetically." He tapped his ash into the crystal ashtray. "Nice touch."

I tried to hide my involuntary shudder. "It all seems so harsh. They didn't even end up doing anything bad."

"We're at war, Miss Smith. Roosevelt needed to send a strong signal to Hitler."

"Maybe they were just trying to defect." I paused for his reaction. "Some of them were U.S. citizens."

"They accepted Hitler's mission to come here and blow up public places. Popular tourist destinations. Mount Rushmore. Army installations. Vital government infrastructure. The Hoover Dam."

"How do we know that?" I asked.

"They testified at the trial that they were sent here to frighten the U.S. public into withdrawing from the war." He took a serious drag from his cigarette. "And by the way, usually only prominent citizens of oppressed countries defect."

"What if that Coastie hadn't turned those Germans in?" I asked.

"He'd be in jail for a long time. Hard labor." He gave me a searching look. "But he's a good citizen. Anyone would do the same, don't you think? On this island. Nothing but patriots."

"What if it had happened here?"

He waved that thought away. "I don't deal in hypotheticals."

"Just a guess?"

He looked out the window to the harbor in the distance. "Well, if it was made public, it would send this place into chaos. Reporters everywhere. Summer people leaving in droves. Say goodbye to tourism for the duration of the war."

"I read that the saboteurs' families were in trouble, too," I said, as nonchalantly as I could.

"Still locked up, awaiting sentences. They should've thought twice about harboring criminals, even relatives. One of their mothers is in the clink."

I swallowed hard. Was he on to me? My stomach started up again. "You don't say."

"Older folks don't do well in prison. Saw it myself when I toured Leavenworth last summer."

"Fun."

"Did you know there's a seventy-six percent mortality rate for inmates aged seventy-plus? The stress of lockup is harder on them. One old guy chewed off the tip of his own thumb. Not that it's easy on the younger ones."

Was he referring to Gram? I closed my pad. How stupid I'd been to come here. "Well, this has been enlightening, Captain."

"Did you know you're not even allowed to whistle in prison? It reminds the other inmates of birds. And freedom. Drives them crazy. As if criminals are not crazy already, am I right?" He stared me down. "Although some are pretty coolheaded."

I stood. "I'd better be going."

"A person's gotta be nuts to think they can get away with these things. Or just stupid." He set his cigarette on the ashtray. "Keeps me in business, I guess."

I stepped to the door, in need of air.

"Hope you win that trip," he said.

I turned. "What?"

"To Atlantic City."

"Oh, yes."

"Thought I might stop by your farm soon. I hear it has quite the view."

I forced myself to meet his gaze. "Sure."

"Good. I may not call, though. I'm not great with details, either."

19

CADENCE

—

1942

I FELT A LITTLE DIZZY STANDING THERE IN THE HOT SUN WITH Major Gilbert. "Jeffers went to the boathouse? Just *now*?"

"Right before I came up here. Whatever is the matter?"

I wanted to run at breakneck speed for the boathouse, since Jeffers could've already found Peter, but instead I walked off in that direction. "I'll go make sure he finds it."

"Happy to lend a hand," the major said.

"*No.*"

He took a step back. "Well, then. Simply offering a spot of help."

Did he have to choose that moment to suddenly become a human being?

"Thank you. But I just want to make sure he gets that anchor quickly. Don't want the boat drifting off."

"Of course. I'll leave you to it. But I was thinking: That tour your grandmother mentioned. Would you still be willing to give it a go?"

"Sure," I said.

"Good, then. I'll pop by sometime."

"Call first. Our life is a little . . . It's best to call."

"Of course. Well. Good, then."

"You'd better get back down to your men. I'll have Jeffers bring the anchor over."

I ran down the path, my abrupt manner seemingly piquing the major's interest.

He called after me. "I'll get that tour on the schedule."

Once out of sight of Major Gilbert, I dashed to the boathouse and made it to the doorway. Through an opening in the window curtains, I saw Peter inside on the sofa, wearing one of Tom's shirts, sound asleep, just as a soldier came up from the beach.

"Hello there," I said, hands on my knees, gulping air. "Jeffers?"

"Yes, ma'am. Come for some sort of anchor to secure the boat down at the beach. Tide's coming in."

"So I heard. How did you find this place? It's so overgrown."

"Major said I should come over this way, and I followed orders, ma'am. I'll just get the anchor." He started toward the boathouse door.

I blocked his path. "No. I'll get it. It's hard to find in there, with all the mess."

"Oh, that's not a problem for me, ma'am. I grew up around boats. On a lake back home. Idaho may be landlocked, but the lakes are beautiful."

"Let me grab the anchor, Private. I'll be right out."

As I stepped inside the boathouse, I closed the curtains as best I could, then shut the door behind me. I gently smoothed a blanket over Peter, willing him to stay asleep. I pulled the sand anchor from the wall, held it by the rope attached to one end, and walked back past the sleeping German and out the door.

"Here it is," I said, handing Jeffers the rope.

"In Idaho we don't use anchors much, just toss a line at the dock. No tides, you see. Makes it so much easier."

I glanced through the gap in the curtains, at the German rousing and pushing off the blanket.

"Rumor has it your grandmother will make a pie from a fellow's home state if he asks."

I nudged Private Jeffers along the path. "Sign your name and the town you come from in the book at the farm stand at the head of the road."

He smiled. "That sure is kind of her. And they say New Englanders are not so nice."

"You'd better hurry, before the tide is in. And please don't come back here to the boathouse. The building is unstable, and I'd hate for you to get hurt."

"Wouldn't get my chance to serve," he said over his shoulder, still smiling.

Private Jeffers made his way down the path to the beach, anchor in one hand, waving back at me as he went. In the distance I could hear the men around the bend at Salt Cove going through their paces. What was to stop more of them from wandering over—even Major Gilbert himself? What if Peter woke and spoke in German? The longer we kept him, the harder it would be to say he'd just washed up here. And if caught, the German would certainly be honest about how long we'd harbored him.

I went back to the boathouse and found him asleep again, open-mouthed and softly snoring. He didn't seem a sinister sort, and if Tom were in that situation, I'd hope some German women would take pity on him. But we had to be realistic, too.

Briar came into the boathouse with a grave look on her face. Bad news from Captain McManus, no doubt.

"Gram's on her way down," she said. "Bess, too."

"Did you see Major Gilbert?" I asked.

"He went back to the beach."

Gram and Bess joined us.

"What did McManus say?" I asked.

"There's no chance of defection," Briar said, her eyes dark. "They would take Peter to Washington for probable execution, just like the Operation Pastorius men."

"Surely there would be a trial," Gram said. "They'd know he's innocent."

"A quick trial, behind closed doors." Briar checked to make sure the German was still sleeping and lowered her voice. "Then it would be the electric chair for him."

"Don't be so dramatic," I said.

"That's what the others got," Bess said.

The German roused and then settled back into sleep.

"I'm sorry, Briar," I said, keeping my voice low. "I know he's probably a good person, and under different circumstances I'd say we should try to help him, but we didn't ask for him to arrive at our doorstep. And one of Major Gilbert's men almost saw him. Can you imagine?"

"I know." Briar shared a bleak glance with Bess.

"How do you suggest we do it?" Gram asked.

"Probably best to call McManus and have him come over," Briar said.

"Well, let's do it," I said.

Briar gave me her there's-another-feral-cat-you-need-to-buy-a-can-of-cat-food-for look. "McManus also said that the island will never be the same if word gets out. People will panic. No one will summer here."

"Well, that's not our problem," I said. "I'm sure Tom would agree."

Bess shook her head. "Of all people, Tom would want Peter to get back to his family. His dear child."

"They'll probably give Tom a dishonorable discharge just for being in the same family as us," Briar said.

"Tom wouldn't want Peter to die. He grew up in this country, for goodness' sake."

I turned to Gram. "If he's found here, we'll all go to jail. We need to be together on this."

Gram nodded. "I hate to say it, but I suppose it's best."

Bess turned away, arms folded across her chest. "You talk about the Christian thing to do."

"I'm sorry, Bess, but I can't risk you all being arrested. I'll call." Gram glanced at Peter. "I hate to do it, though. He's a good man."

The German stirred, and Briar sat next to him on the sofa. "You seem to be feeling better."

"Yes," he said. "I'm happy to help with farmwork."

"I'm afraid the minute you open your mouth, people will know who you really are."

"I can speak in a very believable Midwestern accent. I used to entertain my friends at school with it."

Briar shook her head. "I'm sorry to tell you this, but I'm afraid we're going to have to turn you in. To a friend of mine. In the FBI."

"To help me defect?" he asked.

I stuffed down the guilt. He seemed so innocent.

"You can request it," Briar said. "But I'm not sure it will be granted."

"I see." He looked down at his hands. "Can I call my grandmother? It's a long-distance call, but I can have her send you the payment for it later. I would like to hear my daughter's voice just once."

"I'm afraid we don't want to risk the operator hearing that call," I said. "They can be nosy here, listening in."

"Once Gram makes the call, they'll come very quickly," Briar said to him.

Gram set off for the door.

"Please wait," the German called to her. "Before you do that, I have one more thing to tell you. It may change your decision."

20

BRIAR

—

1942

"If you have something to tell us, you need to make it quick," Cadence said.

"Let the man speak," I said.

Peter attempted a smile. "I appreciate the thoughtful way you have dealt with my situation. I'm sorry to put you in such a position." He looked around the room at our faces. "Truly. I was raised in a home much like this, full of kindness and generosity."

"We need to move this along," Cadence said.

"So you should know, before you surrender me to the authorities, that they will no doubt debrief me."

"Just say you've been here only a few hours," Cadence said.

"They will know the truth. The dryness of my clothes. A complete medical evaluation. My blood-oxygen levels. They will know I have been out of the water for more than just a few hours. They'll know you did not turn me in immediately."

"We can say we were trying to figure out how to hand you over," Cadence said. "That's the truth."

"But that is only part of the problem," Peter said. "They will perform a rigorous interrogation."

"So?" I asked.

"They are highly trained at finding the truth, and it will be in my best interest to give it to them."

"I don't understand," Cadence said.

"They will want to know every detail about the U-boat I came from."

Cadence leaned toward him. "Fine. Tell them. That doesn't implicate us."

He looked at me. "I'm afraid it does."

A spike of fear went through me. "How so?"

"As the ship's medic, I had a unique vantage point, privy to conversations that took place while I was ministering to the sick and wounded on board. Part therapist, part confidant to the ship's captain."

"And?" I asked, steeling myself. Did they have some sort of surveillance? Somehow know about the metal box? The classified documents I took?

"What you may not realize is that, while our main mission is to sink Allied ships, we gather intelligence out there offshore. The radio operator intercepts everything he can—often just bits of conversation between fishermen on their radios or routine police calls we'd all joke about. Like a mean turkey on the loose. But they were particularly interested in Sailfish Five."

My whole body went cold. How could I have been so careless?

"What is Sailfish Five?" Cadence asked. She turned to me. "*Briar?*"

I met her gaze, my heart pounding. "Mr. Schmidt's shortwave handle."

"He's been dead for more than a month," she said. "Who's using it now?"

I looked away. "I maybe talk to his friends once in a while."

Cadence pulled me around to face her. "About what? And please don't tell me it's anything sensitive."

I tried to walk away. "Just things."

She tugged me back to her. "It's against *the law* to use a shortwave radio right now, Briar."

The German sat up straighter. "The radio operator transcribed a conversation about some impending war maneuvers taking place on these beaches soon."

Cadence wrapped her arms across her belly. "Oh, no, Briar."

"I said very little." I raced through what I'd said to Mr. Schmidt's

Squad—just three conversations that referenced the maneuvers, two with detailed descriptions of the amphibious vehicle they'd been testing in the dunes.

"So what?" Bess asked. "I'm sure they pick up chatter all the time."

"Everyone's heard that some sort of war games are happening," Cadence said. "It was in the paper. I wrote about it in my column."

"Maybe so," Peter said. "But the conversation the captain referenced included precise descriptions of military practices and schedules of deliveries, including a new type of landing craft. They noted it was a young woman making the report."

McManus would have reason to come and take the radio and search the whole place. He'd find the German box and the classified pages. But the fact that they'd been out there listening this whole time vindicated me. I wasn't crazy. Or a liar.

Gram squeezed in on the sofa next to me. "Oh, Briar."

"I obviously didn't think anyone was listening."

"You never think," Cadence said. "How could you be so stupid, chatting with your old-man pals? Showing off your war smarts?" She paced. "I can't believe this is happening."

Peter turned to me. "I'm not accusing you. Just explaining what I will need to include in the course of my interrogation."

"Are you saying Briar will go to jail if you tell them all that?" Gram asked.

"You're blackmailing us," Cadence said. "Of course. Is that part of the Mennonite religion, too?"

Peter kept his gaze on me. "I don't want to implicate you, but if I'm turned over to the authorities, I must. My grandmother and daughter need me, and sharing this information is my only hope of surviving. Perhaps the judge will be lenient if I cooperate and show my allegiance by sharing sensitive information."

"What would happen to you, Briar?" Bess asked.

I ran my fingers through my hair. "Arrested for sure. McManus already suspects me of something. Adults go to Leavenworth."

"Maybe you'd go to some sort of juvenile facility," Bess said. "Tom would be dishonorably discharged."

"He had nothing to do with it," I said.

Cadence stepped closer to me, her face flushed. "It is your own hubris that's landed us here, Briar. Maybe prison would do you some good."

Gram suffered one of her little coughing fits and then said, "Stop that. This is your *sister*."

"What now?" Bess asked.

Cadence paced again. "Now it's either turn him in and Briar goes to jail, or we keep him here, under the nose of the army, and probably *all* go to jail soon. Nice choice, sister."

Gram took my hand in hers. "I know you didn't mean for this to happen."

"There's only one thing we can do, Gram." Cadence went to the door. "And we're going to have to be quick about it."

21

MARI

B Y THE TIME MRS. DEVEREAUX STOPPED TALKING, THE SUN WAS
setting, causing the sky to turn deep tangerine and magenta over the
almost-purple sea. I checked out her canvas, nicely primed, her landscape study feathered in. I had tried to paint while she talked, even laid
out my palette, neutral to chromatic, but my canvas sat blank.

"You're stopping?" I asked.

She cleaned her brush. "I'm afraid I've about talked your ear off."

"So, did they keep the German?" I asked.

"Oh, that's enough for one day, Mari. Looks like you missed that
seven-thirty ferry."

Something about the way she said the part about the ferry irked me.
Practically giddy. What did she care that I was giving up the last good
plane fare to be had? And Nate would probably assume I'd been kid-
napped. If he thought about me at all.

Would she just string out this story forever? Clearly she thought I
was related to this Smith family somehow.

"If my mother was connected to all this, then how come she never
said anything? We shared everything. It was just the two of us."

"I can't promise all the answers, but why not stay the weekend?"
Mrs. Devereaux asked. "I have plenty of room, and I can show you the
island a bit tomorrow. Then maybe you can even get something down
on canvas. And you can hear the whole story."

"I guess. Sometimes it takes me a while to get painting."

When my mother was alive, we used to paint together, sometimes all weekend, her banging out one of her amazing Van-Gogh-on-steroids landscapes, me, a postmodern portrait or floral still life. But ever since she'd died, I could barely sketch in pencil, never mind paint.

"All the more reason to stay. We'll go to the Chilmark Flea. You'll enjoy that very much. They sell all sorts of things. And the best brownies."

"Maybe I can stick around. Just one more day." If there was a God, Mrs. Devereaux would get to the point of the story soon.

She smiled. "Good, then. I'll rebook your flight."

We packed up our paints and hung out in the kitchen and ate Cracker Barrel cheddar and Ritz crackers, and she brought out a really good Sonoma chardonnay. Then she scrambled some eggs and I made the toast.

"My mom and I would make this very meal," I said. "We called it din-din fest. Like, breakfast for dinner. I'd make the toast, my specialty. She liked it timed so it was still warm when the eggs were done. And with plenty of butter. But any meal was fun with her. She was a total extrovert; everyone loved her."

"Really." Mrs. D. smiled. "Was she a good cook?"

"Pretty good. She was tired after work most nights. But baking was her thing. I swear, any holiday was an excuse to bake. She made Groundhog Day cookies. Before she died, she'd started making You-Tube videos of how to bake obscure cookies, and she was blowing up."

"Is that right?" Mrs. D. tried to look away, but I saw the tears in her glassy eyes. Was it because Ginny Smith was a baker, too?

"I'll put you in Cadence's old room," she said. "You'll sleep like the dead."

That seemed like a creepy choice of words, since I'd be sleeping in an actual dead person's room, but I was so tired I didn't have the strength to mention it.

I said good night and closed the door to the snug room, which barely fit the full-sized bed and dresser. I ran my hand down the tufts of the white chenille coverlet, which was like something from George Washington's old feather bed. The little milk-glass lamp on the dresser lit up the wallpaper, the cabbage roses now faded. I loved the old green-painted dresser, like the one my mother and I had seen at a shop at Big Bear. *Eastlake,* she called it.

Were Cadence's clothes still in here? I slid open the top drawer and found a yellow blouse, neatly folded. I lifted it out, breathing in the scent of laundry bluing, which my mother had always washed our sheets with, and rose sachet. I loved that someone had used old wrapping paper as drawer liners. No IKEA in those days.

I opened the small closet and hung the one dress I'd brought. I counted six suitcases stacked on the top shelf. Cadence, the would-be traveler. Had she ever seen the world? Was I related to her? I'd never had much wanderlust.

I read the titles of the books stacked on top of the dresser: *Anna Karenina. Jane Eyre.* What must have been her brother Tom's *Emerson's Essays.* Probably her Never-Lend books.

The golden hearts at my wrist glowed in the lamplight. Cadence's good-luck bracelet. How did Nancy Starwood of Los Angeles, California, end up with it?

I changed into my sleep T-shirt and climbed into bed. Was this the very one Bess and Cadence had shared? I eased my head down onto the pillow and tried to remember Nate's face as I drifted off. To the sleep of the dead.

I WOKE AT DAWN the next day, the sun streaming through the curtainless windows, and emerged to find Mrs. D. looking like she was dressed for an African safari, all in khaki, with a straw hat the size of an actual sombrero.

"We'll get breakfast sandwiches at 7a and eat them in the car," she said. "The good antiques are gone by ten o'clock."

Appreciating a fellow treasure hunter, I hurried to the jeep, and after pretty amazing bacon-egg-and-cheese croissants and hazelnut coffees, we made our way to a small flea market in a field a short drive away.

As I got out of the car, Mrs. D. claimed she had somewhere to be.

"I'll pick you up in an hour," she called as she drove off. "Get me a brownie!"

I strolled the booths, the hot sun warming the top of my head, happy to shop by myself. If it wasn't with my mother, I preferred to browse alone. Mrs. D. was right about getting there early, and I spotted some good things as the vendors unloaded their wares onto their tables, some sold right out of their car trunks. A fun white macrame bikini, lots of great jewelry, and a good amount of corny New England antiques, old washboards, white ironstone pitchers, and orphan teacups. But the vintage clothes were the star of the place, and two different dealers offered racks of them. I lost all sense of space and time as I looked through the coats and dresses. I tried on one short tomato-red rayon dress over my clothes that the vendor encouraged me to buy but I couldn't afford.

Once I realized that more than an hour had passed, I hurried to the bakery table under a tree, the sign advertising cold drinks and *the best island brownies.* The line was a mile long, but I could see right away why Mrs. D. had pushed the brownies so hard. Not only did they look scrumptious, glistening in their Saran Wrap, but the booth proprietor greeted me with a little wave—Bike Man.

"Hey," Ronan said as he waited on customers, a girl a bit younger than me at his side. She was so confident, laughing with some guy. Birkenstocks and wispy Dutch-girl braids. Sweet and silly. Perhaps my complete opposite.

I made my way through the crowd around the table to Ronan, suddenly more interested in him. What is it about a guy having a girlfriend that makes him more attractive? He was a bit on the older side to be unmarried. But I guess he could say the same for me. "I hear you have the best brownies."

"We did. Just sold the last one, though."

There was something sweet about Mrs. D. dropping me here and obviously trying to set me up with Ronan. But also incredibly awkward.

"So, you stayed longer," he said.

"I did."

From the direction of the parking lot came the sound of someone laying on a car horn, and I turned to find Mrs. D. waving from her jeep.

"She'll be crushed you're out of brownies," I said.

He made change for a customer. "I don't want to shock you, but she's trying to set us up."

"Clearly." I released an awkward little hyena laugh and started off toward the jeep, mortified.

"Hey, you should come to the bonfire tonight," he called after me. "Down at Black Point Beach. Just chill."

"Oh, I don't know."

He turned to the girl at his side. "She should come, right?"

The girl glanced at me. "Totally." And then went back to serving customers.

"Maybe," I said. I nodded toward the parking lot. "Not sure what's on the schedule."

I skittered off toward the jeep, wishing I was more like Dutch-Braid Girl, able to chat so easily with people. Mrs D. drove me home, unfazed that they'd run out of brownies, proof that she'd sent me there only for a meet-cute with Ronan.

"Ronan White asked me to come to a bonfire down on the beach tonight."

"Isn't that nice of him," Mrs. D. said. "Are you going?"

"I don't think so. I'd have to stay another night."

"Fine with me. Why don't we see how it goes?"

We rode along in silence, the wind warm on my face. Maybe it was the breakfast sandwich or just the change of scenery from the Jamba juice bar, but I hadn't felt this relaxed in a long time.

I turned to Mrs. D. as she drove. "You know, I'm dying to know how that whole story ends. I have so many questions."

"Is that right?"

I stretched my arm outside the jeep and let it float in the breeze. "Like, what happened with that German guy?"

"Oh, Peter?"

"Briar really kept it together. I would have lost my mind with all that going on."

"How serendipitous it was that he washed up on their beach. It changed their lives and those of their friends forever. One of them in an especially profound way."

22

CADENCE

1942

W E ENDED UP KEEPING THE GERMAN. I WAS OVERRULED. SO MUCH for being the sensible older sister.

I forged up the hill from the boathouse, and Bess followed. Why couldn't things go well just one day? Not only was Margaret on her way to Manhattan, soon to be sleeping in the bed intended for me at the hotel, but we now were forced to keep a German fugitive.

"I need to fertilize the Burbanks," I said over my shoulder to Bess. "After that, once it's dark, we'll bring him up to the house. It's not safe to keep him in the boathouse anymore. Any soldier could just come off the beach and find him. We'll keep him in Briar's room upstairs."

Bess rushed to catch up with me, out of breath.

I stopped walking and turned. "You can't be running uphill like this, Bess. The baby—"

"I know—I'm *fine*. Sorry we ganged up on you like that, Cade. But I think it's the right choice."

"What else can I do, Bess? My sister—your future sister-in-law— will probably go to prison if we turn Peter in. I honestly don't think Tom would want you to risk having the baby in jail, but Briar has given us no choice. I just wonder if we can trust him."

"I think he's a good person," Bess said.

For all her worldliness, Bess could be so naïve sometimes.

I continued on up the path. "I guess we'll see, won't we?"

———

LATER THAT NIGHT, after I'd fertilized the Burbanks, Briar and Bess snuck Peter up to the cottage. They dressed him in more of Tom's clothes and sat him at the kitchen table. I could barely watch as Bess helped him into one of Tom's flannel shirts, a little long in the sleeves.

"Hold on now," Gram said. "We need some ground rules here. Peter, you will take Briar's room up in the attic, after she moves in with me in my bedroom."

Briar knew she was on extra-thin ice and didn't complain, as she ordinarily would, that Gram snored too loudly for her to sleep.

"And, Briar, you'll bring him his food on a tray up in your room."

Gram bent at the waist and coughed into her hankie, then continued, "And, Peter, if you're going to stay here, you'll earn your keep working the farm—at night, when there's no risk of being seen." Gram took her Bible from the table. "Also, I know you were raised in a Christian household, but I want you to swear on this holy Bible that you will be a perfect gentleman while you're under my roof."

He hesitated for a moment and then set his hand on the black cover. "I swear."

"I think you're a good person, but I don't know who you really are or what your true intention is. However, if you help us, we'll help you. Understand?"

Peter nodded. "Thank you." He stood. "I will go upstairs."

"Good," I said.

Peter walked past me, stopped, and turned. "Why do you smell like fertilizer?"

"I've been working the field," I said.

"Which one?"

I looked at him more closely. Why was he so interested? "The upper one. Potatoes my brother planted. Burbanks. A new kind—"

"We planted those right before I left home for service. Every farmer in Germany wanted to grow them."

I shrugged. "I fertilized them."

He stepped to me. "Just now? Tonight?"

"What's wrong?" Gram asked.

"Relax," I told him. "Yes, just now."

"I hope you watered deeply," he said.

I waved that thought away. "I'll do it tomorrow."

"*No*—you must do it now. Fertilizer without water will kill the plants. They'll be dead by morning if your irrigation system is not running at medium capacity, *minimum,* all night."

A hot, liquid feeling surged through me. I'd killed Tom's Burbanks.

"We water by hand," Briar said. "My father built an irrigation system, but it's been broken for years."

Peter threw up his hands. "It must be fixed."

"Tell me how," I said.

"It's dark—I won't be seen."

"You're still recovering," Gram said. "In no condition to climb up there."

"We will need a shovel and screwdriver, if you have them, and a lamp may be necessary." He went to the door and turned to me. "Are you coming?"

GRAM STAYED BEHIND TO make us tea, while Briar, Bess, and I hurried along the path to the upper field, following the milky thumbnail of a moon up the hill, the pinkletinks and cicadas calling their night songs. I heard Peter's labored breathing as he fell behind. There was no way we could let those potatoes die. Tom would be devastated, and we needed the money from their harvest for the bank loan on the house.

"Please, can you lend an arm?" he asked, and Bess stopped and let him lean on her as they walked.

Soon we stood on the slope of the upper field, among the green Burbank plants, which glowed almost black in the tepid light. Peter inspected the nearby well, a squat cylinder of pale cement, the wooden junction box connected to it.

"So?" I asked, warm wind drying the sweat on my arms.

Peter crouched among the plants. "It doesn't look good. They're about a week from flowering." He looked up at me. "But suffering serious water loss. Diminished size. Pruney jackets."

I barely breathed. Tom would be devastated if they didn't survive.

Peter held the lamp close to one of the lathe boxes, lighting up its shiny black creosote heart. "These are in bad shape." He stepped to the well. "My father built a similar system, but this one has been poorly maintained." He stood. "Is the system connected to this well?"

"Yes," Briar said. "But the boxes are rotted."

He set the lamp closer to the junction box. "True, but the real problem is that this is full of mud. These must be cleaned every year. Did your father not tell you?"

Briar shook her head. "My father died when I was a little girl, so no."

"I am sorry," Peter said. He dug the tip of the shovel into the junction box. "While I do this, you three go to each lathe box and turn it so the open part faces that row of plants."

"There must be twenty boxes," I said.

"Just turn as many boxes as you can," he said to us. "But hurry."

We set off into the night. Bess directed us as Briar and I stopped at the end of each row and, using the full force of our weight, dragged each lathe box into correct position, splinters cutting our hands. Peter mumbled curses in German as we worked, and it felt surreal that a Nazi soldier was standing in our potato field, trying to save our plants.

It seemed to take forever, but then suddenly there came a wonderful deep gurgling sound and water gushed from the lathe box, washing over my ankles and spreading into the field.

Peter blew out the lamp and came to me. "That should be good for now."

I wrapped my arms around Bess and Briar there in the field, and a great swell of gratitude arose in me. Perhaps our strategy to keep Peter around had a silver lining.

AFTER OUR IRRIGATION ADVENTURE, all four of us took a midnight swim in the pond, the cool water like velvet on my skin. When we came back to the cottage, Gram was still awake and was "tickled pink," as she would say, that Peter had helped us fix the system. She set a cup of tea and a plate of Potato Bargain in front of him as his reward.

"By the way, I would just like to tell you, Mrs. Smith, that heart disease is not the cause of your current symptoms," he said in an offhand way as he ate.

"What are you talking about?" I asked. "She needs a heart operation. Dr. Burns told us to schedule it up in Boston."

"That is a misdiagnosis." Peter went to the sink and rinsed his plate. "What you have is a pulmonary embolism."

"You're just a medic," I said.

"True, but four days after we left port, the captain aboard the U-boat had one, so I know the condition intimately. The defining factor in the diagnosis is the cough. It mimics heart disease, but the presence of a cough means a problem with the lungs."

"A blood clot, am I right?" Briar asked.

He nodded. "Yes. Most resolve on their own, but blood pressure must be monitored daily and a strict regimen of rest followed. We had good success with a drink of two aspirin crushed in a glass of apple cider vinegar. If you have those ingredients, I would start right away. And feet up. But I recommend an immediate hospital visit, a teaching hospital if possible. They will have the latest treatments."

"Thank you," Gram said. "I had a feeling it wasn't my heart."

Peter adopted a grave expression. "Before I go upstairs, I just want to say thank you for allowing me to help." He paused. "And I have something else I need to tell you, also time-sensitive."

"What is it?" Gram asked.

"When I was on the ship, I overheard the captain discussing something with the first mate. It's close quarters, as you can imagine. The captain gave an order for the ship not to leave a five-mile radius of this beach."

"What's so important about that?" I asked.

"It's what they're waiting for that you should know about."

"A person?" Briar asked.

He turned to Briar. "Yes, that's right."

Briar stepped closer to him. "A spy?"

He nodded. "I believe so."

It was almost too much to take in at once. "They're waiting for a spy? A German, here?"

"No. Not German. At least that's what they said. I didn't catch all of it."

Gram sat at the table. "An islander?"

"To be honest, I don't know. I got the impression it was someone they had a prearranged commitment to retrieving. A VIP of sorts."

"Who could it possibly be?" Gram asked.

"Fifth Column," Briar said.

"What is that?" Gram asked.

"Secret sympathizers. People born and bred here who choose to work with our enemies to undermine national interests."

"Who would do that on this island?" Gram asked.

Briar looked toward the window. "Apparently someone they're floating out there waiting for."

"The plan is to pick this person up and head back to Germany," Peter said. "On the new moon, which provides no light at all, just cover of darkness. In just about a week from today. And you must be careful. According to the captain, this person is armed with a deadly weapon. And has been authorized to use it."

23

BRIAR

1942

THE DAY AFTER PETER TOLD US ABOUT THE U-BOAT MEETING the spy, Cadence forced me to sit with her in the kitchen, with Bess and Gram, for another book-club meeting. She claimed we had to establish a normal-seeming schedule, since half of the U.S. Army was swarming our property each morning, and we had to at least go through the motions of discussing *The Song of Bernadette*. I'd actually read Gram's copy of that one, though it had sounded insipid—a young peasant girl who sees visions at the town dump and becomes a nun. Turns out it wasn't half bad; it was based on a pretty compelling true story, and people's constant accusations that Bernadette was lying about her visions made it relatable. But I still loathed the idea of rehashing it *ad infinitum*.

I'd taken my time dressing that morning, in Grandpa Smith's jodhpurs, which Gram had let me cut down; a dove-gray young man's cashmere cardigan that I'd found at the thrift shop; and a silk ascot, a real find in the free basket. Cadence hated my outfit. I could always see it in her eyes. She probably wished she had a sister she could introduce with pride to friends. But I couldn't dress in skirts and saddle shoes just to please her. I dressed to keep the people I loved with me always. She once urged me to try on her gartered thigh-high stockings and pantie girdle, and I'd felt ridiculous, rigged up like a horse. So I dressed as I liked.

But I had bigger issues than fashion to focus on. The absurdity of our situation—troops doing jumping jacks on our beach while a German Kriegsmarine sailor slept in my bed in the attic—was not lost on me. My thoughtless actions had caused it, after all. How stupid I'd been to talk to Mr. Schmidt's friends like that. To try to rectify things, I unplugged the shortwave and hid it on Gram's closet shelf in an empty hatbox. I'd barely slept the night before, listening to Gram's gentle snoring, and I ticked off a mental list of possible spies. Catching him or her was a golden opportunity to redeem myself. Tom would want me to step up.

At least Gram was making my favorite dessert, the delectable Kiss Pudding, and one of my favorite cookies, the unfairly named Grandma's Rocks, the only things that made book club tolerable. The scent of allspice and brown sugar wafted from the oven as Gram baked, banging pots around, with the radio in the living room turned up. Since she was so short of breath most days, she had slowed down considerably and didn't get out to church as much as she once had. She rarely left the radio, listening for any news about Tom. We were on tenterhooks waiting to hear where he would end up fighting. The Pacific Theater? Europe somewhere? North Africa?

Cadence sat at the table. "I know you'd rather be up in your tree or something, but it might do you some good to talk books."

"Can we read a Joan of Arc biography?" I asked.

Bess leaned in and smiled. "You've already read them all, Briar. *The Song of Bernadette* isn't our first choice, either, but the idea is to read a book together."

How lucky was I to have Bess Stanhope for an almost-sister-in-law? Just by being there with us, she made living with Cadence so much easier. "I'm fine with staying," I said.

Bess took my hand. "But before we start the meeting, there's something I need to tell you and Gram."

Cadence helped Gram sit in a chair at the table.

"What is it, Bess?" Gram asked.

"I just want you both to know that Tom and I are having a baby." Wearing an anxious expression, she looked back and forth between Gram and me.

I stood and rushed to Bess and hugged her. "How wonderful!"

Gram stood and came to us and embraced us both. "Good news indeed!"

Bess looked relieved. "I thought you might disapprove. With us not married and all."

Gram brought the puddings to the table and smoothed one hand down Bess's back. "This is a blessing, Bess. You and Tom will make it official when he comes home on leave."

"Have you told Tom?" I asked.

"She wrote him yesterday," Cadence said, clearly enjoying watching us all take in the good news.

I could barely wipe the grin off my face. Tom, a father. As I devoured the pudding, I examined Bess more closely. How had I not seen? Seemingly overnight, she had started wearing her shirts untucked and actually did look pregnant. Just the thought of being an aunt made me thrum with joy. This baby was bound to be exceptional. How would Tom react to the letter Bess had written with the news? Definitely out of his mind with joy.

No wonder Bess had cried so piteously when Tom left. Pregnancy hormones famously wreak havoc on moods. She'd also had some rough spells since then and even locked herself in Cade's bedroom and cried most of the day after Gram showed her Tom's pewter baby cup one morning.

Once things settled down after Bess's news, Cadence reached for her book.

"Okay, now on to Bernadette," she said.

Partly to not have to talk about the book and partly to get their help, I pulled from my pocket the photos of the Nazi rally and house I'd found in the metal box. "These were in Mr. Schmidt's things."

Bess looked at the photos with disgust and passed them to Cadence. "It's terrifying how they worship Hitler. How did Conrad get photos that were taken in Germany?"

"I don't know, but he may have not told me everything. Think he could have been the spy? Maybe they're waiting for him, not knowing he passed."

Gram brought a plate of warm Grandma's Rocks to the table.

"Conrad?" Gram asked. "Not a chance in this world. He was a genuine war hero. And there was no better man."

"Well, who, then?" Cadence asked.

Bess took a cookie, then another, and I held back a comment about eating for two. "Could be the German guy out at the Hornblower estate," she said. "He comes into Alley's and barely speaks."

Gram set her teacup down on the table. "No, he's done some work for me. Has a wife he adores and three kids. He's not getting on a U-boat anytime soon."

"Could be Tyson Schmidt," Bess said.

"He's a nice boy," Gram said. "Though he could have been more devoted to his grandfather."

Gram was right about that. It was I who took Conrad to Bert the Barber and to medical appointments, while Tyson enjoyed his friends.

"And so good-looking, don't you think?" Cadence asked me. She'd often floated Tyson as a possible love match for me, probably fond of the idea of our family ending up with Mr. Schmidt's considerable fortune, like something out of one of her gothic novels, where the penniless sister attracts the initially taciturn lord just visiting for the dove hunt.

Gram stepped into the living room and turned up the radio.

"Tyson may be pure German, but his parents were born here," Cadence said, rejecting Bess's theory. "He goes to Hotchkiss, for heaven's sake. Not exactly a den of saboteurs. And he has enlisted. Who else is German?"

There had been a rash of anti-German incidents reported in newspapers across the country and quite a few on the island. Annie Merry started a rumor that Fritz Frankel was a Nazi because he wore a brown shirt to church. And before he died, Mr. Schmidt told me that people had made more than a few anti-German comments right to his face. But it was relatively minor compared to the Great War, when a German man was killed by a mob in Illinois.

"Who says the spy has to be German?" I asked.

"Who says it has to be a man?" Cadence said through a mouthful of cookie. "It could be that Crabby's friend of yours, Briar."

"Sandra?" I asked. "I seriously doubt it."

Not that I'd tell Cadence, but Sandra actually was a likely candidate. She had a shortwave radio of her own and a fondness for German memorabilia. She'd read *Mein Kampf.* Perhaps she was more Nazi-leaning than I realized.

"All I know is, we need to figure it out by next week or we're letting a spy go back to Germany with God knows what information."

Gram came from the living room and stood in the kitchen doorway. "Briar, it was just on the radio—Tyson Schmidt is in the hospital."

I stood. "Is he okay?"

"I'll drive you over to see him, if you like. But you'd better hurry. They said he's in serious condition."

ONCE I GOT TO the hospital and heard Tyson was going to make it, I considered Gram's suggestion to visit him a double victory. I not only got out of book club, but I could ask Tyson some questions about the weird pictures and inscribed Nazi ring I'd found.

Gram dropped me in Oak Bluffs at the hospital, and I had to be less than truthful in order to visit Tyson. I could see him in the glass-walled room just off the nurse's station. I figured that since everyone already thought I was a liar, I might as well reap the benefits.

A nurse sat at the check-in desk—*Judith Darling, R.N.,* printed on her name tag, probably a cousin to the Darling's popcorn shop Darlings. I recognized her as another former Crabby's Hardware employee who'd gone on to better things; I tried to make small talk, but she wasn't in the mood, so I asked to see Tyson.

"Are you a family member?" she asked.

"Cousin," I said, trying to look suitably tragic. "His parents are traveling, and his grandfather died recently, so I'm the only family nearby right now."

Nurse Darling waved me into the room. "Go ahead. But keep your voice down—this is a quiet zone. No raucous talk or laughter."

It was good to see Crabby's had taught her well.

Tyson slept in the hospital bed, hooked up to some sort of machine, his forehead bandaged, his left eye swollen and bruised an Easter-egg purple. He looked so pathetic lying there. Tom would be happy I was visiting his friend, and part of me was happy I got there before Shelby did.

He woke as I entered. "Hi, Briar."

"Came as soon as Gram heard it on the radio. You're famous."

"Swell," he said. "I'm fine, actually. Only a little sore."

"What happened?"

"I was getting ice cream at Vincente's. It was crowded, and as I was leaving, a kid at one of the tables tripped me. Called me a Kraut. I swear it was George Ibbetson."

"Were you wearing your uniform?"

"No. I came from a swim. I fell on the granite step and got my bell rung pretty hard. Next thing I remember is waking up here."

It wasn't Tyson's fault he had German ancestry. It was like what his grandfather had gone through. Mr. Schmidt would have been livid that Tyson was treated so badly.

"Possible you tripped?"

"*No.* And I heard George say 'Kraut' plain as day. Jeez, you don't believe me?"

"Of course I do. Want me to petroleum jelly his bike seat?"

"What? No. I don't know. It's just hard enlisting, and going through basic, and then *this* happens. As if I could be a sympathizer. My grandfather was a *war hero,* for God's sake. I'm ready to die for my country and damned George Ibbetson goes after me like that."

"George Ibbetson eats his own boogers and wouldn't last a day in basic training."

Tyson smiled at my little joke. "At least Shelby's driving over with some friends."

Once Shelby got here, she'd turn me in as non-family for sure.

I bent closer to Tyson so the nurse wouldn't hear. "Hey, not to change the subject, but would you be up for helping me with something kind of critical?"

"I guess." He tried to sit up. "Got a splitting headache, though."

"Some people are saying there might be a spy on the island."

He waved that idea away. "Please. Somebody thought a guy in Edgartown was building a machine-gun bunker, and he was just laying concrete for his tennis court."

"I think this spy thing might be true. Know any Germans new to town?"

"Are you serious, Briar? Somebody just pushed me down the stairs for being a Kraut, and you expect me to chat with you about traitorous Germans? As if I know."

"Sorry. I thought you might want to help me figure it out."

"No, it's fine. I'm kinda sore about it right now, that's all." A few moments of silence passed, probably music to Nurse Darling's ears. "But who says a spy has to be German? There are plenty of non-German Hitler lovers. Look at Wallis Simpson and the former king of England. Cozying up to the führer. Charles Lindbergh. Henry Ford sends Adolf a birthday gift every year, even since he declared war on us."

I glanced toward the nurse's station and kept my voice low. "I was thinking it could be Sandra at Island Treasures."

"Why? I don't know her. Just seen her around town."

"She told me she's read *Mein Kampf.*"

"She must be eighty-something. Seems too old to be a spy."

"And I heard a shortwave radio in her back room."

We were quiet for a minute. The sounds of the hospital seemed to be making Tyson drowsy; me, too.

"She and your grandfather were friends."

"Wait. Are you saying he might have been involved in spying? I hope you're kidding."

I considered waiting until another time to tell him but instead dove right in. "I did find some things."

"What *things?*"

"Something with the name Kuno. Was that a friend of his? Maybe back in Germany?"

"No idea. Where'd you find it?"

"Just cleaning out some of his old things. I actually wanted to show you something." I slid the envelope of photos from my pocket. "Looks like Nazis," I whispered.

Tyson took the pictures and inspected the one of the crowd with their hands raised in the Nazi salute. "Wait. Is this Germany?"

"Not sure. The house in the second picture has a swastika on it."

Tyson pressed one hand against his bandaged head. "Are you sure they were Grandfather's?"

"Believe me, I'm as surprised as you are."

"He was a decorated war hero, Briar. You know that."

"But look again at the second one. It's a neighborhood with ADOLF HITLER STRASSE on the street sign. Did Conrad ever live there?"

Tyson pushed the photos away. "If you're accusing him of being a Nazi, just say it."

"You have to admit it's strange. I won't show anyone, but aren't you curious?"

"When I get sprung from here, I'll go through his things. See if I can find out more. But I'm so tired all of a sudden."

I heard a familiar voice and turned to see Shelby Parker and two friends talking to Nurse Darling at the desk. They must have come from the beach, still in their bathing suit cover-ups and sandals.

I slid the photos back into my pocket. "Let's talk about this later." I glanced at Shelby, who was pointing our way.

Nurse Darling stood and walked toward us, her lips pressed into a hard line. "Briar Smith? It's come to my attention that you are not a Schmidt family member."

Tyson lay back. "No, but it's fine."

The nurse gripped my arm. "Come with me."

She yanked me past Shelby and pals, who stood there shivering in the cool hallway and popping their gum, muttering various forms of "Briar the Liar" as I passed, just loud enough for me to hear. I barely looked at them. Odious individuals. What did it matter what they thought?

Nurse Darling was squeezing my arm so tight I almost passed out. She deposited me outside the front door.

"And don't come back," she said, as she turned and went inside to allow Shelby and friends into Tyson's room to coo over him. It was fine, I thought, rubbing some feeling into my arm and walking through the parking lot to start the long trek home.

At least I'd made some progress, with Tyson offering to help delve into Mr. Schmidt's papers.

I caught a ride back Up-Island with a friend of Gram's, Bev Iorio. She told me her hens weren't laying and we got into the details, and before we knew it, she was dropping me off at the head of our road. As I opened the car door, a news commentator came on the radio and interrupted the music.

"It has been confirmed. British troops have taken losses at Dieppe in France, the largest percentage by far Canadian as well as American Rangers."

Mrs. Iorio looked at me, wide-eyed, two fingers to her lips. "Isn't your Tom a Ranger?" she asked.

"Thank you," I said, and exited the car, trying to keep my voice steady. And ran all the way down Copper Pond Road for home.

UP-ISLAND HAPPENINGS

By CADENCE SMITH

MARGARET COUTINHO HAS SAILED OFF ABOARD THE PUTNAM yacht, bound for glory on New York City's Seventh Avenue. Will she be running the place soon?

The mean turkey dared to show his red wattle again in the yard of Mrs. Imogene Salva on Music Street and flew at her aggressively. Anyone seeing this bird, which seems to hold a grudge, please phone the Chilmark Police immediately.

If you're going to visit Uncle Henry in the coming days, act quickly, before he gets out the family album, and take him to our newest Up-Island hot spot, Humphrey's coffeehouse at Beetlebung Corner. Candlepinners will feel right at home here, for the interior is as sleek and modern as a bowling alley, but Mrs. Virginia Smith of Chilmark says their Molasses Hermits are even better than her own, so we expect their door to be beaten down soon.

The newly formed Martha's Vineyard Beach and Book Club has not settled upon next month's selection, though several have been considered, including *Joan of Arc*, a work vigorously endorsed by one member, who should know better than to suggest a nonfiction title. The club is planning a game of book bingo and will bore everyone with endless details soon.

This week's book to send across the island is *Great Expectations*, by legendary novelist and candidate for world's weirdest beard Charles Dickens. Pick it up at the farm stand, Susie Baldwin, and pass it to your neighbor when you're done. *Caution: Not to be read by candlelight, at least not in a wedding dress.*

24

CADENCE

1942

WE WERE ALL OUT IN THE HOT SUN, WEEDING THE BURBANKS, when Mrs. Stanhope brought the Chilmark Police to our farm.

We'd discussed the news about Tom's regiment, which Briar alerted us to and Gram heard on the radio, as well. The 75th had been hit hard at Dieppe. But being out in the field kept us from obsessively tuning in for more radio reports. The military had many ways to make a death notification. I'd heard of the news being delivered by telegram, or phone call, but usually in person. When Brenda Munson's father was killed at Pearl Harbor, the Navy had sent the local police to deliver the news. Sometimes the Coast Guard did it, too. Usually guys with special training. Often with a priest or chaplain in tow.

My first thought when Mrs. Stanhope and the police arrived was about Peter's whereabouts, but I quickly settled, knowing he was safely in the attic, asleep after working most of the night in the fields.

It was almost midday and I'd been watching Major Gil exercise, shirtless on the beach below us, with his commandos. I tried to look my best each morning when I raised our book-club burgee down at the flagpole on the beach, since the men came every day at seven. Did the major know I was watching from up there? Not that he thought at all about me. Though he'd cared enough to ask me for the tour.

I knelt shoulder to shoulder with Bess, pulling chickweed from around the potato plants. We'd brought up a pillow from the house for Bess to kneel on, and she was dressed that morning in one of Gram's old housecoats. Bess's waistbands were already feeling a bit tighter, and she had started wearing looser clothes, mostly Gram's baggier old things, quite a comedown from the couture she was used to in her former life. Not that she seemed to mind. But if Bess had been at home, her mother would have commissioned a whole closet full of bespoke shifts and jackets for her confinement.

Gram made her come inside to eat lunch and rest periodically, but nothing could keep Bess from helping with Tom's special crop. As much as she doted on our secret German, supplying him with Tom's clothes and books and even his old Boy Scout belt, her care for Tom's potatoes came in a close second.

The police car arrived first and parked in front of the cottage, then Lydia Stanhope arrived, driving herself, in a massive green convertible.

"Ugh," Bess said as she saw her mother pull up in front of the cottage below. "Hide me."

Fred Leo, the chief of the Chilmark Police, had been in my class at Tisbury High. Lanky and dark-haired, he'd been kept out of the war by a damaged heart valve. He unfolded himself from the car and loped up the hill to us.

I stood and walked to meet him. "Hi, Fred. Hot enough for you?"

"Sorry about this, Cadence. Mrs. Stanhope there came into the precinct, goin' on about life and death and needing an escort here. Said you all might be violent when she came to take her daughter home." He leaned in. "She used the word *unwed* in regard to her daughter. Said she's in the family way, but I wasn't sure that was common knowledge."

"It's fine, Fred," I said. "We all know."

He seemed relieved. "I told her the department is short-staffed, due to the war and all, and doesn't get involved with family spats, but she threatened to call my boss."

"You are the boss, Fred," I said.

He grinned at that. "Any chance your Gram will be making more of that rose-hip marmalade for the farm stand? I'm pretty partial to it."

"I'll put in a good word, Fred."

He waved and started down the hill, giving Mrs. Stanhope a wide berth as she ascended and made her way to us.

"Get in the car, Bess Ann," she said. "It's your father's birthday, which you've obviously forgotten, and we're celebrating at the club."

Had Mrs. Stanhope ever stepped foot in a farm field before? She proudly told all who'd listen that she rarely left Edgartown or their townhome on the exclusive flat side of Beacon Hill in Boston.

Bess wiped the sweat from her brow. "Good to see you, too, Mother."

"He's having heart troubles, Dr. Von Prague says, not that you care."

Bess sat up straighter. "Is he all right?"

"Surely it's been brought on by your shenanigans."

Bess went back to her work, and in the distance, Gram started up the hill with Briar, carrying a tray of lemonade.

Lydia crouched next to Bess. "Enough is enough, Bess Ann. It's at least one hundred degrees out here. You should be in bed, not doing farmwork."

Bess pulled another weed. "I'm fine, Mother. These are Tom's plants. Burbank potatoes he thinks will be highly lucrative. And we all pitch in here."

Lydia turned to me. "Shouldn't you be inside, writing that column of yours? Such as it is."

"The whole island loves Cadence's writing," Bess said. "She's going to New York City to be a book editor."

Lydia tapped the sweat off her brow with the back of her hand. "Oh, please. Some of my best friends are in publishing. They won't hire a farm girl with no experience."

Bess smiled. "Winnie Winthrop disagrees."

The glasses on Briar's tray tinkled together like wind chimes as she and Gram approached us.

"Lydia Stanhope," Gram said. "What can we do for you?" Gram knew Mrs. Stanhope from the many times Lydia had commissioned baked goods for her parties from Gram, back before Bess had come to live with us.

Lydia stood up and nodded. "Virginia. You can stop harboring my daughter, for a start."

Out of breath, Gram blotted the sweat from her cheek with the hem of her apron. "Bess likes it here, and we're happy to have her."

"Women doing men's work. It's appalling."

Gram set her fisted hands on her hips. "Here the women work as hard as any man."

"Clearly," Lydia said, and glanced back downhill. "And speaking of men, who's that fellow I saw at your attic window?"

A spike of fear jabbed me. "Just a hand."

"Oh, I see. Is he living in sin with you, Cadence? I know a marriage certificate means little around here. I have a mind to look around a bit."

Gram crossed her arms above her bosom. "You'll do no such thing. Set one foot in that house and I'll get the police back here to cart you off."

"What is it, Virginia?" Lydia faced Gram. "Why are you doing this to me? Just envious of our good fortune? Do you disdain every person of *Mayflower* lineage?"

Gram helped Briar set the tray on the milk crate. "If everybody who says they came off that ship actually did, it would have sunk long before it reached Plymouth Rock."

"You're clearly jealous. Is it because your dairy farm failed? It killed your husband, didn't it, seeing it slide into ruin?"

"*Mother,*" Bess said.

Gram waved that thought away. "I wouldn't trade places with you for all the tea in China, Lydia."

Lydia turned to Bess. "Plainly you don't miss me. Or your father."

Bess stood and faced Lydia. "You know who I miss, Mother? The man I love, who gave me the gift of a lifetime—a cherished child who will be loved properly here. Tommy is off fighting and may be lying dead on a beach in France for all we know, and you don't even ask about him." Bess wiped a tear. "He's the best person I've ever met and this is his beloved family, and each one of them would do anything for me, and I for them, and *that's* what matters, Mother. And if you don't understand it, then just leave us alone and go find someone else to insult."

"You obviously have been indoctrinated into a cult." With a last look at Gram, Lydia sneered, "Don't think you've won this, Virginia. I won't stand by and watch my child preyed upon by the likes of you trashy farm folk."

"Good*bye,* Mother," Bess said.

Lydia started to leave, then turned and said, "Oh, the telegram boy on his bicycle handed me this." She held out the unmistakable yellow envelope, *Copper Pond Farm* typed in the little cellophane window. "Asked *me* to deliver it. Probably feared for his tires coming down that godforsaken road." She lobbed it onto the lemonade tray.

We just stared at the envelope as Lydia made her way back down the hill toward her car. After a stunned few seconds, Briar picked up the envelope and stepped to Gram.

My whole body went cold. The Army only sent telegrams with bad news.

"Go ahead, Briar," Gram said. "Read it."

25

BRIAR

1942

My fingers shook so hard i could barely open the envelope. I couldn't go on living without Tom. How cruel the Army was to just send such a formal message to a downed soldier's family. Not even a phone call.

Gram linked her arm tightly with mine.

"Just *open* it, Briar," Cadence said, clutching Bess's hand.

My eyes blurred with tears.

"Do you want me to read it for you?" Cadence asked.

I slid the letter from the envelope and unfolded it. It took a second for the words to sink in after I read it.

RAN BOOK BY MILDRED AND SHE IS GAME. CRASHING THREE TITLES PULLED FROM COOKIE JAR. COMING SOON TO DROP MARGARET. CONGRATS MVBABC. X WIN

"For God's sake, *read* it, Briar," Bess said, one hand at her throat.

I blinked the tears away. "It's not about Tom." I handed the sheet to Cadence. "It's from Winnie Winthrop."

Gram relaxed her grip. "Thank the Lord."

Cadence read it and a smile spread across her face. "They're making the books."

Gram and Bess huddled around her, hugging one another.

"It's happening," Bess said. "I wonder which titles."

Cadence embraced us all. "Almost can't believe it."

"What does that mean, 'coming soon,' do you think?" Gram asked.

"I don't know, but we did it," Cadence said.

I WAS DESPERATE TO get out of book club the next day, but Cadence roped me into it, insisting she and Bess needed the head count now that Margaret was off to New York City. I was fine with it, though. Before he left, Tom had wanted me to make an effort to get along with Cadence, and it was the least I could do, to sit around and listen to them gush about *Jane Eyre*, a novel I'd been forced to read in junior year. It was a book that Bess, Gram, and Cadence talked about *ad nauseam*, even out of book club, so it seemed redundant to discuss it there, but I just focused on the cookies.

Bess recited a passage from one of the many *Jane Eyre* scenes that pushed the bounds of credulity, where Mr. Rochester, who somehow stays sound asleep in a wildly flaming bed, is doused with water by Jane, who singlehandedly saves the day.

"*I became further aware of a strong smell of burning. . . . Tongues of flame darted round the bed: the curtains were on fire. In the midst of blaze and vapor, Mr. Rochester lay stretched motionless, in deep sleep.*"

I watched Gram and Cadence, as they listened, rapt.

"*The very sheets were kindling,*" Bess continued, a surprisingly good narrator. "*I rushed to his basin and ewer; fortunately, one was wide and the other deep, and both were filled with water. I heaved them up, deluged the bed and its occupant, flew back to my own room, brought my own water-jug, baptized the couch afresh, and by God's aid, succeeded in extinguishing the flames which were devouring it.*"

Bess snapped the book closed, spent.

Gram turned to me. "You have to admit, sweet pea, that's one heck of a book."

"Whatever you say." I bit into a cookie.

"Out with it, Briar," Cadence said.

"It's just improbable. First of all, Rochester doesn't know he's actually on fire? That's a deep sleeper. And second, Jane throws some water on the fire, and it just goes out. That would never happen. Clearly it was triggered by lamp oil, which, like all fuels, isn't extinguished by water. Water only makes it worse, since it's heavier than most fuels."

Cadence set her book down. "What should Miss Brontë, who is considered one of the greatest novelists of the nineteenth century, have used instead, Briar?"

I shrugged. "Salt or baking soda would have been a better choice."

Gram leaned over and picked up the empty cookie plate. "We do learn things at book club, girls."

"Plus, then Rochester calls her a witch and a sorceress," I went on. "He's such a jerk."

"That's true," Cadence said, perhaps thinking of her own Rochester-in-training, Major Gil.

Bess sat. "You really know how to keep the conversation going, Briar. I always liked Rochester. He ends up being the love of Jane's life."

It made me sad that Bess seemed desperate for romance, with Tom gone. She was starting to lose her grip on reality a bit, maybe imprinting Tom onto Peter. She spent so much time with the German, reading aloud and fixing up the attic for him. It didn't help that we'd had no news about Tom, despite multiple calls to Washington.

Finally, I had enough of *Jane Eyre* and squirmed out of the meeting, claiming an urgent need to vet Sandra at Island Treasures as a possible spy. I could also pick up the proceeds from the sale of the ring if Sandra had been successful. That money would go a long way.

Cadence must have wanted out of book club, too, since she immediately volunteered to drive me. Gram wasn't doing great in the breathing department that morning, so she wanted to rest, and Bess had her usual morning sickness and took to her bed, as well.

It was good to be alone with my sister, just the two of us driving, no Bess to come between us. We kept the truck's radio on in case there was more news about our brother at Dieppe. Somehow, the car made us almost friends.

In exchange for the ride, I promised Cadence I'd run into the A&P and ask my old friend Phillip who worked the counter there for one of the French ginger candies that Bess liked so much and helped with her morning sickness. I did that and came out with a little paper bag with three candies, a bumper crop, and handed them to Cadence.

"Thanks, Bri." She tucked the bag into her purse as we drove up Main Street. "Bess will be so happy."

"I got an extra for you," I said.

"Let's keep them all for her."

I envied Cadence and Bess's friendship, but I worried for Cadence, too, since it seemed a bit one-sided, with Cadence always so concerned about Bess, worried she'd somehow be uncomfortable, having to do without. Bess may have embraced our modest farm life, but she still clung to her small indulgences, vestiges of the rich life she once led. She'd brought a whole suitcase of them with her when she first came to live with us but they slowly ran out. Real French perfume, not just toilet water; a jar of Belgian cocoa, which Gram made hot chocolate with on occasions and Bess drank from a special French bowl; ten boxes of Swiss cereal that looked like horse feed, which she ate every morning.

And the clothes. Though Bess dressed as Cadence and I did, in farm clothes, heavy on the denim, she mixed in her few luxury pieces. A Schiaparelli scarf wound around her neck while she weeded the alfalfa. The lace-trimmed Swiss-cotton nightgown that she slept in. Pretty French-blue espadrille sandals as she watered the Burbanks. Sometimes I wondered what Bess would do when the suitcase was empty. Maybe it would be better if Bess went home and had her baby. It would free Cadence to go to New York, the best thing for her.

Cadence needed to get away from Major Gilbert, too. She was obsessed with the major, always watching him down on the beach. Observing him from afar, I thought he seemed a rigid, career-military type, classist and glib, with little interest in a farm girl like Cade. He'd asked her to show him the island, which was no doubt his way of saying, "Let's go neck somewhere," so who was I to tell her she was barking up the wrong tree?

As much as Cadence and I didn't get along most days, I would actually miss her if she left. Hopefully Cadence's new books-for-the-troops venture would vault her to a publishing career. It didn't help that Margaret Coutinho was probably romping around Manhattan, while Cadence dealt with our German-soldier situation.

My sister had borne the brunt of our parents' sudden deaths, Tom's departure, and Gram's illness, taking her to all of her hospital appointments. Not to mention my stupid choices. She deserved better.

Cadence and I entered Island Treasures and looked around. I'd shared the plan: She would keep Sandra occupied while I snuck into the back room. But I was surprised to find that Sandra was not standing behind the display case as usual.

"Who buys this stuff?" Cadence asked, resting two hands on the glass.

I stepped farther into the room. The smell of cigarettes hung in the air. "Sandra?" I called out toward the back room. "It's Briar."

Cadence and I exchanged glances. Sandra practically lived in that shop. Where was she?

I started toward the back room, but suddenly Cadence called out, "Oh, no, Briar!"

I hurried to her and found Sandra lying on her back behind the counter, arms splayed out. I knelt and felt her neck for a pulse—finding none, I stood. There was no sign of aggression that I could see. No gunshot wound. No blood. I was shaken to the core, with a deep sense of sadness and fear. Poor Sandra. Had the ring caused her death? It could also have been a simple accident.

I bent to grip Cadence's arm. "We need to get out of here."

She shook off my grasp. "She needs a doctor."

"No doctor can help her."

Cadence lingered near Sandra's body. "But we have to call someone. An ambulance. Or the coroner."

Was the ring still here somewhere? The money from the sale? I shuffled around the body and crouched behind the counter, searching the shelves.

"We need to find something I brought in here a few days ago. She was selling it for me."

"Did she write you a receipt?" Cadence asked.

"Yes. Not sure she has a copy, though."

The door opened, startling us, and we stood to find Captain Mc-

Manus. My whole world imploded. He'd find out about the ring for sure, come to the farm, and unravel our lives.

Upon seeing me, he ran one hand through his greasy hair. "Smith."

I stepped out from behind the case and introduced Cadence.

"Great. There's more of you."

"We just got here," I said. "How'd you know about it?"

"A tip." He slid on a pair of examination gloves.

"From who?" I asked.

"I hate to break it to you, but you're not a member of the FBI."

Cadence started for the door. "We need to get going, actually."

McManus held up one hand. "Whoa. You're not going anywhere. This is an active crime scene. Gotta wait for more uniforms—you need a debrief."

"Clearly, someone else was here before us," I said. "If they called it in."

"And why are you two here?" he asked.

"We came in to shop and found her like this," I said.

"Shop for what?" he asked.

I waved toward the glass cabinets. "Just stuff."

Cadence added, "I bought a statue from Sandra last year and wanted to tell her how much I'm enjoying it."

"A statue," McManus said.

I cringed. Cadence was only an okay liar, given that she was related to me and all.

McManus knelt and checked Sandra's pulse. "Touch anything?"

"Just the doorknob," I lied, standing over him. "And her carotid artery, checking for a pulse. It must've been recent. There was still cigarette scent in the air. And rigor mortis hasn't set in."

McManus glared up at me. "Put a sock in it, Smith. What were you two doing behind the counter?"

"Trying to find the phone," I said.

He looked pointedly at the phone on the table next to the Barca-Lounger.

"To call an ambulance," Cadence added, staring down at Sandra's body. "We hoped she could be saved.

McManus waved toward the BarcaLounger. "Take a seat and cool your heels."

The idea of sitting in a dead woman's former nap chair was not appealing, but Cadence and I gingerly shared the seat.

"I know she took epilepsy medication," I said. "Could've been a grand mal."

He ignored me and searched the shelves behind the counter, then parted the curtains and entered the back room, which I hadn't even checked for the ring. If it was there, he'd find it for sure.

Cadence felt next to her on the seat, where the cushion and the armrest met, then lifted a small black book held closed by a thick rubber band. Sandra's receipts book.

With a knowing look, she handed it to me, and I slipped it into my pocket.

McManus wandered out of the back room. "Did Sandra have any kind of cashbox?"

"Not that I know of," I said.

Cadence stood and stepped to him. "It's probably not the normal protocol, but can you debrief us now? Our brother Tom's regiment has been hit at Dieppe, and we need to get home in case there's news."

McManus nodded. "Heard about that. Sorry." He turned back to the body.

The black phone on the table next to us rang, and Cadence picked it up. "Island Treasures, Cadence speaking."

McManus lunged for the phone. "I told you not to touch anything. *Jesus.*"

Cadence looked at me and rolled her eyes, and we listened to McManus's side of the conversation. It sounded like something big was happening in Oak Bluffs. As tense as it was, it was fun experiencing it all with Cadence. She had potential.

He hung up. "I need you two outta here."

I stood, the sticky fake leather trying to hold on to the backs of my thighs. "We'll go give our statements at the police station." It was a short walk, next to the fudge shop near the steamship dock.

"You do that," he said, already making another call.

I pulled Cadence out of there, and we headed to Gram's truck. The Totenkopf ring was gone, and there was no sign of the money, but I was just happy to have escaped McManus's long arm. We'd get to the police station another day, maybe. I had a feeling Sandra wasn't the spy we'd been looking for after all.

"That was kind of fun," Cadence said.

I felt my pocket for Sandra's receipts book. And, thanks to Cadence, we might even have the answer to who'd killed her.

26

CADENCE

—

1942

BY THE TIME MAJOR GILBERT FINALLY CAME AND GOT ME FOR our grand tour of the island, I'd plotted the perfect route, all the way to Edgartown. It seemed the ideal destination for him, with its men's shops that offered striped Breton shirts to help bond traders look like simple sailing folk and its chic restaurants where the busboys wore dinner jackets. Why he now insisted on taking the tour, despite having once passed on it, was a mystery. Maybe he just wanted another mention in my column. Maybe all that rudeness was a façade and he actually liked me. I'd felt the attraction at one point.

But either way, I was happy to go. Taking him away from the farm would allow Peter to complete a final irrigation fix, which he needed daylight for. And it was one of the hottest days on record. Perfect for a breezy drive.

The major showed up in his jeep, and I hurried out the front door and got in. No need to risk him seeing Peter.

"Ready?" he asked, and we set off. "Where to?"

As we headed up Copper Pond Road, shoulder to shoulder in the Army jeep, I tried to sell him on driving to the picture-perfectness of Edgartown—the sea captains' homes, the blue hydrangeas in the window boxes—but Gil had other plans.

"I'd rather see where the real islanders go for a spot of fun."

I tied a scarf over my hair, knotting it at the nape, á la Winnie. "I'm not sure you can handle it, actually."

"Is that rather a put-down?" he asked. "Hard to tell sometimes with Americans."

"Why do you even want to see the island, Major?"

"I think we can dispense with the Major."

"Amelia calls you Gilbert."

"I prefer Gil."

"You seem to be finding your way around perfectly well now, Gil. You don't need instruction."

"Just show me what would be good to write about in your column, I suppose."

"Ah, I see. Captain Feldman again?"

"He did like the last one, yes."

"And suggested you continue?"

"That was our bargain, I believe. Your willingness to be a bridge to the community, for my cooperation. I rerouted my men. Let's not rake over that."

Of course this wasn't just a pleasure drive. I sat back and breathed in the fresh sea air. At least I got a free ride out of it.

"Well, Oak Bluffs is the place to go for fun out here," I said. "Though it might be too downscale for you. Certainly for Amelia."

"Amelia, perhaps. But I like a good mess-about."

"She seems to think we all marry our cousins and eat coot stew."

He smiled at that. "Coot stew? Sounds rather unappetizing, I'm afraid."

"Just a duck we have here that eats mostly fish. It's actually quite good."

Oak Bluffs would be a fair test of the major, who'd probably never been pushed off a sidewalk before.

The major glanced at me as he drove. "I received some word on what's happened with your brother's regiment." He downshifted. "Only fifty men from the Seventy-fifth were embedded at the Dieppe raid. I know it's not much, but it's all I could find out."

I breathed a little easier. That was reassuring news.

"Thank you for that."

"I'll ring down to you if I hear anything else."

How nice it was to have someone in a high place looking out for us. And Tom.

"If Tom were here today, he'd be swimming in Copper Pond. It's the only thing to fight this heat."

"The one down by the beach?"

"It has minerals in it—the copper leaves your skin feeling like glass. They say the water has magical properties."

He gave me a long look and then returned his gaze to the road.

"Gram doesn't like us swimming down there at night, but we do anyway."

"You're not much for rules, are you?"

"Depends." I smiled. "Let's just say I'm happy you're respecting the Victory Speed. But some things can be fudged, I think."

"England runs on rules, I'm afraid. Have to say, this is a nice change of pace. The wild frontier."

"I suppose. We could use a decent bookstore."

"By the way, my men have been enjoying the books. Private Jeffers is trying to finish a Faulkner novel before we ship out."

I turned in my seat. "So soon?"

"That is the idea," he said. "Train here and then go engage the enemy."

"Where are you headed after you're done here?"

"Back to England soon, probably, and then the commandos will be assigned. Italy. France. North Africa. Or there's always the Pacific."

"Will you go with them?"

"That's the plan. They're stuck with me."

I would be sad to see him go. Not that I'd show it. Was the lovely and humble Amelia going along, too, with her silk and pearls? She was still on the island, I knew, since Bess had heard her on the local radio channel doing a story about the new airfield under construction in Edgartown.

"Worried about going up against the Germans again after your run-in with them in Norway?"

"Not a bit."

"Amelia referenced some intrigue."

"Don't let's make too much of it. I was just doing my job."

We finally got to Oak Bluffs and parked, joining the crowded sidewalk outside Darling's Old Popcorn Store. People swarmed in and out of shops, casually dressed, many bare-armed and glistening with suntan lotion, wet dogs and children knocking into us with their sand buckets. Darling's had been an island staple for over one hundred years. How often had Gram taken us there for popcorn bars when we were kids, with Tom choosing the famous wintergreen flavor—he didn't care that it was pink—Briar the chocolate, and me the vanilla?

The major smiled and took in the crowd. "Well, this is quite a good show, isn't it?"

I led him into the shop. Popcorn was popping out of the big copper kettle in the front window, and the scent of butter and sugar filled the air.

"Do we queue up?" he asked.

"No. It's every man for himself; just wave down someone behind the counter. No visitor leaves the island without a white box of Darling's saltwater taffy or fudge or penuche in their valise. Though there's a limit of five pieces now, due to rationing."

"So what flavor taffy would your grandmother like?" Gil asked, leaning so close I could smell the remnants of his shave cream.

How surprisingly kind that was of him.

"Molasses nut, for sure," I said.

The major managed to order his taffy and smiled at the cashier as he handed her a dollar and she made change in her lap. He could certainly turn on the charisma when he wanted to.

We emerged and rejoined the fray on the sidewalk, being pushed and bumped at every turn.

"Talk about no rules," I shouted to him. "Everyone does as they please here."

He took my arm and helped me through the crowd. "It's damned good fun, isn't it?"

I loved the come-as-you-are nature of Oak Bluffs, where everyone was welcome. Where the petite Adams sisters, who'd been in Tom Thumb's wedding, strolled next to Wampanoag fishermen, and one might see famous island residents like stage actress Katharine Cornell and film star James Cagney. Black Americans from all over the country came back year after year to Oak Bluffs, the only Vineyard town that welcomed them at their inns and hotels.

The major seemed to relax and soak it all in, but it was hard to know if it was just a show for my column.

"What do you think?" I asked. "It's not exactly Regent Street."

"You might be surprised. If I'm honest, it has all the energy of a Chelsea football match at Stamford Bridge."

"I didn't take you for a soccer fan." I pushed away a massively attractive image of him in a soccer uniform, running the field. It was better to keep things businesslike. "You're allowed to leave the castle now and then?"

"I actually let an apartment in Kensington."

"How common of you."

He pulled me closer and said in my ear, "I need to see the simple folk now and then. This is invigorating, truly."

I laughed and walked ahead. "Can I quote you? Have to make it good for the column, after all."

He pulled me back by the wrist. "Stop saying that."

I just stood there, jostled by passersby.

He pulled me to him, so close. I barely breathed as he searched my face, and everything slowed. He leaned in, lips parted. I closed my eyes and waited for his mouth on mine.

All at once, someone bumped me from behind, knocking me away from him.

I turned to find a sunburned bowling pin of a man wearing a towel draped around his neck like a prizefighter, walking backward and apologizing profusely.

The major averted his gaze and brushed something off his sleeve, and I walked on, too shaken by the moment to look at him.

He took my arm again as we walked. "I hope you don't think I was boiling up to make a pass."

Of course he was, and I'd been happy for it, but I let it go. "Oh, of course not."

Soon we reverted to our former selves, chatting about similar things again, only less chipper somehow.

We pushed through a throng of people on the sidewalk, and a flash of fear spiked in me as I spotted Captain McManus at the doorway of Sone's Japanese gifts store. At least he wasn't at our house, on Peter's trail. He wore his blue windbreaker, despite the August heat, and was certainly not there to watch taffy being made. A crowd gathered as he placed a board across the gift-shop doorway and his associate nailed it in.

"You can't do that!" someone in the crowd called out.

The Sone family had not been on the island to open their shop as usual that season, and rumors swirled about their whereabouts.

"I heard they've been interned in Montana. How can that happen? They haven't done anything remotely nefarious," I said to Gil.

He led me away. "It's an unfortunate product of war, I'm afraid."

"It's not fair," I said. "Their kids went to school here."

"We can't be too careful right now."

I pictured Peter at home, fixing our irrigation box. If only Gil knew.

We finished our whirlwind tour of Oak Bluffs, and he got me back to the farm-road entrance. I hoped Peter was done and out of the field.

"You can drop me out here at the farm stand," I said, hoping to have that long walk to the cottage all to myself to sort through what had happened with him. But he insisted on dropping me at the house, and as the jeep barely came to a stop, I sprang from it, relieved to see Peter was nowhere to be seen. I watched him drive away, then stepped into the cottage and back to the kitchen, to find Gram and Bess shelling peas at the table.

"How was it?" Gram asked.

"Fine, I suppose." I just wanted to go to my bedroom and sort through it all in private.

"I need every detail," Bess said.

"Can Peter come down?" Gram asked. "He's offered to make me more of that aspirin drink. It really has helped—not short-winded at all today."

"Yes, but only quickly," I said.

Peter came downstairs and stood at the sink.

"Major Gilbert said he found out that only fifty Army Rangers from the Seventy-fifth actually landed at Dieppe," I said.

"That's good news," Bess said, almost too brightly. It raised the question: Was Tom among them?

The front screen door banged. "Me again, I'm afraid!" came a voice.

I turned toward the sound. "My God. He's back."

Bess grabbed Peter by the arm and pulled him toward the back staircase.

Gil stepped into the kitchen. "So sorry to waltz in this way."

My heart thumped my ribs, and I smoothed my hair and tried to smile naturally.

Gram stood and rubbed her palms down the front of her skirt. "We didn't hear you arrive, Major Gilbert."

The major stepped into the kitchen and held out the white Darling's box to me. "You forgot this. For your grandmother."

Remarkably composed, Gram accepted the box. "Oh, thank you. I do love that tradition, especially when it benefits me." She pulled out a chair from the table. "Please sit, Major. I've just made some baked apples."

"No, thank you, Mrs. Smith," the major said, his gaze fixed on Peter. "I don't think we've met."

My knees felt about to fail. Gil would turn us all in for sure once he spoke with Peter. Would certainly never contact me again, except maybe to call me in prison.

"This is our cousin," I said. I turned to Peter. "This is Major Gilbert."

Bess stood between Peter and the major. "He doesn't say much."

Peter stepped to the major.

I swallowed hard and readied myself. It was the end of the line for us.

27

BRIAR

1942

THE MORNING AFTER CADENCE AND I HAD OUR AGATHA CHRISTIE moment at Island Treasures, I woke in Gram's bed and reached for Sandra's black receipts book in the bedside table drawer. Earlier I'd heard Cadence go off with England's finest, Major Crab, for a tour of the island, and I wished she'd been there to talk possible spy suspects. She'd proven herself an able fellow detective, and I could have used her help sorting it out.

I ran one finger across the word *Receipts,* embossed into the pebbled faux-leather cover in faded gold. It made me sad for Sandra, her life summed up in that grubby little book. I avoided something encrusted on the lower corner and yanked off the rubber band, causing all the papers and receipts inside to kind of explode out. Sandra had done some big business through the years.

I flipped the grease-stained pages, trying to keep all the pieces together, turning to the more recent entries. She'd included all sorts of notes and scribblings in there, like dates for estate sales and grocery lists, heavy on the Dinty Moore beef stew.

I wasn't even sure what I was looking for. The names of some of her customers, maybe. Possible leads to who may have wanted her dead. And info about past sales. I found a receipt for a World War I sword sold to a fancy Boston Back Bay antiques shop for two hundred dollars. And it turned out she'd sold the German life preserver I brought her, to a dealer in Quincy, for fifty bucks. She'd paid me two. A receipt for a World War I knife was made out to Shelby Parker. *WWI German trench dagger.* I looked closer at the barely legible signature. What was Shelby doing with that?

I flipped to the last pages and read a line written in Sandra's handwriting toward the bottom of one. *T. Schmidt. Do not leave at his grandfather's house.* I sat up in bed and read it again. So Sandra did know Tyson. She'd lied to me. And he'd skillfully avoided telling me he knew her. What did he buy from her? I rifled through the book for a receipt made out to him but didn't find one. Why would he deny knowing her? Clearly Shelby did, too.

I snapped the rubber band back around it all, stowed it in the bedside table drawer, and got out of bed. With Tyson in the hospital, his house would be easy to search.

FOR ALL MY YEARS of friendship with Mr. Schmidt, I'd never been to his home in Vineyard Haven. It was one of the prettiest houses on William Street, close to town, a white Victorian with a sloping lawn. Mr. Schmidt had lived there full time for decades but in his later years moved to what he called his "camp" on the shore, next door to us.

I shifted my canvas shoulder bag, heavy with reconnaissance supplies—scissors, binoculars, and a pad of paper and pencil—and approached from the back of the house, not gutsy enough to just barge in the front door. Though that's what most people who weren't snooping would have done. No one locked their doors on the island. I stepped through the rear entrance into the kitchen, that big room so bright and sunny, with dust dancing in a light beam shining through the soaring window. It was warm in there—the house had been closed up since Tyson went to the hospital.

I got teary thinking of Mr. Schmidt with his wife, making his peppermint tea, sitting together at the little yellow-painted table. It had been his wife's family home. I never knew Maria Von Weber, but she'd been the love of Conrad's life, pure German, second-generation American. Tyson's grandma. I stepped to the sink and checked out the cereal bowl there, a few cornflakes petrified to the side of it, the milk dried up. Probably Tyson's pre-accident breakfast.

I tiptoed into the main part of the house, not because I had to be quiet but because I was nervous, I suppose. It was a big place, and I ducked into a room that looked like an office. Tyson had taken over the wide mahogany desk as his school study area and filled it with open textbooks and notes. I hadn't taken him for the type who would actually study in the summer.

I opened one of the desk drawers, looking for anything suspicious. Correspondence. German artifacts that could have come from Island Treasures. Papers that shed more light on Mr. Schmidt's ties to Germany.

The only interesting thing I found was a stash of coins in the pencil drawer, which I helped myself to. Tyson wouldn't miss them.

After checking all the drawers, I stepped to the built-in bookcase next to the fireplace, which was crammed with World War I military books and mementos. I was happy to find the little tugboat that I'd given Mr. Schmidt for his birthday just two years ago, after we'd made it together from a kit. I pulled it from the lower shelf. Light dust covered the deck of the *LUCKY XI*, a harbor tug with a rust-and-black hull and little pilot's house. The tiny captain figure and the two seamen we'd painted to look like Mr. Schmidt and me were still glued to the deck. We'd finished it in three days. No doubt Mr. Schmidt had displayed it in a place of honor when he was alive, and now Tyson had relegated it to a bottom shelf.

I replaced the model and continued my search. Before I headed out, I checked the gray file cabinet that stood along the wall across from the desk. I slid out the top drawer and felt papers along the bottom, and then my hand met cold metal. I pulled out a gun, what looked like an old Luger. German? I was no firearms expert, but it was definitely a candidate for Tyson's purchase from Island Treasures. *Do not leave at his grandfather's house.*

I set the gun back in the file cabinet, and as I ran through my options of what to do next, I heard something in the house. I crept out of the office, barely breathing, and inched down the hallway toward the sound.

28

CADENCE

———

1942

I COULD BARELY LOOK AS PETER HELD OUT HIS HAND TO THE major.

"Pleased to meet you, Major Gilbert," Peter said, in a passable Midwestern accent. "I'm cousin Donald. Lindquist."

Major Gilbert shook his hand. "Cadence didn't mention you."

Peter smiled and jammed his hands in his pockets. "Cousin twice removed. Here to help with the farm now that Tom's off serving."

It was hard to breathe. Did Gil suspect? I glanced at his face. If he did, he was a good actor.

"Are you considering joining up?" Gil asked.

Peter frowned. "Astigmatism, gosh darn it."

"Tough luck." Gil waved in the direction of the Army base. "I'm just up at Peaked Hill."

Peter assumed the stance men take when they chat with like-minded fellows, feet spread wide, arms folded across the chest. "For Pete's sake, are you? Go Army."

The major smiled. "That's American football, but yes."

"I prefer soccer myself," Peter said, apparently enjoying his role. "Played as a kid back in Minnesota."

"Indoors, no doubt."

"Oh, no. You've never heard of snow soccer? It's a hoot, I'll tell ya. You'll be able to play it soon here. Gets cold as the north woods on this island come November."

The more he spoke, he got the Minnesota accent down, elongating his *a*'s and *o*'s.

"What position do you play?" the major asked.

"Forward mostly. We went to the state championship when I was in middle school."

"Really?" Gil asked, looking impressed.

"Pride of the Twin Cities."

Gil stepped closer to Peter. "We're having a little game up at the base this weekend. Against the Navy chaps. Maybe you'd like to play for us?"

A fresh spike of fear ran through me, and I looked at Bess. Of course Peter had to beg off immediately.

Peter glanced at me. "Oh, no, I'm pretty dang out of shape. Not like you all."

"Farmwork is great conditioning. And you're welcome to join our morning workouts. We run right by here every day." Gil turned to Gram. "Assuming you don't mind, Mrs. Smith?"

Gram busied herself at the stove. "We do have to get the upper field plowed."

"Navy won last time." Gil turned back to Peter. "There's a trophy involved, and we're quite interested in nicking it back, you see. Word is Navy's got a ringer, and we could use one, too."

"I'm not sure I'm feeling up to it after working the fields," Peter said.

"How about we see how you are tomorrow?"

Gil didn't seem to suspect Peter, but he was opening up a whole new occasion for disaster.

"You bet," Peter said.

"Right, then." Gil sent him a little salute. "I'll be in touch soon. Good meeting you, Donald."

Gil started to leave, then addressed the rest of us. "The general public is not invited to the match, but we'd certainly make an exception for you all if you'd like to attend to cheer on your cousin. If he's feeling up to it, that is."

And make sure he doesn't reveal his true roots with a slip of his German tongue. I sent him a little wave. "Certainly, Major. *Gil.* Thanks for the invitation."

"I'll have one of my men come round and check tomorrow morning," he said.

I just smiled and said goodbye to Major Gilbert. Would the nightmare ever end?

"That was a disaster," I said after he drove off.

Bess stepped to Peter's side. "Maybe it would be safer to start calling you Donald."

"Don't worry, I won't go," Peter said. "But, you know, I'm going a bit stir-crazy upstairs. I would like to get out."

I pressed my fingers to my temples. "You will not be going to a soccer game with half of the U.S. military playing. What if you slip and someone hears your real accent? They might ask for your papers. You can't even get on the base without an ID card."

"I understand. I will not go up there tomorrow."

Peter went upstairs, and Bess and I helped Gram start supper.

I could barely think as we peeled potatoes at the sink. Were we all just cursed somehow? One minute I seemed to be making headway with Peter and the farm, the next he was almost dragged into a public soccer game.

"We need to get him on his way, and soon, Gram, once he plows the upper field. He's practically healed now."

"He has no identification," Bess said.

"We can make him an identity card, best we can, and send him off to Minnesota. We'll give him a little money for a train." I carried the potatoes to the stove. "We need to get your hospital appointment made, Gram. And actually finish a book. I'm looking forward to a normal life again, aren't you?"

Bess stepped to the window, drew the curtain aside, and peered out. "Good God."

"What is it, dear?" Gram asked from the stove.

Bess turned from the window. "Normal won't be happening anytime soon, Cadence. Better get over here and look."

29

BRIAR

———

1942

A<small>S I CREPT DOWN THE HALLWAY OF MR. SCHMIDT'S HOUSE, MY</small> steps muted on the thick carpet, I shook my hands to stop them from trembling. I drew closer, trying to place the sound. A wounded animal? No, it was a human voice. Alternately moaning and then panting like a dog. Soon I made it to the living room and got a bird's-eye view of one of those things that's hard to unsee. The shades were drawn and the front door closed, despite the heat, and Tyson lay on the sofa, facing away from me; Shelby Parker sat astride him, caressing his chest.

So Tyson was home after all. And he had certainly recovered quickly.

There were magazines scattered here and there across the floor, and Shelby wore the bathing suit I'd seen her in at the hospital nurse's station.

"Say it again," she said, open-mouthed and breathless. "What have I got?"

"You've got the best ass on the island," Tyson called out.

I clapped my hand over my mouth to stifle the laugh.

"Louder!" Shelby shouted.

I hid around the corner, my back to the wall, heart pounding.

"Wait," Tyson said. "What was that?"

"Hey," Shelby said. "It was just getting good."

"I heard something," he said.

Tyson must have pushed her off, because Shelby let out an annoyed little noise.

"Jeez."

I was trapped there around the corner from them and tried to slink away, but Tyson came through the door and caught me. "*Briar.* What are you doing here?" he shouted, zipping up his pants.

Shelby followed him. "Did she see us?" she asked Tyson. "Tell her if she blabs, my parents will murder me."

Tyson took me by the arm. "Were you *watching* us?"

I frowned. "No. Yuck. I just came to drop off some of your grandfather's things, and I thought someone was getting murdered in here."

"What did you drop off?" he asked.

He had me. I pulled my arm away. "Well . . ."

"I told you she lies," Shelby said.

"Were you trying to steal something?" Tyson asked, with a concerned look. "If you need money . . ."

"No. But I did get a tip."

"From who?"

"It's confidential. But they said you bought something from Sandra Granger."

He turned to Shelby. "Can you give us a minute?"

Shelby strolled off toward the kitchen, maybe on the prowl for chips.

He held on to the doorjamb and leaned in. "Okay, I do know Sandra. And I did buy something from her."

"I figured. The gun, right?"

"What? No. Wait. Did you look in the *office?* For God's sake, Briar. I told you I'd help you. You know, I should call the cops."

"Well, you bought that from her, right?" I knew I had him.

"*No.* That's Grandfather's old World War I pistol. It doesn't even fire anymore. There aren't any bullets." He turned away. "That wasn't what I bought from her."

"Then what?" I asked.

He stepped into the living room, bent to pull a magazine from the floor, and brought it to me. "There. Happy?"

I read the title on the cover aloud. *"Augenfällig."* It translated to *Eyeful* and was subtitled *Glorifying the German Girl.* The cover photo wasn't exactly glorifying that girl, a pretty-much naked blonde wearing cheetah-print stockings and looking through a keyhole cutout.

"You bought German girlie mags from her?" I asked.

"Yes. Happy that you've embarrassed me? Gonna have your sister print it in her stupid column?"

"How was I supposed to know? You said you'd never met Sandra."

"It's not something I go around bragging about, Briar. At least Sandra kept it quiet. My grandfather would have had a fit if he'd found out."

Shelby wandered back in, eating pistachio ice cream out of a cardboard container with a silver spoon. "Is she leaving?"

"Yes, she is," I said.

Tyson was happy to give me the bum's rush and go back to what he was doing. I walked out the way I came, each step drilling in the irritation. How was I supposed to know he was home?

I passed the office and glanced at the tugboat model on a lower shelf as I hurried by. Mr. Schmidt would have helped me figure it all out. I doubled back and grabbed the model from the shelf. If Tyson didn't appreciate it, I would. He wouldn't even notice it was gone, probably. Shelby wouldn't be asking after it.

I walked off, telling myself that the whole trip had been worth it to get the tugboat model back, safely wrapped in one of Maria's dish towels in my satchel.

As I headed down to Main Street to see what picture was playing at the Capawock, I spotted Cadence's Major Gilbert on foot, with his quick British stride. Where was he going in such a hurry? I gave him a little head start and then followed. According to Sandra, he'd been right up there on her spy list. What harm would it do to check him out?

UP-ISLAND HAPPENINGS

By CADENCE SMITH

THE SERVICEMEN AT PEAKED HILL CONTINUE TO CHARM THE citizens of our little island, performing good deeds and acts of charity worthy of St. Vincent de Paul. After Private Jeffers of Preston, Idaho, spent his day off painting her front fence, Mrs. Virginia Smith of Chilmark rewarded him with an authentic Idaho huckleberry pie. The private vouched for the tastiness of the pie, despite the berries being island, not Idaho, grown.

Major Gilbert and his Cape Cod Commandos have been enjoying all the island towns but Oak Bluffs most of all, according to an informal poll. The major claimed, upon a recent trip there, that it was the most picturesque seaside town he'd been to outside of Brighton, with all the energy of a football match, and he has become a devotee of popcorn bars, even the wintergreen.

However, all is not well in the island's jolliest town, since this past week loyal patrons and passersby watched Sone's gift shop, run with care by the beloved Sone family, being shut down. The door was boarded up per order of the island Federal Bureau of Investigation, the Sones' only crime being of Japanese descent. Vigorous letters in their defense may be sent to the Immigration and Naturalization Service in Washington, D.C. Hopefully they will soon be wading through a deluge of mail as high as the Capitol dome.

Sandra Granger of Island Treasures, formerly of Abby's Hardware, passed away this week at the age of 80. A lengthy memorial was held at the hardware store during business hours, where spontaneous eulogies were given in the aisles, as customers attempted to check out. "She loved her clams," friend Sheila

Kenny said. "Even blindfolded, she could tell a customer where a toilet brush was," said one source, who wished to remain anonymous. "She'd tell anyone to go to hell," said friend Phyllis Conrad. "She was hardware-store royalty."

The next book due to pass in our island chain is Enid Bagnold's *National Velvet,* a book close to my heart. Christal Cooper, you are on your way to the pastures of Sussex, England. Just keep plenty of tissues on hand for the trip!

30

CADENCE

———

1942

"YOU WON'T BELIEVE IT," BESS SAID, HOLDING THE KITCHEN curtain open.

I bent to look out the window, not knowing what to expect, and could hardly believe what I saw: The Putnam yacht was moored just off our shore.

"The *Never Moor*," I said, the words not quite registering.

Winnie and her friends, accompanied by a white-uniformed gentleman, climbed down a short ladder into a dinghy to come ashore.

Gram joined us at the window. "Is that your publishing ladies? Nice of them to come by."

The ship's horn blew, and I was afraid Bess would have the baby right there. "My God, it really is them," Bess said, looking out over the water. "And they have Margaret," she added in a glum tone.

The dinghy motored toward shore, with Margaret sitting at the front of it like a ship's figurehead, hair blowing in the breeze. She wore a new jacket the color of violets, and I reminded myself she'd gone on that trip as a favor to us. If she got the job I could have had, there would be others. Would the ladies have more news about our book for the servicemen? Perhaps that would lead to something for me soon.

I plumped the living room pillows, sending dust into the air. Where was Briar? She would miss all the fun.

Gram started toward the stove. "They'll be hungry."

"They have a chef on board, Gram," I said. "You can rest."

Bess and I hurried down to the beach, quick as we could, mindful of Bess's condition, Scout at our heels. As we descended the bluff, Margaret jumped out into the surf, carrying her shoes in one hand, and she ran up to embrace us.

"You won't believe the time we had," Margaret said, out of breath. "We went to Bergdorf Goodman and Bonwit Teller. And to a restaurant like a real pirate ship, where you can walk the plank."

I congratulated Margaret, genuinely happy for her, and when she asked if she could stay over in the boathouse for the next week since her aunt was having guests, I agreed. Then Bess told her about her pregnancy, and she embraced her so sincerely that even Bess started to soften on old Margaret.

From the dinghy, Dolores waved to us, and Celia called out, "Yoo-hoo!"

The yacht's captain—by the look of his white uniform—helped the Putnam ladies and Winnie out of the little boat. All three wore trousers, in various nautical shades. Winnie was in wide-legged navy-blue sailor's pants, with a striped Breton top and a silk scarf to keep her hair back.

Bess pointed to the boat's name, lettered on the stern. "*The Oxford Comma.* Isn't that perfect?"

Winnie came over to me. "We tried to radio ahead for you to meet us at the harbor but couldn't reach anyone, so we had Captain Karl here drop anchor and bring us by."

"I won't even lie and say I hope we're not intruding," Dolores said. "Because I couldn't wait to see this heavenly place."

"We can't stay long," Winnie said. "But I thought we'd impose on you for a quick tour and then host you for dinner out on the boat."

"I'll die happy if I can see a beetlebung," Celia said.

A second small boat launched from the yacht, with what looked like a staff of white-jacketed men. "It's the bar," Winnie said. "We brought our own glasses."

Bess and I led them up the hill to the farm, all of them exclaiming over our little burgee flapping in the breeze atop the beach flagpole.

"The famous book-club burgee," Celia said. "Long may she wave."

"Army cadets called the Cape Cod Commandos work out on this beach every morning," Bess said.

Dolores laughed. "What a glorious sight over morning coffee."

"We've started having our Boston man send us down the *Vineyard Gazette,* just to read your column," Celia said. "Such a lovely paper, and you're one of the best parts of it, frankly."

I stood, so paralyzed with happiness I could barely reply, and watched the phalanx of waiters land from the dinghy.

Winnie linked arms with me. "You look good," she said as we walked together. She studied me as if I were a Ming vase. "Obviously in love."

I smiled, taken aback. With whom? Major Gilbert? She was mistaken. We couldn't even manage a kiss.

"I can always tell." Winnie continued up the hill. "Just make sure he doesn't keep you from Manhattan."

"Margaret seems happy," I said, braced to hear she'd taken a job that might have been saved for me.

Winnie pulled me close. "To be honest, that's part of the reason we're back so soon. Celia wanted to turn around and bring her back after the first hour on board. She can't abide a chatterer. We told dear Margaret the issue, but it didn't help, so Celia just stowed her in the guest room and had her secretary take her out to shop. They didn't even get a chance to pitch the books."

"But the telegram—"

"It seems that great minds think alike: When Celia called the Army, we heard that a fellow by the name of Ray Trautman at the Army Library had already come to them with a similar idea."

I stopped walking. "Oh."

"But the committee liked the authentic way it developed and wants you to be involved. We'll fill you in after dinner."

I wasn't proud to think it, but I was relieved that Margaret had not taken New York by storm in my place and was thrilled I still might get a chance to go to New York, even if Mr. Trautman had beaten us to it.

As we walked, Bess told the Putnam ladies and Winnie why she had to take it slow, and they all fussed over Bess and her baby news, none of them the least bit put off by the lack of a wedding ring. We made it to the cottage and Gram came out, the screen door banging shut behind her. "Welcome to Copper Pond Farm!" she called out, a little out of breath. "Donuts in the kitchen."

"It's just as I pictured it," Dolores said to Winnie, stepping back to take in the stone façade and the barn, the roof as swayed as an old mare's back. "*Rebecca of Sunnybrook Farm* meets *The Grapes of Wrath*."

We all went into the house with Gram and "Chef Delon," as they called him, a young French-trained cook who apparently wasn't allowed a first name. Celia told the story of how she had poached him from the Grand Central Oyster Bar, where she had to bunk when her train got stuck in the tunnel during a snowstorm and the whole city closed down. Chef had been there, glumly shucking drums of the briny bivalves with the rest of *les misérables,* and they all ended up spending the night eating Blue Points, raiding the wine cellar, and sharing stories of their first loves. The next day, once they dug out, Celia packed them all up and took them aboard the *Never Moor.*

Dolores leaned in. "Chef's terribly grateful to her now and will make anything, except chicken for some reason. The more butter the better, so just ask."

The barmen had stayed down at the beach to set up their station and start shaking cocktails. Gram showed Chef how to make her donuts, as they waited for the canapés to heat. Captain Karl sat at the kitchen table watching it all, sipping a glass of aquavit, transfixed by Gram.

Bess, Margaret, and I gave Winnie, Celia, and Dolores a tour of the barn. "We could have a smashing party out here for the book launch," Celia said.

"Which book?" Bess asked.

"Or should I say books?" Winnie asked.

"The ASEs, of course," Dolores said. "At least that's what they're calling them. Armed Services Editions. There's a whole committee being formed."

"They're working on a compromise," Celia said. "Between the

Army and Navy, who want current bestseller titles, and the publishers, who favor more serious fiction."

Dolores held out a thin rectangle to me. "But Putnam ran a prototype of our own, on a magazine press, and here it is. We told them this title would be especially meaningful to you."

I took the little blue book from her and read the cover. *Emerson's Essays.* Tears blurred my view and I handed it to Bess, who hung her head, one hand to her face.

"This is beautiful, thank you, and so good of you to honor Tom. We'll send it to him right away. He'll be thrilled."

"The Army and Navy are full speed ahead on these books," Celia said. "They questioned Plato's *Republic* being on the list, saying it was too scholarly, but didn't want a *Sad Sack* comic, either."

"Everyone's an editor," Dolores said.

Winnie stepped to Gram's red cookie jar on the counter, the lid broken long ago. "They want us to choose ten titles from the cookie jar and tell them as soon as possible."

"Let's get down to the beach for cocktails," Celia said. "And then back to the ship. Chef's making lobster Newburg."

I soaked in the joy of it all. This would be my life one day, hopefully soon, working in publishing with remarkable, smart women.

After a lovely cocktail hour, the captain ferried us all to the *Never Moor,* and I felt like Jay Gatsby rowing out to meet copper magnate Dan Cody's yacht. One of the white-jacketed men took my hand and pulled me up onto the ship, and we entered the main cabin.

I was overcome by the grandeur of it, the entire interior lined in teak, with room for a small round table set for ten people; the fancy linens and silverware alone were worth more than everything in our house. Soft swing music played, piped in from somewhere, as the glorious scent of lobster wafted from Chef's little flambé table. The alcohol was well protected on shelves along the wall above the leather-upholstered bar, the glasses held safe behind wooden slats and the crystal decanters buckled in, in case of rough seas.

"Nice ship," Bess said, as she and Margaret came aboard.

Celia sipped her wine. "It's my only perk. For client lunches, I practically have to eat at the Automat, or accounting calls me up ranting."

"Just go to Coney Island," Dolores said. "Without question the best food, and clients find it amusing."

"Where's your sister?" Celia asked me. "Briar, is it? Is she part of the book club?"

"Yes. But she's not a big fan of fiction."

"I understand." Dolores leaned in. "Try reading ten manuscripts in a day."

Bess poured herself an orange juice. "Not like Cadence. She used to tell her friends she was being punished, so she could stay in and read."

Celia lit a cigarette. "They say television will be the death of reading."

I loved that Celia made sudden pronouncements like that, throwing out literary proclamations like little cyclones, and just moved on.

We had our celebration and then chose titles from the cookie jar, which we'd brought aboard with some of the book club's favorite titles hastily scribbled on scraps of paper. Dolores noted them on her pad. *The Education of Hyman Kaplan*, by Leo Rosten. C. S. Forester's *The African Queen*. My favorite, *The Years*, by Virginia Woolf. *The Good Earth*, by Pearl Buck. The ladies even agreed to include *The Great Gatsby*, despite its lack of commercial success.

"The Council on Books in Wartime plans on printing 1,322 titles— 123 million books altogether—so we may need to come back for more," Celia said with a laugh.

We thoroughly enjoyed our lobster Newburg, though I sat on tenterhooks all through it, wondering what Winnie had to tell me in the way of employment. Finally, as the evening wound down, she came to me at the ship's railing. It was a beautiful night, the moon a waning crescent over the cottage up on the bluff. In just a few days the new moon would rise, and there'd be a different sort of ship out there, waiting for its passenger to go back to Germany. Were they out there this very minute, watching us?

Winnie came to me at the railing. "Your grandmother seems better."

"I think so."

"I wanted to tell you that the committee for the ASEs has offered you a position. Celia just told me this morning and thought it would be nice for me to give you the news."

Joy swelled in me. "How wonderful."

"You'd work for both the ASE committee and Putnam. The pay is pretty good. Enough to keep you fed and some sort of roof over your head."

"When does it start?"

"That's the catch," Winnie said. "They need you right away. If you can get your things and come back with us tonight, we have a stateroom prepared for you."

I looked to Gram, who was still having trouble breathing. How could I leave? And Bess would be having her baby before we knew it. Briar would help, but she couldn't handle it all.

I shook my head, trying not to tear up.

A light came on up at the cottage, in the attic. And there was Peter.

Winnie followed my gaze up to the house and looked back at me. "Want to talk about it?"

"Someday. But I still can't leave. Not right now."

"Oh, well. It's perfectly fine. They'll hire some dull Vassar girl who quotes T. S. Eliot and fines Celia a nickel per profanity, and I'll keep an eye out for the next job. Putnam hasn't stopped pressuring me to work there, so they may wear me down someday." She tapped her cigarette pack on the railing. "Either way, I'm not giving up on you, Cadence Smith. You've got the gift. A real feeling for words that can't be taught." She leaned in. "And I think it's about time life paid you back."

I swallowed hard. "Thank you, Winnie."

"Just keep writing those columns and getting your life's odds and ends wrapped up. Because if I join the workforce, you're coming, too, my dear. So get ready."

I could only nod. How good it was to have someone care.

"And whatever you do, don't have a baby yet. There'll be plenty of time for that once you publish your first novel."

Winnie's encouragement made it even harder to leave them, but we eventually made it into the dinghy and back onto terra firma. I stood there on the beach and watched the *Never Moor* sail off for Manhattan, along with my newly made-up stateroom and the lobster Newburg, the ship's running lights drifting out to sea.

I would get there someday. Or die trying.

31

BRIAR

—

1942

I HAD A GREAT TIME FOLLOWING MAJOR GILBERT AROUND VINE-yard Haven, but he was a challenge to surveil, since he was a fast walker. For an upper-crusty Brit, he had pretty plebeian tastes and, true to the cultural stereotype, started the excursion with fried fish and chips. It took him forever to eat it, down by the beach, and I almost left, until he headed back up to Main Street. He bought a pack of cigarettes and smoked one. I jotted in my notebook.

Next, the major entered L. E. Briggs's jewelry and furniture store. It wasn't the most expensive shop on the island, but it wasn't cheap, either, and he spent some time in there asking the girl behind the jewelry counter to take out a million different things and then put them back. I hurried in there after he left and asked the girl if he bought anything.

"He did," she said. Lucky for me, she was unfamiliar with the con-cept of customer privacy. "He bought a necklace. The most expensive one we have. A fourteen-karat-gold pavé diamond heart, edged in seed pearls. He barely looked at the price," she said disapprovingly.

I didn't have time to discuss that the whole point of retail was to at-tract customers for whom price was no object, but I knew I couldn't let the trail grow cold. I went next door to the drugstore and used one of Mr. Schmidt's nickels to buy a bag of the best candy in the world, Bos-ton Baked Beans, and set out to find Major Gil.

I found the major in line at the post office, at Church Street and Main, and I watched him while pretending to busy myself at the desk with the envelopes and pens. When his turn came, the postmaster behind the window handed him a small white envelope and he walked out.

The woman in line behind the major moved up to the window and inquired about him.

"It was from someone named Greta," the postmaster told her. "Swiss postmark. Don't know why it didn't come through military mail. I'm not allowed to open anything, though. The censors do all that."

"I hear he was snooping around the practice range over at Katama," the woman said.

The postman shrugged. "Never know these days."

I followed the major past the steamship dock, as he walked toward a little French restaurant named Cheri's. A blond woman came out to meet him, and they started arguing before he got within ten feet of her. I couldn't hear the details, but she was mad and stomped off a couple of times, then came back. He just stood there, hands in his pockets, like he was waiting for a bus. I hoped she'd slap Major Gilbert or something more interesting, but that didn't happen, and they finally went their separate ways.

All at once Jerry Whitcomb, my colleague from the model shop, came up from behind, scaring me so bad I almost choked on my candy.

"Hey, Briar." He dug into my bag and pulled out a bean. "Saw you following Major Gilbert earlier."

"On the advice of counsel, I invoke my fifth-amendment privilege against self-incrimination."

He popped the bean in his mouth and crunched. "Ha ha. Hey, I wanted to fill you in on something I heard. On the q.t., of course."

Ordinarily I wouldn't care a whit about harmless Jerry Whitcomb, but something in his tone made me think he might actually have important information.

"I'm training for a position in the FBI office, just grunt-work stuff, but I overheard Captain McManus talking with his assistant about Sandra Granger's death. Said they searched everywhere for some receipts book and it's missing." He aimed a pointed look at me.

I stuffed the candy bag into my pocket. "So?"

"He mentioned your name in connection with it. Said you were already on the scene when he arrived. With your sister."

Fear shot through me. Cadence was a suspect, too?

If McManus was on the hunt for a splashy arrest to make, one that would send him to the big time, I didn't want it to be me.

"Also, Mr. Reed came into the office and told McManus that three pages of a classified document are missing from the model shop, too."

"No kidding," I said. At least I had burned them.

"But remember I saw you in the classified room? You said you were looking for your Japanese subs. In the *M* drawer. That's the drawer with the missing pages."

I wiped my palms down my pant legs. *Since when did Jerry Whitcomb become some sort of savant?*

"Did you tell anyone?" I asked.

"No. Not yet. But that's withholding evidence."

"Not really. Not if they didn't ask. Volunteering information can actually hurt a case."

Jerry mulled that over. "Well, just so you know, in the FBI training manual it says they have a new way to trace the type of paper classified docs are printed on. From the fibers or something. Have a whole kit of chemicals they apply around a crime scene."

All of a sudden, my chest went tight. If McManus searched our house, could he tell from ashes in the fireplace that I'd taken those pages?

"Gotta go," I said.

"One more thing. McManus filed for a couple of search warrants yesterday in Edgartown—one of them for your grandmother's property and one for the house next door."

I walked away from him, my legs jelly beneath me. "Fine by me."

"Thought you should know," he called after me. "Just between us, right?"

"Right, Jerry. Thanks for being a pal." And I headed home to Copper Pond Farm to get rid of every trace.

32

CADENCE

—

1942

THE MORNING AFTER OUR NIGHT ON THE PUTNAM YACHT, I SLEPT in and woke to Bess shaking my arm.

"Cade. Wake up. Peter's gone."

I sat up, heart racing. "*What?*"

"Gram says Major Gilbert's man just came, right after Margaret left for work at the pharmacy, and took him up to the base for that game. Said they needed him badly since they were losing."

"Oh, no."

"Sounds like he tried to protest. Gram tried, too, but he ended up going." She shrugged.

I threw back the covers. "What time's the match?"

"It's been going on for a while. Briar's watering the middle field and said she'd meet us up on the hill. I told her about Peter being Donald."

"Good. Ask Gram if there's gas in the tank. We need to get up there now."

BY THE TIME GRAM, Bess, and I zoomed up to the guard shack at Peaked Hill, we could hear the soccer match in full swing. We caught up with Peter and Major Gilbert's assistant, who'd been stopped at the gate; a sentry inside the shack appeared to be talking to someone on the phone.

Bess stopped the car and I hurried to the jeep, reminding myself to refer to Peter as Donald. "Donald. There you are. We need you at home."

"Sorry, ma'am. Major Gilbert's orders. I'm to bring him up to the field right away. We're just calling the local police for ID verification, since he forgot his at home."

"He really can't stay," I said.

I looked back at Gram and Bess, dread creeping in. Once they dug into Peter's story, it would be clear he was not here legally. Would Fred Leo have to come over and put him in handcuffs? He'd have to say we'd harbored him.

"Sorry," the assistant repeated. He leaned closer to me. "To be honest, we're losing pretty bad. We need the firepower."

Sweat dripped down my back. Would Fred take the rest of us away, too?

A stocky private in workout clothes came running down the hill. "Jenkins, what's the holdup?" he called out.

"No ID," Jenkins called back.

"Get him up here on the double, anyway." He waved us through. "Just let 'em all in."

The sentry in the shack hung up the phone and we all drove to the heart of the camp, where Army and Navy soldiers lined the field, cheering their teams on.

We helped Gram to the sidelines and got her settled in a beach chair Bess had brought. I spotted Gil on the field, playing for Army, of course, in the usual green shorts and shirt; the Navy team was outfitted in blue. They got Peter onto the field as soon as he was dressed, and in no time his shirt was dark with sweat. One card table at the head of the field displayed a silver trophy, catching the sun, and another held a pitcher of water.

It didn't happen immediately, but Peter scored one goal and then Army built on that momentum. It turned out that Peter was pretty good. He was clearly out of shape, after being on a U-boat for two months, unable to walk more than a few feet in any direction; almost dying from hypothermia would do that, too. But Major Gilbert was certainly pleased as the tide turned for the men in green. Part of me thought that even if he knew Peter was a deserting German soldier, Gil would keep him on the team to defend the trophy.

"Peter's doing so well," Bess said.

My stomach lurched. "You mean Donald," I murmured.

"Of course," she said.

She reminded Gram to say Donald. It would be just our luck to have Peter exposed by one of our own.

Briar edged through the crowd and came to stand next to me. It was good to have her there. I could depend on her not slipping up about Peter.

"Who's winning?" Briar asked.

"Army is now," Bess said.

"Men will do anything for a trophy," Briar said, and crouched next to Gram's chair.

"Look who's here," Bess said, nodding to a woman nearby. "Old Silk and Pearls."

It was Gil's Amelia, standing on the sidelines, cheering Army on. It irritated me that she was still hanging around on my island. Didn't she have BBC stories to cover elsewhere? There was a war going on, after all.

I tried to focus on the match and our strategy for getting Peter home immediately after it ended, to lower the risk of some sort of slip.

It was hard not to watch Gil as he ran back and forth along the field. It was funny that Winnie had said I was in love. Was it even possible to love someone you barely knew? I didn't even know his real first name.

Gil ran by us, and our eyes met. I almost waved, but then he looked away and kept running. My future husband was not exactly committing to the relationship. Might have something to do with his girlfriend standing ten feet away.

Suddenly, as if thinking about it made her appear, Amelia was standing next to me.

"Oh, is this the whole Smith family? How lovely." She gave herself a little hug. "And so cozy, all of you here."

I made introductions and we watched the game.

"They're winning," I said, just to make conversation. "Gil must be happy."

Amelia turned with a smile. "Is it *Gil* now? I love you Americans, so familiar."

"Best to be on a first-name basis, with me writing about the Army in my column."

"I enjoyed your last column. Heard about that Oak Bluffs trip. How was it?"

"Crowded."

"If I'm honest, I know things are terribly informal here and all, but where I come from, a single woman doesn't ride alone in a car with another woman's fiancé."

Gil scored a goal, the crowd erupted in cheers, and Amelia clapped. "Good job, you!" She turned to me again. "He's in cracking form."

I checked her ring finger and found it ringless. "I didn't know you were engaged."

Amelia leaned closer to me, eyes on the soccer field. "Well, things were speeding along until you two started joyriding."

"I have no intentions toward him, Amelia."

"Well, that's rubbish. Any woman with a pulse desires him. I completely understand the attraction. But, fair warning, he always comes back to me."

I kept my gaze on the game. "Good to know."

"And you might want to ask him about Greta."

"Who?" I asked nonchalantly.

Amelia smiled. "You see, there's rather a queue forming for dear Gil. So don't say I didn't warn you."

She wandered away, and Bess and I exchanged a glance.

"Those two fight a lot," Briar said.

Bess and I turned to her.

She shrugged. "I saw them in town yesterday. She was giving it to him good."

Sometimes it was helpful to have an overly inquisitive sister.

The game ended up being close, but Army pulled ahead for the win, with Peter assisting on their final goal. The Army team went crazy, patting Peter on the back, and Gil walked away toward the Quonset hut in the distance. Why wasn't he celebrating with his men?

Army raised the trophy high, then both teams lined up and shook one another's hands, in a show of good sportsmanship. Briar went off in search of the bathroom; I left Gram with Bess and approached Peter at the water table. It wouldn't be long before we got him back down to the house and I could breathe freely again.

"Get your things," I said, keeping my voice low. "And we'll go right home."

Peter toweled sweat from his face and nodded. "I could use a break. I'm not fifteen anymore."

Two players for the Navy team approached the water table; I recognized one as the goalie. He downed a cup of water and turned to Peter. "Great playing out there today."

"It's been a while, but thanks," Peter said, in his Midwestern accent, and started to walk away.

The goalie followed Peter. "You're from the Twin Cities? I'd recognize that accent anywhere."

I swallowed hard. Why had Peter said so much?

"Yes, nice to meet ya," Peter said, and moved along.

The goalie kept following him. "My aunt and uncle live there. I swear you look so familiar."

Peter jabbed a thumb in the direction of the field. "Gotta get back to the team."

"Know the Richmonds? From Minneapolis?"

Peter shook his head. "Can't say that I do."

"Their son Oliver, my cousin, went to the championships there, and we went out from New Jersey for it. I was talking to Major Gilbert, and he said you went, too."

"Yup," Peter replied. "Seems like a million years ago now."

The goalie persisted. "You look just like a guy on his team. Kid went back to Germany with his parents, and the team never went to state again."

"Germany, wow."

"Name wasn't Donald, though. Peter something? I bet my mom still has the pictures."

I stepped toward them, ready to intervene. Should I pull Peter away? Claim our cousin Donald was needed elsewhere?

All at once Bess pushed past the players to me. "Cadence—"

"Not *now*, Bess," I said.

I looked beyond her to a crowd gathering at the sidelines, near where we'd been standing.

"Come quick," she said. "It's Gram."

33

BRIAR

1942

I KEPT MY EYE ON MAJOR GILBERT FOR THE WHOLE TEN MINUTES of the soccer match I watched. Once Army won, Major Gilbert high-tailed it to his office in the prefabricated Quonset hut, and I followed, pretending to look for the bathroom. I'd been up there a million times since that base had been built from nothing. The security wasn't exactly top notch, and I just scaled the back chain-link fence, so I knew it pretty well.

I walked along the Quonset hut hallway, listening as the celebrations on the field died down and following the sound of the major's voice. He was on the phone in his office, and I paused near the bathroom door and listened.

"No. I told you. It's happening in three days, no matter what."

I edged closer, my heart thumping. *His rendezvous with the U-boat?*

"That's right. I have to leave my men, but I must do what I have to do, am I right?" His chair scraped back. "I need to get back to the game."

The conversation went on like that for a while longer, and all of a sudden loud shouting came from the field—not celebratory, more panicked.

I ducked into the bathroom as the major hurried out of his office, his footsteps echoing down the hallway and outside. I waited a few seconds, followed him, and quickly saw what was happening at the field. A crowd had gathered where we'd been standing. Gil was running that way, and someone was shouting for an ambulance. I picked up speed and ran, already knowing what it was.

BESS STAYED HOME WITH PETER, and by the time we got to the hospital in Oak Bluffs, Gram was stable but looking pretty shaken. Cadence and I sat in the back of the Army ambulance with her, an Army medic driving like we were escaping tank fire on the battlefield. Major Gil followed in his jeep. Taking a break from his spy activities long enough to accompany Gram to the hospital? Maybe he was covering himself, seeing as Gram had collapsed on Army property. Or maybe he was just after my sister. It didn't add up completely, but I was getting there. For the moment I needed to focus on Gram.

We'd always known she was sick, but seeing her on the field, gasping for breath, scared the hell out of me. Thank God that Army medic was close by and came with oxygen.

It turned out Peter had been right: The problem was her lungs, after all, according to Dr. Nickerson, the intern on duty in the emergency room. He looked not that much older than me and like he'd been used for amphetamine research, his eyes red-rimmed, probably from working around the clock. The island couldn't exactly lure the cream of the medical crop to come down from Boston to treat sunburns and self-inflicted kitchen-knife cuts, but at least he got the diagnosis right.

When Cadence told him we'd been giving Gram a cocktail of aspirin and vinegar, he said it had probably saved her life. I said a silent thanks to Peter and finally relaxed a little. She was going to make it. Gram was more concerned about not being able to go to church the next day than anything else.

They would keep her for observation for a few days and then propose treatment. Whatever Gram needed, it would be expensive. As it was, a few nights in the hospital would eat up our loan-payment money for the month. But Gram's health was all that mattered.

They kicked us out once it started to get dark, and Gil gave us a ride home in his amazing jeep, me in the back seat, flying through the night, watching those two up front. They may have forgotten I was riding with them, since they talked like I wasn't there—a pretty innocuous conversation on the face of it but loaded with innuendo.

"I'd like to come by tomorrow," Gil said, "and check on how your grandmother's doing. I have the day off."

"That's nice of you," Cadence said. "A ride home tomorrow would be helpful. Maybe around six? I imagine we'll be visiting in shifts."

They were so formal with each other and not making much progress toward doing what they really wanted, which was to pull over and make out.

When we left Gil that night, Cadence was more than a little in love and I was more confused than ever. Was Major Gilbert the spy? What about that letter the postmaster gave him? He'd been captured by the Nazis and spent time with them. Maybe he'd been compromised. Maybe a double agent for Churchill? If that was true, perhaps he was just stringing Cadence along for a quick fling. But he did seem genuinely smitten with her, sneaking little glances now and then when she wasn't looking.

It would all unfold very soon. When the crew of the *Leopard* came to call.

34

CADENCE

1942

I DROVE THE TRUCK TO SEE GRAM AT THE HOSPITAL THE NEXT morning and stopped in Edgartown to drop off my column before tomorrow's nine o'clock deadline. It was good to have some time to myself to sort through everything. New York City. Gil. As much as I loved Bess, it was hard to talk to her about those things. She just wanted Tom to come home and me to stick around the Vineyard forever, in that order.

Though Winnie had said she'd keep an eye out for jobs down the road, it would probably be a while before I could leave my responsibilities on the island, not to mention the German in our attic, and it looked like another year would slip by without a real job. To make matters worse, Mr. Wespi was called up for military service and the club abruptly closed, leaving Bess and me without an additional paycheck. I tried to focus on the good things. At least Celia and Dolores said they read my column, the thought of which had caused me to stay up half the night working on the latest one. I was especially proud of the result.

I'd looked at starting salaries in the New York newspapers, and they were pitifully low. I'd barely be able to afford a shared room, never mind decent clothes.

I rolled down the truck window and my thoughts wandered to Gil. I'd never been attracted to anyone this way. It was almost painful to think about how he'd looked on the soccer field the day before. No wonder Amelia was so desperate to hold on to him. They'd probably kissed at least, and no doubt he was good at it. Briar had said they'd been arguing, but that didn't mean he gave a fig about me. Would he just ship out and happily leave me behind?

I parked and headed toward the *Gazette* offices. And as I hurried along the brick sidewalk, someone called from behind.

"You're avoiding me, I see."

I turned to find Mrs. Stanhope following me. She'd dressed for the ambush, in a lemon-yellow suit and white gloves.

"I didn't see you," I said.

"You need to be observant to make it in the publishing world. It's a den of snakes."

"I need to visit my grandmother in the hospital. Please make it quick."

"Has it ever occurred to you that Bess Ann is only using you all?"

I leveled a cool gaze at her. "Is that all you have, Lydia?"

"It's what she does. Has fun with a new concept and moves on. This time it's playing penniless farm girl. Next week it'll be something new."

"Maybe new mother to a child she wants to raise in a loving house. Unlike what she had growing up."

"Aren't you the feisty one?" She stepped closer. "Bess Ann is going to go through a very difficult time with that baby, even under the best circumstances. I want you to convince her to come home to have it."

"She'll never agree to that."

"If you tell her to, she will."

"Why now? You never cared about her when she was growing up. Shipped her off to boarding school."

"She's my only child, and the thought of a grandchild changes everything. It's a chance for us to reconcile. I can give the child everything. And with your grandmother in the hospital, poor woman, it's not a good place for a child right now. I miss my Bess. I think you can understand that. I hear your own mother was such a lovely woman, sweet Emma, running the library and all. I think she'd side with me."

"You didn't even know her."

"I simply want a second chance with my own daughter."

"Bess has a mind of her own."

"Just listen to my proposal. I think you'll find it's quite interesting." A smile teased Mrs. Stanhope's lips. "Why not get something out of this whole mess, a little security once Bess has gone off after the next bright shiny object? My roommate from boarding school is an executive at Simon & Schuster, and we've recently become reacquainted. Seems she's ready to offer you an editorial position. Ten thousand a year, if you can believe it, for a person like you, untrained as you are."

"Not interested," I said.

"And there may even be some cash in it for you."

"I'm not taking your money."

"It's all green and spends the same."

I turned and went on my way along the path. "No."

"Start that job whenever you want. Just convince my daughter to come home to have her baby. It doesn't have to be permanent. Seems a fair trade to me."

"I can get a job on my own," I said, over my shoulder.

"Well, not if you don't have that column anymore."

I turned. "What are you saying?"

"The editor at the *Gazette* is another friend of mine. And would stop printing your column the minute I asked."

"My God." I finally understood what people meant when they said they saw red, I was so angry. "I need to go."

"And if you think your friendship with Winnie Winthrop will help you, think again. I can and will poison the well on that one. All it would take is one call."

I tried to swallow but couldn't. "No, you won't."

"She's been telling everyone who will listen how talented you are. But did you tell her that you dropped out of high school in senior year? Miss Let Me Tell You About Literature, not even a high school graduate."

Of course Lydia Stanhope knew the one skeleton in my cramped little closet. I was so tired of it all. The hiding. The lies. At least she hadn't acted on seeing Peter.

"How did you become such a horrible person, Mrs. Stanhope?"

"Don't breathe a word of this to Bess or I'll go wide with it. I have friends at all the New York papers, long overdue to return favors."

I continued along the sidewalk.

"You've got twenty-four hours before I start reaching out about this, Cadence dear," she called after me. "I want Bess Ann home."

THE NURSE AT THE hospital allowed Gram to have the radio on in her room, and we listened to it for word of Tom, so desperate for news.

Later that afternoon Bess arrived for her turn to stay with Gram. How could I not tell my best friend about Lydia's ultimatum? I'd do it soon. Just not that minute.

After Gram fell asleep, Bess and I heard a full report about Dieppe, for the first time since it took place the week before. The commentator said that, as Gil had told me, only fifty of the men in Tom's regiment had been a part of the forces invading the Nazis on the beach in northern France at the coastal port town of Dieppe. A combination of Allied troops—the largest percentage by far Canadian—had landed and faced intense German forces. "*Though the losses were heavy, the men died bravely,*" he said. My heart went out to the Canadian troops who'd taken the worst of what sounded like a massacre, if you read between the lines; only one third of them had made it back to Britain. But only two American Rangers had died. Was Tom one of them?

I took Bess's hand as she sat in the visitor's chair. "Chances are he's fine," I said. "They would have contacted us by now if he wasn't."

Bess looked up at me. "I'm just so tired of crying, Cade. We need news at this point, even if it's bad."

She was right. The not knowing was the worst. Not even a letter from Tom. But maybe there was one on the way. Mail coming from overseas took forever. Bess and I agreed that it was better that Gram hadn't heard that report. We would tell her soon enough, when she recovered.

Once six o'clock came around, I gave Bess the truck keys and got ready for Gil to pick me up for a ride home.

"You know, I've been thinking that Major Gilbert may not be so bad after all," Bess said. "The way that he has been so helpful with Gram. Not that he isn't a testy sort sometimes, but who isn't some days? And there might be a good bit of humanity in there."

"Winnie told me I'm in love. Says she can always tell."

Bess smiled. "Winnie is positively orphic, I tell you, and completely right, of course. We can't help who we love. But you have to take what you want in that department, Cadence. It won't always come to you. Especially with people like dear Amelia around."

"I was thinking about asking him to come for a swim in the pond."

"There you go. I bet the major looks jolly good in a swimsuit. Or out of it. He can borrow Tom's trunks; they're in my drawer."

"He barely talks about anything important, though. Long stretches of silence."

"You have that effect on men. Tom told me that in seventh grade his friend Mark Ford could barely speak in your presence. Just bring some wine and ask him about war stuff. That'll get him chatty."

"It doesn't feel right leaving you here and having fun, with everything so up in the air about Tom."

"Briar's coming soon to keep us company, after she and Margaret stop for sandwiches to bring. It's going to be an extraordinarily fun time here tonight at Martha's Vineyard Hospital, so don't worry about us. And Tom would want you to go," Bess said, her eyes glassed with tears. "He knows all too well that the right person comes along only once, and you have to enjoy it, my dear friend, while it lasts."

GIL PICKED ME UP at the hospital and brought me back to the cottage, the shadows growing long. We talked about Tom and Dieppe, and little else, on the drive home. He seemed preoccupied, and I started to question the wisdom of asking him to stay for a swim. He had Amelia to think of, after all, even if they'd been quarreling, as Briar said. And he had all of his men to take care of. Also, how uncomfortable would it be if he turned down my invitation?

Gil drove to the front gate and braked, and I gathered myself to climb out.

He turned in his seat. "You know, I'm off duty tonight, and I was wondering if you'd like to . . . well, take that swim you talked about." He met my gaze directly. "In your rather magical pond."

I smiled to myself, relieved I didn't have to ask, and then got lost somehow, staring at his beautiful eyes. Green, but flecked with blue, I saw in that light. He must have taken my quiet as reluctance and continued, "It's just so bloody hot. If I'm being a nuisance—"

"No," I interrupted. "I mean, yes, let's swim. You can use my brother's trunks if you'd like."

He seemed relieved and turned off the engine. "Right, then."

We entered the house, and I switched on the lamp in the entryway. It was nice being with him in that snug cottage, just the two of us—with Peter hiding in the attic, of course, but mostly alone.

I led Gil to my bedroom, happy Bess had made our bed that morning as always, a habit she'd acquired from boarding school. I opened my bureau drawer, releasing the pine smell that had been there since it was my mother's so long ago, when she'd used balsam sachets and lined the drawers with red reindeer Christmas wrapping paper. What would she have thought of Gil? She probably would have liked him, once he'd warmed up to her. If she'd been there to see me going off to swim, she would have said, *Be a lady,* her favorite advice.

I pulled out Tom's old blue bathing suit, handed it to Gil, and then took mine out, as well, a white suit that Mrs. Jantzen had left in the club lost and found.

"I'll leave you to it," I said, and went to Gram's room to change.

Halfway there I turned back, having forgotten my shorts, and watched through the slightly ajar door as he pulled his shirt over his head, then slid off his trousers and underwear. I stood riveted to the spot by the beauty of it, surpassed only by the Adonis Uffizi I'd seen in an art history textbook. Maybe Gil's body was even handsomer, being flesh and not marble, and tanned the lovely color of worn saddle leather everywhere except where his shorts kept out the sun.

I crept away, afraid to be caught a voyeur. Then I stepped to the attic stairs, heard Peter softly snoring up there, and rushed to Gram's bedroom to change into my suit.

Would Gil and I kiss? I slipped on the suit and glanced at myself in Gram's mirror. My breasts weren't perfectly symmetrical, as I'd pointed out to Bess one day when we were changing. I smiled, remembering her reply. "I would kill to be that well-endowed," she said. "And breasts are sisters, not twins. Matching is for socks and eyeballs. Men don't care about symmetrical."

I skipped the shorts—Briar had said they made me look like a gym teacher, anyway—took a bottle of Gram's beetlebung-honey wine from the icebox, and met Gil out front. He was leaning against the front gate, completely re-dressed, his uniform pants cuffed at the ankles. The wind was picking up.

"Ready?" I asked, brandishing the wine bottle. "We need to hurry. It'll be dark soon."

We made it to the beach and the breeze swept his hair, the last of the sun setting his face aglow. My gaze wandered to our catboat, pulled up on the beach, thankfully above the high-tide mark. Of course, Briar had taken it out and forgotten to put it back in the boathouse, again.

"Nice suit," Gil said as we walked.

"To be honest, we don't always wear suits when it's just us girls." I made a mental note to slow down and let him come to me. If this was even anything more than a friendly dip.

"I'm sure the boys up at the base would be happy to hear that," he said.

I stopped and took a sip of wine from the bottle, suddenly overwhelmed by his presence.

"Straight from the bottle, is it?" he asked with a grin.

I set the bottle between us. "Unless you brought the crystal."

He lifted his shirt over his head and removed his trousers to reveal Tom's trunks. They were a bit tight in the seat but still fit well. Bess was right. He really did look jolly good in a suit.

I walked the twenty yards across the beach to Copper Pond, sat at the edge, and rinsed my feet. He followed with the wine, sat next to me, and turned his face to the sky. "It's lovely here. *Twilight drops her curtain down and pins it with a star.*"

I took a deep breath. Quoting Lucy Maud Montgomery? I held myself back from straddling and kissing him.

"So this is the famous Copper Pond," I said instead. "The minerals in the water give it that metallic shine. Make it feel like silk on your skin."

"Brilliant." He took a swig of the wine. "This is remarkably good."

"My Gram's recipe. With the honey the bees make from those trees up there. The beetlebungs."

We were quiet for a moment, listening to the night sounds. "I'll hate leaving here," he said. "Only a couple more days left."

I wasn't crazy about the thought of him leaving, either. Was anything going to happen between us? We exchanged a long look. Perhaps he was still smarting from his failed attempt in Oak Bluffs.

"You have a scar," I said, nodding toward his chest, just below his clavicle.

"My stab-wound souvenir. I don't talk about it much, but we were captured by the Germans. Six of us."

"Amelia mentioned it. You must have been terrified."

"They ambushed us, so it all happened quickly." He looked down at the scar. "They kept us at a POW camp near Schleswig. Two of us escaped, though. Made it back to England eventually."

I longed to smooth my fingers over the scar; to avoid that, I changed the subject.

"Speaking of Amelia," I said. It was the blond elephant in the room. I had to broach it.

He tossed a pebble into the pond. "She left this morning."

I took a long sip from the bottle. "She wasn't happy that I rode alone with you to Oak Bluffs."

He shook his head. "She lives in her own world."

"Your fiancée."

He laughed. "No. In her mind, maybe. I broke it off with her a few days ago, actually. It took her this long to accept it."

"It must be hard."

He looked at me. "It was mostly her doing the pursuing."

I waded into the pond, up to my chest. "I've never had a boyfriend, really."

"I find that hard to believe."

"The boys here aren't the least bit worldly."

He waded in. "That's important to you?"

"I suppose. It would be nice to at least find someone who knew how to kiss properly."

"Vineyard boys don't know how to kiss?"

"Not in my limited experience, with Lawrence Belson at the Chappaquiddick Club bonfire."

He swam to me. "Good to know it's a low bar."

I ran two fingers across the scar on his chest, bent and kissed it, letting my lips linger there.

He kissed my mouth, hard and urgent, with no pretense of softness, the stubble of his beard grazing my lips in a good way. He seemed to want it as much as I did.

I broke free first and touched my lips, bruised, and then went back for more. I lost track of time in that warm water, our bodies smooth against each other.

"Lawrence Belson doesn't know what he's missing," Gil said into my ear. "But I must say, if you'd rather not go down the garden path, we should probably take a cold ocean swim or something."

I had a feeling I knew what "the garden path" was, and nothing was keeping me from that.

"Have you ever skinny-dipped, Major? Is that what they call it across the pond?" It may have been the wine or Bess's urging me to live a little, but I liked my newfound boldness.

He smiled, teeth white in the darkness. "They call it wild swimming."

"It's a much better experience without suits."

I slid off my swimsuit and set it at the pond edge. He did the same and then pulled me close, his arms so warm around me, his chest smooth against my breasts. "You're the most beautiful thing I've seen in my life," he said as he kissed my neck, and I closed my eyes. It started to rain, the drops pattering on the water around us and wetting my upturned face.

"Perhaps we should make our way to somewhere dry," he murmured in my ear.

I smiled. "There's always the boat. It does have a small bed up front in the cabin."

We hurried across the sand, hand in hand, and ducked into the catboat cabin. I lay with Gil in the darkness, the wind gently swaying the boat. And gave myself up to the glorious weight of him.

UP-ISLAND HAPPENINGS

———

By CADENCE SMITH

THE PUTNAM YACHT, *Never Moor,* BELIED ITS NAME AND anchored off Salt Cove on our North Shore last week, and it offered a night worthy of Jay Gatsby. The lovely Putnam ladies, invited to the island by Mrs. Winifred Winthrop, are planning a literary treat for our troops abroad come next spring. Let's just say that, thanks to President Roosevelt, our lucky boys will have better access than the rest of us to the popular-seller shelves of the bookshops.

The dauntless Margaret Coutinho returned from her whirlwind trip to New York City, having emptied Bergdorf Goodman and dined at the Ship Ahoy Chop House on West 51st Street, where you enter from the street on an honest-to-goodness pirate gangplank. There she feasted on seafood rivaling our island's best and, staying loyal to our New England bivalves, insisted on ordering the Woods Hole clams.

If you're as impressed as I am by even the smallest feat of athleticism, such as bending to feed the cat, you'd have been astounded by the athletic prowess on display up at Peaked Hill on Saturday, where the Army soccer team beat Navy, in a battle befitting Julius Caesar, 4–3. Word is, after a rousing tug-of-war and a three-legged race, the Army players were last seen raising the coveted trophy to the sky in celebration before turning in for a 5:00 a.m. wake-up to do even more running. Pity the poor Germans, going up against our boys.

Mrs. Virginia Smith took ill after the soccer game and was escorted to our fine hospital by Private Harwell Dufree, a medic at Peaked Hill who hails from San Saba, Texas. "Mrs. Smith wrote to my mother for her pecan pie recipe and made it for me for my birthday, so I was glad to pay her back and get her to the hospital right quick," Private Dufree told me. All are hoping for a speedy recovery and for the donuts to return to the farm stand.

This week's lucky winner, Kimberly Krautter, gets to go to Manderley again. Come pick up your book, Daphne du Maurier's *Rebecca*, at the Copper Pond farm stand, and send it along to your neighbors when done.

35

BRIAR

1942

THE MERCURY WAS HITTING ONE HUNDRED DEGREES AND A STORM was on the way, as I climbed to my post atop my favorite beetlebung tree to cool off and try to quell my anxiety about everything. I'd cleaned both Mr. Schmidt's house and our whole cottage top to bottom with ammonia, swept the fireplaces clean, and warned Cadence that McManus might be preparing to show up. Our plan was to get Peter down to the boathouse once he woke, since he worked the farm at night and slept during the day.

But that worry was nothing compared to my fears about Tom. Why hadn't he written? We'd heard little from the Army, just a form letter promising an update soon. I checked the casualty list every morning at the post office, but his name hadn't shown up there. Talking to Cadence about it was no help, since she lay on the sofa like some lovesick Victorian on a fainting couch, probably reliving her swim with Major Gil the night before.

I'd heard Cadence tell Bess she'd gone swimming with Gil, which probably concluded in the boat cabin, since Bess had slept alone. If my sister wasn't careful, she'd end up like Bess, sitting around the house in Gram's old housecoat and throwing up every fifteen minutes, and blow her chance to go to New York City. Gil certainly wouldn't be around much longer, with the war going on and whatever sneaky thing he was up to. She'd better get out of here soon, before McManus threw me in prison and tried to take the rest of them with me. He wouldn't rest until he'd made his big score that sent him off to the land of fat cigars and Delmonico steaks. They might even blame Tom somehow.

I climbed to the highest branch and caught a cool breeze. I just felt closer to Tom up there, the sun high in the sky. Also, I could see if a car was coming with bad news. Before Gram went to the hospital, it had been hard to watch her at the window, waiting for someone to come down that drive, black Anglican prayer beads in her hand. And almost harder to see Scout at the front gate, at her post, waiting for Tom.

My gaze drifted to the rows of emerald potato plants in the upper field, Tom's Burbanks. That morning, before dawn, Peter had snapped off a flower bud and opened it with his thumb. "Won't be long now," he said. "Two days. Maybe three. But we'll need at least twenty men to harvest them."

I counted the available hands. Cadence and me, with Bess driving the truck. Peter, if he could help load them at night. Margaret could put us over the finish line. The proceeds would help Gram get better. And maybe keep the lights on awhile longer.

Out on the sound, the wind was starting to whip up some whitecaps. Was the U-boat out there, watching and waiting for their spy? Just one more day to go. If Peter was even telling the truth.

I looked toward the white steeple of the Chilmark Methodist Church in the distance as the bell tolled once, on a limited schedule due to the war. We were lucky to even have a bell. Throughout Europe, so many had been taken by the Nazis and melted down.

I loved that I could see all the way out to the main road—a good slice of it, anyway—through the trees, to the farm stand at the head of our road, which Tom and I had painted ourselves.

A movement caught my eye. It was a car. Not Margaret's, since she was at work. As it drove closer, I thought it might be the old Pontiac that I'd seen McManus around town in. I could see a man in the passenger seat. They turned onto our road, and I broke out in a cold sweat. It would take roughly six minutes for them to make it down Copper Pond Road and emerge from the woods at our house, depending on how concerned the driver was for his tires and how many potholes the car could take.

I scrambled down the tree, two branches at a time, and took my shortcut to the cottage, running like hell. I reached the front of the cottage and ducked inside.

I stepped out the front door as McManus pulled up and he and his minion got out.

"Hey," I said with a wave.

McManus nodded toward the flowers along the fence. "Nice lilies. Hope you don't mind us stopping by."

I stayed on my side of the fence. "It's not a good time, actually. My sister is sleeping." Would Peter hear us and wake? Be smart enough to hide in the closet upstairs? They'd probably look everywhere.

"Oh," McManus said, as he tried to see past me through the open front door. "Mind if we come in? Won't disturb your sister."

I stepped back toward the house, about to lose my lunch. "I'm not feeling well." All at once, a second car came down the road and emerged from the woods, with two uniformed men in the front seat. They parked and exited the car, both wearing the white pants and shirt of the Coast Guard. They strode to us with that all-business military step. It was like it was happening to someone else, in slow motion, a newsreel maybe.

"I'm Lieutenant Kiligrew of the Coast Guard at Woods Hole, ma'am. Is there a Virginia Smith at home?"

I wrapped my arms around my waist. "Tom."

How baby-faced the officer was, his pale cheeks flushed salmon pink. This was our notification team. They sent two in case a family member collapsed or went nuts and attacked them. We didn't get the chaplain, though.

Captain McManus and his deputy started toward their car. "We'll come back another time."

I could barely speak. "Gram's at the hospital," I said to the coast-guardsman. "I'm her granddaughter."

"Full name, please, miss?" he asked.

"Briar Rose Smith."

"If you don't mind, Miss Smith, I'd like to come in."

36

MARI

2016

$\mathbb{I}$ DECIDED TO STAY ANOTHER NIGHT AND MRS. DEVEREAUX MUST have used a tank of gas driving around the island as she told that tale. The last time I'd been that transfixed by a story was during an episode of *Long Island Medium,* when Theresa Caputo stopped a woman in a coffee shop and told her that her deceased father forgave her. But the tension was starting to get to me with this one.

"Can you tell me if Tom's going to be okay," I asked, as night began to fall. "Let's just cut to the end so I can know how this all applies to my mother."

At this rate I'd never paint anything, and I'd miss the next boat, too.

"I'm almost done," Mrs. Devereaux said, as she focused on the road, the old headlights barely piercing the darkness. I assumed we were on the way back to the farm and hoped she'd open a bottle of the good chardonnay when we got home. And more Ritz crackers and Cracker Barrel cheese. Rich people always ate the most surprisingly basic stuff. In L.A., Tori Spelling, our favorite customer at Jamba, came in every Monday for a water and a breakfast wrap, no meat or cheese—basically a warmed-up naked tortilla.

"Women were so awful to each other back then. That Mrs. Stanhope. And Amelia. And what was up with Peter? Why didn't he just leave?"

"It wasn't that easy getting off the island then. You needed to show identification. If he'd been caught, it would have been bad for them all."

I turned to Mrs. D. "You don't have to stop telling the story, you know. Happy to pull an all-nighter. My mom and I once sat up all night at a hotel in Joshua Tree, out there for her birthday. We weren't even tired the next day."

"Just talking?" she asked.

"About everything. Her best friend that moved away in grade school. My dad and how they met at a high school dance. How he died driving a truck cross-country. We had each other, but she would've had a whole different life if she'd grown up here. Of course, I wouldn't have been born."

Mrs. Devereaux pulled over at the head of a dirt road, next to a row of ten mailboxes. We sat in silence for a long moment, listening to the crickets and cicadas, and then she waved toward the glove box. "I'll tell you more soon. But first I need you to get something out of there for me."

I opened the glove box and found it practically empty, only an old silver flashlight atop the registration.

"Take out the flashlight?" she asked.

I pulled it out and tried to hand it to her, but she waved toward my door. "You can get out now."

"Are you serious?"

"I need you to do something for me."

I stepped out of the jeep, flashlight in hand, and closed the door. "Okay, what do you want me to do? Steal someone's *New York Times*?"

"Just walk down that road until you hear the ocean," she said, and then rolled off in the direction of the farm. "Turn right at the split in the road," she called as she zoomed away.

I stood in the dark for a bit, under a canopy of stars. Was this her way of getting me to go to Ronan's bonfire? We hadn't seen another car on that road in over an hour, so, not having much faith in the prospect of hitchhiking home, I switched on my flashlight and hit the dirt road.

—

I WALKED FOR OVER half an hour before I heard anything other than cicadas and an occasional noise from one of the few houses along the dirt road. The going was slow, since the flashlight kept flickering out and was so weak I could barely see the road in front of me. My phone wasn't much better. Was this some sort of Yoda lesson Mrs. D. was trying to teach me?

By the time I made it to the right fork, I could hear the ocean. I quickened my pace, stepped around a locked gate, and soon came to a long bridge over a pond, the moon rising, finally, for some more light. There must have been twenty swans on that pond, as still as could be, some bending their long necks to feed on something in the water.

I watched the swans for a while, then heard voices and moved on to the beach. The bonfire.

I emerged through the dunes and found them all there. Ronan White. Dutch-Braid Girl and a bunch of other equally laughy and *Vogue*-magazine-just-hanging-out-on-a-private-beach-photo-shoot-on-Martha's-Vineyard types. Waves pounded the shore as they all lounged around the perfect bonfire, in their plaid flannel shirts or hooded sweatshirts, as a whole burning tree trunk shot a column of flame into the night sky. The only thing that could've made the scene more absurdly perfect would have been s'mores.

I had no choice but to join them, since they saw me, and if I didn't get someone to drive me home, I'd have to make that walk back.

Ronan stood and came to me as I trudged through the sand toward them, my gauzy blouse not the right layer for the strong ocean wind.

"You made it," he said.

He took off his sweatshirt and wrapped it around my shoulders, the fleecy part still warm from him.

"Mrs. D. dropped me off," I said. "Kind of a forced situation. Though I'm happy I made it."

We sat on a log near the fire and hung out for a while, taking cold beers from the cooler someone had brought. His friends were actually pretty nice. And Dutch-Braid Girl turned out to be his stepsister—she was not as annoying as I thought she might be and told me about a clothing store called Pandora's Box that I had to check out in Menemsha, which she said was my vibe.

Ronan wasn't my usual type, which was emotionally unavailable with a splash of narcissism, but maybe it was good to switch things up. We talked about everything and nothing. How he made amazing bluefish pâté. And what bread to use for the perfect breakfast sandwich, with us agreeing that it was croissant, not biscuit.

We were quiet for a while, listening to the pop of the fire. "Mrs. Devereaux's telling me some long, rambling story."

"About what?" He stood and got us both another beer.

"The history of that farm. About the sisters who lived there."

"That's so personal." He opened my beer and handed it to me. "She doesn't seem like the type to just share like that."

"Not sure it's all true. She might be a little senile."

He tipped his head to one side. "To be honest, I think she's pretty *compos mentis*. She remembered me, and I met her only once."

I sipped my beer and considered that. Who wouldn't remember Ronan White? He looked amazing, unshaven, with the fire shining in his eyes, his hair loose and tousled by the wind. And if he kept throwing around the Latin, I might have to force myself on him right there. For some reason it was a huge aphrodisiac for me and was something rare to hear in L.A., unless you counted the theme song of Super Smash Bros., sung entirely in Latin.

"This may be way off base, but I'm pretty sure the whole story is connected to me somehow. Like that's my long-lost family or something."

He toasted me and drank his beer. "That would be wild. But I wouldn't be surprised." He leaned over and smoothed back a lock of my hair. "You strike me as a real Vineyard girl. There aren't many of those left anymore. Everyone's a washashore now, imported from somewhere else."

A real Vineyard girl. Something about that sent a velvety warmth down my shoulders. That *would* be wild.

I rubbed the label off my beer with my thumb. "Well, it's getting kind of intense, to be honest. I wish she'd cut to the chase."

"If you're connected to that place, you'd better figure it out soon. Some big Boston construction company is trying to buy it. They want to develop it."

"No way. She never said anything."

"It's been in the paper. Mrs. Devereaux tried to give it to the land bank, but the developer is challenging the will. Saying she's not related to the original owners."

I was silent for a while. How tragic would that be? Is that why she'd encouraged me to come?

"Painted anything?" Ronan asked.

I shook my head. "Nothing."

He threw a stick into the fire. "That happened to me a while ago. It comes back. You can't force it. Sometimes just getting your life sorted out helps. If you're clogged, how are you supposed to paint?"

"I'm not that good, anyway." I finished my beer. "No great loss."

He looked at me so seriously. "It's not always about the finished product. And, anyway, who's to say what's good?"

Once things started winding down, we walked across the bridge to his car—a beat-up Volkswagen, but at least it would get us out of there and back to civilization.

"Winter must be terrible here," I said as he drove me home.

"Not at all. It's my favorite time. Quiet. And you can get into the best restaurants. I paint and read and cook and fish. I'm in the bluefish derby coming up this fall."

I tried to remember what Nate and I had watched on Netflix that month on my account, our go-to for fun.

Every light in the place was on when we got to the cottage, and he parked at the fence gate, motor running.

"If you ever want to just talk, I'm here. I lost my mom, too, so, you know, I get it."

He took my hand and held it for a moment. Such a simple thing, but it made me want to cry.

Ronan waited for me to get inside, and I let the screen door bang behind me. I found Mrs. Devereaux at the kitchen table, playing soli-taire and munching on Ritz crackers and cheese. She was drinking what looked like a martini in a jelly-jar glass, if the olive was any indication.

"Join me?" she asked.

"Are you kidding? Yes."

She stood and fixed me a martini, adding two olives on a toothpick.

"Thanks for abandoning me. I saw Ronan White, of course."

She looked over her shoulder at me. "Wasn't that a surprise."

"He told me developers want this place."

"Did he?" she asked.

"Yes. Is that why I'm here? Can you get to that part in the story?"

She handed me the martini. "Did you have fun with Ronan? He had a girlfriend, you know, but she moved to Santa Fe last year and married a hotel manager."

I took a second to process that—it made me feel oddly effervescent. "Yes, but now you owe me." I pulled out a chair and sat. My paints, brushes, and a canvas lay stacked on the table, and just seeing them made me want to paint.

"You need to tell me how my mother and I fit into this story," I said, and set up my canvas. "And I'm not leaving this chair until you finish it."

37

CADENCE

1942

I HURRIED INTO THE COTTAGE AND FOUND BESS AND BRIAR SIT-
ting on chairs in the living room, a Coast Guard lieutenant on the sofa,
his white uniform hat and a leather case next to him. There was another
officer standing near the door, outside.

"Why didn't you call me?" I asked no one in particular, pulsing
with jagged, aching fear. He was here about Tom, of course. They
didn't take an officer from his duties to chat. Why did they send the
Coast Guard when there was a whole camp of Army men right up the
hill?

"He just got here," Briar said, with a haunted look I'd never seen on
her. All at once I wanted my mother.

Briar introduced me and I sat on the sofa next to the lieutenant,
folded my hands in my lap, and floated in that gauzy place between
hope and reality, running through the options. *The lieutenant could be
here to tell us Tom is missing. Or wounded. Why did they send someone so
young?* I glanced up at the ceiling. *Is Peter down in the boathouse or upstairs listening to it all?*

I stood. "Would you like a molasses cookie, Lieutenant? My Gram
made them."

"No, thank you—"

"We have some scones, too, but those are a bit stale now, I'm afraid.
You must be hungry, though, all the way from Woods Hole."

He looked up at me. "You may want to sit down, Miss Smith."

I walked to the kitchen and back. "My brother, Tom, considered your branch of the service before he became an Army Ranger."

Briar reached for my hand. "Come sit, Cade."

"Not that the Coast Guard is inferior, not at all, but his friends were going to the Army."

"For God's sake, just sit down, Cadence," Bess said, her face drained of all color.

"Yes, of course." I sat. "Go ahead, Lieutenant."

"The commandant of the U.S. Army has entrusted me to express his deep regret that Thomas Smith"—

Bess made a frantic little wave. "Please don't say it."

—"was killed in action in Dieppe, France, on August nineteenth. The commandant extends his deepest sympathy to you and your family in your loss."

He handed me a certificate from his case, and I read aloud, "*Missing in action and presumed dead. Died in the service of his country.*"

Bess bent over and let out a sob. "Oh, no."

The horror of it hung in the room. I sat there, numb, and could not even cry. None of it seemed real.

"So, there's no body?" Briar asked.

The lieutenant gathered his things and prepared to leave. "We will be in touch with a follow-up appointment to discuss the details."

Tom was dead. I tried to poke myself with the thought to make it seem real. Thank God our parents weren't here to see it. And Gram. But I would have to tell her.

"Wait," Briar said. "You're *leaving*?" She nodded toward us. "If this were your family, would you leave them this way? With no details? You need to tell us more."

I brought the certificate to Bess and tried to console her, but she pushed me away.

Briar stood. "Not that you Coasties will ever be in danger, safe here in happy land. A hard day of condolence calls and it's back to the barracks for some poker, am I right?"

"*Briar,*" I said.

He sat up straighter. Apparently, the Coast Guard handbook didn't offer guidance on a grieving family that didn't accept the scripted message.

Tears stung my eyes as Briar fought on. It was hard to accept such brutal news, but Briar, the original doubting Thomas, would not go easily without definite proof. I had my doubts, as well, but her desperate denials only made it harder on all of us, especially Bess.

The lieutenant stood. "There's a number on the back of the certificate in case you have more questions."

"Did he suffer?" Bess asked, her face puffy and tearstained. "Tommy?"

"No, ma'am." The lieutenant stepped out of the door, into the sunshine, and walked back to his car with his fellow officer. Mission completed.

Briar wrapped her arms across her waist. "I don't understand. How can they just assume he's dead?"

"Leave it for now, Briar," I said, sinking deeper into despair. Only two Rangers had died. Why did Tom have to be one of them?

Tom would want us to tell Gram gently. How could I even speak those words? *Our Tom didn't make it.* That would almost be worse than hearing the news myself.

"Until we have his body, we shouldn't even tell Gram," Briar said.

"Sometimes you have to accept things, Briar," I said.

"Not this," Briar said. "Never. Tom would want us to find the truth."

I heard steps in the kitchen, and Peter appeared at the doorway. "I'm sorry for your loss."

"Thanks," I said, wishing he'd stayed upstairs. I could barely look at him.

"I can tell you what I think is the truth," he said quietly.

"Please," Briar said.

He exhaled. "Clearly the raid was a failed operation."

"So you're the expert?" I asked, stepping next to him.

"I'm sure the Germans would have returned intense fire, and the regiment probably had to leave him behind."

I examined Peter's German face, his square jaw and blue eyes. He was a part of the machine that caused Tom's death.

"You know what?" I raised my hand, and he didn't even flinch as I landed a slap, hard, across his face. "I wish it had been you instead of Tom." I paused, happy to see the red patch blooming on his cheek. "How's that for truth?"

Peter looked at me like he was about to say something, then slowly climbed the stairs.

Briar turned to me. "It's not his fault."

My hand buzzed with the slap, so satisfying, and I itched to do it again. "Really? He's one of them, like it or not."

"How can you be so unfeeling?" Briar asked. "Accept it so easily?"

I faced Briar. "Don't you dare tell me how I feel, you spoiled brat. I loved Tom more than you can ever know."

Bess stood, unsteady on her feet. "Stop it! Both of you. We have to stay together."

I went to the phone. "I'll call Pastor Harshfield to arrange the service, and Briar and I will go tell Gram. And you'd both better make sure Peter stays upstairs. Things could actually get worse."

THE MARTHA'S VINEYARD BEACH and Book Club took up the front pew of the Chilmark Methodist Church for Tom's service. *Full attendance for once*, I thought. Tom, always a good audience, would have laughed at that.

Briar and I sat on either side of Gram, each of us holding one of her hands; she'd been sprung from the hospital for two hours only, on strict orders from Dr. Nickerson. We all sang Tom's favorite hymn, "Christ the Lord Is Risen Today," which was usually sung only on Easter, but an exception was made. Pastor Harshfield had made an exception for Scout, too. She lay at Gram's feet, head resting on the kneeler, perhaps knowing how much Gram needed her. The pastor told stories about Tom as a child and how, years before, he'd helped our father hang the new bell in the church steeple, a gift from the Odd Fellows of Oak Bluffs.

My thoughts collided. There was no casket. No body to bury. There was a chance Tom was still out there somewhere, but it was almost more painful to hold out hope. A dull buzz of despair coursed through me. I was tired of being strong, slogging through suffering with that New England stiff upper lip.

All cried out, I tried to remember the good days with Tom. Catching eels through the ice on Quitsa Pond. The time he left the heart bracelet under my pillow for my sixteenth birthday. I'd worn it that day as an homage to Tom, and I ran one finger along it. So much for good luck. It felt strange to not have Tom here with us. He always sat on the end of the pew so he could jump up to help with the offering, holding the rectangular basket by the long handle, shaming everyone to donate, jingling it when he passed it by his friends.

I turned and checked the crowd. The church was packed, with many of the soldiers from Peaked Hill, all Gram's church ladies, and almost everyone from town. Tyson Schmidt was there, looking good in his uniform, sitting with Shelby Parker in a back pew. Worrying he might be going off to meet a similar fate?

But there was no sign of Major Gilbert.

Tonight would be the new moon, and if Peter was right, someone would be paddling out to meet a U-boat off our coast. I checked the crowd for possible spies and immediately felt ridiculous. I'd known most of the people in that community my whole life. None of them would betray their country.

At the reception line after the service, Gram sat in a chair and shook hands with guests, and I helped her recall names. "I can't remember from the latch to the door these days, I'm afraid," she would say if she couldn't put a name to a face.

Tyson Schmidt, his face tear-streaked, greeted Briar in line. Tom's friend. Tom had taught Tyson to sail. I tried to picture him as a spy. With his baby face and earnest way, not to mention the uniform, it seemed doubtful.

Briar came to me. "Captain McManus is here. I just want you to know that he was at the house yesterday. Probably wants to come back."

I greeted more guests until the front church doors opened and Gil hurried in from outside. He pressed his warm hand in mine. "I'm sorry to be so late, Cadence."

How good it was to see him. "Gil." I held on to his hand. He looked tired.

He leaned closer. "I couldn't get away from a meeting, and I'm sorry to ask this of you, but could we speak privately after this is over, perhaps back at your house?"

"Of course," I said, and he left as quickly as he'd come.

What was that about? It seemed like a positive thing, but one never knew with the major.

Captain McManus approached me soon after, murmuring platitudes. "I'd like to come by the hospital, if I could, and talk with you and your grandmother."

"Talk about what, Captain?"

"Your sister. There have been some irregularities and—"

"*Really*, Captain? This is my brother's funeral and you're here to do business?"

"I have a job to do."

"Perhaps look for someone a little more mature to stalk. Why are you going after a troubled sixteen-year-old girl who grew up without a mother?"

"You may not know what she's been up to."

"*Captain*. Look around you. We are grieving. My grandmother has a lung condition, which they haven't yet figured out how to treat, and she just lost her grandson who meant the world to her and to all of us, so if you don't back off, I will ask Chief Leo to have you removed."

He had the decency to look chastened. "Another time, then."

He walked off and I greeted the next well-wisher in line. I could barely think, going through the motions of interacting with the guests, everything tumbling down on me. No matter how I stalled, no matter how well we hid Peter, McManus would find him. That's what he did for a living, and despite the crusty exterior, he was probably really good at it. Why had we been so stupid, keeping Peter? Letting him kick a soccer ball around Peaked Hill? Were those Navy guys on to him? It was time to send him on his way. He'd helped with the farm, but what was the point of that anymore?

A dreadful sucking feeling weighed me down. Tom would not be coming home to us. He would never see Bess again. Or their child. He would never see his Burbanks harvested. It seemed selfish to think of it, but I'd never have the money to go to New York, to send money home to help Gram. At least Mrs. Stanhope wasn't there, lowering the boom, but that loomed over me, as well.

My gaze wandered to Briar there in line, doing her best to greet family friends and neighbors. She was so young and brilliant and would probably end up in juvenile detention somewhere for all of this. Maybe she was just too smart. Bess stood next to her, doing her rich-girl I-can-talk-to-anyone thing. Would she have her baby in prison? And Putnam would never hire a felon.

I exhaled. I had to compose myself and think straight. *If you can't move heaven, then just raise hell.* We didn't have Tom, but soon we'd have his child to raise. We would need to get Peter out of our house sooner than planned. He'd require an identity card and some money and he'd be on his way to Minneapolis. We just needed another meeting of the book club.

38

BRIAR

1942

I GOT THROUGH TOM'S FUNERAL IN ONE PIECE, JUST GLAD I DIDN'T have to get up and speak or something. That crowd wouldn't have reacted well to my eulogy, the main point being that my brother was not actually dead and they were all pawns in the military's scheme to use up our servicemen and discard them.

I walked back to the house with Scout at my heels and left everyone else at the church hall, eating the slightly stale donuts Gram had made before her hospitalization. It was hard to watch all of them standing around so sorrowfully, accepting whatever the U.S. military told them. Making themselves feel better by chatting about what a hero Tom had been. Why did people just believe everything they were told without questioning and not think for themselves? Hitler had done pretty well with that. The German people swallowed whatever he told them. Mr. Schmidt had always said that's what would eventually be Germany's downfall—hearing only what they wanted to believe.

I had tried to shake the constant loop of horrible thoughts about Tom by examining the church crowd for spies. That church was full of islanders, mostly women and soldiers, with so many off at war, but I checked each row. Young Fred Fisher. Chief Leo. Mr. Reed. None of them in a million years. My thoughts went to Peter, at home. What if he had planted this red herring and he was actually the one going out to the boat?

Tyson Schmidt had shown up with Shelby, who'd even changed out of her sandals for once. In the receiving line Tyson said some nice things, and he seemed genuinely saddened by the news of Tom's death, but our conversation ended in a quarrel when he asked me to give the tugboat model back.

"C'mon, Briar. I know you have it somewhere. One day you're at my house and the next day it's gone."

"This is Tom's funeral," I said. "Can you live without it for another day? You didn't even care about it until I wanted it."

My mind spun with options about who would be meeting the U-boat that night. The new moon, which reflected none of the sun's light, would provide someone with complete cover out there. I had narrowed down my suspects to two. I was glad it would finally come to a head.

When I got to the cottage, I noticed Margaret's car parked down near the path to the boathouse. She'd made it home quickly. Since she returned from her yacht trip, she'd been staying in the boathouse, practically living with us when she wasn't at work at the drugstore. Gram, ever generous, had insisted she stay as long as she wanted. I could barely think about Gram not being here with us someday. Not so close on the heels of Tom's supposed death.

Peter was probably upstairs, staying out of sight. He'd had quite a scare when the Navy guys almost exposed him. There was no reason why they couldn't just call the cops about him.

I took the binoculars to the bluff and searched the sound for the U-boat. If they were out there, they were staying submerged. I fed Scout and went to Gram's room to change out of my funeral clothes— and found that the shortwave was missing from the hatbox on the closet's top shelf. I tossed the hatbox to the floor and felt around the whole shelf, my heart whacking against my sternum. How long had it been gone? And who'd been in the house to take it?

I heard footsteps above me in the attic.

Peter. Of course it was him. He'd been there throughout the funeral. He was such a talented actor and so good at gaining our trust. He was probably using the shortwave the whole time we'd been gone, communicating with the U-boat. Of course he was the one going back to Germany. Taking something with him the Germans wanted badly.

I had to be careful. What if he had a gun? I strode to the kitchen and grabbed Gram's fish knife from the drawer, then crept up the back stairway to the attic.

I found Peter on the bed, belly down, shining Gram's silver flashlight out the little window, clicking it on and off. Obviously communicating with the U-boat.

Blood pounded in my ears. How had I not seen?

I APPROACHED THE BED and held out the knife. "So, when were you going to tell us?"

Peter turned and sat up.

I moved closer. "Communicating with your friends? How could you?"

"I'm not—"

"*Quiet.*" I waved the knife. "Don't move. And hands up."

He raised his arms. "I can explain, if you allow me to speak."

"Where's the radio?" I asked.

Peter shook his head. "I don't understand."

"*Please.* I'll search your things. Or do you have it stashed in the house somewhere?"

Behind me, I heard footsteps on the stairs—Margaret. "My God, Briar."

I kept my gaze on Peter. "I caught him signaling his U-boat friends."

Margaret came to my side. "Put the knife down, Briar."

I held it steady. "He's the one meeting them tonight, and I'm sure he has Gram's shortwave. Took it from Gram's closet." I glanced at her. "Get some rope."

"No," Margaret said. She stepped toward the bed and turned. "He was signaling me."

I looked from her to Peter. "I don't understand."

Margaret went to sit on the bed next to him. "Since Peter can't use the phone, he uses the flashlight to tell me when it's safe to come up from the boathouse and . . . well, visit. Please don't tell the others."

Peter took her hand. "I know it was a breach of trust."

"I wanted to tell everyone," Margaret said. "But I wasn't sure you'd understand."

They seemed to be genuinely affectionate, but what did I know about that? I wasn't sure how I felt about the two of them bunking up behind our backs. It seemed to me an inconvenient time to suddenly fall in love.

I lowered the knife. "Well, someone took that radio from Gram's room."

Peter waved toward his knapsack. "You may search my things, the room. It is not here, I assure you."

"Then who took it? We're kind of getting down to the wire here. Someone's meeting the U-boat tonight."

"Any theories?" Margaret asked.

Could I speak freely in front of Peter? Or Margaret, for that matter? None of us knew her all that well. Peter seemed like such a caring person, but he could easily be scamming Margaret, who wasn't exactly experienced with men, and the rest of us, too. But my gut said he was telling the truth. And I needed his help, so I hurried to my room to get the photos, then returned to the attic.

"This is getting serious," I said. "Someone's going out there tonight. I've narrowed the spy possibilities to two: Major Gilbert and Tyson Schmidt."

Peter sat forward. "I know the major, obviously, but who is Tyson?"

"Our neighbor, the grandson of my deceased friend Conrad Schmidt."

"The one decorated in World War I?" Peter asked. "I actually overhear a lot up here."

"Yes. Mr. Schmidt was a true hero. And his grandson is eighteen." I handed Peter the photos. "I found some pictures in Mr. Schmidt's house that maybe you could look at?"

Peter took the photos and examined them. First was the crowd in the forest, with their arms raised in a Nazi salute.

"The one of the crowd is clearly a Nazi rally," I said. "I'm thinking it was probably taken in the woods near Hitler's house in the mountains."

How many newsreels had we all seen of Hitler at his vacation home in the Bavarian Alps? Staged footage of him with Eva Braun, smiling with his advisers.

Peter then looked at the house with the swastika embedded in the stucco beneath the eaves.

"And in that one, do you recognize the architecture?" I asked.

"No," Peter said. "Because these photos were not taken in Germany."

"I know they're not wearing armbands," I continued, "but I'm thinking—"

"If you would listen for a moment, I will tell you how I know." Peter held up the photo of the rally in the forest. "First of all, those are hickory trees behind them. There hasn't been a hickory tree in Europe since the Ice Age, when they all died off and became extinct. Plus, see the man here in the brown shirt?"

"In the Nazi uniform?" Margaret asked.

"Nazi uniform, yes. German man, no. He is giving a military-style salute. In Germany, they salute with only one arm raised."

How had I missed that? "You're right, of course."

Peter considered the photo of the house. "And this one was taken here in the United States, as well."

I pulled a chair closer and sat down. "But there's a swastika under the eave there. And ADOLF HITLER STRASSE?"

"This is not a German town. Our street signs don't look like this."

"I just don't understand why Mr. Schmidt would have these. He's lived here on the island ever since he left the military."

"But where did his family live? His children?"

"He had one son, Tyson's father," I said. "He and his wife lived somewhere in New York, where Tyson grew up. Visited the island for a few weeks each summer, I think. But Conrad never talked about them much."

Peter said, "Do you have a magnifying glass?"

Margaret fetched Gram's, which lived downstairs on her folded newspaper.

Peter examined the photos again. "This one of the crowd is definitely not Germany." He looked up at me. "It is Camp Siegfried, in Yaphank, Long Island, at least according to the sign there—very small."

"What? No."

"And the house with the swastika is here in America, as well." He offered me the magnifying glass. "Look for yourself."

I waved it away. "I believe you. But why would Mr. Schmidt have these?"

"My bet would be they belong to his son. Perhaps Tyson grew up in Yaphank," Peter said. "They have a large German American population. I read about it in *Frauen-Warte* magazine, back in Germany. One of my crewmates was joking about defecting there. To the Bund."

I swallowed hard. I'd read about the Bund—Nazi wannabes who assembled in Manhattan at large rallies. They'd had a sellout crowd at Madison Square Garden. A group of Bund leaders had even traveled to Germany, hoping to meet Hitler. After Pearl Harbor, the Bund had not been so open about their activities, but they likely hadn't lost their ardor for Hitler, either.

I hesitated. Could I trust Peter about the ring? "To be honest, I also found a ring in Mr. Schmidt's things."

"What kind?" Peter asked.

"A Totenkopf."

Peter shook his head. "Impossible. Those are for Himmler's most trusted advisers. It must be a fake."

"I don't think so. And it was inscribed *To Kuno*."

"*Kuno* is another word for *Conrad* in German, but it also means *Junior*. Perhaps those are Mr. Schmidt's son's things. Perhaps he gave the ring to his grandson?"

"It's hard to believe it might be Tyson," I said. "He's in uniform, due to ship out. And he was Tom's friend. Though he has been having some trouble with German prejudice."

"If he grew up around the Bund, then he may be sympathetic to Hitler. Like his parents. Where are they?"

"Traveling."

Peter shrugged. "To Germany, maybe?"

"What about that girlfriend of his?" Margaret asked.

I thought for a moment. "Shelby? I hadn't considered her."

"Any other suspects?" Peter asked.

"Major Gilbert," I said.

Peter exhaled and looked away. "I've had a strange feeling about him since I met him."

"Me, too," I said. "And a local antiquities dealer said Major Gilbert knew a lot about the Nazi stuff she had in her shop. Plus, he was a German POW."

"This is a hard choice, if it even is one of them," Peter said. "Tyson fits the profile of a traitor in some ways. Young. Headstrong. Ostracized by his own country for his German name, perhaps. But the major may fit, as well. A man once held by the Nazis. It's not outside the realm of possibility that a British officer would become sympathetic to the German cause and end up spying here."

"And it could be Shelby, to be honest. She'd be easily manipulated. Her father works for Hitler's friend Henry Ford. Probably big Charles Lindbergh fans."

Margaret stood. "Can we follow all leads?"

"Why not?" I asked.

Down below, I heard Cadence come home. "Cadence can check out Major Gil. And I'll take Tyson."

Peter sent me a dark look. "In the end we may just have to wait and see what happens tonight. Someone is meeting that boat."

39

CADENCE

———

1942

Gram was exhausted by the time the funeral reception wrapped up and I brought her back to the hospital. Though she'd already buried two children—my mother and uncle—the news of Tom's death was the one to finally break her physically.

I drove home and went to the kitchen, trying not to look at Scout stretched out by the hearth, resting her head on her paws. Gil would be here soon to distract me from the pain of missing Tom.

I found an envelope addressed to me on the kitchen table. A telegram. I opened it, thinking for a moment it might be the Army with news. They had made a mistake. Tom was still alive. I pulled the telegram from the envelope and read, *OUR DEEPEST CONDOLENCES. WINNIE AND YOUR PUTNAM FRIENDS.* I held the paper to my chest. Of course there had been no mistake. That infinitely kind gesture from Winnie and the girls made me wish we could rewind and go back to our night on the yacht, still unaware of Tom's death.

Gil pulled up out front, and I called upstairs to warn Peter of his arrival and to stay in the attic. I met Gil at the front door, and we stood in the darkened living room.

He removed his hat when he entered. "I know this is highly unusual, and I apologize in advance for speaking of it on the night of your brother's service."

"Shall we sit?" I asked, putting the telegram on the table.

"There's no time. I just want you to know that my life is complicated right now."

I braced for it. *He was married.*

"No, I don't have a wife stashed away in my attic," he said, as if reading my thoughts. "But I am leaving sooner than expected, and I need to know if you'd be willing to follow me in a life that is . . . well, unorthodox to say the least."

"Follow you where?"

He stepped close to me. "I know I've been a most irritating boor to you, and I'll be happy later to enumerate the ways. But please know that I've wanted you from the day I met you."

I laughed. "That's hard to believe."

"I'm sure of it. I have the brain of a kipper sometimes, though. Petrified of happiness, or some other dodgy male affliction."

I was dizzy at the thought. It was such a turnaround. He looked so sincere, but it was almost too good to be true.

"I know it's sudden, but I don't want you to slip away. Who knows how long the war will go on, but please consider coming to London when all this is over. Meet my mother."

I barely knew what to think. "Are you serious?"

He took my hands in his. "I couldn't be more so. You just need to wait for me. Not get snapped up by Lawrence Belson. I'm not the get-down-on-one-knee type, and that may be premature anyway, but I want to be with you. Of that, I'm sure."

I stepped away from him. "It's all so unexpected." Tom's death. Gil's abrupt declaration of love. His ex-fiancée's recent departure from the island.

He followed. "I like to think you return a *bit* of what I'm describing?"

It could be wonderful. There were publishing houses in London. But there was something odd about it all. People often fell in love very quickly—I already had immense feelings for him, as well—but marriage?

I nodded. "You know I do."

Gil kissed me quickly. "I need to go. But I'll be in touch, my darling."

He left the way he came, and I touched my fingers to my lips. He'd loved me the whole time? Not that he used the word *love*, but I felt it. Meet his mother? It was practically a proposal.

Briar stepped into the kitchen. "I hope you're not serious about marrying him."

I turned to her. "You've been hiding here all this time?"

She nodded. "Isn't it all a bit odd? Last week he barely spoke to you. Now he wants you to meet Mummy."

Of course Briar couldn't be happy for me. "People change, Briar. You'll see when you find someone you care about."

"He told you he's leading an unorthodox life, Cade."

"He does have an unusual life. Including shipping off to war soon."

"Sounded to me like he was warning you he might be involved in something more nefarious. 'I'm leaving sooner than expected'?" Briar stepped closer. "If he's the spy, he might be trying to lull you into inaction with a marriage proposal."

I waved that thought away. "Oh, please don't tell me you're serious. He was appointed by Churchill himself."

"Allegedly."

"I'm tired, Briar. Can't you just be happy for me? After everything we've been through with Tom, I need some sort of hope."

"You'll believe anything if it gets you out of here."

"Is it so bad that I want something better for us all?"

"Your attraction for him is clouding your judgment. What if he really is the one meeting the U-boat tonight?"

"*Gil?* Are you insane?"

"Sandra at Island Treasures had her doubts. Said he knew a lot about the Nazi merchandise."

"You do, as well."

"And I heard him on the phone the day of the soccer match, saying he had to leave his men."

"Perhaps he's being reassigned. He's an officer in the British Army, for God's sake."

"He spent time behind enemy lines. Could have been compromised. It's not unprecedented."

"His family is extremely wealthy."

"And has contacts with Germany probably, am I right? But things aren't always done for money. Ideological reasons, too." Briar paused, then, "I saw him pick up a letter at the post office. And overheard the postmaster saying it was from Switzerland. A woman named Greta."

"So much for postal privacy."

"They thought it odd that it had been sent through regular mail, not Army. They also said he'd been snooping around at the Katama firing range."

"You've been following him."

"The clerk at Briggs's told me he bought a diamond-and-pearl necklace, too, which hasn't materialized for you, right? You have to admit it's all very odd."

I moved away from her. "Well, this is your wildest theory yet, Briar. And that's saying a lot. This entire spy thing is ridiculous. What we need to do is find Peter an identity card and get him out of here. Or tell McManus and be done with it. I'm sick of it all."

"Want me to go to prison? You, too, probably. Major Gil would be history, and Gram would probably die in prison. Like it or not, this is the path we chose, and we have to see it through. And I don't think you want to marry a spy, right? Tom wouldn't want that."

I bit the inside of my cheek. "Of course not."

"A U-boat is picking someone up tonight. Isn't it smart to at least rule the major out?"

"I can't just ask him about his spy past."

"Go up to Peaked Hill—you might even uncover someone else we haven't thought of. Bring some more books for the troops or something, as cover, and leave them in his office. It's right across from the bathroom."

"How do you know these things?" I asked.

"Have a look in his drawers. His closet if there is one. Really drill down. You may find something."

"Piano wire? A vial of cyanide?"

Briar looked gravely serious. "That letter from Greta, for a start. Photos. Reconnaissance. You'll know it when you see it."

"I can't believe I'm considering this," I said.

"I'm hunting down leads on my end, too. Thinking about Tyson Schmidt."

"Oh, please. Peter is probably wrong about all of this."

"We can't just let someone board a U-boat tonight to report back to Hitler."

I studied Briar's face, so earnest. What would it hurt to make her happy? We owed it to Tom to follow every lead.

"Fine. I'll go up there now."

40

BRIAR

———

1942

ONCE CADENCE HAD GONE UP TO PEAKED HILL TO CHECK OUT Major Gil, I made one last sweep of the cottage for the shortwave. Maybe Gram moved it? I stepped to the mantel and took down the tugboat model Mr. Schmidt and I had made. I turned it in my hands. Why did Tyson want it so badly? He'd relegated it to the back of a bookshelf, after all. It was a powerful symbol, though, of the bond I had with his grandfather, which Tyson never had. I considered bringing him the little model as an olive branch of sorts. Would that inspire him to open up to me?

No. It might only fan the flames of his envy.

I started to set the model back on the mantel, caught the bottom of it on the edge, and it dropped to the floor and cracked open, the whole hull releasing from the deck. From the interior sprang short lengths of brown photo negatives, which landed on the kitchen floor between the two halves of the ruined boat.

Everything slowed as I crouched and picked up the negatives, my heart beating out of my chest. I held them to the kitchen lamp. They were pictures of someone's vacation. Tyson's? One of Mount Rushmore. One of a massive waterfall—Niagara Falls? And several shots of an Army base, cacti in the background. Had Tyson hidden them in the model? Mr. Schmidt? Tyson had been so intent on getting the model back.

I snapped the model together, set it back on the mantel, and hurried through the woods to the camp for answers, hoping Tyson was there. It was going to rain; the air was heavy and the undersides of the leaves on the trees upturned. The Burbanks could use the extra help.

I approached the house in the distance. I was close to the answer, I could feel it. There is always a point in any pursuit when all factors seem to coalesce. "The quickening," Mr. Schmidt called it. Perhaps Tyson had grown up with German-sympathizing parents, steeped in Nazi culture. In Yaphank, Long Island? He'd never mentioned where he lived before going to boarding school. But, being of German descent, people mistrusted him. And there was the incident at the ice cream parlor. A new thought struck me. Maybe Tyson and Gil were working together. Shelby, too?

I carefully opened the side door and crept into the darkening living room. I followed the glow of a light in one of the back bedrooms and found him sitting on the bed, his back to the door. As I drew closer, I saw he was turning something in his fingers, examining it beneath the bedside table lamp. The *ring*. My breath caught in my throat: I saw the shortwave radio, as well, on the bed next to him.

"What are you doing?" I asked.

He looked at me, startled. "I was just coming to find you, Briar. You're not going to believe it. You were right about the spy. It's Shelby."

I stepped into the room. "How do you know?"

"This. She had the shortwave in her bag."

"I don't understand."

"Don't you *see*? She's been playing me all along. I should have known—her father works for Henry Ford, for heaven's sake. They're sympathizers. She's probably been communicating with the U-boat for a while now."

She had been oddly interested in the radio on that day she and Tyson went swimming.

He looked so defeated, there in his uniform, slumped over, elbows on his knees. "I really thought she was the one. Feels rotten, you know? Gonna have to ship out without a girl back home."

"Are you sure?" I asked. "Is she smart enough to do something like this?"

"*Yes,* Briar. She's actually very smart. Not everyone gets into Miss Porter's."

That was debatable, especially when it came to parents with money, but Tyson didn't seem open to that conversation right now.

I turned toward the doorway. "If you're sure, we should confront her. Call Chief Leo, maybe."

"Okay. But I ran out of gas on State Road. Gotta go back." Tyson took the radio, shoved it into his knapsack, slid one strap over his shoulder, and went down the basement steps. He came back up with a can of gasoline. "Let's go."

He hurried outside, lugging the can of gasoline, and I rushed after him, past the concrete steps to the beach. He continued on and I stopped there, a little dizzy at the height of them, and suddenly it was all so clear.

I looked around, the mourning doves cooing in the pines, waves lapping the shore. The colors sharpened, the spruce green of the trees and the white of the concrete stairs. Finally. The quickening.

41

CADENCE

—

1942

I WALKED UP TO PEAKED HILL WITH MY MEAGER CARTON OF BOOKS. The one sentry glanced at my ID card, let me through, and waved toward the silver Quonset hut in the distance. I thought about my night on the beach with Gil, in the cabin of the *Tyche*, our bodies intertwined. There was no chance he'd been faking his affection for me.

It was strangely quiet up there with everyone gone off somewhere. I walked to the top of the hill and stood on the bluff that overlooked the North Shore, all the way down to Lambert's Cove Beach. There was a low ceiling of clouds, darkness coming on. They were preparing for something big along the distant coast, where lanterns glowed as twilight fell and trucks drove on the beach. The mock invasion I'd written about? Whatever was happening, it was imminent.

Would Gil leave his men to meet a German U-boat tonight? Not in a million years. It was someone else, I was sure of it. Probably Tyson Schmidt. He wore a uniform but was sort of a hothead. Or it could be someone we hadn't thought of. Briar claimed she'd vetted the entire island population, but even she had her limits. Or perhaps it was no one at all. Maybe Peter had heard wrong.

I stepped into the Quonset hut, down the hallway toward Gil's office. There was no sign of him, or anyone else, and it felt like a betrayal to be there, ready to paw through his things. *My future husband.* Gram and her tea leaves had been right. But this was not the best way to start a life together. It was absurd to think he'd betray America, after training those men with such dedication, and take secrets back to Germany.

He loved his commandos like his own brothers, I was sure of it. But Tom would want me to do all I could to join forces with Briar. For all her faults, she was a genius when it came to puzzles. And there was no greater one than this.

I flicked on the lights, set my carton on the chair, and took in Gil's office. He had packed up much of it, but I could tell he was a neat sort, which I liked. It looked the same as every other in that prefabricated building, with the government-issued metal desk and the venetian blinds covering the window, but Gil had put his stamp on it with a leather desk blotter and a framed engraving of an English town on the wall next to the closet.

I opened the left-hand file drawers at his desk. In the unlikely event that anyone found me there, I would say I was looking for tape to seal the book box. Rifling through the files, I found nothing out of the ordinary; I felt along the back of the drawer, then moved on to the right side and repeated the same—my hand met leather. I pulled out an empty gun holster. His service revolver. So, he had a gun. That wasn't particularly surprising for an Army officer.

Next I opened his closet, which smelled like him, of shave cream and some sort of lovely British bay-rum aftershave. Two coats hung in there, both heavy, one a canvas raincoat. Perhaps he'd packed them thinking that August on Martha's Vineyard would be more like his own island, since England was so rainy. I felt in the pockets of one, finding only a pack of cigarettes. In the pocket of the other I felt a box and pulled it out. It was a white jewelry box, a gold L. E. Briggs sticker on the lid. The necklace Briar saw him buy.

Intended for me? I paused. If it was, I'd be ruining the surprise. I listened hard to make sure no one was about, then lifted off the lid to find a black velvet box. I snapped it open. A necklace. A diamond-covered heart edged with pearls on a gold chain lay there on the velvet. I'd never seen anything so beautiful.

I closed the lid and replaced the box just as I found it. If it was an engagement gift, then why had he not already given it to me? Today's quasi-proposal would have been the perfect time to do so. And there were pearls. Was it intended for Amelia? Was he still seeing her? What about the Greta person Briar had told me about?

I was ready to give up and head home when I felt inside the breast pocket of his coat and pulled out a letter. Everything sharpened, colors enhanced somehow. It was postmarked *Geneva,* in handwriting feminine yet bold, and addressed to *John Gilbert in care of the Vineyard Haven Post Office.* So, John was his first name. It suited him. But why did he not want that letter sent via the usual military post? He hadn't even read it.

I took a letter opener from the desk and gently worked it under the envelope flap, pulled out the letter, and sat down hard in his desk chair to take it all in.

I opened the folded sheets and a photo slid out of Gil and an attractive woman, perhaps in her early thirties, sitting at a café table. It looked like somewhere in Europe—maybe Switzerland, from the half-timber style of the houses around the cobblestone square. I examined it more closely. There was something else in the background. I swallowed hard: A Nazi flag hung from a building. The letter was three pages long and written in German, certain words so close to English. *Großvater. Foto.* But some were French, as well. *Mon chéri.*

My whole body felt blank. Briar was right all along: Gil had been compromised. Somehow he'd been just fine behind German lines, toasting with some German woman. Not exactly escaping from his German captors. And what about the *mon chéri* part? Clearly they were lovers.

I slid the letter into my pocket, hurried out of the building, and found the path down the hill back to the farm. Hopefully Bess, Margaret, and Briar would all be home. Together we'd figure out who to call.

42

BRIAR

1942

I RAN BACK THROUGH THE WOODS TO THE COTTAGE. I NEEDED Cadence. And a phone, as soon as possible.

"Wait, Briar!" Tyson called, following me. "Where are you going? We have to find Shelby."

I kept running, digesting it all as I went. Tyson was a good liar.

The sun had set, and a cool breeze came up as I hurried into the cottage. I found Margaret and Bess at the kitchen table, making Peter's fake ID card.

I took the tugboat model from the mantel and held it to my chest. "Tyson's coming. He may be the spy."

"What?" Margaret turned in her chair and looked out the window. "Well, he's right outside."

A terrible sense of dread seeped through me. "Margaret, go up and tell Peter we need his help."

Bess sniffed the air. "What's that smell?"

"Gasoline," Margaret said.

Both of them went to the window and looked out.

"My God," Bess said. "He's shaking gas around the foundation."

Tyson was definitely the one we'd been looking for. Why else would he try to burn our house down with us in it? At least Gram wasn't here. And Cadence was still up at Peaked Hill.

Tyson stepped inside and splashed gasoline from the can onto the kitchen floor and counter.

"You're going to burn the house down?" I asked, holding the tug-boat to my chest.

He dropped the gas can and pulled a gun from the rear of his waistband. Mr. Schmidt's Luger.

He held out one hand for the model. "Give it to me."

I suspended the little boat over the gas pooled on the floor. "I know what's in it, Tyson. And once the negatives hit gasoline, they'll melt."

He came closer. "Give it to me. *Now.*"

"You've been going around the country taking pictures. To bring back to Germany, right? Did your father have you do it? To show your loyalty? Is he back in Germany now, waiting for you? The son with the info on all the American places to blow up? Cause panic here and make sure we get out of the war?"

"Give it to me."

I held the model closer. "You got the ring from Sandra, didn't you?"

"What ring?" he asked.

"You know. The Totenkopf. I'm not stupid, Tyson. It's your father's, isn't it? Kuno?"

"That ring was *mine*. Father gave it to me before he left, his most prized possession, but Grandfather found it and took it away. He had no right."

"So you killed Sandra to get it."

"She wanted me to pay for something that was *mine*. And I didn't kill her. She had some sort of fit."

"But you didn't help her. And you killed your grandfather, didn't you? When he took the ring away. Pushed him down the beach stairs."

"He was always ashamed he came from Germany. But my parents weren't. Yaphank was a place we could be ourselves for a change."

"Following Hitler here in the States."

"You don't understand, do you? He tells the truth."

"So you're the one meeting the U-boat?" I asked.

He pulled a matchbox from his pocket with his free hand. "Give it to me or this place burns."

I froze. "You wouldn't." Gram's kitchen would go up like dry kindling. Along with everything we owned. All we had left of Tom.

I heard footsteps in the attic, and then Peter walked slowly down the stairs.

"Hurry up, if you want to go back," Tyson shouted to him. "I know you love Germany."

Peter slowly approached Tyson and stood next to him, barely meeting Margaret's eyes.

Margaret gasped. Maybe she didn't know her Peter that well, after all.

I tried to remember where Gram kept her fire extinguisher. Under the sink? I hoped Cadence would get here soon and possibly disarm him, but he could just as easily shoot her.

Tyson held us at gunpoint and handed the matches to Peter. "Light one."

Peter hesitated.

Tyson waved the gun at him. "Do it!" he shouted, and Peter slowly opened the matchbox. He looked at me and then struck one wooden match along the side of it. The blue flame sprang to life.

Fear crawled up my spine. We might all die.

"My God," Bess said. "Give it to him, Briar."

Tyson reached out his hand. "Now, Briar. Or this place goes up."

It wasn't worth risking our lives over. I tossed the model to Tyson. "There," I said. "Put out the match."

Tyson caught the model, tucked it under one arm, and took the match from Peter.

"Thanks, sweet pea," he said with a smile, and dropped the match onto the kitchen floor.

43

CADENCE

1942

I RAN DOWN THE HILL, READY TO TELL BRIAR AND THE OTHERS about the letter I'd found in Gil's office, trying to make sense of it all. Who was Greta? They'd been relaxing in Nazi Germany. I'd definitely been blinded by love. Gram's whole stupid tea-leaves thing.

I smelled the smoke before I even got to the cottage, and as I came out of the woods, I saw black clouds of it billowing from the rear windows of the house. I ran through the front door and back to the kitchen, where flames licked the curtains and cabinets. Briar and Margaret were trying to smother the fire with a blanket, while Bess struggled to pull the garden hose in through the window.

"It's Tyson," Briar yelled when she saw me. "He doused it with gas. Just left to meet the U-boat. Peter, too."

Tyson and Peter together? Is Gil involved? Thank God Gram isn't here, I thought, as the flames spread toward her bedroom. "The fire extinguisher is in the cabinet under the sink," I called out.

"You may notice that's on fire," Briar said.

I turned to her. "Salt," I said.

"*What?*"

"Remember? *Jane Eyre.* You said, 'Salt or baking soda would have been a better choice.' The salt's outside the door."

All four of us raced to the front door, lugged in the coal buckets of rock salt, and flung scoopfuls of it onto the flames. When it was safe to open the cupboard under the sink, I rescued the fire extinguisher, took off the safety cap, and aimed the flow of white powder at the flames.

Once the bulk of the fire was out, we stood in the ruins, the kitchen full of smoke and the whole back wall charred. Rain pattered the roof. That might help with any remaining embers outside. I asked Bess and Margaret to stay and extinguish every spark, and Briar and I turned our attention to Tyson and Peter. We raced down the path to the boathouse in near darkness, the arches of trees above shielding us from the rain.

"They have a gun," Briar said as we ran.

I tried to stay a few mental steps ahead of Tyson. He was obviously the one meeting the U-boat. Peter, too? So much for his pacifist act. Why didn't I follow my instincts on Peter? We wouldn't be here, risking our lives, if I'd sent him away from the start.

The wind picked up, and we slowed as we came to the boathouse. They had turned a lamp on, and through the open door I saw Peter holding the gun in one hand and the tugboat model in the other. He stood looking at Tyson, who lay face down, bleeding on the floor. I entered the room and Briar followed, the smell of gunpowder in the air.

Peter turned to us, still holding the Luger. Fear grabbed me, and I pushed Briar behind me. Would he kill us, too?

"Peter, don't," I said.

Peter set the gun down and gazed, horrified, at Tyson's body. "I couldn't let him leave. He tried to get me to take the boat out, and when I refused to help, he aimed the gun at me, so I rushed him and wrestled it away from him."

"It must have just gone off," I said.

Briar took the tugboat from him.

"No," he said with a sob. "I pulled the trigger. I killed him."

An eerie quiet surrounded us, as wind and rain battered the sides of the boathouse. Peter knelt and felt the side of Tyson's neck for a pulse; finding none, he sat back on his heels. "He's gone." Peter started to murmur a prayer but then placed his hands over his face and cried.

For a man who'd been raised as a pacifist, it must have been hard to do it.

I rubbed his back. "You saved our lives. He would have shot us once we got here."

Peter dried his eyes and looked at me. "Did you extinguish the fire?"

"We did. A lot of damage, though."

Peter stood, his eyes red-rimmed. "I hope you understand—Tyson approached me when I was out in the field this morning, when everyone was at the funeral. He'd been in touch with the U-boat through the shortwave, and they gave him a description of me. He threatened to expose me to the authorities if I didn't come back to Germany or if I said anything to you all. So I had to pretend to go along. I'm sorry I didn't stop him from burning the kitchen. But I had to make him think I was on his side."

"I was hoping you were just playing along," Briar said.

"I wanted to get him away from the house before he shot you. He was on the verge of it. I had to catch him unawares, use the element of surprise to disarm him."

I nodded, overcome by the moment. Peter had done us a favor.

I asked Peter, "The U-boat—is it really still out there?"

"Probably, considering photos and information Tyson had for them. On our way down to the boathouse, he told me his father had arranged the collection of intelligence on American sites and Army installations, the whole thing, before he went back to Germany. But chances are the U-boat won't stick around long."

"Not with half of the U.S. military about to land up and down the North Shore," Briar said.

"We must clean up the blood," Peter said. "And get him buried." He looked out the window at the storm. "I'm afraid I can't do it alone."

I nodded. "I know four women who will help."

44

BRIAR

—

1942

ONCE BESS AND MARGARET HAD PUT OUT ALL TRACES OF THE fire, they came down to the boathouse, as shocked as we were about Tyson, and we discussed our options for disposing of the body. Bess suggested we bury him under one of the boulders on the hill, and Peter, Cadence, and I took turns digging the grave. Margaret secured a chain around a boulder in the field, and Bess drove the tractor to drag it into place over the spot. It wasn't easy pulling the body on a tarp up from the boathouse. Only days before, I'd dragged Peter from the beach.

I was more energized than tired, though the task had taken us most of the night, but we were a determined lot. I slid the negatives into Tyson's pocket before we wrapped him in a blanket and buried him. After I'd found the negatives, I didn't replace them, just in case he was planning to take them back to Germany. If anyone ever found the body, those negatives would be proof that Tyson had been a traitor.

My emotions about Tyson were all over the place—sad about our friendship one minute, and mad as hell at him the next. If he hadn't killed his own grandfather, Mr. Schmidt would still be here. And Sandra would still be enjoying life behind her glass counter. And none of this would have happened, probably.

Bess climbed down from the tractor and slapped the dirt from her hands. "Rest in peace."

The weather had cleared, and Cadence and I stood looking along the coast as dawn broke over Vineyard Sound, Lambert's Cove Beach in the distance. "I suppose the mock invasion is going to start anytime now," I said. "Looks like lots of activity."

"At least Tyson won't be reporting back to Berlin about that, too," Margaret said.

"But is the U-boat still out there?" Cadence asked.

I searched the water just off Pepper Cove with my binoculars, slowly checking the sea for any sign. "No, I don't see—oh, wait." I paused. "There it is."

I handed Cadence the glasses. "Straight off Pepper Cove. See?"

She saw something among the whitecaps and I focused the glasses for her. "Yes. Yes, I see it. Like a metal fence?"

"That's it," I said. Warmth spread through me. How good it felt to have someone else finally see it.

Cadence reached out one hand to me. "Quick. Come with me."

She hurried down the hill to the beach, pulling me behind her, and followed the phone line to the call box.

"What are you doing?" I asked.

She lifted the receiver and turned the crank on the box until a male voice answered.

"Shore Patrol Main Station," I heard the voice through the phone. "What is the nature of your call, Chilmark Eighteen?"

"This is Cadence Smith, and Major Gilbert has asked me to report that a U-boat has been spotted just off Pepper Cove."

"Not the one Briar Smith is fantasizing about."

"Yes, the very same," Cadence said coolly. "Briar Smith is my sister, and yes, she's been right about it all along. Please send immediate water assistance."

"Best we can do is scare it off—"

"I urge you to do so immediately. With what is happening on our North Shore beaches this morning, I'd hate to have to tell the major it couldn't be done."

"Roger, Miss Smith. Right away."

I smiled as my sister hung up the phone. Tom would have loved to see that.

We started back up the hill, and before we'd gone even halfway, the whir of a Coast Guard cutter's engine caught our attention; we turned to watch as it made a wide sweep through Pepper Cove.

Cadence took my hand in hers. "That was something I should have done eons ago," she said. "But better late than never."

We continued up the hill to Peter, Bess, and Margaret, who were eager for the binoculars. Even with the naked eye we could see the mock invasion starting, and the breath caught in my throat as we watched the beaches along the North Shore. Sunlight had breached the dunes, and fleets of ships appeared in Vineyard Sound, approaching our island so silently, amphibious boats like none I'd ever seen, flat-hulled and open, plowing through the surf. One hit the beach and disgorged its men, full packs on their backs, and then another hit the beach, and another.

Waves of troops swarmed ashore, avoiding enemy machine-gun fire—blanks, of course. Explosions shook the earth as red bombs and smoke screens blasted into the sky, and what must have been flour-bag grenades gave the action a touch of realism. Flare rockets shot into the sky, and massive white balloons floated like dirigibles above the beach.

"What are those balloons?" Cadence asked.

"Barrage balloons. Tethered to the beach. They're used to protect troops on the ground from hostile aircraft," I said, not accustomed to Cadence asking me questions and actually listening to the answers. "They raise steel cables from the ground to deter enemy planes."

I focused my binoculars on a group of top military brass, generals and admirals, as they stood on a bluff overlooking it all, watching troops dash across the sand and take cover in bushes along the shore. Was Major Gil there with them or down on the beach with his men?

Planes roared overhead, dropping paratroopers along the dunes behind the beach to support the ground forces and the medical units swarming in with supplies. Soon they would be doing it for real on another beach somewhere, perhaps in North Africa or along France's vast coastline, having practiced on our beach. Our boys.

I was overcome by the enormity of it all. It might be too late for Tom, but Gil's men would have a fighting chance when they had to storm the beaches of Le Havre or Calais or wherever they landed to battle Hitler.

"I guess Gil wasn't the spy," I said to Cadence. "Sorry I suspected him."

Cadence turned to me. "Let's not waste our time on regrets." She took my hand as we watched America's finest storm the beach and fan out across Martha's Vineyard. "Life is short. Tom would have wanted us to enjoy every minute of it."

45

CADENCE

—

1942

LATER THAT MORNING, WE SWEPT THE ASHES FROM THE KITCHEN and hauled out most of the charred cabinets. Peter led the way, with Briar in her sentry tree, ready to signal in case McManus or any other intruder came down the road. We all tried to keep a cheerful face on, but the kitchen was pretty much ruined. At least we saved the mantel that Grandfather had carved. That was a bright spot. We'd also avoided a visit from the fire department. And we would rebuild. But Gram couldn't come home. She'd need to go to a nursing home after discharge from the hospital, and we didn't have the money.

"I have some money saved up," Margaret said, handing me a Leslie's Drugs bag with cash in it. "One hundred dollars almost."

How incredibly kind that was of her.

"Thank you, Margaret, but we can't take your money," I said. With little family available to help her, she needed to keep her nest egg.

We took a break from our cleanup and carried our books and towels down to the beach for a swim in Copper Pond, while Peter pried out one stubborn cabinet that needed replacing.

I wanted to try to regain the book-club feeling we had before the Tyson incident, back when we fought about what books to read and Bess and Margaret were at each other's throats. We toweled off and Bess stepped to the flagpole and raised our burgee.

But Tyson's death had shaken us to the core and made it hard to chat about books, so instead we discussed how to explain his disappearance.

We would float a rumor that he had gone to live with his parents or that he left the Army to travel some more. Would Shelby believe it? And when we'd exhausted that conversation, we took to our towels and read on our own. At least we could count on books to get us through.

I dove back into my mother's copy of *Anna Karenina* to finish my third read, always my go-to for a good escape, but soon my attention went to the boulder up on the hill. Would word of what we'd done get out somehow? And Peter was still a big problem. I worried every minute that McManus would turn up looking for him. I could tell Peter knew it was time to go.

The shrill tone of Briar's whistle sounded from the hill, and I sat up on my towel. A car was coming. I ran as fast as I could to warn Peter. Hopefully he'd heard the whistle, too, and had taken cover.

I made it to the front gate just as Private Jeffers pulled up in Major Gilbert's jeep and saluted me, which seemed kind of him, since I held no rank.

"A message from Major Gilbert, Miss Smith," he said, the motor running. "The major had to ship out but wanted me to give you this."

Jeffers took a white paper bag from the passenger seat and handed it to me. "Said I needed to get it down here on the double."

"Thank you, Private."

"I won't be seeing you for a while," he said. "I ship out tomorrow. Headed for the Pacific, splitting off from Major Gil's group."

"You'll miss them, I'm sure."

"Like mad. But it's been nice knowing you Smiths. And I'll be back here. I told my mom I'll bring her around to see the island."

"You're welcome anytime."

"Please tell your grandmother thanks for making me that huckleberry pie, will you? Guys couldn't get over that she went and found huckleberries."

Private Jeffers went on his way and Briar came at a run from the direction of her tree, relieved to find it was simply Gil's messenger. We took the bag inside to my room and sat on the bed to open it. Briar stared at me with anticipation as I took the card from its envelope. How good it was to have her there with me.

The card was written on Army letterhead, *Peaked Hill* printed at the top, and I read aloud:

"My dear Cadence, I hope this letter finds you well. Upon returning to my office this morning, I found a box of books the gate sentry said you'd left and a letter missing, which I must assume is in your hands, since it would be quite a coincidence otherwise. Perhaps you will allow me to explain about the letter, which I received from the local postal office, as your sister probably told you, since she followed me through half of Vineyard Haven that day, I'm assuming due to the protective nature of a beloved sister.

When I was captured by the Germans in Norway, we were taken to a POW camp, Stalag 10A in Schleswig, Germany; there a woman named Greta Sternberg, a happily married mother of two, helped my friend and me escape. We hid in plain sight in some German towns as we made our way home, thanks to Greta and her husband, and even after I returned safely to London, I continued to stay in touch with her. I chose to pick her letter up off base, in Vineyard Haven, since she often sends me photos of her children, which military airmail regulations do not allow.

As I explained, my life is a bit chaotic at the moment. I have been reassigned, away from my men for now. I hate to leave you and this beautiful island, since I've come to love you both, and I most ardently hope you will come to London soon, where I shall promptly and unconditionally explain anything more you still wonder about. I hope to do that over potted shrimps at Sweetings, where their signature beverage, the Sweetings Black Velvet (Guinness and champagne), has been known to lead to more than one marriage proposal, so consider yourself forewarned.

In the meantime, I hope you accept this token you might wear to keep me in your thoughts now and then. I will write, in care of Copper Pond Farm, from whatever outpost they are sending me to and hope we all come home soon.

> *Yours with unending love*
> *and devotion,*
>
> *Gil"*

Briar and I sat for a moment and let the letter sink in.

"I think he likes you," Briar said.

I opened the velvet box to find the necklace I'd seen in Gil's coat pocket, which Briar seemed astounded could be purchased from any jeweler on the island. She helped me with the clasp, and I looked down at the diamonds and seed pearls there at my throat. I was thrilled at the prospect of a London trip, of course, and delighted that the necklace had been for me after all.

I stood and held out my hand to Briar. "It's the perfect accessory to wear to finish cleaning a kitchen."

I WOKE UP THE next morning, the bed next to me cold. I assumed Bess had risen early, ready to warm the last of the chocolate for breakfast, since Peter had gotten the stove working again yesterday. I stepped to the kitchen and found Briar there, still in her pajamas.

"Peter's gone," Briar said. "Margaret, too."

We went to the boathouse and found no sign of them.

"They must have walked to the docks last night," I said.

They'd just taken the clothes on their backs and disappeared. Somehow, I knew they'd be okay and would make it safely to Minnesota. I smiled, happy for Margaret—hopefully she'd start a new book club there. They would certainly be all set in terms of discussion questions.

"Where's Bess?" I asked Briar.

"I don't know," Briar said. "She took the truck and told me to tell you she'd be back later so we can visit Gram."

With Gram at the hospital, and Peter and Margaret now gone, the house felt so empty.

And it wasn't like Bess to just leave without telling me.

46

BESS

——

1942

I DROVE GRAM'S TRUCK TO MY PARENTS' HOUSE IN EDGARTOWN the next morning. I'd finally figured it out. There was only one way for us all to go on.

I parked out front along the fence. "The prettiest house in Edgartown," they called it. It may have been—a former sea captain's home Mother inherited from her parents, with its perfectly proportioned, white-painted clapboard façade. It was set back from the road just far enough, a riot of blooms at the fence. But the idea that anyone even judged which house was the prettiest, in that town so full of astonishingly handsome homes, spoke volumes. It was so important to be the best.

I hurried through the black-painted front door into the living room. While the exterior of Mother's house was certainly lovely, the inside was a true Lydia Stanhope work of art and the envy of every person at the club with any taste. She'd had good architectural bones to work with, the original wide-planked floors and soundproof walls insulated with horsehair. She'd been wise to use the classic colonial fireplace to set the tone for the décor—traditional, but not too George Washington—the sofa and club chairs slipcovered in chintz for a restrained yet modern effect, the too-casual-for-a-coaster-but-you-probably-should-use-one-anyway side tables arranged just so. Her decorators had taken a tea cart about the rooms and stripped them of most of the personal and decorative objects Mother once set about the place. On the mantel they left only a wedding picture of Mother holding a bouquet of cascading roses, the single blight on the otherwise carefully arranged colonial charm.

I called up the front stairs for Mother and, hearing no reply, walked through the enormous kitchen, with its English stove, two refrigerators, and miles of marble counters. What would Gram Smith think of that room? Probably prefer her own humble galley—pre-fire, at least.

I hurried on into Mother's glass-walled flower-arranging room, my steps echoing on the pillowed Belgian bluestone floor. Where was she? I wanted to get the whole thing over with before I lost my nerve. Just a whiff of rose triggered my pregnancy nausea, and I fanned my face with a nearby garden brochure. The morning sickness was the least of my problems, not that I had told the Smiths. I wore trousers to conceal my swollen ankles and could barely breathe some days. Dr. Von Prague had been right about the diagnosis. I would need to start following his advice if I wanted a healthy baby.

Mother's gardener, a kind man built like the Great Buddha of Kamakura, waved to me from the side yard. "She's out in the back garden."

"No, she isn't." Mother came into the room, wearing a pink dress and stacked heels, her hair pulled back in a bow that would have been better on a schoolgirl. She carried her myrtle-wood garden trug, with its pile of subjugated roses, like a purse, looped over one skinny arm.

She glanced at me. "You look dreadful."

My poor mother, incapable of a pleasant greeting.

"Hello, Mother."

She stepped to the porcelain garden sink. "I'm assuming you're ready to come home. Is that why you're here?"

Despite her usual disdainful manner, I could tell she was happy to see me, probably hoping my return would quell the rumors in town. Or maybe she really did miss me. "I just want to talk."

She set her trug on the counter. "What's left for you on that farm, anyway, now that Tom is dead?"

"You could've come to the funeral." I tried to keep my voice from wavering. "It's been really hard."

She turned to me. "I'm sorry, dear. I would have, but I had a long-standing appointment."

I was too hollowed out to be anything but honest. "You and Father would never have accepted Tom, would you? Unless I'd met him at the club and he was wearing white tennis flannels and sopping up the highballs."

Mother brushed off the counter. "Are you hungry? Deirdre can fix you something. An omelet, perhaps. With Swiss cheese. Your favorite."

Was it my imagination, or did she look much older now, her face more gaunt? Perhaps my moving out had affected her more than I knew.

"No, thank you, Mother."

"Deirdre!" Mother called out toward the kitchen. "I don't know where she goes half the time." She lifted a rose from the trug and snipped the stem. "They tell me her name means 'sorrowful' in Irish, and I think she feels it necessary to act in a manner befitting her name."

"Maybe because you make her sleep in the attic and it's two hundred degrees up there."

"The Irish don't feel the heat as we do. But she can toast you some of that bread with raisins that she made, which your father won't eat. Just be careful with the butter. You'll regret overeating once the baby comes. I had a terrible time getting the weight off after I had you."

"I want to talk about the Smiths, Mother."

"I guess you're now chained to those people for life, Bess Ann. I suppose Cadence told you that I made her a proposition."

"What? No. She never mentioned it. Probably didn't want to worry me." I paused, listening to the water from the sprinkler hit the side of the house. "I have a proposition for *you*, Mother."

She snipped another stem. "I'm listening."

I drew a deep breath and forced myself to say the words. "I'll come back if you help them."

Mother set down the snippers and looked at me. "For good this time? To Boston?"

I rubbed my wet palms down my trouser legs and nodded.

Mother smiled and chose a vase from the shelf. "I suppose we can have your room at home aired out. You left so many old clothes in there it smells like a thrift shop."

"I need a check for their bank in Vineyard Haven. I want to deposit it today. Gram needs hospital treatment."

"Oh, *Gram* you call her now? You were barely civil to your own grandmother."

"She used to hit me with her cane if I pushed my doll carriage over her grass."

"She was a strong woman, that's all."

"Really, Mother?" I exhaled. This was harder than I'd imagined. "I want to give them five thousand dollars."

Mother laughed. "I hope you're joking, Bess Ann. They'll probably just spend it on liquor."

"I want to make sure they're financially stable."

"You know how it is with that sort. They don't know the first thing about thrift. They'll fritter it away in no time and be right back to squalor."

"And they need some house repairs."

"Of course they do, living in that place. It's unsanitary, really." Mother turned and considered me for a moment, as she kneaded Pond's cold cream into her hands. "How do I know you won't go running back there the minute the check clears?"

"I keep my word. I'll need help with the baby—I'm sure you'll want to get to know your grandchild. And I'd like to give birth in a hospital. This is all I have left of Tom, and I don't want to take any chances."

"Maybe it's for the best, Bess dear. Now you can move on. Men are always a disappointment anyway."

"I'm not moving on, Mother. I just want to help them. Please."

"It's unseemly to just hand someone that kind of money. It's not the way we do things."

"You and Father have never been particularly charitable."

"Well, if you mean we don't go around chiseling our names into buildings, you'd be correct."

"Help them. No one will know. Just this one time, Mother."

She eyed me and then looked at her roses. "I feel like all I do is write checks these days, for one thing or another. You know we had to replace the greenhouse floor? So many cracked tiles."

"Will you agree to this or not?"

"Your father will have a fit if he finds out. But I could take it from my household budget—he never looks at that."

"So you'll do it?"

"I suppose." Mother went to the living room for her purse and returned with her checkbook. "But only if you agree not to go back there, write, or contact those Smiths in any way."

I swallowed hard. "I will. But I need one more night there. To gather my things."

"Very well, then." She wrote out the check and handed it to me. "I'll send William with the car tomorrow evening at six, so you'll be back well before seven. I want to catch the last boat." She paused. "You're finally doing something smart, Bess Ann, coming home to your real family."

I didn't reply, already halfway out the door, shattered, having just agreed to leave my Tommy's house and the only real family I'd ever had.

That night I came home and tried to drift off, back to back with Cadence in the bed where I'd slept since Tom left, pale moonglow lighting the room. I felt her warmth against me, her breath slow and regular, such a good sleeper, as always. Scout lay curled up at my feet, and cool, almost-autumn air wafted through the curtainless window.

I would miss that perfect little American bedroom, with the pink cabbage-rose wallpaper Gram had gifted Cadence for her sixteenth birthday, the white milk-glass lamp on the bureau, Cadence's pictures and postcards arranged around her mirror. A Paris postcard I'd found for her at a thrift store. A picture of Tom in the *Tyche,* squinting up at the camera. How handsome he was. Would our child be like him, hopefully have his charm? I felt a stab of longing for him but tried to think about books. The baby. What to pack the next day. Anything but him.

Our child moved inside me, and I set one palm on my belly. How marvelous it was to feel the baby turn. An elbow? Knee?

I leaned over to Cadence and gently shook her arm. "Cade. Sorry to wake you. But I think I'm going to go home to Boston for a while. To have the baby."

Cadence turned, her lovely blue eyes full of sleep. "Why?"

"Mother found a doctor at Boston Lying-In who specializes in high-risk birth. It's just what I need. They've pioneered obstetrics programs there. And Mother offered to pay for it all, so I thought it best to take her up on it. Better to be safe than sorry." I hated lying to her.

She looked at me so trustingly. "I see."

How could I have the baby without her by my side? Her brother's child. It was such a cruel thing to take from them.

"You're coming back, though, right?" she asked sleepily.

I nodded, fighting the tears. "Of course."

She took my hand and we fell asleep together, my last night at Copper Pond Farm.

I WOKE THE NEXT MORNING and breathed in the scent of coffee someone must have made in our burned kitchen, then I remembered, with a sinking feeling.

I was going home.

Mother would be waiting for me, bags packed for Boston, to leave promptly at seven tonight. I had delivered the check. There was no going back now.

It would all be fine. I'd have the baby safely in Boston and return one day, when Mother forgot about the arrangement. Two, three years, maybe? Lydia Stanhope couldn't stay angry about it forever. I tried to push it all away and enjoy my last day at the farm. Someday I would tell Cadence why I made my pact with the devil. But for the time being I would have to keep up the pretense. The most important thing was to get medical help for Gram and the house rebuilt so she could return. Tom would have wanted that. And I would be able to visit eventually, to show our child where their brave and talented father once lived and loved and fished. His legacy would never die.

The dinner bell clanged from the front of the house. "Cadence! Bess! Come quick!" Briar called out.

Cadence and I scrambled out of bed, threw on our robes, and hurried to the front door, where Briar stood, dressed in her boys' red tartan pajama set, pulling the bell cord.

"What is it?" Cadence asked.

"The Burbanks!" she exclaimed over the clang of the bell. "They've flowered!"

We all dressed for the job at hand: to dig those five hundred potatoes out of the ground and get them into the back of the truck for market. Cadence suggested that, given my condition, I should drive the truck from the barn to where they were harvesting and stay in it, out of the sun.

I watched as Cadence and Briar worked side by side, digging their spades into the rich loam. Tom would be happy his sisters had finally come together. Cadence would need Briar more than ever once I left.

"Think we can get a decent price today?" Cadence asked.

Briar nodded. "Broker said if we were the first crop to harvest, we'd get two dollars a pound from one of the markets." She smiled. "That's almost two hundred dollars."

It was not exactly the fortune Tom had anticipated, but I was happy for them. It was a start. Chief Leo stopped by to check on news about Gram and promised to come back later and help.

As the sun climbed in the sky, we checked the back of the truck, barely a quarter filled with potatoes. Cadence leaned on her shovel. "We can't get these all out of the ground in one day."

All at once a car bumped down Copper Pond Road, passed the cottage, and parked, and people started up the hill. Billy Sullivan, the dump-shack guard. Then more cars came. Gram's friends Effie Littlefield, Ethel Vincent, and Agnes Morris from church. Young Eddie Cottle and his friend came on foot. Fred Fisher was in his white T-shirt and suspenders.

"We were over at the Ag hall and heard Chief Leo say you needed help," Billy said as he hurried toward them.

"Isn't this just extraordinary?" I called out to Cadence. It was hard not to feel Tom's presence in that field.

We worked the rest of the day, with half of Chilmark there pulling

Tom's little brown money bags out of the earth and Gram's church ladies plying everyone with the Windfall Apple Cake that Gram always
made. By the time the sun started to set, the truck was piled so high we
had to tie it down with a tarp.

Cadence and I watched the truck rumble down the hill, with Billy
driving and Briar in the passenger seat, off to Vineyard Haven to make
the sale.

"Tom would be jumping for joy," Cadence said.

"Guess who else is." I took Cadence's hand and pressed it against
my apron front. "Wait a second—there it is."

I felt the baby move against Cadence's hand, and she shook her
head. "I love this baby so much already. You need to get back here
right after the birth."

"You bet," I said, as we walked toward the cottage.

"I'll miss you," she said. "Promise you'll write?"

Mother would make sure that didn't happen. "Not sure if I'll be able
to for a while. Busy with the baby and all."

Cadence linked her arm in mine. "I expect daily letters."

"I'll try."

We walked along in silence, listening to our helpers up on the hill
saying their goodbyes.

"You know, Tom changed when he met you," Cadence said. "He
grew so much happier."

I searched my pockets for a handkerchief. "I have to go before I
turn into a mass of hideous sobs."

As we approached the cottage, Mother's black limousine pulled up
and idled at the front door. I grabbed my bag from the house, accepted
a never-ending hug from Cade and a kiss from Scout.

Cadence tucked a stray curl behind my ear, in the simple way Tom
had always done. "I feel like you're not telling me everything."

Of course she knew I was withholding something.

I broke away and climbed into the back seat of the car, part of me
happy I was finally getting it over with. I rolled down the window.
"You won't know me the next time you see me, dressed in a muumuu
and pushing a baby carriage," I said, sounding much too bright.

Cadence hurried into the cottage, came back to the car, and held her golden heart bracelet out to me through the window.

I shook my head. "You can't give me this. Tom's birthday gift to you?"

"I've seen how you look at it when I wear it. You should have it. You never got your ring. You need some sort of keepsake from him."

I did love that bracelet. I let Cadence fasten it around my wrist and held it up for her to see. There was something about those golden hearts that made me feel happy.

As I watched Cadence standing there, arms wrapped across her chest, waiting for me to go, I almost sprang from the car and stayed. At least Gram would get her treatment. And the house would be repaired.

William glanced at me in the rearview mirror. "All set, Miss Stanhope?"

I took one last look at the sea view, the little cottage, the flowers at the fence. "Just drive, before I never leave," I said, and we set off, bumping up the road.

"Isn't this an extraordinary place?" I asked William.

"It certainly is, Miss Stanhope."

I'd be back one day, I was sure. Home to Copper Pond Farm.

47

CADENCE

———

1942

THE DAY AFTER BESS LEFT, I WAS GETTING READY TO VISIT GRAM at the hospital when the phone rang. I answered it to find Martha's Vineyard National Bank on the line, saying that a check in the amount of five thousand dollars had been deposited into our account. I told the man he was mistaken, said my goodbyes, and hung up. Two attempts later he simply called into the phone, "Your money is here and will be credited to your account. The memo line reads, *For Mass General,*" and he hung up.

That's when I realized it was Bess. She'd somehow convinced her mother to help Gram. And then some. It was just like her to be that generous and thoughtful. But at what cost? If Lydia Stanhope was involved, Bess might never be back.

The phone rang again, and I answered it, ready to thank the bank man and apologize for hanging up on him, but he'd given up on me and was attending to more important bank matters, it seemed. Someone else was on the line.

"Get over here straightaway, Cadence. I think you know the address."

IT DIDN'T TAKE ME LONG to drive to Winnie's house, out on West Chop, slowing only as I passed the Bayside Club, closed for the season, Mr. Wespi off at war. It was hard to picture him in combat, attacking the enemy, but passing there made me oddly nostalgic for the times Bess and I had served in the Bayside uniform.

Winnie was right about me knowing her address, since I'd often glided by her house on an ocean "tide ride" with Tom around the island. How fun those were, both of us floating on our backs in the sea, letting the current sweep us around that lovely peninsula of stately homes, doing my best to peek in and get at least a glimpse of how Winnie lived.

Hers was one of my favorites of the big old places along the shore, "the *grande dames*," Gram called them, with whole third-floor spaces for the maids. I drove Gram's truck down a short road to the house, a massive gray-shingled place with the door flung wide. As I walked up the porch steps, I could see clear through the house to Vineyard Haven Harbor. What could Winnie possibly want? Had more ASEs arrived? Did she need more titles pulled from Gram's cookie jar?

I knocked and then entered, since there was no bell, assuming Winnie and I were well enough acquainted to just walk in like that. I stepped into the living room, expecting to find it arranged in the traditional way those big houses were. I'd been inside one only once: After our parents died, Gram did housework for a rich Vineyard Haven lady, Mrs. Cooper, and she took Briar and me there. While the lady of the house was away, Gram made dinner and served it to us on Mrs. Cooper's fine china. She allowed us to drink water from the crystal goblets and even let us press the button under the table with our foot to ring the servants' bell in the kitchen. That house had been full of white wicker chairs and tables, with sterling-silver picture frames on every surface, as if Mrs. Cooper would forget who was in her family unless reminded.

I was happy to see there wasn't a piece of white wicker to be found in Winnie's house—and there wasn't even a chair, for every inch of her living room was covered in what looked like East Indian saris, draped like a white circus tent from the ceiling and gently swaying in the breeze of the open doors beyond. The floor was covered in every sort of pillow, scattered around low tables. Pink velvet. Lime-green raw silk.

My knees grew weak when I saw the stacks of books arranged about the room, many of them current bestsellers.

"Cadence, my darling, come in."

Winnie glided toward me, dressed in a flowing lemon-yellow caftan, hair slicked back, and gold hoops at her ears. She pulled me in for an embrace, the silk brushing my bare arms, her bracelets jangling, and I breathed in her exotic scent, at once spicy and sweet.

"I hope you got the telegram. We were all so sorry to hear about dear Tom."

I thanked her for the telegram, and she ushered me in, poured some brown liquid into a glass, and handed it to me.

She poured herself some of the same. "Such a sad time for you. We sent a first edition of *Emerson's Essays* to the Library of Congress in his honor."

Tears stung my eyes. "That's lovely, Winnie, thank you."

Winnie pressed a small bottle into my hand and stepped off down the hallway, caftan fluttering behind her. I opened the lid to find it full of sky-blue capsules.

"What are these?" I called to her.

"Effective," Winnie replied, from the butler's pantry.

I set the bottle on a side table. "Thank you, Winnie, but I'm fine. I just try not to think about it."

"Excellent. A skill you'll need in the publishing world."

I followed her into the butler's pantry. "Did Mrs. Stanhope talk to you about me?" I braced myself.

"She did. Came by and tried to share her dreadful secret about you. I suggested she find a better use of her time and needlepoint a pillow, with some snippy Edith Wharton quote or a declaration of love for sauvignon blanc."

"She told you I never got my diploma?"

Winnie brushed that thought away. "If stellar high school performance was a prerequisite for literary success, half the authors in the world would never have published. In France they prefer their authors self-taught, you know. Makes them more authentic. I myself barely made it through Radcliffe, and look where I am now. With a perfectly wonderful new position at Putnam."

"Oh, Winnie! Congratulations."

"That's why I've asked you to drop everything and scurry over here, my dear. Celia persuaded some bigwig there that I'm just what they need to get them through the war. They want a colorful lineup of travel books and think I'm the one to do it, since I've been practically everywhere. I'm not sure if I should be flattered or terrified by the offer. I start next week. Since my ex-husband is gone for good—last seen in the Amazon, wearing only a gorget of pig's teeth around his neck—I figured, why not?"

I sipped the brown liquor, which tasted like warm, liquid almonds going down. Everyone was leaving. Was it too much to hope that she might need me, as well? "The job sounds perfect for you."

"For *us,* you mean," Winnie said. "Of course you're coming with me as my editorial assistant. I told them that I'd already offered it to you and that I certainly couldn't do it without you, which is true."

I could barely string a sentence together.

"They'd floated some *cum laude* Barnard girl with perfect paragraph-reading scores, but I nixed that, unless you'd like an assistant, as well. The first few months will be terribly dull, I'm afraid. I'll be in Mexico City for the first book; *Where the Coffee Comes From* is the working title. What do you think? I'll be supervising the pictures and will send the rough copy home to you, which you can dish up any way you like. I know it's not fiction, but it's only until the war's end, and then we'll get back to serious literature."

"That—"

"So you can stay here on the island—in this house, if you want—tie up loose ends, and come to New York whenever you like. The pay isn't anything to brag about, but it will get you started. Plus, you'll get to travel like mad, if you like that sort of thing." Winnie looked at me, rocks glass suspended in midair, perhaps mistaking my shocked look for reluctance. "I hope that's suitable."

I knocked back the rest of my drink and set the glass down. And prepared to give her my answer.

UP-ISLAND HAPPENINGS

—

By CADENCE SMITH

WHILE OUR TROOPS MUSTER FOR BATTLE IN NORTH AFRICA and Europe, and Hitler's men add more books to their bonfires, work is afoot here on the home front to provide our troops with more books, in a new, smaller format. Thanks to G. P. Putnam's Sons and others, Armed Services Editions, aka ASEs, will feature some of the world's greatest authors and will be distributed to every service member serving abroad. Diverse titles, from *Ethan Frome* to *Dracula*, will be keeping our men amused and their minds challenged while they go about the business of winning the war.

In news closer to home, the Up-Island community came together on Copper Pond Farm and harvested a colossal crop of the newest potato variety, the mighty Burbank, for which the Smiths received a more-than-fair price from Bangs Market.

Margaret Coutinho has moved off-island to live in Cleveland, where there is sure to be a drugstore to take advantage of her pharmaceutical talents. We'll miss you, Margaret!

Mrs. Virginia Smith of Chilmark spent her first week away from this storied island since her birth and has returned in renewed health and with the assurances of half the doctors at Massachusetts General Hospital that she will continue to flourish. In her suitcase are countless requests for the recipe for her Molasses Hermits, the treats that accompanied her upon check-in and were distributed to the staff. She continues to write to the families of downed servicemen who once graced our little island with their boundless good humor and friendship. She hopes it is a small comfort for the loved ones of those who so valiantly served their country.

This will be the last column penned by this author, for she will be traveling to and from New York City soon to work in publishing, as personal editorial assistant to Mrs. Winnie Winthrop at Putnam. It has been her greatest pleasure to take up this little corner of the world each week, and she hopes you wish her well, off to see the world.

48

BRIAR

—

September 2, 1945

THREE YEARS AFTER THAT TERRIBLE NIGHT WITH TYSON, THE war finally came to an end. Cadence heard on the radio that the Japanese surrender seemed likely at any time and said small groups were gathering across the island, waiting to share the joyous news with neighbors and friends. She suggested I go join one, but I told her I'd rather watch the celebrations from my sentry tree, and there I sat, on top of the world.

My eye went to the cottage below and to Gram's flowers along the front fence. The whole back of the house had been rebuilt, thanks to Bess. Gram would have loved being there to see that bumper crop of lilies, but she had died the year before, asleep in her bed at home, two years after her successful treatment at Mass General. We'd never told her the truth about Tyson and how the fire started. Cadence took the blame and said she'd left the linguica frying on the stove too long. Gram never did recover from the terrible news about Tom. And she was right. We really did miss her when she was gone.

At nineteen, I lived like a dormant cicada, burrowed deep in the ground, working the farm, waiting on war news, ready for it to end. Someone had a car radio turned up loud out by the Methodist church in Chilmark Center, probably in order to hear the announcement once it came. Even miles away I could feel the anticipation.

It had been a long five years of war and the island had matured, grown a thicker skin through it all. Sandra's house had been turned into a coffee shop, and McManus was kicked upstairs to New York City, with bigger fish to fry than us. The summer people would still come and go, and the carousel of seasons would still turn. Just not like before.

I tried to picture Tom's face and tensed, having trouble conjuring it. If he'd been here, what would he be doing to celebrate? Certainly be at the church tolling the bells himself.

A great cheer went up in the distance, and I turned in the direction of the church. First the Chilmark bell began to toll, and then West Tisbury joined in. And people started blaring their automobile horns, something no one had done since the start of the war.

It was over.

I tried to soak in the joy of the moment, but I felt blank. Maybe I just missed Tom too much. He'd given his life, and it was hard to celebrate while carrying that weight. They'd never even found Tom's body.

I looked to the upper field. I missed Peter and Margaret, too. I hoped they were in Minnesota with his grandmother and daughter. I missed Bess, as well, but much as Cadence held out hope, I had a feeling she'd never return. Once she left, she cut off all contact with us. Tom had a two-and-a-half-year-old child out there somewhere.

My gaze wandered to the boulder near the grove of beetlebungs where Tyson lay. Only the postmaster had inquired about him, and Cadence said he'd had to ship out unexpectedly. Cadence heard from her friend at the draft board that they assumed Tyson had left the country to evade service. Shelby had asked about him only once, then married a Cornell student from Nantucket one year later and moved to Ithaca. It still gave me the willies to walk near that boulder. Even Scout gave it a wide berth.

I never did find the Totenkopf ring in the belongings Tyson left behind. It was better he'd probably been buried with it, one less piece of evil out there in the world.

I looked down the coast toward Lambert's Cove Beach, a haze over it, and thought of all our island-trained boys who'd been lost on the beaches at Normandy. The rumors had been right: The Army was practicing here for the Allied invasion of western Europe. I liked to think that their training had at least given them an advantage as they landed and so bravely faced the German machine guns at Pointe du Hoc. Almost half of them never came home. But perhaps the casualties would have been even greater if Tyson had succeeded in divulging American strategies to Hitler.

I felt a vibration below and up came Cadence, working her way through the leafy branches. That was a first, my sister climbing a tree. Cadence clumsily reached the branch below mine and sat.

"Thought I'd come report on the end-of-the-war happenings," she said. "But you already have a good view of it all." Cadence took in the vista. "No wonder you like it up here."

"Welcome."

"Nice outfit," she said, nodding at my tweed waistcoat and cap. "I just got back from driving around a bit. It's quite a scene in town. Everyone out of their minds, crying with happiness. Rose Miller, more than anyone, was a wreck, with her two boys still serving."

"Glad they'll be coming home."

"Everyone was ripping up their gas-ration cards and making confetti out of them and driving up and down South and North Roads leaning on their horn buttons. Two privates from Peaked Hill were dragged off the road and forced to tolerate kisses from Gram's church ladies."

"Poor guys," I said. "You should go back and celebrate more."

"It'll be going on for a long time. I'm enjoying being here with you." Cadence paused, then said, "I was thinking. With Tom gone, you might need a new sailing partner."

"That'd be great," I said, but couldn't quite warm to the idea. With a little work, Cadence would make a fine partner, but I had a hard time even thinking about sailing the boat without Tom.

"And we still have a book club, you know. Agnes and Ethel want to join, Gram's pals. I know you hate fiction, but we're reading *Brideshead Revisited* before I go. Winnie sent us copies."

I'd flipped through one of those books when the box arrived from New York City, and it didn't look half bad for fiction. "Not sure I want to read a book about men calling each other 'old sponge,'" I said.

But I liked the story. Figured I'd give it a try.

I looked down at the beach, where Cadence and Bess's little book-club flag still waved. I liked the way that, no matter the weather, Cadence still raised it every morning and lowered it each night. Maybe I'd keep that going when she left.

Perhaps I was just maturing, my frontal cortex developing, but something about the idea of being with Gram's friends and eating Grandma's Rocks with a beetlebung-honey wine chaser appealed to me.

I moved over to make room for Cadence next to me on the branch. "Do you miss Gil?" I asked.

Cadence had kept in touch with Major Gil, and he was still hot to trot. He'd survived the war and was even decorated for combat in Italy, but he seemed pretty ensconced in London, and she was working for Winnie long distance and planning to make the move to New York City later that fall. Turned out Cadence wasn't so quick to rush off as I figured she'd be.

We heard that our Private Jeffers from Preston, Idaho, had been awarded the Medal of Honor for heroism after dying on the battlefield. He had stayed at his post, on a beach in New Guinea, wounded, and fought off the Japanese until the end. We'd found out about it not long before Gram passed, and she had sent Mrs. Jeffers a note, telling her how much we'd enjoyed her son.

"I'll see Gil soon enough," Cadence said. "He's coming over from London. Just a look-see, whatever that means. I hope you'll be okay when I'm gone. You can always come to New York with me."

I looked down on the barn. I would be better than okay. Once we had acquired the exclusive sale of Burbanks on the island, I pushed Gram to invest in ten cows and resume production as a dairy farm. We flourished after Gil arranged a contract for us to sell our Copper Pond Creamery products to the military. I suggested they print a drawing Bess had made of a sweet cow on every milk bottle. What would Tom have thought to see me here running the whole operation? At least it helped me get up every day.

"Gil said they used the *Naushon* as a hospital ship at Normandy,"

Cadence said, referencing the beloved steamship that had been requisitioned for war duty in Europe. "One of his commandos recognized it when they picked him up off the beach at Pointe du Hoc. Gave him a good bit of comfort."

"Tom would have liked that." I pulled at a twig. "Maybe you should go visit Gil in London. Try to see Bess."

I had watched Cadence slowly give up on expecting letters from Bess. At first she'd sent daily letters to Boston, only to find them back at the post office, *Return to Sender* stamped on the front. Cadence had even taken the train there and knocked on the Stanhopes' townhouse door in Beacon Hill, but the house was closed up tight. Cadence heard through the grapevine that the Stanhopes had moved to Paris, but we knew little else. I figured Tom's child would be talking by now, in French no less.

"Maybe," Cadence said. "I think she has moved on. We were only a phase for her."

"Don't say that. Maybe we remind her too much of Tom."

A movement caught my eye down at the cottage, as Scout walked along the front fence and lay in her spot. Still waiting for Tom? Maybe just watching for squirrels.

"I'll try to look Bess up," Cadence said. "But in the meantime, don't you want to at least come and have some fun? Celebrate?"

Something pulled at me, a gentle tug of positivity. Tom had wanted me to grow up and become a citizen of the world. Why had I resisted for so long? It was something I could do for my brother.

I worked my way to the branch below. "Let's go down."

"Are you sure?" Cadence asked, perhaps surprised that her coaching had worked.

"Come on." I reached up to take her hand. "Let's go join the living."

A MONTH AFTER THE END of the war, the confetti was still sprinkled on the ground, but the island was busy getting back to normal. I still heard the sounds of a few soldiers at Peaked Hill now and then, but most had moved on, the manic hum of activity up there now quiet. Fewer airplanes came and went from the new airport, a relief from the near-constant drone overhead. And even though the Sones had not returned to their gift shop, I hoped they'd come back next summer, after an outpouring of letters on the part of their devoted island fans. At least Bert the Barber was at his chair again. Cadence and I had driven by his Main Street shop and the line was out the door.

The island welcomed October, always my favorite month, when the summer people were long gone and fall arrived in full force. I'd craved the smell of wood fires and baked apples, the crisp nights with the stars on show. Walking the beach, the sand cold on my feet.

Scout took up the rear as I brought the cows to the barn for milking, our lead cow Louise forging ahead, the bell at her throat clanking a little song. Scout, now almost nine, still followed us everywhere, just a little more slowly. At the cottage Cadence took the wash from the line, gathering a sheet in her arms as it ballooned in the cool breeze, and I felt a surge of love for her, always so willing to go on, no matter the headwinds.

In the distance along Copper Pond Road, something caught my eye, starch white in the sunlight, like a great swan floating toward us. I looked harder. It was a nun of some order, wearing an enormous white cornette. I shaded my eyes with one hand and squinted. The nun held the arm of an elderly man as they made their way down the road.

My heart thumped and I walked, as if levitated, toward them. The man wasn't elderly, I saw, though he picked his steps carefully.

Was I hallucinating?

"My God," I said, and took off at a run, Scout close behind. I could barely breathe by the time I made it to them, and I took in Tom, his face more lined and pale, but it was him. I threw my arms around his neck, and he was so thin I could feel his vertebrae. I held him out to get a good look, letting it all sink in. "You're home."

He looked at me and smiled a bit, perhaps taken aback by my enthusiastic welcome. I would be gentler. He was recovering, after all.

Tom was back.

Cadence threw down her sheet and ran to us, crying and kissing Tom's cheeks, and we hugged our brother.

"It might be good for him to find a chair," the little nun almost whispered in a breathy French accent.

We apologized for not greeting her sooner. The young woman introduced herself as Sister Claire, a Sister of Charity, and Scout led us into the cottage, Cadence still smothering Tom with kisses along the way.

We took seats at the kitchen table as Cadence boiled water for tea and I held Tom's hand, his skin smooth and opaque, the skin of a shut-in. *Where had he been?*

I watched him closely while he surveyed the kitchen, as if just having landed on Neptune. He looked much older than his twenty-three years, stooped and gaunt but well-dressed, in his hand-knit sweater and linen trousers.

I tried not to cry when Scout came to sit at Tom's side, as if her master had never left. "Good girl," Tom said, caressing the dog's ear with his free hand. His voice was a bit lower and a touch gravelly, but a trill of joy ran through me at the sound of it.

"That's the first thing you've spoken, Tom," I said. Tom turned and regarded me, as if looking at some new acquaintance on the street. *He doesn't remember me.* The thought heaved through me.

Cadence smiled at Sister Claire. "We've never let poor Tom get a word in edgewise."

As Cadence plied us all with scones and clotted cream, I slowly realized, with a sinking heart, that Tom was alive and healthy but he wasn't "all there," as Gram would have said.

Tom removed his stocking cap to reveal a scar at his temple, almost proud of it, and Sister Claire explained the story she herself had pieced together over the years. She'd spent most of the war corresponding with the nun in France who'd found him.

"Sister Agnès, have you heard of her?" she asked. "They call her the Angel of Dieppe. After the battle there, she walked the coast of France, searching for fallen men who were still alive. She didn't give up on finding survivors, though the Allies had moved on."

As if in a dream, I listened to her explain that Tom had been left for dead and taken to Sister Agnès's convent, where they assumed he was Canadian, seeing no dog tags and hearing only the French phrases Tom muttered.

"He repeated, *Je t'aime plus*," Sister Claire said.

One of the phrases Bess had taught him. *I love you more.*

"The Germans had stripped him of everything," Sister Claire said.

She told us that Sister Agnès sent Tom by ship to Canada, to the Sisters of Charity, a cloistered order in Quebec, hoping they could find his family. Once Tom recovered enough to sketch in some of his history, Sister Claire eventually traced him to Copper Pond Farm, and the Holy Mother of the convent funded their trip there by train. Being cloistered, the nuns were not allowed to use the phone, but they had sent letters—to a wrong address that Tom had misremembered. He'd told them he was in the Coast Guard, which he might have thought was true. There were sixty-three Thomas Smiths in the military, and that letter of inquiry was probably still on someone's desk.

I sat back, exhausted after taking it all in. It was the most incredible story I had ever heard, and I longed to get Tom alone so I could learn more details. And I itched to thoroughly test his faculties.

He'd been lucky to survive a gunshot wound to the head; I assumed that's what caused Tom's amnesia. And he was exhibiting the same symptoms our grandfather had after his stroke: aphasia and minor facial paralysis. I made a mental list of treatments. I'd start with flash cards of words. Everyday objects and place names.

Tom looked toward the kitchen door. "Is she . . ."

"Who?" Cadence asked. She paused a moment. "Bess?"

He nodded.

Of course he remembered that name. The love of his life.

Cadence frowned, in that trembly way she always did when she tried not to cry. "Bess left a few years ago. We think she's in Europe."

He nodded, seemed satisfied with that answer, and looked to Sister Claire for direction. Had he ever gotten Bess's letter about the baby?

I told him about Gram, and he looked down at his hands. Was he even able to take it all in? Did he remember her? In time the memory might come back. Grandfather's had. Tom and I would paint together—that was a start. Maybe I'd help him write a letter to Bess. Take the boat out.

I nudged his arm with my elbow. "What do you say we go out for a sail sometime? Cadence has agreed to come along."

He turned to me and met my gaze. "Hi, Port."

I saw it there, the light of recognition, and gave in to the sweet surge of joy.

"Hi, Starboard," I said with a smile. "I've missed you."

49

MARI

2 0 1 6

I SAT BACK IN MY CHAIR AS MRS. DEVEREAUX FINISHED, SUNLIGHT filling the little kitchen. So many questions swirled in me. Was this my actual family?

I had painted all night as Mrs. D. talked and now sat, spent, at the kitchen table, listening to the sound of waves hitting the shore in the distance. I'd finished a piece at last. It wasn't perfect, little more than a rough study, but I knew it was one of the best things I'd painted.

Mrs. Devereaux came over and sat down next to me. "She's lovely."

It was my mother, just head and shoulders, and I'd painted her there at the table, the fireplace as a background. It was almost as if I hadn't painted it myself, and I loved the brushwork, bold and layered, the palette much softer than anything I'd done before, almost monochromatic, in beiges and muted pinks. She wasn't forcing some fake smile, just wearing what I called her Happy Nancy face, in her best place, mellowed out, like she was listening to music, ready for us to have a glass of wine and talk about stupid little stuff about work or her yoga class.

"She looks exactly like you," I said to Mrs. Devereaux. Why had it taken me so long? Mrs. D. was my grandmother. Maybe I'd known it the whole time.

I turned to her. "My mother was Tom and Bess's baby, wasn't she?"

She nodded. "Yes."

"And you're Bess. You're my grandmother."

She nodded, eyes bright.

I wanted to laugh and cry, overcome by it all. I was a Smith after all. But my mom had never even gotten to meet her own mother, at least not that she remembered. How close they'd come to a reunion.

"I know it's a lot to take in," she said. "At least you know the whole story now. I feel like I haven't let you get a word in edgewise."

"Tom was my grandfather—did you two ever see each other again when he came back?"

She looked at her hands. "No."

"Why not?" My eyes stung with tears. "He loved you so much."

"After I went home to Boston, I delivered the baby early. Mother arranged to have the infant removed from the nursery; she claimed the child had died, but she'd secretly put her up for adoption. I eventually found out what my mother had done."

"She was a witch," I said. My great-grandmother.

"Then Mother sent me to the Sorbonne to learn painting, which she hoped would snap me out of my depression over losing the child, and it did, I suppose."

"That's where you married?"

"Yes. Happily at first. But in time we ended up divorcing, since I couldn't bring myself to try for another child."

"So you and Tom never reunited? How is that even possible?"

"I never reached out to the Smiths again. I assumed Tom was dead and knew Mother would bring the wrath of God down on them if I contacted Cadence. And then, before Mother passed, she confessed the whole thing. I was happy to know my baby had lived, but I was overcome with grief and anger."

"You never told Cadence?" I asked.

"No. I was too crippled by the shame of having lost my child to reconnect with the Smiths."

I stood and walked the room. "How awful for you."

"I hired a private detective, took out ads. Collected a whole scrapbook of clues to my baby's whereabouts. Once I found her, I thought, I would reconnect with the Smiths. But Mother had made certain the child could not be found."

I sat and pulled my chair closer to Mrs. Devereaux.

"Eventually, Cadence died and then Briar followed, and I received a letter in Paris. Ever the detective, Briar had hired her own private eye, and he'd finally found me after she passed. The letter said that Briar had left me this farm, as caretaker, so I moved back here and painted, turned the barn into my studio. And then one day my own detective told me he had a lead. Meanwhile, your mother had been looking for her own birth parents."

I sat back in my chair. It was like a dream. "It makes sense Tom was my mom's dad. She had his personality for sure. The same kind of charisma."

Mrs. D. pulled out a photo of Tom sailing in a boat. "Here's your grandfather. Briar took this one."

I searched Mrs. D.'s face. "But my mom was definitely a combo of you both. His eyes and coloring but your expressions, too."

"Do you think?" she said, her eyes bright with tears.

I took out my phone and opened my videos. "Here's one of her baking. Flag Day shortbread. Don't you see it? There. The way she does that thing with her nose when she smiles. And look—the way she bites her lip like you do?"

She dried her eyes. "I'm so dreadfully sorry we never met."

I took her hand in mine. "Me, too. She would have loved you and this place and that story. But at least she knew you existed. And at least I finally found you. It was kind of a miracle, don't you think?"

She nodded and looked to the painting. "Indeed."

"What happened to the Smith girls?" I asked. "My great-aunts, right? Did Cadence go to New York?"

"They tell me she traveled extensively with Winnie Winthrop after the war and became quite well known in literary circles as a book critic, rivaling even Mary McCarthy herself."

"And Gil?"

"He made it back to England in one piece, though with only about a quarter of his Cape Cod Commandos."

"Did Gil and Cadence marry?"

"They did, and he came to join her in New York City and became an advertising executive. They eventually bought Winnie Winthrop's

Sutton Place apartment, after Win moved to Zanzibar to start a publishing company for the sultan, and the two of them lived there quite happily, though childless."

"And Briar? She was amazing."

"She ended up living here for years, with Tom, never feeling the need to marry, I suppose. That's her yellow jeep I still drive. She got Tommy much rehabilitated—though never quite the same, of course—and under their watch, Copper Pond Creamery reached new heights just after the war. But then years later, once Tom passed, Briar scaled back the dairy. She made some incredible ship models in her later years. You can see them at the Martha's Vineyard Museum, which was once the old Marine Hospital."

"And the cops never found Tyson Schmidt's body?"

"No. His parents were Hitler devotees and, later, folks found out they'd moved to Germany, so by the time he was officially missing, people just assumed he'd joined his family."

"It's creepy to think Tyson Schmidt's buried here."

"What we did helped. If he'd been allowed to escape to Germany with all he knew, more boys could have died. As it was, we lost almost half of the ones who were stationed here."

I looked out the window, down toward the beach in the distance. So many of them had trained right there.

On the flagpole, the little pink flag swayed in the breeze.

"You still raise the book-club burgee," I said.

"Every morning that I'm vertical. Though it's getting grungy. Maybe time for a new one."

I stood and set my painting on the fireplace mantel, next to the tugboat model. It felt surreal to suddenly have a new grandmother. Good, but somewhat awkward.

"Who do you think I'm most like?" I asked.

That set her off crying again, so she could barely get the words out. "My Tom. I knew the minute I saw you. His beautiful eyes. His gentle way. Even your laugh. I feel like I have my Tommy back."

I felt my face and it was wet, though I didn't even know I was crying. I set my hand over hers. "So what do we do now?"

She dried her eyes again. "I have so many questions about your mother, and you, as well, but I suppose we should discuss the business end of things. Briar's will specifies that I'm the caretaker in perpetuity of this place, unless a Smith child presents him or herself. So, if you want the farm, you can claim it."

"Wait. What?" For some reason I hadn't tracked that far on all of it. She was *giving* it to me.

She pulled a document from a drawer. "There are stipulations. *Conditional on transfer of the property, the beneficiary must oversee the dairy operation in order to pay the taxes and maintain the property.*"

"You mean I'd run this place?" I held out one hand. "I can't do that."

"It contributes a great deal to the food bank and helps feed a lot of people out here, so it requires a healthy amount of oversight, but I believe you could handle it. Twelve employees. Payroll. It barely breaks even, so it's not like you'll make tons of money from it, but it's an immensely satisfying life."

It was one thing to discover my family but another to have the weight of that land on me.

"Wow. I have to tell you, I'm not the most organized person in the world. I work at a juice bar. I barely figured out how to refill the condiments station." I scraped the chair back and stood. "I need to go."

"Don't be silly. The last boat isn't until seven-thirty."

"I just can't." It was all so much. Good and bad, but mostly scary. Dizzy, I tried hard to breathe but couldn't catch my breath.

"Are you all right?" Mrs. D. asked.

"Do you have a paper bag?"

I could see it all coming. The big expectations, high hopes for the long-lost Smith girl, and then would come the fall. I shook my hands to warm them. I was catastrophizing—one thing I was actually good at, according to my therapist.

Mrs. D. brought me a bag and I breathed into it and held up one finger. She rubbed my back sweetly, and soon I started to feel better.

"I need a minute," I said, setting the bag down and inhaling deeply.

"Take as long as you like."

I sat up straighter. "I'm sorry. Go ahead. How do the developers factor in?"

"Well, the will stipulates that if no Smith descendant claims the property, it cannot be sold, since I am just a caretaker. I wanted to donate it to the land bank upon my death, but that's what the developers are challenging. They claim that once I'm gone, the property should go into public domain for them to purchase. For a song, of course."

"They only care about money."

"I've seen the plans. They want to build a luxury community with a golf course."

The thought of it made me sick. The mega-mansions, the tennis courts.

"You could challenge them," she said. "It won't be easy. They'll fight you even with genetic proof you're a Smith, but my money's on you. Does your job require notice?"

I imagined that conversation with Jamba assistant manager Kevin, who barely knew I worked there and called me Mandy. "No."

"A boyfriend?"

Would Nate even know I'd gone? "Kind of. So, I'll have to do a DNA test? Like spit in a tube? I've never done one."

"Yes. They'll require genetic proof. But to me, this is proof positive you're a Smith." She ran her finger along the heart bracelet at my wrist. "Cadence gave me that the day I left the farm for good. Her sixteenth-birthday gift from Tom."

"How did my mother get it?"

"When she was born, I doubled it and slipped it onto her wrist. Silly, I know, but it was my gift to our baby from him."

"So you knew your baby was a girl."

Bess lost herself in the painting. "Yes. I remember holding her right after the birth. But they'd given me some sort of drugs, and I didn't know it was the last time I'd see her. Mother barely looked at the baby before she had her sent off—the doctor in charge handled it all, paid handsomely. Didn't even get a chance to name her." She shifted her gaze to me. "And now here we are. With you, the last of the Smith girls."

"This is a lot." I ran my fingers through my hair. "It's amazing and a great story, but my mother *just* died. I'm still cleaning out our apartment."

"I completely understand," she said. "And this life and this island aren't for everyone. If you prefer to stay in California, the land bank will fight for this place and hopefully win. They're set to begin opening arguments next week."

Being handed a farm on Martha's Vineyard, while incredible, was something I was totally unprepared for. Court? Even if we won, I'd have to run a business. Payroll? I'd have to move all of my stuff here and then learn to actually farm. Drive a tractor? I hadn't even driven a car in five years. And Nate was not about to give up his tech thing to come out east and run a farm.

"I don't want to seem ungrateful. I'm incredibly glad I found my birth family, and *you,* after all these years. It's just that I'm terrible at public speaking—I'm not sure I could stand up in a courtroom and make any sense. And I'm absolutely hopeless with machinery of any kind. And calendars and organizational stuff, too. Can I tell you once I sleep on it?"

"Of course. But you might want to make a quick decision." She leaned in. "I don't buy green bananas, as they say. And I booked a new flight for you, by the way. But for now let's spend some time on the beach, and then we'll get you packed up and to the boat."

THE RIDE TO THE ferry in Vineyard Haven was a blur as I sorted through a tangle of thoughts. Was I turning down the opportunity of a lifetime? But there was no way I could handle running a farm on Martha's Vineyard, never mind fighting for it in court. I already felt such a deep connection to this place after that story, and I was flattered that my newfound grandmother thought I could do it, but she didn't know the real Mari Starwood, mess-up extraordinaire.

She dropped me at the ferry and drove away. I'd heard of the Irish goodbye, where people leave without a farewell, but this must've been the Martha's Vineyard goodbye.

"Hey!" I called after her. "Are we gonna write or text or stay in touch somehow?"

She just waved, and I went ahead and boarded the ferry, right back where I'd started only two days ago. I made my way past the cars parked in the belly of the ship and climbed the stairs to the top deck.

I stood at the railing, next to other passengers waving to people on shore. I checked my phone and finally had a few bars and a full battery. No missed call from Nate. I rang his number, and the call went to voicemail, so I hung up and took in the view of the harbor and the sweet town, so old-fashioned and unspoiled. How did big developers live with themselves, ruining places like this purely for money? Did they even live here?

Suddenly I spotted Mrs. D. below, standing next to the jeep in the parking lot, as the orange-vested workers guided the last of the cars onto the ferry.

It was cooler up here with night falling. The lights started coming on along what I figured must be West Chop, and a couple strolled along the harbor beach, past a ritzy-looking club, probably where my grandmother and great-aunt had worked as waitresses. Over at his bike shop across from the ferry, Ronan White wheeled a bike in from the front porch. It was that moment between light and dark when anything seems possible.

Maybe I was just freaked out by the enormity of it all. And the prospect of failing. It seemed like someone else's life. A movie where they tell Anne Hathaway she's been royalty all along. But it wasn't as if living here would be all farmers markets and yoga in the barn. And relocating wouldn't be easy. And I'd only seen snow at Big Bear. I'd need sweaters. And a winter coat.

Down in the parking lot, my grandmother was trying to get my attention. Where had I seen that before? How she stood on her toes and waved her arm like a metronome, trying a little too hard to be happy about me leaving? My mother had waved like that when she saw me off on the bus to Camp Hollywoodland the summer when I was eight. How did they have the same wave?

Chances were, my own mother would have preferred it here on the island, the place where she should have been raised by Bess and the Smiths. What a different life she would have had, fishing and foraging, loved and fed big dreams, safely tethered to the invisible thread of her family. Maybe it was the best place for me, too.

What would it be like to fight the developers? Like badass Mariska Hargitay on *Law & Order*. She always won. The more I thought about it, the idea of taking on a bunch of greedy contractors made me feel lighter somehow. I could at least try. L.A. was great, but the only things left for me there were a reluctant boyfriend and a rented apartment. My landlady could send me the few things I'd left. Or just donate them.

Ronan White would at least be one friend. And I could always restart that book club.

And I'd have my grandmother beside me.

I watched the final car drive onto the boat, and the man in the orange vest gave the cutoff signal to someone below. I hurried to the stairs and took them two at a time down to the belly of the ferry, now packed with cars, and ran between them to the man putting the chain across the mouth of the ship.

"You gotta take the passenger ramp," he said, as I stepped over the chain.

"Sorry," I called over my shoulder, and ran for the parking lot.

I made it to the yellow jeep and found it empty. Catching my breath, I scanned the lot, and then the fudge store, and the T-shirt shop. Where had she gone? The ferry whistle blew, and I turned and watched the ship sail away, happy I wasn't on it. But where was Mrs. D.? I'd expected to return to her, triumphant, hoping to bring a smile to her face.

I hurried up the hill and walked Main Street, checking stores and even the public-bathroom stalls. I finally found her sitting under a tree, on a bench next to the old movie theater.

"You're back," she said.

"There you are." I sighed, relieved. "Where did you go?"

She raised the cardboard coffee cup in her hand. "Matcha may be good for you, but it tastes like fish-tank water, don't you agree?"

I sat next to her on the bench. "I was thinking. Maybe I wouldn't be such a bad farmer, actually."

"Oh, really?" She stood and headed toward the parking lot, sipping her matcha as we walked. "Why the change of heart?"

I slipped my hand through the crook of her arm and held her closer. "I don't know. It isn't every day you find your long-lost family."

We came to the jeep, and she slid behind the wheel and waved for me to get in. "It won't be easy. You're open to taking them on?"

"If we can't move heaven, then we'll just raise hell, right?"

She looked at me and nodded. "I think you'll do just fine."

"I'm a Smith girl, after all," I said with a smile.

"Isn't that just extraordinary," my grandmother said, as she started the jeep.

And we drove off together. Home to Copper Pond Farm.

AUTHOR'S NOTE

I BASED THE CHARACTER OF CADENCE SMITH ON MY MOTHER, Joanne Finnegan Hall, who grew up on Martha's Vineyard and loved the island but always wanted to leave it.

The youngest of four children, Joanne was raised on her Smith grandparents' family farm in West Tisbury. Her grandparents, Emma Melling Smith and William Smith, now buried in Oak Grove Cemetery in Vineyard Haven, came to the island in 1891, after meeting in the New Bedford textile mills, where Emma had worked since the age of six, picking up spools from the mill floors. They hoped to earn a living growing flowers on the Vineyard, in the yard of the farmhouse they bought, which still stands today on State Road, next door to North Tisbury Farm Market.

Their daughter, my mother's mother, Emma Louise, enrolled in teachers' college off-island and came home at school break via steamship. She disembarked at Aquinnah—then named Gay Head—and caught a ride home from Bart Mayhew in his oxcart. She married Christopher Finnegan from Bridgewater, Massachusetts, and they opened a grocery store in Westmoreland, New Hampshire, but moved back to the island to care for Emma's mother when her father died.

My mother told great stories of what sounded like a tranquil but poor childhood. How people Up-Island spoke Martha's Vineyard Sign Language back in the day, and how she found her tricycle and her books at the town dump, where the summer people discarded their belongings at the season's end. She wasn't picky about where her books came from, just as long as she had a new one in her hands.

On the heels of the Depression, her father, Christopher Finnegan, supported the family by working at Bangs Market in Vineyard Haven. After he died at the kitchen table one morning, unable to get to his nitroglycerine pills, her mother was left with four children and no income, so they sold flowers and vegetables, took in laundry, and sold donuts out front of their home (much to my aunt Mary's embarrassment) for twenty-five cents a dozen.

My favorite stories my mother told were about World War II on the island. The rumors of Germans coming ashore from U-boats. How at night they could hear the subs recharging their batteries just offshore. She described how, when she was fourteen years old, the convoys of Army jeeps would drive by their farm, on their way up to Peaked Hill Army base, and how friendly and kind the soldiers were. How she and her friends Betty Cottle and Shirley Kennedy, too young to go to USO dances, were so happy to see all the handsome soldiers in town and how they called them "their boys."

And how after the war so many of their boys never came home.

The character Tom Smith was inspired by my uncle John "Sonny" Finnegan, who left Martha's Vineyard to enlist in the Army Air Corps in 1941, became a B-17 ball-turret gunner in World War II, and was shot down over Messina, Sicily. The only survivor of his downed plane, he was rescued, hidden, and healed by nuns in a convent there, who eventually returned him to his family on the Vineyard, and he went on to marry and raise a family in California.

From the soup-can ankles and ample bosom to the tea-leaf reading, my childhood memories of my infinitely kind grandmother Emma Louise helped me create my fictional Virginia "Gram" Smith. The originator of the phrase "You'll miss me when I'm gone," which she would half-jokingly say, Emma Louise was pure love. Even when she could only afford to make Potato Bargain for supper, she always set a formal table, with a tablecloth and her best napkins, thinking that made the food seem more substantial somehow. Though maybe not quite the baker the fictional Gram Smith was, Emma Louise did her best. My sister Polly Simpkins, who now owns my parents' house on William Street in Vineyard Haven, found Emma Louise's *First Baptist Church of*

Vineyard Haven Cookbook, the recipes from which I used as my fictional Gram's recipes. Emma Louise's cookie contribution to the cookbook, Grandma's Rocks, has only one instruction: *Drop from spoon.* They're simple and delicious, perfect for a woman who had a lot going on. I wish she could see how inspired her great-grandchildren are by her resilience.

To create the character Bess Stanhope, I combined my mother's friends Betty Cottle and Shirley Kennedy—smart, funny, principled New England women, my mother's stalwart friends from childhood until the day she died. We have wonderful photos of the three of them in my mother's new yellow convertible Willys jeep, her prized possession. Though my mother died in 2000, and Betty in 2021, Shirley is doing beautifully, still living in her house in Vineyard Haven, and she helped me fill in the gaps, happily recounting stories of their war years: The Jive Hive rec center for the teens not old enough to go to USO dances. Her fond memories of Katharine Cornell and Darling's popcorn shop. Shirley even filled me in on the give-a-little-take-a-little dump rule.

After the war, my mother worked as a medical secretary at the Marine Hospital in Vineyard Haven, now the home of the splendid Martha's Vineyard Museum. There she met my father, William Hall, a Coast Guard ensign from Arlington, Massachusetts, who became a patient at the hospital. Joanne checked his chart and, finding him healthy, allowed him to call on her, and they had their first kiss while sitting on a bench at the West Chop overlook. They soon married and left on the *Islander* steamship in 1948. Finally, off to see the world.

My mother's first love was always reading, and her friends and their love for books and for one another inspired the book club in this novel. When my parents moved back to the island in 1979 and bought a sea captain's home on William Street in Vineyard Haven, my mother was so happy to be back within walking distance of the Bunch of Grapes Bookstore, her cathedral of sorts for years. Every Christmas my father gave her a bookstore gift card, and the next day she kept one eye on the door, waiting for him to carry home her best gift, a sky-high stack of books. I think she'd be thrilled to see how the Vineyard book scene has flourished, including Bunch of Grapes, in its new home; Edgartown Books, more vibrant than ever; and all six island town libraries, thriving.

My mother loved reuniting with Betty and Shirley and, together with Jan Van Riper, Dorothy Bangs, and Jacquie Renear, they would sit on Lambert's Cove Beach, snack on Ritz crackers and cheese, and read books and play cards—the original Martha's Vineyard Beach and Book Club.

I was lucky to have Bow Van Riper, the research director of the Martha's Vineyard Museum, on my side. Bow helped me navigate the 1940s, including his family's Van Ryper Model Shop, a world-class modeling business that once operated in our own little Vineyard Haven, the best of the old Vineyard. In 1933, Bow's grandfather Charles opened the shop, which made yachts and favorite ships for boat lovers, as well as recognition models for the military once the war started. Today the models are extremely rare and collectible, and two even ended up in the hands of U.S. presidents. Though the shop worked on many government contracts, the classified room and Briar's pilfering of documents is purely fictional.

Bow also generously lent me his own sailboat's name, *Tyche*, and sent me his father Tony's hand-drawn map of 1941 downtown Vineyard Haven, complete with store names penciled in. It was invaluable in helping me bring Main Street alive, even down to the four grocery stores in town, including the A&P where my mother had worked; she often told us how she added up the grocery prices on the back of a brown paper bag with a pencil. Our parents were the best of friends, and some days it felt like Bow's mother, Jan, and my mother were right there with us, piecing together island history.

As my former co–room mother of our daughters' third-grade class in Fairfield, Connecticut, Sissy Biggers, now the community engagement and program director of the Carnegie Heritage Center in Edgartown, was a tremendous research help, as well. She filled me in on Edgartown during the war years and made introductions to help me tour some of the most beautiful homes in Edgartown, which helped make Mrs. Stanhope's house come alive.

The wonderful Tom Dresser also so generously helped me with Vineyard wartime research. When we met at his house for tea, he was surprised to see I'd dog-eared almost every page of his extraordinary book, *Martha's Vineyard in World War II,* which he co-wrote with two friends. It includes the Peaked Hill Army base, which a sure-footed hiker can still climb up to today for a breathtaking view of the island.

After the attack on Pearl Harbor, it was clear that the Japanese were well ahead of the United States in amphibious ship-to-shore invasions. At a U.S.–U.K. conference in London, Lord Louis Mountbatten suggested assembling battalions of highly trained American amphibious specialists that would receive their initial training in the United States and their final in England. The U.S. War Department established a boat training center at Camp Edwards, in Falmouth, Massachusetts, brought over several British Army and Navy officers, and placed ads to recruit civilian boat operators from across America. There was an outpouring of volunteers from every part of the country: Masters of Great Lakes vessels. Amateur yachtsmen from Long Island and Lake St. Clair. Boatbuilders from small boatyards. Small-town blacksmiths and New York City longshoremen. And the 2nd Engineer Amphibian Brigade was born.

The waters and beaches of Cape Cod and Martha's Vineyard were ideal for training the amphibians. The mock invasion of August 1942 was an enormous military exercise executed to test the new amphibious landing craft and commando training. The invasion originated at Camp Edwards, and the top military brass chose the Vineyard's North Shore for its similarities to Normandy's rocky coast. The landing craft were manned by the Engineer Brigade, who became known by locals as the Cape Cod Commandos. That nickname stuck and followed them across the Pacific Ocean to Australia, New Guinea, and the Philippines. Whenever they were in a tight spot, or just lonely and tired, someone would bolster them with a "Come on, you Cape Cod Commandos" and a laugh.

During the "Martha's Vineyard Maneuvers," troops clambered out of the boats and up the beaches, simulating a beach landing under hostile fire. They proceeded to the newly built airport to "capture" it, the commandos crawling through the gardens and yards of Vineyard residents.

The mock invasion was a great success, on target and on schedule, and the lessons learned laid the groundwork for tactics later used under battle conditions. Later in the war, local residents rooted for their Cape Cod Commandos as the troops spearheaded campaigns in North Africa, Sicily, Salerno, Normandy, and many islands in the Pacific.

The character of Private Jeffers, one of Major Gilbert's Cape Cod Commandos, is based on an Amphibian Brigade soldier who died in the Pacific, Private Nathan K. Van Noy, Jr., from Grace, Idaho; the son of Pauline Pedersen and Nathan K. Van Noy, Sr., he was a member of the 532nd Engineer Boat & Shore Regiment. In combat in New Guinea, Private Van Noy defended a beachhead while grievously wounded, ignoring calls from nearby soldiers to withdraw and save himself. Van Noy was posthumously awarded the Medal of Honor, the nation's highest military award for valor, and I wanted to remember him for his incredible bravery in action and for giving his life for his country, as so many of our servicemen still do today.

Hitler's use of U-boats along the Eastern Seaboard has become well-known history through the years. During the early part of World War II, he sent his submarines in astounding numbers, and they cruised the Atlantic coast to prevent essential war materials from reaching the U.K., sinking ships bound for Europe. The Navy draped anti-submarine nets across harbors, built concrete lookout bunkers along the East Coast to try to spot the U-boats, and employed aviators like my father-in-law, Lieutenant Michael J. Kelly, to fly dive-bombers to drop depth charges on the U-boats. But despite the Navy's valiant efforts, German U-boats sank more than one hundred ships off the East Coast of North America, in the Gulf of Mexico, and in the Caribbean Sea in the first three months of 1942 alone, some of them within sight of land.

The residents of Vineyard Haven reported hearing the hum of U-boat batteries at night, as the ships surfaced to recharge and lingered offshore, the crews often interacting with fishermen and local sailors. I found several reports of U-boat soldiers coming ashore. One described a pair of Germans trying to board a Martha's Vineyard steamship bound for the mainland, and another reported two Germans having dinner at the Beach Plum Inn, an Up-Island restaurant still popular today. Upon seeing the Germans cut their meat in the European way, the waitress turned them in to the authorities. And thanks to Joe Yukna, co-founder of the Cape Cod Military Museum, we have the story of the U-boat surfacing and taking the Portuguese fisherman's lobsters and returning to the depths. Such incidents were quickly hushed up, perhaps to avoid panic on the island and the loss of tourist revenue. Chamber of commerce ads run at the time in local magazines and newspapers decried U-boat incidents as rumors, but locals insist they happened.

The threat of a Fifth Column was also very real, and Nazi sympathizers worked within America to sabotage factories and heavily populated tourist sites, with the intention of weakening morale and the American will to stay in the war. Operation Pastorius was a failed German plan during which U-boats dropped eight former U.S.-resident Germans on Long Island and the beach at Ponte Vedra, Florida. They did little to meet their mission of blowing up targets to scare the American people into staying out of the war and were apprehended and later tried. Only the leader and his friend who turned the operation in were spared the electric chair—Roosevelt was eager to send a message back to Hitler that the United States would not be deterred.

The character Tyson Schmidt's indoctrination into National Socialism was inspired by an article I read about the German American Bund-operated summer youth camps, patterned after the German Hitler Youth program, which operated in the United States and taught anti-Semitic Nazi ideology at locations like Camp Hindenburg in Wisconsin and Camp Siegfried on Long Island. Equally chilling is the German Gardens neighborhood in Yaphank, Long Island, that still stands today, where the streets were once named Adolf Hitler Strasse and the houses had swastikas bricked into their façades. I thought it would be a good backstory to give young Tyson and a reminder that Hitler had a healthy cult-like following here in the United States, not just among prominent isolationist figures like Henry Ford and Charles Lindbergh but everyday Americans, as well.

I loved the idea of incorporating the creation of Armed Services

Editions into my story and discovered them in a wonderful book at a flea market, *Books in Action: The Armed Services Editions*, edited by John Y. Cole. It chronicles the creation of low-cost, highly portable books for servicemen, reprinted from the bestselling titles of the day. When I read in Mr. Cole's book that they had pulled the original titles to print from a cookie jar, I thought it would be a great thing to give Cadence in my story. In truth, Ray L. Trautman, who headed up the U.S. Army Library section, came up with the idea, along with Army graphic artist H. Stanley Thompson.

The Council on Books in Wartime ended up taking that good idea from the Army and turning it into a cooperative enterprise between all branches of the military and over seventy publishing houses. The council viewed the ASEs as "weapons in the war of ideas" and, instead of banning and burning books as the Nazis did, published 1,322 titles in a wide variety of genres, 122,951,031 total copies.

Distributed throughout Europe and the Pacific Theater, the ASEs were credited with creating a nation of readers after the war and catapulting many titles to bestsellerdom. The popularity of *The Great Gatsby*, a title whose sales initially didn't live up to those of F. Scott Fitzgerald's previous books, surged after the war, perhaps owing to the 155,000 ASE copies distributed to troops, compared to the meager 25,000 copies printed by Scribner in the first seventeen years after the book debuted.

The little books were an instant success with the troops, and stories abound of soldiers reading during combat, including one about how Americans in the trenches laughed out loud while reading Betty Smith's *A Tree Grows in Brooklyn* and how Kay Boyle's *Avalanche* helped a group of American soldiers navigate the French countryside during combat. Every soldier who landed in the invasion barges at the beaches of Normandy carried one.

I think my mother would have liked this book, happy to revisit the island as it once was, back in that gentler time, since, as much as she always wanted to leave the Vineyard, she finally came home here for good. And I bet she would have added this book to her Never-Lend collection. And I hope she'd be happy to see how much we really do miss her now that she's gone.

But I think she'd be happiest to see the island's troops immortalized, their boys who drove in the jeeps past her house, waving and stopping for warm donuts. She'd be happy to know they have not been forgotten.

ACKNOWLEDGMENTS

To my husband, MICHAEL KELLY, THE LOVE OF MY LIFE FROM day one, who so eagerly and expertly reads every manuscript draft and makes me so glad the compact went click.

To my daughter Mary Elizabeth Kelly, a phenomenal editor and friend, who helped me give birth to this book. She and her husband, Chase Altenbern, suggested the topic and she read every iteration, no matter how busy she was, and helped me shape the characters and story. I truly couldn't have done it without you, Mare.

To my daughter Katherine Kelly, who shared her wise editorial opinions and her own book club, aptly named the Book Club, whose adventures and fellowship inspired many scenes in the book. Extra thanks to Katherine and the Book Club for providing valuable cover input, as well.

To my son, Michael, my go-to science consultant, who's always up for talking book plots and scenes.

To my mother, Joanne Finnegan Hall, who could have done anything with her life but chose to raise four children, dedicated readers all. And to my father, William Hall, who never stopped trying to come back to the island.

To Kara Cesare, the most wonderful person and editor a writer could ask for—kind, funny, and infinitely wise. I feel lucky every day that I get to work with you and am filled with gratitude that the universe (and Alexandra Machinist) brought us together.

To the brilliant crew at Ballantine: Debbie Aroff, Allison Schuster, and Corina Diez in marketing; Melissa Folds and Chelsea Woodward in publicity; Jennifer Hershey, Kim Hovey, and Kara Welsh in the publisher's office; Dennis Ambrose in production editorial; Elena Giavaldi in the art department; and editorial assistants Jesse Shuman and Gabby Colangelo. Thank you for your guidance, unflagging support, and inspiration.

To my literary agent, Alexandra Machinist, who pulled me out of the slush pile years ago and who continues to be my stalwart champion.

To my sister Polly Simpkins, thank you for your incredible generosity in support of this book, and for patiently helping me comb through endless variations of plot as we walked West Chop, and for always providing boundless, enthusiastic support and love.

To Brad Simpkins, master of the art of the tide ride around West Chop, thank you to you and Polly for being such loving caretakers of our parents' former home on William Street, which would make them incredibly happy.

To my sister Sally Hatcher, always my stalwart supporter, and my brilliant nephew Will Hatcher, whose close reading and popping up at book events is always a lovely surprise.

To Shirley Kennedy, one of my mother's best friends and longtime Martha's Vineyard resident, who supplemented my own recollections and my mother's stories by generously sharing her memories of growing up on the Vineyard during World War II. Thank you for filling me in on it all, including Humberto "Bert" J. Colaneri, aka Bert the Barber, who was married to my cousin Hazel Smith. And thank you for so often telling me that my mother would have loved the book.

To Bow Van Riper, director of research at the Martha's Vineyard Museum and an endless font of Vineyard knowledge, who so generously answered my ten million questions about Martha's Vineyard during World War II and gave me access to the museum's incredible archives.

To Bow's father, Anthony Van Riper, who gifted my ship-broker, tugboat-loving father a Van Ryper tugboat model, which sits on my mantel today and inspired the one in this book.

To Tom Dresser, co-author of the book *Martha's Vineyard in World War II,* which was an invaluable tool for the writing of this novel. He didn't hesitate a moment when I asked him to meet with me about research, and he and his wife, Joyce, so kindly welcomed me to their Martha's Vineyard home with true island hospitality.

To Sissy Biggers for her unflagging support and for so generously arranging entrée into some of Edgartown's loveliest homes.

To Lynn Allegaert and Kim Booker and to Rosalie Ripaldi Shane, for so generously opening their glorious Edgartown homes to me as research for the fictitious Stanhope house.

To the immensely talented Meg Mercier, who not only hosted me at the Edgartown Yacht Club but answered my barrage of questions about her life and process as a painter, as well.

To Joe Yukna of the wonderful Cape Cod Military Museum in Falmouth, Massachusetts, for sharing his deep knowledge of World War II, including the Engineer Brigade, the mock invasion, and for his story of the Portuguese fisherman and his startling encounter with a U-boat.

To Robin Kall Homonoff @robinkallink for being my go-to for author advice, and the funniest and most loyal friend.

To my lovely sister-in-law Mickey Murray, who generously gave us free range of the house she rented on the North Shore one summer, Soundings, on which I based Copper Pond Farm. There is no more glorious place on earth.

To John Hough, for helping me research the mock invasion of 1942 on the Vineyard.

To William Ewen, author of *Steamboats to Martha's Vineyard and Nantucket,* published by Arcadia, who brought me into the fascinating world of the steamships, and for getting the Steamship Authority to install historic steamboat whistles on their larger ferries. There's no more iconic island sound than that whistle.

To Gabrielle Spears, research archivist, and Heidrun Perez, MLS technical information specialist, Navy Department Library Histories and Archives Division Naval History and Heritage Command, Washington, D.C., for their help with U-boat research.

To Heidi Pitlor, book-and-author-nurturer extraordinaire, who helped me bring Cadence and Briar to life.

To Fran Keilty at the helm of the Hickory Stick Bookshop in Washington Depot, Connecticut, my hometown bookstore, for her support and enthusiasm.

To Peg Shimer, site administrator of the Bellamy-Ferriday House and Garden, who continues to be a wonderful friend and my most wholehearted cheerleader.

To the Bunch of Grapes Bookstore in Vineyard Haven, for hosting so many lovely book events and for endless reading inspiration from childhood to today.

To my mother's friend Betty Cottle, who waitressed at the Bayside Club in Vineyard Haven and inspired Cadence and Bess's work there, and to her lovely garden for inspiring Gram's garden in this book, and for being the best friend my mother could have asked for, sitting at our kitchen table every afternoon talking books and island news.

To Amy Cottle and Martha Fisher, for their friendship and great memories of the Vineyard as kids.

To Sarah Fitzpatrick of Abel's Hill, who long ago introduced me to *It Began with a Whale,* one of my favorite nonfiction histories of Martha's Vineyard, and for inspiring us with her amazing paintings.

To Morgan Burke, who let me borrow her dog Scout's name for Tom Smith's, and for being my biggest fan.

To my hairstylist, Maddie Carlson of the Sunraes and Waves Hair Boutique in Hobe Sound, Florida, and owner Alex Krueger, who are not only great readers but actual hair geniuses, as well.

To journalist Karen Bakofsky, who told me that when she was a child she would tell people she was grounded so she could stay in and read.

To islanders Larry Hepler and Alice Early, for their fabulous Black Point Beach bonfires, which inspired the ones in this book.

To Kari Scott and the Life's Little Blessings Book Club, who sent me emails urging me to "Save Tom!" when I shared early plot outlines of this book, in which Tom Smith never came home. I'm so glad you did.

ABOUT THE AUTHOR

MARTHA HALL KELLY is the *New York Times* bestselling author of *Lilac Girls, Lost Roses, Sunflower Sisters, The Golden Doves,* and *The Martha's Vineyard Beach and Book Club.* She lives in Connecticut, New York City, and Hobe Sound, Florida.

marthahallkelly.com

Facebook.com/marthahallkelly

X: @marthahallkelly

Instagram: @marthahallkelly

This book was set in Fournier, a typeface named for Pierre-Simon Fournier (1712–68), the youngest son of a French printing family. He started out engraving woodblocks and large capitals, then moved on to fonts of type. In 1736 he began his own foundry and made several important contributions in the field of type design; he is said to have cut 147 alphabets of his own creation. Fournier is probably best remembered as the designer of St. Augustine Ordinaire, a face that served as the model for the Monotype Corporation's Fournier, which was released in 1925.